MEMORIES OF YOU

BROOKE HARRIS

Storm
PUBLISHING

Copyright © Brooke Harris, 2023

The moral right of the author has been asserted.

To request permissions, contact the publisher at rights@stormpublishing.co

Ebook ISBN: 978-1-80508-076-3
Paperback ISBN: 978-1-80508-078-7

Cover design: Emma Rogers
Cover images: Shutterstock

Published by Storm Publishing.
For further information, visit:
www.stormpublishing.co

ALSO BY BROOKE HARRIS

The Promise of Forever

When You're Gone

My Daughter's Choice

For all the New Year's resolutions-makers.

'Find out where joy resides, and give it a voice far beyond singing. For to miss the joy is to miss all'

– Robert Louis Stevenson

PROLOGUE

It's a midsummer's day when I read a life-affirming article about New Year's resolutions in a dog-eared magazine! I flick through the pages between the wash and blow-dry stages at my local hairdressers. I chose the most recently dated magazine to peruse – one that still has a cover; front and back. Jennifer Lopez smiles brightly on the front cover. Her teeth are as white as the snowy backdrop behind her. She wears a matching bobble hat and scarf and offers her tips for an eight-step beauty regime. My beauty regime stretches as far as two moisturisers. One for day and one for night, and I still manage to mix them up sometimes. I make an instant decision to add *try a beauty regime* to my list of New Year's resolutions next year.

The hairdresser is chatting away about beer gardens and barbecues, although it's hard to hear her above the hum of the hairdryer.

'The guy on the radio this morning said it's the hottest day of the year,' she says, while dragging a brush painfully through my easily tangled hair. 'Thirty-one degrees. That must be a new record for Dublin, right?'

I have no idea, but I nod and smile. People pass by the

window wearing as few clothes as legally possible, all while my
mind is transported to snowy scenes and mulled wine. I wonder
if it's ironic that even on a glorious summer's day, I can't take my
mind off New Year's resolutions and how important they are
to me.

The actual irony comes when I take my phone out of my
pocket and text my sister.

Tabs: So, you know the way one of my new year's resolutions
was to spend less time on my phone this year? Well, I was
reading a magazine in the hairdressers just now and do you
know what it said?

Avery: That you fail? Because your on your phone right now.
LMAO 😂

Tabs: It's you're. And haha very funny. But I'm only on my
phone cos I HAD to tell you. Look at this...

I take a photograph of the magazine article and attach it. I
wait for Avery's reply and read back over the words that feel as
if they could be written for me, personally.

*Did you know that last year 66.8% of people said they would
make at least one New Year's resolution? Imagine, two-thirds of
people want to make their life better in some way. Did you make
one? If you did, and you failed, then worry not; you are not alone.
More than 96.4% of people fail by the end of January. So, drink
the wine, folks. Skip the gym and eat the chocolate. Life is too
damn short not to.*

Avery: I like the gym. This is BS. YOU'RE still on YOU'RE
phone btw.

I laugh out loud. Then blush. As I feel the hairdresser's eyes on me and the eyes of the woman beside me. Who is also on her phone. Quietly.

'My sister,' I say, feeling the heat in my cheeks creep across my nose.

The woman smiles and returns her gaze to her phone screen. I do the same.

Tabs: I love you

Avery: You too. Can't wait to see the new hair.

Tabs: Nothing new. Just a trim.

Avery: I know 😊

I fumble about under the hairdresser's cape and shove my phone back into my pocket and I reread the article once more. The final line feels cold and messy like the ice cream sliding down the face of a little boy outside the window. Most people fail. But that means *some* people succeed. I want so badly to be in that small group of succeeders. I am determined that some year I will be.

Every December I make twelve new resolutions. One resolution to be followed each month for the whole year. A sort of month-by-month, step-by-step plan to a better me. Has it worked? Not exactly. It never *really* works, to be honest. I've been writing New Year's resolutions for more than a decade and I keep waiting for *that* year. That year that will change everything. What is everything? I have no idea. But when it changes, I will know. It will finally be my year!

I read somewhere once (probably in another tatty magazine) that humans are, by nature, creatures of habit. One day you're a teenager placing your first cigarette between your lips and the next you're a fifty-year-old smoker, puffing away on twenty a day. Or, that couch to 5k that used to burn the legs off you has somehow become two marathons a year and an ambition to better your personal best. You may not remember when or why you started something; you just know that something is an integral part of who you are now.

However, I do remember when and why I began writing New Year's resolutions. It was a Tuesday morning in October, shortly before my thirteenth birthday. I was one of the youngest in my class. Last to become a teenager. The shift between childhood and adolescence seemed to bring with it a strange and almost forced maturity. All of a sudden, we were supposed to know what we wanted to be when we grew up.

'I want to be a pop star,' I giggled, turning my drink bottle upside down to create a makeshift microphone before I burst into out-of-tune song.

'Be serious, Tabby,' someone said. 'A real job.'

They meant a solicitor or a dentist or an architect. The types of jobs their parents had. If it was fun, then it wasn't a job, clearly. My mother was an artist. A painter. Always with her hair tied up in a messy bun and with a splash of paint on her cheek. I saw the way the other parents looked her up and down at the school gates. Her floral dresses and Dr Martens boots stood out like an eyesore next to their tailored suits and kitten heels. But she smiled so much more than they did.

Later that morning, instead of joining my classmates for PE, I convinced my sister, Avery, to ditch school and come to the park with me instead. Our imaginations ran wild as we scaled knobbly bark and swung from high branches like brave explorers on a jungle expedition. The other kids were wrong, I thought. When life is fun, then it is *most* real.

'Look at me, look at me,' I squealed excitedly as I clung to one of the highest branches on one of the tallest trees. 'I bet I can hold on one-handed.'

'Bet you can't,' Avery shouted back from her position on the ground with her head tilting towards the sky, staring up at me.

'I can too,' I said, indignant, dropping my left arm down by my side.

The fingers of my right hand began to slip almost instantly and, before I could reach up to grab on with both hands again, I found myself sprawled flat on my back on the icy ground crying for my mother.

'Oh no, Tabby. We're going to get in so much trouble,' Avery said before she ran as fast as she could to get help.

'I don't know what I'm going to do with her,' Mam told the doctor later as he wrapped my broken leg in a bright purple cast.

Purple had always been Avery's and my favourite colour. But I didn't like it so much anymore.

'I've two daughters. Both as wild as goats,' Mam told the doctor. 'I worry about them so much.'

'Well, I'm sure this one has learned her lesson. Haven't you, Tabitha?' the doctor said. 'No more climbing trees. You'll be the death of your mother.'

My mother was my favourite person in the whole world. On the outside she looked like Avery and me – short with dark, wild hair and round chocolate eyes. But inside she was calm and softly spoken and her hugs melted away all our problems. Mam passed away two days before my cast came off and I knew I would never climb another tree again.

The other kids were right. It was time to grow up. No more days spent drawing or playing games of make-believe. It was time to make a plan and be the good, sensible girl who would make my mother proud. It was time to change but I wasn't sure how. Mrs Applegate – my favourite teacher – had an idea. Or rather, she gave me an idea. She taught us all about the Babylonians and the origins of New Year's resolutions. Mrs Applegate explained that these ancient people believed that if they resolved to live their best life every year, their crops would grow and their king and their gods would be delighted. New Year's resolutions may have changed slightly over the years – I doubt the Babylonians had to worry about dry January or joining the gym – but a deal was a deal and I liked the idea of living my best life. And just like that I had a plan. So now, ever since I was thirteen years old, I start every year with a fresh set of resolutions. Always with the same aim – to be the very best version of myself that I can be. My mother was full of colour. Like a rainbow. I was so determined to shine too.

ONE

31 DECEMBER

'Tabby, are you nearly ready?' Mark, my fiancé, shouts from the bathroom.

'Nearly,' I call back, my fingers tapping the keyboard of my laptop as I sit cross-legged on the floor in the spare room, crammed between some storage boxes, my old easel and the ironing board. 'I just need two more minutes.'

I said that ten minutes ago, and ten minutes before that, but this time I really am nearly ready. I scroll back to the top of my Word document and read my chosen header. *New Year, New Me.* Then I count the bullet points. Twelve. Twelve carefully crafted New Year's resolutions – one resolution to be completed each month for the whole year. *Perfect.* I open my email and attach the file. My fingertips tingle with anticipation as I hit send.

'Tabitha, seriously. We're going to be late.' Mark opens the spare room door as I close my laptop and set it down on top of one of the boxes. 'What are you doing in here?'

'Just sending a quick email.'

Mark rolls his eyes. 'This self-improvement stuff again.'

'Resolutions,' I whisper under my breath as I stand up.

I pull a large Velcro curler from the front of my hair and straighten out my somewhat creased trouser suit.

'How far did you get last year?' Mark asks. 'April?'

'March, actually. And that doesn't matter because this year is different.'

'Do any of your "resolutions" include being on time, for once?' Mark asks, adding air quotes, then taps his watch. 'The party starts in twenty-five minutes and I don't want to have to explain to everyone why we're late. It's embarrassing.'

'I know. I know. I'm ready now. Promise.'

I hurry towards the mirror in the hall and run my fingers through the giant curl to break it into softer waves that frame my face and I slip my feet into the waiting, uncomfortable but elegant, black patent heels. Mark fetches my coat and drapes it over my shoulders.

'Oh God, what is that smell?' he says, taking a deep, exaggerated inhale of the air around me. 'Is that perfume?'

'Yes. It's new. Do you like it?'

Mark pulls away. His nostrils are wide and his face is twisted.

'It's the one your mam gave me for Christmas,' I say.

His expression relaxes and he steps closer again, placing his hand on the small of my back to guide me out the door.

'It suits you, Tabs. You smell lovely,' he says, as he closes the front door behind us with a gentle click.

I pull my coat hood over my hair as we hurry towards the car, dodging giant raindrops. But before we sit in, Mark pauses. Rain trickles down the side of his nose as he locks his narrowed, blue eyes on mine and shakes his head. 'Don't you think it's time you gave up these nonsense resolutions? Nothing ever changes.'

I cross my fingers behind my back and say, 'Maybe this year will be different.'

TWO

'Three. Two. One... HAPPY NEW YEAR!'

A cork pops. Glasses clang. And a sweet chorus of 'Auld Lang Syne' fills the air. I wait for the laughter, cheers and celebration to follow. But all I hear are busy feet walking away.

I open my eyes, only then realising they were closed, and stare upward. There are no fireworks overhead, just greyish ceiling tiles that I assume were once white. The lingering scents of Christmas – pine cones and fir trees – are quashed by the overbearing smell of chemical cleaner and a metallic tang hanging in the air. I take a deep breath. It hurts. I try another but it hurts more. So, with a shallow exhale, I whisper, 'Happy New Year.'

My sister's short, spiky purple hair shoots into view, hovering over me. She's trembling as she nods and says, 'You're awake. Oh, Tabs. You're awake. You scared me there for a minute.'

'Hospital,' I say, my throat dry and stinting.

'Yes. You're in St Martin's. But you're okay. You're going to be just fine.'

'Mark,' I try to add, but no sound comes out.

'Did you hear the singing?' Avery asks.

I nod and the sudden movement sends pain darting up and down my spine. Worry flashes across Avery's face but she hides it quickly and well.

'It was the nurses singing,' she says. Then she turns back and raises a half-full glass of what looks like prosecco and tilts it towards me. 'It's fizzy grape juice. The best they can do when they're on duty. I want to say it's not half-bad. But...' She pokes her tongue out and scrunches her nose.

I stare at her as she squeezes my hand, gently.

'Anyway, trust a blast of "Auld Lang Syne" to wake you up,' she says. 'I should have remembered your obsession with New Year's Eve and started singing hours ago.'

'Hours ago?' I croak.

Avery lets go of my clammy hand and stands up to pour some water from the jug that's waiting on the bedside table.

'I dunno if you're supposed to drink anything or not. But, here, you look parched.'

I pull myself into a sitting position and take the glass of room-temperature water and sip. 'Thank you.'

Avery sits in the plastic chair next to my bed again and soon the only sound is the heel of her shoe tapping insistently against the metal chair leg.

I cough and my eyes water.

'The seatbelt,' Avery says, pointing towards my chest, where the pain is the worst. 'Your ribs are badly bruised and there's some swelling. The doctor said it's a miracle nothing was broken considering—'

She cuts herself off and stands up suddenly. The chair legs squeak in protest against the floor tiles. 'More?' she asks, reaching for the water jug again.

I raise my glass so she can see it's still almost full and I ask, 'Considering what?'

'You know, I should probably tell someone you're awake.'

'Considering what, Avery?' I say, my voice a little louder and my chest a little sorer.

'Hey. Hey. Just relax.' Avery takes the glass from me and eases me back until the mound of pillows swallows me up. She backs out of the room slowly and for the first time I notice she's been crying. Her porcelain skin is puffy and blotchy and her signature fiery-red lipstick and dark mascara are smudged.

I close my eyes, but I open them quickly when I don't like where the darkness takes me. *A scream. Screeching brakes. A bang.* I distract myself by listening to voices in the corridor, but I can't make out words, just mumbles in hushed tones.

'Well, hello there,' someone chirps, and I shift my gaze towards the door, where a woman in blue scrubs stands with a clipboard tucked under her arm.

'She's awake,' Avery says, appearing at the doctor's side.

'She is indeed, and sitting up too.' The doctor nods approvingly as she pulls a pen from her chest pocket and clicks on the top. 'How are you feeling? Any pain? Dizziness? Nausea?'

I'm not sure. There's a strange ache somewhere inside me. I'm not sure where, just deep inside. It's not a broken bone or bleeding or anything physical, but I feel it nonetheless.

'Mark,' I whisper.

'I'll give you a minute,' Avery says as her puffy eyes glisten with tears. She closes the door behind her but I still hear her begin to cry.

Then there are voices again and I guess someone is comforting her. And slowly the sound fades as they walk away.

'I'm Doctor Lauren Shapiro,' the doctor says. 'We met earlier when the ambulance brought you in. Do you remember?'

Dr Shapiro glances at the edge of my bed and I nod, letting her know it's okay to come closer.

'It's okay. I know this is all a little overwhelming,' she says, edging slowly forward until her thigh is pressed against the side of my bed. 'Let's start with something a bit easier, shall we? Can you tell me your name?'

I swallow and my dry throat croaks out, 'Tabitha Greenwood.'

'Good. Great. And how old are you, Tabitha?'

'Thirty-three.'

She smiles and makes a note on her clipboard. 'Can you tell me what you remember?'

I'm Tabitha Greenwood. Tabby. Tabs. I live in Pentsbrooke – the posh part of Dublin, my sister teases – and I'm a chef. I have shoulder-length mousy-brown hair and brown eyes. I'm short, five foot-ish, and curvy. Six months ago, Mark Buchanan asked me to marry him. I said yes. And, last night I said something I really, really wish I hadn't.

At least, that's what I could say. It's what I *want* to say. But instead, I lick my dry lips and whisper, 'I'm not sure.'

The lines around Dr Shapiro's eyes deepen and exaggerate the dull, grey hammocks underneath. She shakes her head and her blond ponytail swishes. The ache inside me hurts a little more.

'You were in a car accident,' she says, 'on your way to a party. Can you remember?'

I glance at a chair shoved in the corner by the window. There's a clear plastic bag resting on top. Inside I can make out spindly black stilettos and my silky black trouser suit.

Dr Shapiro follows my gaze and says, 'One of the nurses popped all your stuff in this bag for you. Your sister said she'd take it home later and bring you in some clean jammies and that sort of thing. I know these hospital gowns aren't the most comfortable. A bit breezy in the back, unfortunately.'

I open my mouth but no words come out.

'Your sister's been beside you for hours. I couldn't even convince her to grab a coffee or stretch her legs. She didn't want you to wake up alone.'

I try speaking again but I still have nothing.

Dr Shapiro takes a small torch from her pocket and shines it in one of my eyes and then the other as she continues talking.

'You're so alike. I thought you might be twins, but your sister proudly tells me she is thirteen months older than you. Gosh, I can only imagine your parents had their hands full when the two of you were babies.'

Finally, I find my voice and ask, 'Is she coming back?'

'Of course. I think she's just grabbing that coffee at last.' Dr Shapiro palpates round my neck with her fingertips, smiles and writes something more on her clipboard. 'You two must be very close.'

'Yeah. We are.'

My breath catches as she straightens up and takes a step back and I notice her expression become a little more serious.

'Do you remember getting ready for the party, Tabitha?'

'Yes,' I whisper as I stare at the clear plastic bag again and at the suit Mark asked me to wear crumpled inside. 'I remember.'

I had splashed out on a beautiful long, backless black dress with lace sleeves. But Mark said that with my figure trousers would be more appropriate.

'Let's not put anyone off their food with your thunder thighs,' he'd joked, and I laughed as if it was funny.

I returned the dress and bought a black satin trouser suit instead. It was fine. Lovely even. But I couldn't shake off Mark's comments. *Thunder-thighs Tabby.* I spent ages trying to get my hair and make-up just right. I figured if my face looked good it might compensate for my body. I so badly wanted to feel pretty. I wanted Mark to notice. I wanted him to look at me the way I'd seen him look at other girls. But I took so long getting ready that we were running late. Mark hates to be late and he was speeding. The rain was heavy and visibility was poor. I should have asked him to slow down. Instead, I said something else. Something I really, really wish I hadn't. The ache inside of me sharpens and it makes me want to be sick.

There's a gentle knock and the door creaks open. Purple hair peeks round, followed sheepishly by the rest of my sister. She's carrying a murky grey takeaway tray holding two paper cups, and the scent of slightly acidy coffee wafts towards me.

'Tea for you, coffee for me,' Avery says, placing the tray down on the bedside table.

There's a sudden silence. It's cumbersome and heavy and it seems to suck all the air out of the room.

Avery backs toward the door. 'I can come back if—'

'Is Mark okay?' I ask, cutting her off, and I don't miss Avery and the doctor exchanging a knowing glance.

Avery runs her fingertips under her eyes and shakes her head. 'I'm sorry, Tabs,' she says. 'I'm so, so sorry.'

There's a noise, suddenly. Loud and animalistic and it takes me a moment to realise it's coming from inside me. I close my mouth and cover it with my hands. But the noise becomes so big and strong trapped inside me that I feel as if it will burst through my chest.

Avery's eyes are wide and locked on mine – full of sympathy and sadness. It hurts my heart to look at her so I focus on Dr Shapiro instead. She tilts her head and the lines around her eyes seem to soften slightly as she says, 'Mark died in surgery, Tabitha. We tried everything we could but his injuries were too great. I'm so very sorry.'

'This is my fault,' I say, gasping for air as if I'm coming up from under water.

'No. God, no,' Avery says, stepping forward and clutching her arms as if she's cold. 'It was an accident, Tabby. An icy patch. This was no one's fault.'

I pull my knees into my chest and wrap my arms round them. It makes my already shallow breath harder to draw, but I don't budge. 'We were running late. He was so mad. And, I... I-I—'

'Would you like to speak to someone?' Dr Shapiro asks. 'When you're ready. We have an excellent counselling service.'

'No,' I snap. 'I mean, no, no thank you. There's nothing to say. Not really.'

'Okay.' Dr Shapiro nods. 'That's okay. But if you change your mind...'

I shake my head and she smiles.

'I'll leave you two alone now,' she says. 'The nurses' station is right outside if you need anything, and I'll be back later to check on you.'

'Thank you, Doctor,' Avery says, showing Dr Shapiro to the door as if she's a guest we've just had over for coffee and a few biscuits. When Dr Shapiro is out of view, Avery turns back towards me and says, 'She seems nice.'

'Yeah. Nice.'

Tears trickle down my cheeks and I finally realise what the sensation deep inside me is. It's relief. Relief that I'm still here, that I'm still alive. But the solace is quickly squashed by guilt. I'm here and Mark is gone and my whole world is upside down.

'Oh, Tabs.' Avery's nutmeg eyes round and she climbs onto my bed, knees first, bouncing us. She throws herself over me like a warm, familiar blanket. 'Shh,' she whispers. 'Shh. Shh.'

I wrap my arms round her and hold on tight.

THREE

Like with most people, there are certain important dates that punctuate my year. The fourth of October, for example: it's my birthday! And the eleventh of November is the day my mam died suddenly. I lost my dad on the eighteenth of November. Exactly five years and five days after Mam. The doctors said it was a heart attack, but to this day Avery insists it was because Dad's heart never healed after losing Mam. The tenth of July is the day Mark and I should be getting married. But instead, I have a new, important date to remember. Today. Today is the fourth of January and it's the day of Mark's funeral. Everyone is there to say their final goodbye. Everyone except me.

When one of the nurses appears by my bed with a gentle smile and her hands tucked behind her back, I groan inwardly, not sure I can bring myself to make conversation. I hope she will take my blood pressure or bloods, or whatever this morning's ritual is, quickly, and leave me be. But as she edges slowly closer and tilts her head, I know this is not going to be quick and silent.

'Hello,' she says.

'Hi,' I reply.

'Um, your sister asked me to pass something on to you, if that's okay?' She seems unsure as she removes her hands from behind her back to reveal she's holding an iPad.

I stare blankly. I have my phone. Why would I need an iPad?

'It's a hospital device,' she explains. 'So unfortunately, I'll need it back later, but there's a live link there for you to click.'

'I don't understand.'

'Um.' I watch her swallow hard. 'It's a livestream of your fiancé's funeral.'

'Oh God. Avery is recording it,' I say, suddenly so conflicted I don't know whether to cry or scream.

'Your sister wasn't sure if you'd want to click the link or not, but she wanted you to have the option. I hope I've done the right thing bringing this in.' She grips the iPad a fraction tighter. 'Phone screens are a bit small, and we have all these fancy iPads.' She glances over her shoulder at the nurses' station as if there's an invisible stack of iPads weighing down the desk. 'And your sister just thought... well, she thought you'd want to say goodbye. I know I would.'

I nod and she steps closer and passes me the device.

'I'll give you some time,' she says. 'We can check your blood pressure later.'

I want to thank her, but there's a lump so huge in my throat it's all I can do to breathe. But as she slowly turns and walks away, I think she knows how grateful I am. I take a deep breath and tap my finger against the blue writing on the screen.

The music is instant. Violins and cellos and an angelic voice. The church is packed and I can only guess Avery is sitting somewhere near the back. And I am grateful as I imagine she's the only mourner with her phone pointed towards the altar. It's hard to make out much in the distance. I squint but it doesn't help. All I see are the heaving shoulders of crying friends or relatives. I can't find Mark's family. Or the altar, or even Mark's coffin.

'I can't,' I say, aloud as if anyone can hear me. 'I can't.'

I turn off the iPad and set it down on the bedside table. Then I cry myself to sleep.

FOUR

On the sixth of January, one whole week after the accident, Dr Shapiro says I'm well enough to go home. I can't wait to get away from blood pressure checks and bland food, but the thought of returning to my flat – my and Mark's flat – makes tiny goosebumps appear up and down my arms.

Avery and I sit side by side on the edge of my bed, our shoulders and thighs brushing against each other. I'm dressed for the first time; skinny jeans and an oversized woolly jumper with a floppy roll-neck that tries to swallow me up. And some-times I want to let it. Avery sips coffee from the machine down the hall and she stops talking every so often to pull a face and tell me it's terrible before drinking some more.

'I bought your favourite bath bombs,' she says, swinging her legs back and forth, gently rocking us both, 'the cute ones that look and smell like lemon meringue pie.'

'Lemon meringue is *your* favourite.'

'Well, the blueberry muffin ones are gross.' Avery smiles. 'And I bought that fancy prosecco you like – with the shiny silver label.' She sighs, noticing my blank expression, and elaborates, 'From the Tesco Metro on the corner round from your flat.'

'Are we celebrating?' I ask.

'Shouldn't we?' Avery stops swinging her legs and turns towards me. 'You're getting out of this place at last. I've missed you so much.'

Avery has never once said the word hospital. Instead, she defaults to calling it *this place*. I've noticed how the incessant beeping of electronics and the squeaking of rubber-soled shoes hurrying up and down the corridors makes her twitch. Nonetheless she has been to visit me every single day without fail. By now, most of the staff know her by name; she's spent hours offering them unsolicited life advice. Avery comforted Lorna, the cleaner, after a disastrous Tinder date. She shared some yoga tips with Nurse Davenport to help with her bad back, and she even offered to teach Dr Shapiro salsa dancing in her spare time.

'There's the doc now,' Avery says, jumping off my bed and whipping out her phone as she sees Dr Shapiro pass by in the hallway. 'I must show her this YouTube video I found. It'll help her with the tricky cross-body turn.'

The video begins to play and upbeat, guitar-led music fills the air.

'Mark's brother stopped by,' I blurt suddenly, pulling Avery's attention away from the hall and back into the room. 'Alan. You know, the oldest one, with the long-ish hair.'

'Oh.'

I raise my voice so she can hear me over the music. 'Yeah. After the funeral. He just wanted to see how I was doing.'

Avery's eyes narrow, disapprovingly. 'Right. Okay.'

'Can you turn that off for a second, please?'

Avery taps her phone and shoves it back into her pocket.

The sudden silence is sharp and my stomach clenches as I

say, 'He said there will be some paperwork coming my way soon.'

Avery's eyes round like two shining pennies. 'Oh God. Do you think it's Mark's will?'

'Mark didn't have a will.'

'Really?'

'Yes, really. Why would he? He was thirty-four.' My tone is clipped and angry. I'm not angry with Avery. But I am angry. Bitter and angry. Because Mark was thirty-four. He was only thirty-four years old.

'I just thought...' Avery pauses and draws invisible shapes on the ground with the tip of her shoe. 'I just thought you guys own a bistro together so you'd have all legal stuff like that sorted out.'

'It's not something we ever talked about,' I say. 'Who thinks about dying at our age, you know?'

Avery swallows hard. 'Yeah. I know.'

'Anyway,' I say, drawing a deep breath and ignoring how it still hurts. 'Alan said everyone missed me at the funeral.'

'I bet it suited Catherine just fine that you were stuck in this place,' Avery mumbles, folding her arms. 'No one to steal her thunder as chief mourner.'

'Catherine was Mark's mother,' I say.

'And you were his fiancée. It's disgusting that they didn't wait until you were out of hospital to have the funeral. But that's Catherine for you. Ever the bitch. Even when she's heartbroken.'

'Alan didn't mention Catherine, actually,' I say, trying to hide how much my heart hurts. How horribly painful it is that I never got to say goodbye to the man I loved for so long. Colleagues, neighbours and acquaintances got to see Mark one last time but I didn't. But it hurts so much more knowing that Avery is right. Catherine wouldn't have wanted me there, especially not if she knew what I'd done.

'Did Alan say if they got the flowers we sent, at least?' Avery asks, folding her arms. 'Or did he explain why Catherine is not replying to any of your texts? You know she barely made eye contact with me in the church. It was all just so... so...'

'Weird,' I finish for her.

'That whole family is weird.'

'Avery.' I say her name as if she's a small child who has done something naughty. 'You can't say stuff like that.'

'I can.' Avery shrugs. 'I just did.'

'Then you shouldn't,' I puff out. 'Especially not right now.'

'I'm sorry, Tabs. I know you loved Mark but Catherine was going to be your mother-in-law and she hasn't come to see you. Not even once. She never picked up the phone to check in. Never texted back. I mean, who does that?'

'She lost her son,' I reiterate. 'She's not thinking straight.'

'And you lost everything.'

I don't have a reply so I stare at Avery. I can see her emotions bubbling up and I know at any second they're going to reach spilling point and all her worries and fear and concern that she's tried so hard to hide all week are going to come bursting past her lips.

But Avery surprises me when she holds her head high and calmly says, 'It's a text, Tabs. Just a text. I feel so sorry for her. I do. But it would be nice if she got in touch. That's all I'm saying.'

'Thank you,' I say, knowing how hard it was for her to hold back. I can see the corners of her lips twitch, and her fingers are tapping against her folded arms restlessly.

There's a gentle knock on the already open door and Dr Shapiro's head appears in the gap. 'Ready?' she asks, grinning brightly.

Avery's eyes light up and she scurries off the bed like a petite, purple-haired pixie to grab my case. 'We are soooo ready,' she says, picking it up.

I am surprised Avery spoke for me. But I'm also relieved. Because as Dr Shapiro's concerned eyes burn into mine, I know the answer written all over my face is, 'No. No, I am not ready to go home and I'm not sure I ever will be.'

Avery's phone pings and she pulls it from her pocket. 'Perfect timing,' she says, reading a text. 'Our taxi is here. Let's get you out of this place.'

I smile and clutch the prescription for painkillers in my hand as I slide off the bed like a women fifty years my senior.

'Yeah,' I say, my voice shaking slightly. 'Let's go.'

FIVE

The flat feels bigger than I remember. Though big still isn't a word I would use to describe the two-bedroomed ground-floor space.

'Just imagine us jogging here on sunny afternoons,' Mark said three years ago, as we followed an estate agent into the master bedroom that overlooks a pretty park across the street. 'And wouldn't this make a cute nursery?' he gushed when we squeezed into the single bedroom. Although babies were nowhere on my radar and I couldn't see myself running, unless for some unfortunate reason I was being chased, I still, somehow, found myself agreeing to buy this flat.

'Slippery little fecker,' Avery says, struggling with the key in my front door. Her cheeks pinken and she glances over her shoulder at me, apologetically. 'Nearly have it. Nearly, nearly.'

My chest tightens and I almost ask Avery to stop. Stop turning the key. Don't open the door. Let me stay on this side for ever, where there are no memories to be faced.

Avery scrunches her nose and pokes the tip of her tongue between her teeth as we hear the clink of the lock releasing.

'Got it,' she says, triumphantly. 'Now, c'mon, let's get you out of the cold.'

She steps aside so I can walk in first, but it takes me a long time to finally put one shaky foot in front of the other to brush past her. Avery picks up my case and follows me. My heart jumps when I hear her close the door behind us. *I'm home.*

The familiar smells of my flat hit me first. The subtle hint of Mark's aftershave mixed with my perfume. And the fresh scent of cotton breeze fabric softener from some of Mark's clothes, hanging on the clothes horse in the hall.

Avery bends to pick up some post off the floor and places the stack of envelopes on the console table next to the Christmas tree. It's started to wilt and the lower branches are grazing the tiles. A couple of the larger baubles have fallen off and are dotted around the bottom. Avery reaches for them and tries to rehang them, but the tired tree can't hold their weight and they roll to the ground once more. Avery tries again and again and again. When she finally gives up the branch springs back, almost knocking a photo off the wall.

Avery jumps to steady it and when she turns back her glistening eyes tell me she's sharing my thoughts.

'It's a great picture of Mark, isn't it?' I say.

'It's a great photo of you both. The bistro's opening night.' She inhales sharply as if the memory hurts.

I watch as she pushes the branch aside and runs her finger over the photo of Mark and me. We're all dressed up and posing with Mark's arm draped casually over my shoulder as the picture-perfect facade of La Bella Vita peeks through in the background. Our pretty bistro with pebble-dashed white walls and a mint sash window.

'Can you believe that was almost four years ago?' I ask.

'Time flies,' Avery says with a wistful look in her eyes that reminds me so much of our mother. 'I still can't believe you guys owned your own bistro before you were even thirty.'

'Mark was ambitious, that's for sure. And besides, I had no idea what to do with all that inheritance.'

'Eh, Coachella.' Avery laughs, reminding me that she spent her half of Mam's legacy on festivals and travelling the world. There isn't a penny left and I know she has absolutely no regrets.

'Investing made sense.' I sigh, and I'm not sure if I'm trying to convince Avery or myself.

'Well, it's your bistro now,' Avery says, letting the branch snap back, and the frame wobbles and I hold my breath as I watch and wait for it to steady itself.

I flash Avery a pointed look that says, *I'm not ready to hear that.* And when an awkward silence descends Avery jumps in with, 'Tea?' followed quickly by, 'Or cake? You always have cake in the freezer, don't you? What's that awesome one you bake? Red velvet, isn't it. But oh, the chocolate biscuit is amazing too. Or the coffee one, I love the coffee one. And now I'm hungry. Officially starving. Are you hungry? Should we order pizza or something?'

'I'm okay,' I say. I'm finding it hard to take my eyes off Mark's face in the photo. 'I'm not very hungry. More tired, really. I might go for a lie-down.'

Avery's bright smile falters.

'But you go ahead. Please? The number for the pizza place is on the fridge and they're usually pretty quick to deliver.'

'Tabs,' Avery says, suddenly so serious and so not herself.

'It's okay. I'm okay. Order one for me too and I'll have it when I wake up.'

'Spicy pepperoni?' Avery asks, smiling again, but it's much less confident than before.

I nod. 'Sounds great.'

I turn away and drag myself towards my bedroom. I just want to be on my own. And at the same time I am so aware that, from now on, I am alone.

SIX

My foam hair curlers and a bottle of fake tan are scattered on the bed, reminding me of the last time I was in my bedroom. I was so full of hope and eagerness. I had written my most important New Year's resolutions yet and I could hardly wait for the stroke of midnight, for the new year to begin and for the new me to follow.

It all seems so silly and pointless now as I push the neon pink canister and curlers off the bed and finally flop in. I wrap myself in the duvet and roll onto Mark's side. I take a deep breath and wait to get a sense of him. When it doesn't come, silent tears trickle down my cheeks.

I lie still with my eyes closed for a long time but I don't sleep. Instead, I think about us. About Mark and me. About all the times we laughed in this room. Mark telling his terrible dad jokes. The worse they were the more we laughed, and he would remind me often that he couldn't wait to be a father some day. I think about all the times we made love in this bed. Where I tried very hard to make sure I didn't make Mark a father any time soon. I think about when we argued and when we made up right here between these sheets. And for the first time since I woke up in hospital, in a world without Mark, I think about New Year's Eve. About the party. The one we never made it to. And all Mark's friends who were waiting there for us.

'It'll be a great night,' Mark had said. 'All the lads will be there. And their wives and girlfriends. I know you don't really know the girls – they're intellectual types. But no one is expecting you to be clever, Tabs. Just tell them about your cakes. Everyone likes cake.' Then he slapped my arse and said, 'Although not as much as you. Actually, why don't you make that one of your resolutions this year? Tabitha Greenwood must eat less cake – has a nice ring to it, eh?'

I must drift off to sleep because when I open my eyes again it's dark outside. The room is wrapped in a warm orangish-yellow glow as the street light across the road shines through the window. Groggily, I get up and close the curtains. The sound of laughter carries from the sitting room. Jealousy pinches. And leaves a sting. Because I hate that something – anything – can make Avery giggle right now.

I take some time before I leave my bedroom. My eyes are red and puffy and advertise that I've been crying in my sleep. I try freshening up with a make-up wipe but it stings my face and I curse and toss it aside. I change into my favourite fluffy pyjamas – they're old and have a hole under the left armpit, but Mark bought them for me shortly after we moved into our flat and wearing them now feels as close to hugging him as possible. I brush my hair and twist it until it sits neatly like a chocolate doughnut on top of my head. Finally, feeling semi-functional, I open the door.

Avery's on the phone but she senses me behind her straight away.

'I gotta go,' she whispers. 'I'll call you later.'

She slides her phone into her pocket, untangles her legs from underneath her and stands up. She looks at me with wide, concerned eyes and says, 'Hey, you.'

'Hey.'

I'm curious about who Avery was chatting to – someone who can make her giggle so heartily; but before I have a chance to ask about the call, Avery is hopping from one foot to the other, shouting, 'Oh, shit. Pins and needles. Pins and needles. Ouch, crap, ouch.'

I smile and almost laugh.

'It's not funny,' she says, pointing a finger at me. 'I'm in real pain. You've no idea how much I'm hurting—' She cuts herself off, clamps her hand over her mouth and shakes her head. 'Shit, sorry, Tabs, that was a stupid thing to say. I know stupid pins and needles can't compare to how you're feeling.'

'It's okay.' I sigh. 'Fizzy feet hurt.'

'They do,' she says, lowering her hand. 'They bloody do. Anyway, did you get some sleep? You don't look as bad as you did. I mean, you still look absolutely rotten, I won't lie. But not *as* rotten.'

Avery's familiar lack of filter feels oddly comforting and I manage a throaty, 'Thanks,' before I change the subject. 'Was your pizza nice?'

The empty box and some crumbs litter my coffee table.

Avery rubs her bloated belly. 'So good. Yours is in the kitchen. Will I heat it up for you?'

I'm still not hungry, but Avery looks at me with pity-heavy eyes so I smile and say, 'Sure. That'd be great. Thanks.'

Avery walks towards the kitchen and I flop onto the couch, unable to hold myself up any longer. Loneliness sits next to me like a physical thing. I can sense it holding my hand, rubbing my back, promising me it will never leave me.

'*I like your flat,*' it says. '*I bet you were happy here, once upon a time.*'

I sweep my eyes over my home. Over the space Mark and I shared for so long. The cream couch takes up the bulk of the floor space in the small living area, with cream walls, cream carpet and cream curtains. The only splash of colour comes from the wall-mounted television and the bookcase with my cookbooks, organised in order of size, underneath. I never liked cream so much. But Mark loved it.

I'm halfway through an episode of *Friends* – one I've seen countless times before – when I'm distracted by the smell coming from the kitchen. Instinctively, I clamp my nose as I follow the pungent scent.

'I can't do this,' Avery grunts as she points to a pot of something bubbling on the cooker hob. 'How do you make this look so easy? I've been stirring non-stop for ten minutes and it's still lumpy and looks like dog shit.'

'Smells a bit like it too,' I say, retching a little. 'What happened to pizza?'

'I just wanted to make your favourite. I thought it might cheer you up.'

'Nobody's favourite should be this colour.'

'I'm sorry, Tabs,' Avery says, pouring the pot of greeny-brown gloop down the sink. 'I wanted to do something nice for you and instead I've just made your whole flat smell like fart.'

'It's the thought that counts,' I sigh, cracking the window. 'And anyway, pizza *is* my favourite.'

She nods and pops a couple of slices of pizza in the microwave. Then she fills the sink with steaming water and washing-up liquid and eases the pot in. I take her hands in mine as she reaches for the wire scrubbing brush.

'Thank you,' I say, giving her sudsy hands a gentle squeeze. 'Thank you for taking such good care of me. I know it's not easy for you either.'

Avery's eyes glisten with tears and she pulls away from me to start scrubbing. I cringe as metal grates against the sides of my best non-stick pot. But I don't stop her. I wish I had something to scrub, or fidget with. Instead, my idle hands hang like weights by my side, dragging me down.

The microwave dings and Avery rolls her shoulders back, takes a deep breath and tries so hard to sounds cheerful when she announces, 'Pizza's ready.'

'It's okay, you know. You don't have to try this hard,' I say.

Avery nods and fetches the plate from the microwave. The sight of slightly shrivelled cheese and limp pepperoni makes my stomach clench.

'I'll try to tone it down a bit, eh,' she says. 'I'm just worried about you. You haven't really talked about what happened and I don't know what to say or do and—'

'Maybe don't say anything at all,' I sigh, knowing how great an ask that is of my sister. 'Let's just watch some TV, eat some pizza and not say much at all.'

'Sure,' she says, slightly tetchily. 'What do you want to watch? I started watching this new documentary about elephant babies. It's really good. You'll love it, Tabs. They're so cute and big-eared and all.'

'Mark loved documentaries,' I say. 'Not about animals, to be fair. But all the crime ones. He'd try to outguess the detectives.'

'Of course he would,' Avery says under her breath, and I pretend I don't hear her as silent tears trickle down my cheeks.

Avery drops the scrubbing brush and throws her arms round me. 'Oh, Tabs. This is shit. It's so fucking shit that Mark is gone. I'm sorry.'

Her hands are wet but I hug her close. I drop my head onto her shoulder and I finally let myself cry.

'I love you,' she whispers. 'And, I'm here for you. Whatever it takes, whatever you need. I'm here.'

'What do I do now?' I sniffle. 'I just don't know what to do now.'

'Oh. My. God!' Avery jumps back suddenly, and my tear-soaked breath catches. She throws her hands in the air. 'That's it. That's totally it. Tabitha Greenwood, you *do* know what to do. You've always known what to do.'

'I... I... I...'

Avery darts away and I stand alone and aching all over. Finally, I take a deep breath and follow her into the sitting room. She bends and looks under the coffee table.

'Nope. Not here,' she says.

She searches the bookshelf under the television and shakes her head.

'What are you looking for?' I ask, although I know not to expect an answer as she concentrates.

For a while I watch as purple hair dives into drawers and ducks under cushions. And I wrap my arms round myself as I hear Mark's voice in my head. *'Your sister is bonkers, you know that, right? Thank God you're nothing like her.'*

SEVEN

I sit on the couch hugging a cushion and watching Avery's elephant documentary. A shrivelled-skinned baby elephant wraps his trunk round his mother's tail and tries not to fall over his own feet as he follows her through the savanna. *At least he has someone to guide him*, I think. Then I turn off the television, realising it's not helpful to be jealous of the simple life of animals on the far side of the world.

I don't know how long I stare blankly ahead before Avery reappears with a laptop tucked under her arm. My laptop. She points at the plate on the coffee table that I've ignored.

'You haven't touched your pizza,' she says, her voice slightly distorted by a lollipop in her mouth. 'Never mind. I'll cook us something later. These are lovely, by the way.' She pulls the lollipop out to show me the colour. 'Strawberry. Or raspberry maybe. It's hard to tell. Anyway, I found a stack of 'em in one of the boxes.'

'They're for kids at the bistro,' I say.

Avery shrugs and pops the lollipop back in her mouth. 'People say I'm a big kid.'

'I'm not sure that's a compliment.'

'Yeah it is! Kids are fun. Grown-ups are boring.'

'Did you find what you were looking for?' I ask, changing the subject. The last thing I want is a conversation about adulting. Or Avery's lack of, to be more precise.

'I did.' Avery pushes the plate of shrivelled pizza aside and places my laptop in the centre of the coffee table.

'You said you don't know what to do now, right?' she says, as she opens it and the screen comes to life.

I nod and I feel tears swell again. My desktop background is a picture of Mark and me, taken in Paris not long after we first started dating. The reflection of the Seine shimmers in Mark's sunglasses and we're both smiling like a couple in love. In love with the beautiful city. In love with each other. In love with life.

Behind us is the Pont des Arts, where we attached a silver padlock and threw our key in the water. We promised to love each other for ever. I had no idea for ever would be this short.

'Those leaflets we got at the hospital aren't much help, are they?' Avery bites and I hear the lollipop crack into tiny pieces in her mouth. She shoves the sticky stick into her pocket and continues speaking. 'All full of big words and diagrams.'

She's right. I couldn't bring myself to read past the second page of *Living with loss*.

'But we don't need any of that mumbo-jumbo,' Avery says between loud crunches.

'Jumbo,' I say, flicking my eyes to the television, desperate for a distraction. 'That's the baby elephant's name.'

'You started watching without me?' Avery huffs.

'You were busy,' I say, in a barely audible whisper.

'You're right. I was. Busy finding these beauties.'

Avery swirls her finger around the mousepad. The arrow comes to a stop just above Mark's and my smiling faces and lands on a Word document. A Word document clearly sign-posted *New Year, New Me*. My words, which just a week ago I thought were so clever, stare at me now, painful in their irony.

Before Avery has time to say another word, I slap the laptop shut, nearly catching her fingers.

She clutches her hands close to her chest and stares at me with round, slightly confused eyes.

'What the hell are you doing?' I snap.

Avery swallows hard and I can almost see the fragments of sugary lollipop making their way down.

'I just want to help...'

'Help yourself to my files, you mean. What the actual hell, Avery. They're private.'

'I know, I know,' Avery says, nodding repeatedly. 'I didn't mean to upset you, it's just—'

'Did you read it?'

I feel winded. As if someone has slapped me hard in the back. And I just want to open my mouth and scream until all the pain spills out.

'Did you read it?' I say again, louder.

'Tabby, what's wrong? Have I done something wrong?'

My heart begins to race and I can't bring my eyes to meet hers. She must think what I wrote are the most horrible words in the world. *I do.*

'Did you read it? Did you read my New Year's resolutions?' I'm shouting now. So loudly my words scratch at the back of my throat.

'No. No, I didn't, I swear.'

I can breathe again. I inhale sharply and for a moment I see stars.

'What is it? What's wrong. What have I done?' Avery asks.

Avery asks this question often. Usually, I reassure her with a smile and a run through her faux pas. But not this time. Because Avery hasn't done anything wrong. It's me. It's all me.

Avery gingerly opens my laptop again and says, 'Please don't be mad, Tabs. Won't you just take a look? Your resolutions could be the perfect roadmap to get you through this year.'

'They. Are. Private,' I reiterate through clenched teeth.

'What? No, they're not! You spent all of December banging on about your resolutions, and half of November too, come to think of it. You're the same every year. January this. February that. March the other. What's changed?'

'Mark's dead. That's what. He's gone.'

Avery shifts uncomfortably and cream leather squeaks under her bum as she takes my hand.

'I know,' she says. 'And that's why they're more important than ever. They will help. I know they will.'

'They won't.'

'You don't know that unless you try. Let's start small. How about we take a look at January's resolution. If it helps, then next month we move on to February's and so on. Do you see what I mean, a roadmap?'

'Avery, stop,' I say, raising my hand. 'I don't want to try. I don't want to think about New Year's Eve ever again. And I really, really don't want to think about any stupid bloody resolutions.'

'Tabby, c'mon, don't be like that.'

'Leave me alone. For once can you just stop being so extra and give me some bloody space.' I pull myself off the couch and storm into my bedroom. 'Do. Not. Follow me,' I shout, slamming the door behind me. My body is aching with tiredness and heartbreak as I flop onto the bed and sob into Mark's pillow.

EIGHT

It's quite a while before I'm all cried out and finally ready to leave my room again. It's almost midnight and the flat is still. Too still. I'm grateful for the low hum of the television or radio trickling from the flat above as I shuffle into the hall, rubbing my stinging eyes. The droopy Christmas tree is gone and in its place are plastic bags filled with fairy lights and baubles, ready to be put away until next year. Avery's coat is still here, draped haphazardly over the console table. I sigh, relieved.

I find her asleep on the couch. In the absence of a blanket, she's covered herself with the large bath towel from the main bathroom. The coffee table is cleared and polished and the television is switched off.

I drag myself into the kitchen to check if there's any pizza left. There's a box I didn't notice earlier on the countertop with a sticky note on top.

Tabby,
I ordered some more in case you got hungry.
I'm sorry.
A xx

I don't bother to heat the slice I stuff into my mouth and I relax my stiff shoulders as flavour explodes over my tastebuds.

'You're up,' I hear a groggy voice behind me whisper.

I turn round to find Avery wearing the towel over her shoulders like a superhero cape. It suits her.

I swallow down a half-chewed mouthful and say, 'They usually come round to check blood pressure and stuff at this time on the ward, so...'

Avery rubs her sleepy eyes and nods. 'Tabs, I'm sorry,' she says, stepping closer. 'I shouldn't have been so pushy. I just know how much you love your resolutions and I want you to be happy and—'

'My resolutions won't make me happy. Not this year.'

'Oh, Tabby.'

'It's not fair.' I begin to blubber. 'We were both in that car. We were going to the same party. How come I'm still here and Mark's gone?'

'You had no control over this.'

'I did something terrible,' I say as I wrap my arms round my quivering body and loud, heartbroken crying takes me over. 'Just before the crash. I said something I shouldn't have. Something I'm not even sure I meant.'

'Okay,' Avery says slowly.

I want her to hug me. But instead she takes a step back to give me the personal space I demanded earlier.

'What did you say?'

I sniffle and drag the sleeve of my pyjamas under my nose. 'I'll show you.'

Without a word Avery follows me back into the sitting room. We sit on the couch, our calves brushing against each other, and I'm not certain but I think Avery is holding her breath. I open the laptop and click into the *New Year, New Me* file.

'Yay,' Avery says, and claps her hands like an excited seal

tapping its flippers. 'I just know this is a good idea. I really, really think that sticking to your resolutions will give you focus and help you through the first few months...'

As Avery rambles on, I angle the laptop away from me and towards her so she can see the screen and I can't anymore. Then I inhale until my lungs feel ready to burst and wait for her to start reading.

She clears her throat and begins. 'New Year, New Me, by Tabitha Greenwood, smiley face emoji. Or is that a winky face?' She squints and nudges closer to the screen. 'It's kinda hard to tell with your brightness down this low. Is your battery dying? Hang on, I'll go get the charger.'

She shifts to stand up but I catch her hand and tug. 'Please. Just keep reading.'

'I'll only be a sec, the charger is on top of the—'

'Please. Before I change my mind.'

Avery settles back onto the couch, presses her knee against mine once more and nods. 'Okay, where was I?' She clears her throat with a gentle cough before she continues. 'January. Step one. Break up with Mark.'

I want to break up. I want to break up. I want to break up.

The last words I ever said to Mark play on a loop in my mind as I wait for Avery's explosion. I'm ready to catch the laptop if she jumps off the couch in surprise and knocks it. I'm ready to catch a cushion she might throw in a knee-jerk shock reaction. And, most of all I'm ready to catch myself when her disgust knocks my heart out of my chest. I don't have a reaction prepared for when she continues to read on, cool and focused.

'February. Step two. Give up sugar.' Avery rolls her eyes. 'Well, that's never going to happen. You're a bag of cats without a pain au chocolat for breakfast. March. Step three. Walk ten thousand steps a day. Ugh. Boorrriiinnnggg. You don't even own a Fitbit.' She flicks her gaze to me and shakes her head. 'April. Step four—'

'Stop. Stop, please,' I say, dropping my head into my hands, unable to listen to any more. 'Aren't you going to say something?'

Avery pauses. And long, silent seconds tick by before she says, 'Would it change anything if I did?'

'No.'

She straightens the laptop and rolls her shoulders back. 'Right then. What's all this about giving up sugar?'

'Sugar is bad for you,' I murmur without lifting my head.

'Yeah. And hangry Tabby is bad for the rest of us.'

I want to break up. I want to break up. I want to break up.

My last words to Mark play on a loop in my mind. I hear the crack in my voice as I said them and I see the look on his face as he heard them. They're the last words I think of before I fall asleep. And they're the first words that come into my head every time I wake up again. And they were the last words Mark heard before he died. Five words that changed everything.

I begin to cry. It's louder and angrier and more painful than I've ever experienced before. 'I didn't want to be with Mark anymore. And now he's gone. For ever. I guess I got what I was asking for.'

'You're not responsible for this,' she says. 'Who do you think you are – some sort of traffic god?'

I struggle to catch my breath between snotty, slurpy sniffles.

'It's my fault. It's all my fault. Mark is dead because of what I said.'

'Stop it,' Avery scolds, suddenly matronly. 'It was an accident. A car crash, for Christ's sake.'

I wipe my fingers under my eyes and trail off as the memory floods my senses. The shiny black paint of Mark's Audi that he took to the car wash once a week. The smell of pine forest air freshener that sometimes made my eyes sting. The feel of his leather seat in my hands when I gripped the sides, willing him to slow down as he weaved in and out among motorway traffic, racing to the party. The sound of his laughter as he said, 'Myself and the lads have a bet on how far you'll get this year. My money is on March. Don't let me down.'

'You bet on me?'

I tried to slacken the seatbelt that suddenly felt as if it was crushing me. But tugging on it only made it hug me tighter.

'Oh, lighten up, Tabs. No one takes New Year's resolutions seriously.'

'I do,' I whispered.

'I know. It's embarrassing.'

And then I said it. Those five bloody words. They burst past my lips so furiously they almost winded me.

'What?' Mark took his eyes off the road to glare at me and I had to shout at him to watch where he was going. 'You can't be serious.'

'I am. I'm sorry. Breaking up with you is my January resolution. I don't think we should be together anymore.'

'Fuck this,' he snorted, tipping the accelerator harder. 'You're telling me this now, right before we walk into a room full of our friends.'

'Your friends,' I reminded him. 'And I *am* sorry. I know the timing is bad. I was going to wait until after midnight. Until January first, but—'

'No. Just no.' His knuckles whitened as he gripped the wheel tighter. 'If anyone is leaving anyone, it's me. I'm leaving you.'

Mark didn't see the truck until it was too late. He swerved into the outside lane so suddenly the truck had nowhere to go except straight into us.

'Tabs, are you even listening?' Avery taps my shoulder and pulls me back to the here and now.

'I miss him,' I say.

The raw honesty comes out of nowhere and shocks me. Avery looks at me with pursed lips and I wait to hear something comforting, but as uselessly generic as she thinks my resolutions are.

'You broke up with Mark,' she tells me slowly, as if I didn't know or had somehow forgotten and she is gently reminding me. 'That was huge. A long time overdue, but still a big deal.'

My chest hurts. 'Avery, please. I'm tired.'

'I'll just say this...' she begins.

I close my eyes and press the tips of my fingers against my temples as I listen.

'I'm proud of you. Breaking up is hard, especially when you've been together for what? Nine, nearly ten years. But it was the right decision. Mark didn't make you happy.'

'He did. Once,' I say, silent tears trickling down my cheeks as I remember.

'But he hasn't for a long time. I know you loved him. I not sure why, but I know you did.'

'Avery!' I open my eyes and roll them.

'I'm sorry he died. I really am. It's awful and tragic and so, so sad. But I'm not sorry that everything will change now. You haven't been happy in ages, Tabs. And I want you to be. You deserve to be.'

Sometimes I wish I could climb inside my sister's head and take a walk around. I imagine it's full of colour and music. And I find myself smiling through my tears.

'I want to be happy,' I whisper, as if admitting it out loud is shameful. 'I just don't know how anymore.'

'I do,' Avery says, and her enthusiasm is punctuated with a single clap of her hands. 'I'm going to write new resolutions for you. Good ones. Bloody awesome ones. You've forgotten who you are, Tabitha Greenwood. I am going to remind you. This year you are going to remember how to be happy.'

'Oh, Avery, I don't—'

'Don't worry, I won't try to make you sky-dive again.

Although I still think if you had just jumped with the rest of us you really would have enjoyed it.'

I yawn and tiredness weighs heavy over my eyes. I've never felt tiredness like this before. Eating, or showering, or just moments of conversation leave me physically aching for my bed. I stand up and kiss the top of my sister's head. 'I love you. Goodnight.'

Avery slides onto the floor and sits cross-legged in front of the coffee table.

'Na'night,' she says, as she pulls my laptop closer to her and opens it. I hear her banging the keys as I fetch some blankets and a sheet, and I leave them folded on the end of the bed in the spare room for her. Back in my room I take one of Mark's t-shirts out of the drawer and hold it to my nose. It smells of fabric softener. I think about wearing it, but Mark didn't like it if I borrowed any of his clothes, so I fold it and place it back in the drawer. I climb into bed, and like every night since New Year's Eve, I cry myself to sleep.

NINE

FEBRUARY

I'm grateful that time seems to move faster at home than it did in the hospital. And yet being in my flat – the memory box of my once-upon-a-time-life – grows steadily harder. Netflix and junk-food-fuelled days are divided up by how often I change from one set of pyjamas into another. I haven't worn anything that isn't fluffy, or without a drawstring waist, in weeks. I've lost track of what day it is and the nights are long and restless and full of what-ifs. But the clock ticks, time passes and life doesn't stop.

Without discussing it, Avery seems to have moved in with me. She's taken over the spare room, and most of the rest of the flat, and some item of her clothing is almost permanently draped over the back of the couch. Hairspray and boxes of neon hair dye occupy the bathroom cabinet and I wake up most mornings to the smell of incense wafting from the sitting room. But I'm so grateful not to be alone right now. We eat together. Watch TV together. Laugh together. Cry together. There's very little we don't do together, but we don't talk about Mark, the crash or New Year's resolutions. When Avery tries to broach the subject, I shoot her down quickly, and she lets me.

I start every morning staring out the kitchen window, cradling a cup of warm tea against my chest. This morning I watch a robin hop from one tree branch to another. He's charming as he pushes his swollen ruby belly forward and flaps his tiny wings. I read once that robins appear when loved ones are nearby. I believed it then, when I was young and desperate to feel my parents' presence. Now I lean over the sink and pull down the window blind. I hear the pitter-patter of Avery's feet cross the tiles behind me and I turn round and smile, finding her barefoot in a pair of skinny jeans and one of my old Westlife t-shirts. Her sketchbook is under her arm, a pencil is tucked above her ear and the half-moons under her eyes are as purple as her hair.

'Morning,' she chirps. 'Sleep okay?'

'Yeah,' I lie. 'You?'

'Not great. Stayed up late finishing these.' She slides her sketchbook onto the table and flicks through the pages to show me beautiful watercolour paintings of farm animals.

'Oh wow, Avery.'

'I hope the publisher likes them. I emailed them over this morning.' She inhales sharply and I can feel her nerves. 'So, I'm all yours today.'

I sip tea that is too hot for my mouth and spit it into the sink. Avery has been all mine, all day, all month.

'Soooo do you fancy some shopping? If we go to town we can pop into the hairdresser while we're there.'

I gaze at her purple hair as she swirls the kettle, checking if there's water inside. 'Is this boiled?'

'A while ago. It's probably gone cold by now.'

She flicks the switch, and takes the biggest mug from the cupboard. The one that says *World's Best Fiancé* in jazzy letter-ing. She spoons in some instant coffee as my eyes trace over each letter.

'Well. Whatcha think? Town?'

'Erm.'

'I've gotta get this stripped if I want to go green for spring,' she says, tugging a purple tuffet of hair.

I try not to smirk. Avery will never keep a hair colour for an entire season. She'll be pink, or blue, or red, by Valentine's Day.

'You haven't checked your email this morning, have you?' she says.

I haven't checked my email all month.

'Not yet. Why?'

Avery produces my phone from her back pocket. 'Check now.'

'You were in my room?' I say in a tone reminiscent of our teenage years, as I set my cup down on the countertop a little roughly and some tea sloshes over the side.

'God, you are so not a morning person,' she complains, passing me my phone as the kettle beings to boil loudly. 'Check your emails. Please.'

My *what have you done?* alarm bells start ringing as I unlock my phone and stare at the screen.

From: Avery Greenwood <averypaints@mymail.com>
To: Tabby Greenwood <tabitha.l.greenwood@mymail.com>
Date: 1 February
Subject: The Remember Plan

I drag my eyes from the screen and to Avery as she lifts the kettle and pours the water.

Oh God.

'I've sorted it all out,' she says as she stirs. 'Twelve resolutions. One a month, yada, yada, yada. It's just the way you do it. Except' – she pauses for dramatic effect – 'these resolutions are actually life-changing, if I do say so myself.'

'Oh. I don't know about this.'

'It's too late to change your mind. It's all set up.' She begins stirring again. 'A new resolution will arrive in your email inbox on the first of every month. And oh God, it took me for ever to figure out how to do that, so you have to read them all. I'm never getting that week of my life back. But I do feel a bit brainier now, I won't lie.'

I shake my head. I can't think a day ahead right now, never mind a whole year.

'Just read it. I'm trying to help you and you're acting like I'm asking for a kidney. Which, by the way, I would totally expect you to give me if I needed it. Just FYI.'

'I would rather give you a kidney—'

'C'mon, read it. You promised you would try my resolutions.'

'I didn't promise anything,' I remind her. 'I just didn't have the energy to argue that I wouldn't.'

Avery swirls the spoon round and round, dragging the silver against the ceramic cup. The noise grates as if she is twisting the spoon inside my head. Finally, she stops stirring, and taps the spoon on the edge of the cup three times.

'Here. Give it to me.' She takes my phone again and begins reading. 'The Remember Plan. February. Step two.' She lifts her eyes from the screen to regard my jammies and bed hair. 'We're on resolution two because it's month two. Today is the first of February, by the way.'

And just like that January is over. A whole month without Mark gone. Done. Finished.

'And we're not skipping a month because you already completed January's resolution. I know technically you dumped Mark while it was still December, but it counts. So, eh, yeah. We're on resolution number two now. Yay!'

My chest tightens. There is a stack of sympathy cards on my hall table. My phone beeps regularly with messages and emails of condolence. There is a stain on my pillow where my tears fall every night and dry out the next day. But I don't deserve kind words or to wallow in my grief. I didn't lose my fiancé; I lost a man I no longer wanted to share a life with. The guilt is crushing as I lean my back against the sink edge and plead with my knees not to buckle.

'So, what do you think?' Avery asks.

'Hmm.'

My phone is in my hand again – I didn't notice her pass it back to me – and she's watching me with expectant eyes. Her words stare at me from the screen, equally expectantly.

Start with a small change. Try a new haircut.

'That's it?' I say.

'That's it.'

I run my fingers through my hair and they catch in a clump at the back and I realise I can't remember the last time I brushed it.

'I thought we'd start with something simple. And no offence, but your hair is kind of a mess.'

'At least it doesn't glow in the dark.'

Hurt flashes across Avery's face but she shakes it off quickly. 'You've had long hair for ever. Change it up a bit, have some fun. How d'ya feel about a bob?' She steps back and makes a square shape with her fingers. She squints and tilts her hands from left to right, framing my face the way the idiosyncratic photographer does with the girl-next-door type in movies, right before he tells her he's going to make her famous. 'I'll book an appointment for this afternoon. I'm sure Barney could squeeze you in.'

I don't know who Barney is and I don't want anyone to squeeze me anywhere.

I raise the cup to my lips and remember just in time that it's too hot. 'Actually, I was thinking of going into work this morning.'

Avery is expressionless as she shoves her hands in her pockets and traces an invisible shape on the ground with her foot.

'There are boxes of merchandise in the spare room and they're not doing much good here,' I say, trying hard to sound casual and not as if I might burst into tears at any moment. 'But you should go. Go get your hair done. Green will suit you.'

Her face twists a fraction and I can feel her disappointment.

'I have to go back some time,' I say. 'The bistro has been closed for almost a month. I need to get some money coming in again.'

Mark's voice creeps into my head. Not for the first time I hear him say, *'What are you doing, Tabby? Think of the staff out of work. Think of the mounting bills and cancelled bookings. How could you make such a mess of it all, Tabby? How could you?'*

'The lollipops are all gone. I'm sorry,' Avery blurts. 'I was only going to have one or two, but they were so yummy and right there. Right beside my bed.'

I smile.

'You can get more, right?'

'Of course. It's no problem.'

'More for the flat, I mean.'

I nod. I knew what she meant.

'I'll put the order in today. When I'm in work.'

'No. No. Please. You can't. Not today. There's someone I really want you to meet today. I thought we could all have lunch together.'

'Becca?' I say, testing the name I've overhead Avery say often on Zoom or late-night calls when she thinks I'm asleep.

Avery's eyebrows pinch. 'Yes. Becca. How did you know about her?'

'The walls in this place are paper-thin. And you two talk a lot.'

'Oh, Tabby. I'm sorry. I wanted to tell you about her. Really, I did. But Becca said the timing wasn't right. She still thinks it's too soon.'

'So, is it serious between you two?'

Avery's cheeks pinken as she nods. 'I think so. I mean, I hope so. I like her, Tabs. I like her a lot. And I think she actually likes me too. No one ever really likes me but I think Becca does.'

'Everyone likes you,' I say, but I know I'm lying.

'Mark didn't.'

'Your sister drives me crazy. Don't invite her to the party/barbecue/dinner. No one will want to come if she's there. She's sooo loud and annoying.'

Mark was always kind and polite to Avery's face. But behind her back his words cut deep. It was exhausting trying to hide how much they hurt. I thought I hid it from both of them. I guess Avery was better at seeing through me.

'He liked you,' I try again.

'He didn't.' Avery shrugs. 'But who cares? Can't be everyone's cup of tea, eh?'

I smile. Avery is my favourite cup of tea. I really would like to meet the woman who is making my sister so happy. But nonetheless, I say, 'I'm sorry. I really do have to go back to work. New month, new start.' I swallow, trying to convince myself as much as Avery.

'Okay. Fine.' She nods. 'We'll come with you.'

'To work?'

'Yes.'

'But—'

'I'm not letting you face that place alone. Not yet.'

I open my mouth but no words come out.

'Becca and I will come with you and we can all have lunch there. I've told Becca all about La Bella Vita. I'm sure she'll be excited to see it. And I know she's excited to meet you. A bit nervous maybe. But excited too. I've told her all about you. She loves shopping. You love shopping. She loves cake. You love baking. Oh, Tabs, I just know you're going to love her.'

My insides flutter as if there is a tiny bird trapped inside. Maybe Becca is right. Maybe it is too soon. Too soon for everything. Suddenly all I want to do is go back to bed. I want to climb into Mark's and my bed. Close my eyes and wish I could feel him beside me.

'Right. I'm going to grab a shower,' Avery says.

She takes the mug of coffee in one hand and her sketchbook in the other and her feet pitter-patter away.

'Don't use all the hot water,' I call after her, as if anything like that matters right now.

TEN

I shower and dress in black jeans, a cream jumper that isn't woolly enough for February, and I look for my long, grey winter coat. I spend at least twenty minutes searching before I remember it was in the back seat of the car. I grab my leather jacket instead, just as Avery announces, 'Becca is here. She's just pulling into the car park. I can see her.'

Avery points out the sitting room window as a hot-pink Mini Cooper parks in the space reserved for next door and a tall woman in a pinstripe trouser suit steps out. Avery opens the door and beckons for me to follow. At first I'm glad she doesn't suggest inviting Becca in but as we exchange a handshake in the car park and Becca says, 'Hi, Tabitha. It's so nice to finally meet you,' it all feels weird and I wish for the distraction of making tea or opening a packet of biscuits as we sit round a table and get to know one another.

'Nice to meet you too,' I say.

'Avery has told me so much about you,' Becca continues, and I can tell she's keen to make a good first impression.

I don't tell her that Avery only mentioned her to me for the first time an hour ago.

Becca asks the best route to the bistro as we all get into the car, and Avery offers to direct as if Google Maps wasn't the obvious answer. I sit in the back, not really listening as I stare out the window. I'm surprised when Avery tells Becca to turn left at the end of the road instead of right.

'I want to show you all the best parts of Dublin,' Avery says.

Becca reminds Avery that in spite of her thick South African accent she's been living in Ireland for ten years and in Dublin for six. I'm glad she doesn't realise that Avery is clearly avoiding the regular, relatively short route that Mark and I travelled together every morning for the last few years.

So, I find myself in the back of Becca's Mini Cooper, staring out the window. Traffic is heavy and we're stationary more often than not as I watch packed double-deckers whizz by in the bus lane.

'Look, Tabs, it's our old college,' Avery says, pointing towards a large building set back from the road, with tall, leafless trees dotted haphazardly in front.

'You went to college together?' Becca sounds surprised.

'Yeah, of course,' Avery says as if it would be odd if we hadn't. 'We used to do everything together before...'

Before Mark, I want to finish for her but I bite my tongue.

'I studied art and design and Tabs studied culinary arts,' Avery continues.

'Sounds fancy,' I say. 'But it's just cooking, really. You don't need a degree to boil spuds,' I add, regurgitating Mark's exact words.

I wait to hear a laugh or a giggle at least but it doesn't come.

'Did you meet your fiancé in college?' Becca asks.

'No. I, eh, I met Mark after college.'

'Tabby taught Mark to cook,' Avery says, proudly. Then her tone changes as she adds, 'And then Mark became head chef.'

'Oh,' Becca says, and I notice her head turn, just for a

second, to catch Avery's eye before she returns her gaze to the road. Traffic moves and Becca drives on.

'Oh. My. God. Ohmygod. There's Flaherty's. Look. Look. Flaherty's is just the best, Becca.' Avery is giddy with memories.

I glance at the unassuming pub on the street corner. FLAHERTY'S hangs over the door in chunky gold lettering and there's a light-up TIME FOR GUINNESS sign that's coming away from the wall and looks as if it might fall on some unfortunate passer-by at any moment.

'They do the best karaoke nights every Friday,' Avery explains. 'Tabs loves this place. She was here almost every week when we were in college.'

'You can sing?' Becca asks, impressed.

'No. God no. I really can't.'

'But enough gins in us and that doesn't matter.' Avery laughs. 'We butchered "My Heart Will Go On" so often we should probably write a letter of apology to Celine Dion.'

I smile, remembering. Our throats would be sore the next day because of our screeching.

'I can't remember why we ever stopped going,' Avery says. 'I miss it. I loved laughing with you.'

I think about the first night Mark and I took to the stage together. I was so looking forward to our duet, but before the fuzzy lyrics appeared on the screen he scurried back to his friends, leaving me standing with the microphone in my hand and a crowded bar demanding to be entertained. Later that night, after we made love, Mark slapped my arse and said, 'That was the best laugh I had in ages, you sounded like a frog under water. You're so much fun. I love laughing at you.'

'We should go. This Friday. All of us.' Avery battles with her seatbelt as she tries to twist her whole body round to look at me. 'Pleeeaaassseee…'

'I have physio on Fridays,' I say, quicky.

'No problem. We'll go after.'

Becca's eyes shift to the rear-view mirror so she can see me as I shake my head. 'You know, karaoke bars aren't really my thing,' she says.

'Oh.' Avery deflates and turns back to squeeze Becca's knee. 'No worries. Singing isn't for everyone.'

Thank you, I mouth, catching Becca's eye in the mirror once more.

Finally, Becca turns out of the heavy traffic and down a narrower, less busy road.

'This is nice,' she says, taking in the view of brick Georgian houses that line both sides of the street like tall concrete soldiers in red coats and black top hats. 'I've never been over this side of the city before.'

'I keep telling Tabs it's snazzy round here and she should put her prices up. But does she listen?' Avery says as she points at the colourful shop and café fronts that adorn the bottom half of all the buildings.

I don't reiterate that there's more to pricing up a menu than picking numbers off the top of my head, because the conversation has already moved on.

Becca has spotted a beautician above a boutique and Avery thinks we should all go for a facial.

'Could cheer you up, Tabs?' she says, and before I have time to reply she adds, 'This'll be much better than karaoke.'

Becca slows and looks for on-street parking and finally she tucks between two flashy cars both a little too big for the spaces they're crammed into. She turns off the engine and Avery hops out first and hurries round to open the boot. She appears at my side seconds later with a woolly scarf and hat and she wraps me up. The weatherman said on the radio this morning that it was surprisingly mild for early February, but I'm cold and I appreciate Avery's thoughtfulness.

'Ready?' she asks, linking my arm as if I'm a paper doll who might blow away in the wind.

Becca joins us on the path, smiling as she enjoys Avery's overzealous need to take care of me.

I snuggle into the colourful scarf that smells of appley perfume and looks as if someone hand-knitted it. And I like how the hat keeps the wind away from my ears.

'I'm ready,' I say.

The walk feels longer than usual and by the time we reach the familiar cobblestoned, pedestrianised part of the street, I'm flagging.

'We're here,' Avery announces and Becca steps off the footpath to take in a better view of my pride and joy. La Bella Vita.

The large mint window is sweet but needs a lick of paint, and the cream canopy is slightly wonky, and tilts lower on the left than the right. The dissymmetry bothers me more than usual and I stare until my eyes blur.

'Oh, I know this place,' Becca says. 'We had our work Christmas party here. The mini pizzas were amazing. The whole office is still talking about them.'

'Pizza was Mark's speciality,' I say.

Becca's smile flatlines. 'I'm sorry, I didn't mean—'

'It's okay. Mark was talented. I'm glad you liked them.'

'I prefer your pizza,' Avery says. 'I always have.'

Suddenly the ground is made of quicksand and I'm sinking. I can't make pizza and desserts and manage staff and fix a wonky canopy. I can't do this. Not on my own.

Becca places her hand on my shoulder and squeezes gently. 'If it's all too much for one day, we can come back.'

'I... I...' I can't find words.

'Look.' Avery smiles with concerned eyes. 'Why don't we pop in and make coffee. Or some of that toothpaste-flavoured water that you like?'

'Peppermint tea,' I explain for Becca, who's suddenly looking a little lost.

'And then if it's all too much—'

Avery is distracted by a silver Mercedes passing by and parking in the 'set down only' area for deliveries. The door opens and a middle-aged woman with silver hair as shiny as her car steps out.

'Oh, you have got to be kidding me.' Avery makes a chocking sound as if distaste is lodged in her throat. 'What is Catherine doing here?'

'I'm not sure,' I say. 'Checking on the bistro, I suppose.'

Mark's mother notices me as soon as she looks up, and she doubles back with her hands cupping her face. She's even thinner than usual, and her rounded shoulders seem to whittle inches off her. My heart aches until it feels as if it might fall out of my chest.

My eyes shift to Avery for a moment and she nods support-ively as if to say, *you've got this.* But her eyes don't tell me what to do, or say, or how to meet this woman for the first time under such a cloud of sadness. I need time. I need a chance to shuffle my thoughts and try to arrange them in some sort of order. But Catherine is approaching with heartbreak-heavy eyes and a doleful smile.

Before I have a chance to find words, Catherine lunges forward and wraps her arms round me.

'Oh, Tabitha. Oh, Tabitha, sweetheart.'

She cries and cries and we sway on the spot and when we finally come to a standstill, I notice Becca and Avery have stepped back. Catherine lets go of me and gathers herself straighter.

She drags a tissue from the sleeve of her coat and dabs under her eyes and says, 'I'm sorry, Tabitha. I'm so sorry I didn't come to see you in the hospital. It's just... it's just—' Her shoulders round again and her chest heaves. 'It's too hard.'

I nod. I understand. Catherine should soon be my mother-in-law. Now that will never happen.

Catherine blows her nose and when she straightens again she takes a deep breath and says, 'I didn't see you at the funeral.'

'They wouldn't let me out of the hospital.'

'Yes. Your injuries.'

She looks me up and down, searching from some broken part. Some part of me held together with a bandage or a stitch. She searches for the part of me the accident has scarred. If she could see inside of me, inside my head and my heart, she'd find what she's looking for.

'Are you visiting the bistro?' she asks.

'I thought maybe I should put a notice in the window. Explain there's been a bereavement. People might think we've gone out of business and I just want to let them know.'

'Of course. Of course,' Catherine says, and there's a sudden shift in her tone, a hint that she doesn't approve.

'Are you, er, visiting too? The bistro. Eh, are you here to *check* on the bistro?' My palms are sweating.

'Yes. I thought someone should,' Catherine says, shoving the tissue back up her sleeve. 'It's my first time since... since...'

'Since Mark died.' Avery finally speaks, finding the words that nobody else seems able to.

Mark died. For a moment it's like hearing those words for the first time all over again and I am paralysed with grief as I stand face to face with his broken mother.

'I'm so sorry for your loss, Mrs Buchanan,' Avery adds. 'I know how close you and Mark were.'

Catherine's eyes narrow and she glares at Avery is if she is made of something that sours her stomach. She turns back to me and says, 'It was so good to see you, Tabitha. Let's not be strangers.' Then she wraps one side of her coat over the other, lowers her head into the wind and walks towards La Bella Vita.

'That woman,' Avery snorts, as Catherine opens the door and disappears inside. 'Are you all right?'

'She has a key,' I say, watching through the window as

Catherine takes off her coat and drapes it over a chair before she heads towards the kitchen in the back. 'Mark's key is still in the flat. And mine is here.' I tap my pocket, reassuring myself. 'So where did she get one?'

Avery drapes her arm over my shoulder and whispers, 'Let's get you home. We can come back tomorrow.'

The warmth of the car is a welcome relief and I close my eyes and wait for the sound of the engine. Instead, I hear the squeak of someone restlessly shifting on leather seats, and then Avery says, 'What do you think she meant by *let's not be strangers*?' She mimics Catherine's accentuated vowels effortlessly.

Becca shrugs. 'No idea. I thought that was a strange thing to say, though. And why did she ask Tabby if she's visiting her own bistro?'

'The doctors said Tabs could go back to work whenever she's ready,' Avery says.

'Um-hm.'

The engine purrs to life and Avery and Becca continue to talk about me as if I'm not here. I try to block them out and imagine myself back in work, whipping cream and spinning sugar. But the idea feels alien, and my mind wanders towards Catherine's words. Strangers. *Let's not be strangers*. Lately, my life is filled with strangers; loved ones tiptoeing around me in case one wrong word shatters my blown-glass exterior and all my emotion comes spilling out. Avery, Catherine, Mark – the familiar all lost. And Tabitha Greenwood is gone with them. I am walking around in a stranger's skin. It doesn't fit properly. It's too tight across the chest and sometimes I can barely breathe. Other times it's so loose and gaping that I'm cold and numb.

'I have to go,' I say suddenly, opening the door and stepping onto the footpath. 'I need to make sure Catherine is okay. Mark would want me to. *I* want to.'

Avery's door opens too and she swings her legs out, but before she stands up, I raise my hand. Becca smiles at me with knowing eyes and places her hand on Avery's shoulder.

'Call us when you're ready. We'll come back and pick you up,' she says.

Polarised, Avery looks from Becca to me and back to Becca. I can sense her mind racing.

'Go. Enjoy a day together,' I say. 'I'll be fine. I *am* fine.'

'Call us,' Becca reiterates. 'Whenever.'

I nod and walk away. I don't look back to check if Avery pulled her legs back into the car. I don't look back to see if they argue or hug. I don't look back to watch them drive away. I walk with my head lowered and my hands cupping my elbows and I don't look up until I am standing under a wonky cream canopy.

I count backward from five, take a deep breath and use my key. The brass bell above the door chimes and proudly announces my arrival.

ELEVEN

'Hello,' I call, tiptoeing forward as if I'm exploring some foreign land. 'Helloooo.'

I wait for Catherine to answer back but silence hangs heavy. I notice her coat is gone from the chair in the window and I can only imagine this was all too much for her and she left. I feel it too, the overwhelming sense of Mark everywhere. I feel him in the black and white chequered floor tiles that clash with the red-and-white-chequered tablecloths. In the pebble-dashed cream walls and rustic, dark brown and black furnishings. Every inch of La Bella Vita is Mark. People often asked us what our Italian connection was and Mark's face would light up when he told them about summers with his family skiing in the Alps, or boating on Lake Como. I would nod and smile, but the nearest I ever got to Mediterranean holidays as a kid was gazing at one of my mother's beautiful paintings.

I step away from the door and concentrate on measured breaths as I take off my coat, hat and scarf, fold them and place them in the wicker basket for employees' belongings that we keep under the reception desk.

Thursday is typically our busiest day. The place usually

heaves with suits from the business district round the corner. The smells of woody cologne and fruity perfume dance in the air as people with flawless hair, expensive tailored clothes and high-paying jobs laugh and enjoy the perfect lunch to complement their perfect lives. Sometimes a table of suits insist on meeting the chef to thank him for their delicious meal. Those words have nowhere to fall now.

'I'm too busy for this nonsense,' Mark would complain, but nonetheless he would leave the kitchen and head to their table, smiling and waving as if he was a Hollywood A-lister walking the red carpet. Occasionally one of the staff would tell me that a suit raved about the sticky toffee pudding or the basil and black pepper ice cream. No one ever said Mark took credit for my desserts and I never asked. He would return to the kitchen glowing with pride and reeking of superiority.

Today the bistro smells of pine floor cleaner and abeyance. I search the supply closet for air refresher, but when I finally find a canister of lavender fresh, it's empty. I wander into the kitchen and leave the door open behind me. I rack my brain for something to bake with a warm and homely scent that will wrap around the whole bistro like a comforting hug. I grab an apron and gather flour, eggs, butter and sugar. Unfortunately we're all out of fresh cinnamon, and I'm just leaving to buy some in the local market when I hear voices. I hold my breath and listen. Within seconds the door of the office creeps open and a man appears. He's tall and broad, with tight hair – or maybe he's bald – and a smart black beard. His eyes are big and round with a dark chocolate centre and they seem surprised to see me. He steps forward and I back into the kitchen, knocking the bag of flour onto the tiles. A white cloud engulfs me and, when it settles, I'm sprinkled in flour from the waist down.

He takes another step.

'I'll scream,' I say, my voice a barely audible whisper. 'If you come any closer, I will. I'll scream.'

'I'm sorry. I didn't mean to freak you out. You must be Tabitha. I'm Scott,' he says, stepping around the flour on the floor and extending his hand.

I don't shake it as I stare him down.

'I'm the new head chef. Scott Wilson.'

'Excuse me?'

'I start today.'

I begin to dust the flour off myself. 'I think there's been some sort of mistake. We're not looking for a new chef. We're not even open.'

The dust gets in my throat and I start to cough. Scott brushes past me to pour a glass of water. He leaves it on the countertop beside me and fetches the sweeping brush.

'Didn't Catherine tell you about me?' he says as he sweeps.

I've no doubt the look on my face gives him an answer.

'I'm so sorry for your loss,' he says. 'I can't even imagine.'

I swallow hard as tears prick my eyes. 'Look, I'm not sure what's going on here,' I say. 'Or what you think is happening. But as I said, we are not looking to hire any new staff right now.'

Scott stops sweeping and makes cautious eye contact. 'But I signed a contract. Literally five minutes ago. In Catherine's office.'

'Right. Well, Catherine doesn't work here, so...' I take the brush from him.

'I think there's some crossed wires. You should probably talk to Catherine. But I *need* this job.'

'Is this a joke? Is this some sort of sick joke?'

Scott shoves his hands in his pockets and stares at the ground as he says, 'I really am so very sorry for everything you've been through. But Catherine has offered to double my salary. I called La Vie D'Amour straight away and told them that I quit.'

'La Vie D'Amour,' I echo, finding it hard to catch my breath.

'That place is very good. It's booked out for something like three months in advance.'

'Six. But since they lost their head chef this morning...'

I shake my head. 'I'm sorry. There's no way I can afford to pay you. I doubt I could match your old salary, never mind double it. Catherine has made a terrible mistake. I'm sure if you explain to your boss he'll understand.'

'I called him a pompous fart-bag on the phone. So, eh, no. I don't think he'd welcome me back with open arms.'

'Tabitha. Tabitha, sweetheart, what are you doing back here?' Catherine says, appearing from Mark's office with a piece of paper in her hands.

My eyes home in on the large lettering at the top. *La Bella Vita – Employment Contract.*

'I wasn't expecting you back so soon,' she says. 'You've lost the most important person in your whole world.'

She looks me up and down, disgust rippling across her face as she stares at the flour explosion.

'It's understandable that you're falling apart, sweetheart,' she continues. 'No one is judging you.'

'You're here,' I say. I mean it as a compliment to her strength but it comes out like an accusation. 'I can be here too. I *should* be here too.'

Catherine's eyes water and her bottom lip quivers. 'I loved him with all my heart. That's why I'm here. It's what Mark would want. Us Buchanans are fighters. When the going gets tough, we get tougher. But I know not everyone is as strong. I know it's harder for you, sweetheart. You've always had your struggles and no one is expecting you to cope with this. But I'm here now. And I've hired Scott. Only the best chef is good enough for my Mark's legacy. We are going to take care of everything. Don't you worry.'

'We can't afford this,' I say.

'No. I don't expect you can. But I am happy to pay. With

personal funds, of course. Lord knows there's not much in the kitty with the way this place was managed for the last few years.'

'I really don't think—'

'Tabitha, please. It's already settled. I will be paying Scott's salary until business is booming. Mark has left me his share of the bistro and I intend to make my son proud. Now, don't you think it's time you went home and got yourself cleaned up?'

My heart is beating out of my chest.

'Scott, if you could clean this up, please?' Catherine says. 'Put those expensive hands of yours to use.'

Scott looks at me, apologising with his eyes, as he takes the brush from me and begins sweeping again.

I walk away, creating dusty footprints as I go.

Catherine calls after me, 'This is for the best, sweetheart. I know you're not good with change but trust me. It's what Mark would have wanted.'

I fetch my coat, hat and gloves and barge through the door, gulping in air as I reach the street. I dial Avery's number, hardly able to punch the digits into my phone fast enough.

'Hey. How did it go?' Avery asks. 'Are you ready to go home?'

'Actually, is it too late to call your hairdresser friend?'

'Barney? No. Why?'

'Okay. Good. Can you call him now? Can you book an appointment for me, please? For today.'

'Sure. No problem. But why the sudden change of heart?'

'I just think you're right. I think it's time I changed.'

TWELVE

I've had long, mousy-brown hair all my life. I was born with a full head of wiry curls. My mother always said that's why she had such bad heartburn while she was pregnant. By the time I was a toddler, my wavy hair cascaded all the way down my back. When I was a little girl, I used to pretend I was Rapunzel. I would lie on my bed and hang my head over the edge until my hair swept the floor and I would pretend my Prince Charming was on his way. Avery would laugh and tease me but I kept pretending nevertheless.

On Monday morning, I stare in the bathroom mirror at ash-blond hair that sits above my shoulders. My eyes look a little browner, my cheeks a tad pinker and my lips a hint redder. I spent all weekend mulling over what to wear on my first full day back at work. I settled on my favourite jeans and a pinstripe white-and-navy blouse. The weight I've lost since Mark died is particularly noticeable and I add a belt to stop my jeans from slipping down, but I feel smart and ready.

Avery and Becca are in the kitchen when I walk in.

'Swit-swoo,' Avery whistles. 'My God, you look unreal.'

I blush.

'Are you ready to knock 'em dead?'

'I'm actually really nervous. I feel like I'm the one starting a new job.'

'I still can't believe bloody Catherine. Throwing her weight around like that. Who does she think she is?'

'Mark's mother,' I sigh. 'And apparently as the new co-owner she has every right to hire staff.'

'She should have run it by you first. That's just manners. Now we know where Mark got it from,' Avery says.

Normally I would feel obliged to defend the Buchanans, especially in front of Becca, but I'm tired and Avery is right. Mark was so like this mother in both appearance and personality. It came as no real surprise when I called my solicitor and he confirmed that Mark had indeed left his share of our bistro to his mother.

'Mark's share of the flat will go to you, of course. As I'm sure you're aware, there are laws and agreements to protect home owners. But unfortunately, there are no such laws in business. Mark can leave his share of La Bella Vita to whomever he chooses.'

I didn't even know Mark had a will. I'd told Avery he didn't. It wasn't something we ever discussed. I took for granted that we were young and had so much more time. But soon Mark's 49 per cent of the bistro will legally transfer to Catherine. That, combined with the 2 per cent he insisted we gift her when she loaned us the deposit for elaborate pizza ovens, gives Catherine the presiding share of La Bella Vita. However, my solicitor explained that nothing is official until the paperwork is signed and I would be well within my rights to contest Scott's employment if I see fit.

I didn't mention the later part of the call to Avery. I've no doubt she would advise me to put Catherine in her place while I still can. But I'm not strong enough for any drama. And, despite Catherine's best efforts to appear otherwise, I know neither is she.

'I haven't shared a kitchen with anyone other than Mark for years,' I say. 'What if I can't work with Scott?'

'Is he hot?' Avery asks.

'What?'

'The way you described him, he sounds hot.'

'I dunno. I didn't really notice.'

'He's hot,' Avery tells Becca. 'That means he's hot.'

'Hot or not, he's one of the best chefs in the whole country. The last place he worked has a whole heap of awards. You know those plaques that we have hanging on the front wall?'

Avery stares blankly.

'The ones that you say look like ugly plates.'

'Oh, those yokes.'

'Yes, those. We have two silver ones that we nearly killed ourselves to earn. La Vie D'Amour have so many gold ones that they're running out of wall.'

'And they've a better name too.' Avery nods.

Becca digs her elbow into Avery's side and says, 'Well, I think it sounds like their loss is your gain.'

'Or, it's as intimidating as hell. I mean, how am I supposed to be his boss when he's like Gordon Ramsay junior.' I tug at the lapel of my blazer. 'Maybe I should change. I should change, shouldn't I? This looks shit. What was I thinking?'

Avery rubs her side and smiles. 'Your jeans look great. Your hair looks A-mazing. And you're a talented chef. You've got this.'

THIRTEEN

The sun isn't up yet when Becca unwittingly drives the wrong way up a one-way street and then pulls over at the side of the road.

'Thanks so much for the lift,' I say awkwardly.

'No problem. I'm showing flats on this side of town today. La Bella Vita was on my way.'

I don't believe her. And not just because it's obvious she's unfamiliar with this side of the city. But because Avery's eyes were practically bulging out of her head this morning as she encouraged Becca to chaperone me.

'The bus! Are you mad?' Avery had said when I attempted to leave the flat. 'You can't get the bus alone. What if something happens?'

I didn't bother to ask what my sister was worried might happen. I knew she would have a long list of hypotheticals and I had too much on my mind to argue about travel. So I strapped myself into the front seat of Becca's Mini and we made small talk the whole way here.

'What time will I pick you up?'

'Oh, em. I don't know what time I'll finish at. It's probably best if I just get the bus home.'

Her eyebrows pinch. 'I'll be passing by again later. Around six,' she says. 'As I said, I have to come this way anyway.'

'Becca,' I say slowly. 'I'm fine. I promise. I've been getting the 54X almost every day for the last three years. I'm not going to get lost. Or pass out. Or fall under the wheels. Or whatever other crazy scenario Avery is worried about.'

Becca smiles. 'So would you like to break it to her or shall I?'

'If you wouldn't mind talking to her...'

'Oh God.' She laughs. 'I better buy some flowers on my way home from work. It's always best to lead with flowers, isn't it?'

'I *do* know how much she cares,' I say, feeling Becca needs to hear it more than I need to say it.

'I know.' She nods. 'Good luck today. Just remember you're the boss, yeah?'

'Thank you.'

I open the car door and a gust of sharp wind pinches my cheeks. I watch as Becca U-turns and we both wave as she drives away.

The street is eerily still as cafés and shops sleep soundly with their canopies retracted and their shutters down. I'm surprised to find La Bella Vita is awake, light from inside shining through the sash window to cast a yellow waffle-shaped shadow on the footpath. I don't bother to root for my key as I take a deep breath and push open the unlocked door.

'Good morning,' I say, announcing my arrival to an empty bistro. I cringe when I hear how hard I'm trying to be chipper.

I go through my regular cold-morning routine: peel off layers, stuff them under the reception desk and make my way straight to the kitchen to boil the kettle for a much-needed cup of tea.

'Oh. Hello,' Scott says, looking up, as I push the door open with my hip.

He's head to toe in uniform. His double-breasted jacket is blindingly white and 'La Bella Vita' is embroidered in gold lettering above his chest pocket. Mark and I have never worn jackets with the bistro name on them. I hand-made a couple of uniforms when we first opened and we've been wearing them since. They're greying over time, no matter how often I boil-wash them.

Scott has a carrot in one hand and a knife in the other. He stares at me with the same wide, surprised-to-see-me eyes as last week and I don't try to hide how much it irritates me.

'Nice hat,' I say, pointing at his *toque blanche*, which looks like an oversized mushroom on top of his head.

'Thank you.'

'You know a hairnet would do, if you'd be more comfortable,' I say.

'Bald,' he says, smiling. 'This thing is a bit itchy. But Catherine said—'

'I won't tell if you don't.'

'It's okay, I'm getting used to it,' he says, as he goes back to chopping carrots.

I catch my reflection in the shiny metal countertop and realise Scott's wide-eyed gaze was for my new hair. Last week he met a long-haired brunette and I arrived today as a made-over blonde. I cringe for a moment and try to squash the feeling of trying way too hard in my own kitchen. I run my hand over the back of my hair and, although *I'm trying something new* or *I just fancied a change* are on the tip of my tongue, I press my lips firmly together and walk towards the kettle. Except it isn't there. I glance around the countertops. There's no sign of it anywhere.

'Did you move the kettle?' I ask. 'It's usually here, by the sink.'

'I put it in the staffroom. I thought that's where it belonged.'

'There's no sink in the staffroom.'

'I can get it for you—'

'No, thank you.'

'It's no trouble.'

'It's fine!'

I fetch a pot, pour some water and light the hob. Soon the only sounds are water bubbling and Scott's steel blade slicing against the chopping board.

Finally, when I can't take the silence any longer, I say, 'Why are you here so early?'

'Veg prep.'

'Veg prep.'

I glance out the window where the orangey hue of morning is slowly starting to push the darkness aside. If we are opening today – which, from the fancy new uniform, preposterous hat and vegetable chopping, I'm guessing Catherine has decided we are – we don't open until after twelve.

'You don't need to come in before nine,' I say. 'The rest of the staff won't be here until eleven.'

'I know,' he says, and the sound of the knife against the board feels as if he is slicing carrots inside my head. 'But I've put some challenging dishes on the menu and I—'

'You changed the menu?'

He adjusts his hat and scratches his head. 'It's just some minor tweaks to freshen things up a little.'

I pause to catch my breath as pain burrows between my eyes. I've become used to headaches in recent weeks but this one is almost blinding. 'Did Catherine ask you to change it?' I say.

Scott's face is painfully serious and I can tell that walking the tightrope between impressing Catherine and not pissing me off is already taking its toll on him. 'Would you like to see the menu?'

I don't speak but I'm sure my narrowed eyes and folded arms answer for me. Without another word he sets down the knife and hurries away. The pot on the hob begins to hiss and smoke and I realise all the water has boiled off and left a murky brown burn mark in its place. I lift the pot into the sink and concentrate on deep, even breathing but, if anything, my headache worsens.

I yelp at a tap on my shoulder, and turn round to find Scott with a piece of paper in his hand. He extends his arm and I take the page. He returns to the chopping board and it's obvious he doesn't like me, or he feels sorry for me. Maybe both. I try not to think about it as I scan the appetisers. *Soup, prawns, wings, antipasti.* A little boring. But not terrible, I decide. The mains are more imaginative and I feel the pangs of hunger as I read on. I pause and a lump gathers in my throat as I read the desserts. I scan them again. And once more before I say, 'You didn't change them. The desserts. You kept it the exact same.'

'You can't improve on perfection,' he says.

I laugh. 'Wow. You're cheesier than your menu.'

Scott grins shamelessly and tosses a slice of carrot into his mouth. 'I haven't printed these up yet,' he says between crunches. 'So, if you want to change anything...'

'No. It's good. I like it.'

'Okay. Great. Brilliant. And I thought we could change it up every few weeks. Move with what's in season.'

My head is spinning.

'I don't mind doing it. I can work them up and you can just give a thumbs-up or -down. If you don't like it, we won't change it.'

Scott's enthusiasm is both exhilarating and exhausting. He reminds me of me when La Bella Vita first opened. I was full of bright ideas and I was so excited to experiment with dishes I hoped would become signature. But Mark was more concerned with building a stellar menu of staples. Favourites customers would order over and over. He was right, I know: returning customers was worth more than any number of awards or plaques on the wall; but nonetheless the monotony got to me. Slowly I focused my ideas more and more on desserts. Mark wasn't very sweet-toothed and left me to my own devices.

'I mean, pizza is great. And a real crowd-pleaser,' Scott says, 'but maybe not every Friday, you know?'

I nod and he smiles. Then he unbuttons his double-breasted jacket and hangs it up. I hate that I notice how strong and defined his arms are.

'Are you leaving?' I ask.

'I'm going to get us some breakfast.'

I look around the kitchen. 'I usually just whip something up.'

'First-day treat,' he says, and it's more of a question than a statement. 'It's on me.'

'Sure. Sounds good.'

'There's this vendor on the corner. He should be arriving with his cart any minute and I want to catch him while his bagels are still fresh from the oven.'

'Rashidi's Bagels?'

'Yes. Yes. You're a fan too, I take it.'

'They're the best.'

Scott's tense shoulders relax and his unsure smile widens and becomes less forced.

'Rashidi used to park up at the other end of town,' he says. 'For almost a year I started every morning with a fresh bagel and a chat.'

'Really? I didn't know that. I thought this street was always his spot.'

'About four years ago, a group of retail owners got together and reported Rashidi to the council,' Scott says. 'They gave him hell over permits and whatnot but he fought tooth and nail for his little business. But then, suddenly, one morning he just wasn't there anymore.'

My heart aches to think of the frail old man with wiry salt-

and-pepper hair and a heart as big as his cart being swept away by the council like rubbish.

'For years I wondered where he went and if he was okay,' Scott says. 'Until last week when I came here for my interview with Catherine. There Rashidi was. Right outside. His bagels as delicious as I remembered and his cart looking shinier than ever.'

'He does like a shiny cart,' I say.

I think about the day I met Rashidi. I could hear the commotion on the street from the kitchen. I hurried outside to find Mark screaming at an elderly man standing next to a hand-pushed street cart.

'You can't be here,' Mark bellowed. 'This is a classy place and my customers don't want to look outside at this piece of shit while they're enjoying their meal.'

Rashidi explained that all café and shop owners felt the same way and he had nowhere to go.

'Not my problem, mate,' Mark said. 'Move along or I'll move you.'

The worry and oppression in Rashidi's eyes broke my heart. He nodded and agreed that he'd be gone the next day. Later, when Mark was distracted by the accounts, I went back outside and bought a bagel.

'My partner doesn't work Mondays or Wednesday afternoons. Feel free to park here then,' I said.

Rashidi took my hands in his and squeezed so tight that his gratitude should have filled me up, but all I felt was sadness. Sadness that a day and a half at the side of the street meant so much to him. So, together we called in to every business along the street. We asked for half-days outside the beauticians and mornings next to the dentist. We secured hours here and there until, finally, we managed to fill up the whole week. Rashidi is synonymous with our street now, moving like the hands of a clock up and down both sides of the road. He's there on the

sunniest afternoons and the coldest mornings. And our street is
so lucky to have the best bagels in town.

'Do you want to know why I took this job?' Scott asks,
fetching a smart leather jacket and his wallet. 'Rashidi is why.
Working with people who are threatened by an old man trying
to earn a living can really drag you down after a while. I should
have left sooner, to be honest.'

'Well,' I say, swallowing hard so my emotion doesn't tip
over. 'Sounds like a sign.'

'I never thought about it like that. Do you believe the
universe led me towards Rashidi so I'd take this job? Like a sign
this is where I'm supposed to be?'

'Erm, I think it's a sign you should start mornings with a
bagel.' I smile. 'But yeah, sure... all that universe stuff too.'

Scott blushes and there something endearing about his
embarrassment as he finally takes off his *toque blanche*.

'Bagels,' he says. 'I'm on it.'

FOURTEEN

MARCH

Just because you're boring doesn't mean La Bella Vita needs to be. It's about time you joined the rest of the rest of the world online. You're a star, little sister, don't forget to shine.

I smell tea and biscuits before I even open my eyes. My body is heavy with sleep after another restless night and pulling myself to sit up in bed feels like a workout. I stuff a couple of pillows between my back and the headboard and rub my eyes that don't want to focus. As suspected, I find a mug of tea and two chocolate Hobnobs waiting on my bedside table. There's a sheet of La Bella Vita–headed paper peeping out from under the cup and saucer. I slide it out, laughing at the perfectly round tea stain created by the bottom of the cup, and squint as I try to read Avery's writing.

Happy March 1st. Check your emails.
Love,
A x

P.S. Bikkies might be stale. Bite with caution.

I sip tea and bite into a biscuit, then immediately spit it back onto the saucer. My phone is full of the usual emails that seems to gather in the night. A supplier letting me know they sent baby gem lettuce instead of iceberg. Staff asking to swap shifts and book holidays. Bills, bills and more bills. My inbox mirrors my real life with rather strange accuracy. I can be crying over the wrong lettuce one day and swooning over the waiting staff's holiday snaps the next. The last month back at work has seen many, many tears but I have smiled and laughed too. And even on the hardest days – the days when the weight of grief is heaviest – my sister is there for me. Trying her best to put a smile on my face. Like now. Avery's email arrived at exactly midnight in my inbox, where it patiently waited all night until I was ready to take on a new month and a new resolution.

As I read Avery's words, my skin tingles thinking about an online space for icing and spun sugar and stiff peaks and tortes. My phone is running out of memory – bursting at the seams – with photos of my favourite treats, and I would love an opportunity to share them. But I don't know the first thing about website design and neither does Avery. I imagine professional design is expensive and, with a stack of bills demanding my attention, *BellaVita.ie* will have to wait.

Nevertheless, I can't help but muse about fonts and a colour scheme and a button in the shape of a macaron that you click when you want to make a booking. By the time I finally return to the here and now and drag myself out of bed, I've already missed the bus. I grab my phone and begin typing.

Tabs: Fancy a bagel this morning?

Scott: Are you running late again?

I resist the urge to send an angry emoji – a middle-finger one. But Scott's question isn't unjustified. I've been late almost every morning this week. Partially because I'm exhausted from broken sleep, but mostly because I dread bumping into Catherine. She has taken to dropping by the bistro unannounced; before a nail appointment, after the hairdresser, for lunch with a friend. It's always under the guise of checking up on Scott, but I suspect that *really* she is checking up on me. Which is why it's both awkward and frustrating that I've never actually been there when she does. The more time that passes without me physically seeing her, the more I dread when I will. She is so like Mark in so many ways. Facing her hurts my heart. I try to put the thought of my almost mother-in-law out of my head and take on the Trojan effort of sliding my legs out of bed to place my two feet on the floor.

Tabs: Missed my bus

Scott: Is this a peace offering?

Tabs: Do you want a bagel or not?

Scott: Sure

Tabs: What type?

Scott: Surprise me 👍

Two overcrowded buses pass by without stopping and I'm frozen by the time a third stops. Traffic is bumper-to-bumper the whole journey and, by the way woman beside me looks up from her Kindle every so often to smile at me, I've no doubt she can hear my stomach rumbling.

Rashidi's spot is next to the bus stop this morning. As

soon as the bus doors open, he winks at me, opens a wonky shelf on the side of his cart and says, 'The last bacon bagel of the day.'

'Rashidi, I could kiss you.'

The delicious smell calls me, but I don't reach to take it. Instead, I ask, 'Am I really that predictable?'

'You like what you like,' he says.

'I think that means I'm boring.' I try to make it sound like a joke but we both know it's not. 'Maybe I'll try something different today.'

His wise eyes narrow. 'Everything okay?'

'Um-hmm.' I scan the menu stuck to the side of the cart. The sun has faded the text over the years and I can't make much out. 'You know what, could you surprise me? I'll take two of your best bagels, please.'

'Two,' he says, and curiosity twitches in the corners of his smile.

'One for my co-worker.'

'Ah, that new boy.'

I don't know how old Scott is. He hasn't asked me and I haven't asked him. I assume he's in his thirties, a year or two either side of my age. Certainly not a boy. But Rashidi refers to anyone under fifty as a boy or a girl.

'The tall fellow. Not much hair,' Rashidi says as he makes up fresh bagels.

'Yes. That's Scott.'

'Scott,' Rashidi says, as if he's trying the name on for size, and his widening smile tells me he likes how it fits. 'Nice boy. Very nice boy.'

We chat as he finishes. When I pay and turn to leave, he calls me back.

'Aren't you forgetting something?'

I have a bagel in each hand and change in my pocket. I shake my head.

'My kiss.' He chuckles. 'You said, you could kiss me and I expect you to be as good as your word.'

I double back and kiss Rashidi's cheek. 'Thank you. See you tomorrow.'

'Tomorrow,' he says, and he turns to serve his next customer.

Scott is waiting for me at the door of La Bella Vita and his face is the colour of barley water.

'What's wrong?'

He grabs the bagels as he ushers me inside. He drops them on the nearest table and throws his coat over them.

'Catherine's here,' he says. 'In the kitchen. Pacing.'

'Pacing?'

'She's been reading the new menu and wearing a track in the floor without a word for ten minutes. Not a single word.'

'That doesn't mean anything,' I say, knowing it means everything. Mark could dig a trench with pacing when he was frustrated.

'Right,' Scott says, marching towards the kitchen as if he's a soldier going into battle. 'Let's get this over with.'

My stomach rumbles as I follow him, leaving the delicious smell of warm bagels behind.

'Oh my goodness,' Catherine says, lowering the menu to stare at me. She brushes past Scott to take my hands. 'Look at you. Just look at you. Have you lost weight?'

'A little, yeah. I think it's just everything that's been going on,' I say, wishing I was wearing my uniform, which hides my new shape better.

'And your hair. Wow. Isn't that lovely. What a change. I almost didn't recognise you.' Catherine is smiling widely. I can see her gums. 'I'm so glad you're putting this effort in at last. If only my Mark could see you. He'd be so proud. He was always trying to get you to shed those extra pounds, wasn't he?'

Scott can't seem to wipe the disgust off his face as he glares at Catherine from behind. And then I feel it. His pity. His gaze shifts to me and his eyes tell me to ignore her, or that I look great, or any number of those generic, peppy phrases people use to try to make someone feel better.

'Scott tells me you've been checking out the new menu,' I say, desperate to move the conversation away from my waistline.

Catherine's glare pulls slowly away from me, dragging part of my soul with it, and she returns her attention to the piece of paper in her hand. 'Yes. Yes indeed.'

Scott folds his arms.

'This here for example.' She runs a ruby-red nail across the paper as if she's highlighting a word. 'Foey grass.'

'Foie gras,' Scott corrects her pronunciation with a hint of smugness. 'It's really just a fancy way of saying pâté.'

'Oh, pâté,' Catherine says, nodding. 'And this...' she reads on, 'beurre blanc. Is that a wine?'

'A butter sauce. Delicious with fish,' Scott explains.

Catherine's nodding grows faster. 'Good. Good. I like the sound of that.'

'I can promise you they taste even better than they sound,' Scott says.

Catherine's eyes flick onto Scott with an intensity that warns him that they better. He doesn't seem to notice. Thankfully.

'And here. The desserts.' Catherine's nail is tapping the paper again and I think she is going to punch a hole straight through it. 'They're the same as before, are they not?'

'They are.' Scott smiles. 'They're so well thought out. A little something for everyone. I couldn't possibly improve them.'

'Hmm.'

'I'd be more than happy to revise the desserts,' I say. 'In fact, I've wanted to shake up the menu for a long time, so—'

'Oh good,' Catherine says, cutting me off. 'It's great that we're on the same page.'

I smile. It *is* good.

'I've spoken to the accountant and he agrees.'

My smile fades.

'He says buying in ready-made desserts will save us a small fortune.'

'Ready-made?' Scott sounds as disgusted as I feel. 'I really don't think—'

'It's decision made, I'm afraid,' Catherine says. 'The accountant says we're haemorrhaging money and we have to save where we can. And no one ever makes it that far down the menu anyway.'

Winded, I just about catch my breath enough to say, 'Let me speak to him. Go over the numbers again.'

'Do you know Bill?' Catherine asks.

'Who?'

'Bill Jenkins, the new accountant. I had to let that other chap go.'

'You fired our accountant?'

'Bill has been managing my finances for years. I wasn't about to let some stranger dip his hands into my pockets. Let's not forget who is paying for what, shall we?'

A tiny vein at the side of my head pulses. I want to tell Catherine to shove her money. But I catch the words just as they're on the tip of my tongue, and swallow them down. Scott needs this job. La Bella Vita needs Scott. And Catherine damn well knows it.

'I'm grateful for your support,' I say, the words tasting bitter in my mouth. 'But this is a mistake. Desserts are our biggest seller. Especially at the weekend.'

'Please.' Catherine drags a hand over her face and puffs out. 'I don't have the energy for an argument.' She is pale and her hands tremble slightly. I wonder if I should fetch her a seat. But before I have time she continues, 'What has got into you, Tabitha? I'm just trying to help.'

'I know. But Mark would tell you that you're wrong,' I say. The lie sits over me like a dark cloud and I swear it feels as if Catherine can see it.

'I'm doing my best. And this is the thanks I get. My God. I'm glad my Mark isn't here to see this. It would break his heart.'

'Let's all take a deep breath,' Scott says, watching me with concern.

Catherine places her hand on her chest and inhales deeply and exhales slowly. She repeats. Over and over. Until Scott finally breaks the performance by saying, 'Better?'

Catherine's narrowed eyes glare at me as she says, 'Better.'

'I apologise if I'm overstepping the mark here,' Scott says, edging forward. 'But I think fresh confections are very important for reputation. People hold La Bella Vita in high regard. A testimony to Mark's legacy.'

'Oh.'

Tears trickle down Catherine's cheeks and it's hard to hold back my own.

'If you think fresh baking is good for business... if you think it's what our customers want—' she says.

'I do. But as I said, if I've crossed a line...'

Catherine stretches her arm out and passes Scott the menu. 'My son was a fantastic chef,' she says, her voice cracking. 'But he was an even better businessman. He built this place up from scratch and I am immensely proud of all he achieved. If this is a good business decision, then I know my Mark would be behind it. Thank you, Mr Wilson.'

Catherine leaves without saying goodbye and Scott accompanies her to the door. I duck into the office, shaking. There's a photo of Mark and his golfing buddies on his desk. I flop into the swivel chair and stare at it.

I think about some of the arguments we had over the years.

We fought when Mark suggested I lose weight because his mother was worried about my health. We didn't speak for days when I returned from a spa weekend with Avery to find Catherine repainting our bedroom in her choice of colour. We almost called off the wedding a couple of times because Mark's mother didn't like any of the venues I chose. Avery even joked that Catherine would probably have to approve my dress before she'd let me walk down the aisle and embarrass her in front of her friends.

'Oh, Mark. It wasn't supposed to be like this,' I whisper as I blow a kiss at his sunburned cheeks.

FIFTEEN

There's a gentle knock on the door before Scott's head peeps round it. 'Still hungry?' he asks, holding a bagel in each hand.

I nod, but I'm not.

'Mind if I join you?'

I wish he wouldn't but he pulls over a cardboard box, marked 'lollipops', that I keep meaning to bring home to Avery, and uses it as a makeshift stool.

Scott and I munch on our bagels without conversation for a while until, finally, between mouthfuls he says, 'Does Catherine always speak to you like that?'

'Like what?'

'With an air of... I don't know. I can't quite put my finger on it.'

I lower the bagel I'd been eating on autopilot and slowly realise that Rashidi has given me my usual simple bacon.

'That's just Catherine,' I say. 'She doesn't mean any offence.'

'And you don't take any?'

I wince. 'I didn't say that.'

Scott looks away and takes another bite of his bagel.

'What?' I say, knowing he's itching to say more.

He shrugs. 'Nothing.'

'No, c'mon, say it.'

Scott drops his half-eaten bagel onto the wrapper on the desk and says, 'She didn't seem to have a problem anymore once I spoke up.'

'Yeah. You didn't have to do that, by the way.'

'Do what?'

'Take all the heat like that,' I say. 'I'm not afraid to take responsibility. But she lost her son, and, like she said, now isn't the right time for arguments.

Scott nods and we eat in silence for a while, but it's obvious he's chewing on more than his bagel. Finally, he says, 'I respect Catherine. I'm grateful for this job and I'm happy to be working here. But the way she spoke to you earlier...' He pauses and shakes his head. 'Well, if she's like that when she's grieving, I just... I can't imagine what she must have been like before.'

I sigh. This conversation feels unbearably familiar. Avery flagged Mark's choice of phrasing countless times. And each time I would defend him, just as I find myself defending Catherine now.

'The Buchanans don't mince their words,' I say. 'Trust me, you'll get used to it. I don't even hear it anymore.'

'That's kind of sad, don't you think?'

'I don't think about it,' I say, but what I really mean is, I try not to think about it.

Scott stands up, crumples the wrapper off his bagel into a ball and tosses it into the bin.

'I suppose work will be never boring with Catherine around to keep us on our toes,' he says, forcing a laugh. 'Speaking of which, I best get back to it.'

He tilts his head towards the door and his expression seems to ask me if I'm okay to be left on my own.

'Do you think I'm boring?' I blurt.

'What?' Scott shifts his weight from one foot to the other as if my question has unsteadied him slightly. 'Why do you ask that?'

'You said Catherine is never boring. And I think I might be. Actually, I know I am.'

Scott sits back down and puffs out. 'I thought you said Catherine doesn't get into your head anymore.'

'It's not her,' I say.

His face tells me he doesn't believe me.

'See this.' I point at the wrapper from my bagel. 'Every day I order a plain bacon bagel.'

'And...'

'And that's boring, right?'

'If you like bacon, I don't see the problem.'

'Today I told Rashidi to surprise me. I asked him to make me his best bagel and what does he give me?'

Scott stares at me for a moment before he realises I'm waiting for an answer. 'Bacon,' he says, grinning.

'Exactly. Bloody bacon.'

'Was it nice?' he asks.

'What?'

'Was your bagel nice? You polished if off, even cold, so I'm guessing it was good.'

'It was great. But that's not the point.'

'What other point is there? You ordered something you like. It was good. The end.'

I exhale, frustrated. 'Rashidi gave me the same as usual because he knew I wouldn't like something else as much.'

'Okay.' Scott's face scrunches. 'I'm not sure what we're establishing here other than bacon is good.'

'I'm predictable. Always the same. Always a bacon bagel. Always bloody boring.'

'I order the same bagel most mornings. Chicken tikka,' Scott says. 'I don't think that makes me boring. Or predictable. Tikka is delicious. You can't sum up a whole person with just one word. Or one bagel.'

Losing the point, I say, 'My sister thinks I'm boring.'

'Really. Your sister said that?'

'Kind of. It's complicated. Avery's all free-spirited and arty and fun and I'm not.'

'You're not fun?

'I used to be. But that was a long time ago.'

'Running your own bistro must be stressful,' Scott says. 'Sounds to me like you just need to let your hair down a bit.'

I glide my hand over my hair and for the first time I allow myself a moment to absorb the shock I feel when the silky strands come to a stop just above my shoulders.

'Is there anything I can do to help?' Scott asks.

'Really?'

'There is more to me than chopping carrots. I do know how to have a laugh.'

'Do you know anything about building a website?' I ask.

'Are you serious? That's your idea of fun? Website building. Okay, your sister is right. You are boring.' He chuckles.

My face feels hot and I've no doubt I'm blushing.

'It's her idea, actually,' I say. 'It's just this whole thing. I promised her I'd give it a try. And, well, I'm not very techy.'

'My sister is bossy too,' Scott says, offering me a pity smile.

'Avery's not bossy. She's just... um...

Scott laughs again. More relaxed this time.

'I know a guy who knows a guy,' he says. 'I could give him a call, if that helps?'

My mind wanders to the stack of invoices in my email inbox. 'I'm not sure I could afford a professional, to be honest. Plus, I'd have to run anything expensive by Catherine first, and I'd rather boil my head than talk to her right now.'

'Fair enough. What about Instagram?'

'Yeah. Maybe.'

There's nothing to stop me from bending the resolutions a little to make them work, I decide.

'A lot of places use DMs for bookings. La Vie D'Amour has that option and it works really well,' he says.

I don't mention that I suggested utilising Instagram messaging to Mark two years ago and he shot down the idea without discussion.

'People don't want to book online. They like a voice on the end of the phone, Tabs. Don't you know that's good customer service?'

'We could run some competitions too,' Scott continues. 'Romantic dinners for two. That sort of thing. I know it means giving away a free meal, but likes and shares always put La Vie D'Amour all over people's stories. It could give us a lot of visibility.'

'What about Catherine?' I say.

'I'll tell her. I can say it was my idea, if it helps. It's good for business. She won't argue with that.'

'And it's free,' I say. 'So I won't have to listen to any more digs about our finances.'

'Exactly. What's not to love?' Scott takes his phone from his pocket and types something. 'Dammit, the La Bella Vita handle is already in use. We could try La Bella Vita Dublin or Bella Vita—'

'Actually, we have a profile already. Mark set something up when we first opened. But we never got round to doing much with it.'

'Too busy in the kitchen,' Scott says.

'Something like that.'

'Can you remember what it was called— oh, never mind, think I found it. La Bella Vita Bistro. Is this it?'

Scott turns his phone round so I can see the screen.

'That's it.'

'Perfect,' he says. 'What's the password?'

'No idea.'

He sighs.

'Don't worry, Mark writes all this stuff down. He's obsessive when it comes to spreadsheets and filing stuff.' My voice cracks and I swallow. 'Was. I mean Mark was obsessive. He was very organised.'

Silence follows and the warm office is briefly cold and I wrap my arms round myself. Scott looks at me and I can tell he's searching for the right words. He must not find them, because silence lingers.

'You know, we should really get back to work, lunch won't prep itself,' I say, dragging the sleeve of my jumper across my eyes.

I make my way towards the door but Scott's hand on my shoulder stops me in my tracks.

'Why don't you take a moment,' he says, so softly I have to strain to hear him. 'Have a look around, see if you can find that password. I can handle things in the kitchen for a while.'

I nod and silent tears trickle down my cheeks.

SIXTEEN

'I'm so excited about this resolution,' Avery says, her voice big and commanding the small office as my phone sits on the desk on loudspeaker.

'Me too.'

'Really?'

'You sound surprised,' I say as I flick through colourful pieces of paper in the desk drawers.

'No. Not surprised. Just relieved. You didn't seem to like February's resolution all that much.'

I run my hand through my hair and replay Catherine's shocked face as she took in my blond bob.

'Actually, I loved that one too. You're good at this.'

'I am. You're right.' Avery laughs. 'Instagram is even better than a website. It's where all the cool people are.'

'You're just saying that because you have eleven million billion followers over there.'

'Ha. I wish. I'm a small fish with a few thousand. But you have to start somewhere, right?'

Avery regularly receives messages from strangers wanting to commission a painting. It makes up half her workload. The other half is made up of arty brands wanting to collaborate. Avery's gift of the gab shines even online. She can post a video of a ladybird climbing a blade of grass, say something about nature and beauty and bam! The video explodes with likes and shares galore.

'Just wait till people see your cakes, Tabs,' she says. 'It's like art you can eat. You'll be booked out for months.'

'Not unless I can find this bloody password. I just know Mark has it written down here somewhere.'

Honk. Honk.

I jump as Avery's car horn blasts around the office.

'Eejit.' *Honk. Honk.* 'Learn how to drive, lady,' Avery shouts.

'You okay?'

'Yeah. Sorry. Just some stupid cow cut me up. Nearly killed both of us. I swear some people should never get behind the wheel.'

I close the drawer and flop into the chair as if the air has been punched out of me.

'Oh shit, Tabs. I've done it again, haven't I? Put my bloody foot in it. But if you saw this woman you'd understand. Absolute arse truffle she is.'

'Arse truffle?'

'Yeah. Like a shithead, only worse.'

'Ah. Right. Gotcha. I think Catherine is one of those.'

'Nah. Catherine is more your classic bitch—'

'Avery, I have to go,' I say, cutting her off with a smile she can't see as I notice the light reflecting on something small and silver next to the desk.

'Eh, okay. Sure. I haven't upset you, have I? I didn't mean anything about bad drivers, honest.'

'No. No. You didn't. I'm fine. Something has come up, that's all.'

I crane my neck and squint, my eyes straining to see better.

'Wait. Wait. Becca's coming over for dinner later. Is that okay?' Avery says.

'Cool. Cool. I really have to go. Talk to you later.'

I end the call, turn my phone to silent and place it face down on the table so I'm not disturbed. I stand up and creep slowly towards the box as if it could come to life at any moment and attack me. I must have knocked it out of the drawer when I was sifting through papers. The small, square-shaped box is wrapped in high-gloss silver paper and purple ribbon adds the finishing touch. Purple is my favourite colour. I crouch and pick it up. My fingers are trembling as I tug at the ends of the bow and it comes undone in my hands. The shiny paper parts easily too and a red velvet box waits inside. It opens with a subtle creak, the way jewellery boxes in the movies do, and I can scarcely see through my tears as I stare inside at a beautiful bracelet.

'Oh my God, it's beautiful,' I say, as if someone is here to listen. 'It's really, really beautiful.'

And I gasp and cry as I realise I'm telling Mark. I want him to know how much I love it. How much I loved him. And how terribly much I wish everything was different.

I pick up the solid rose-gold bangle gently as if it's a dried flower that I'm afraid will crumble at my touch. The engraved ivy pattern swirling all around is subtle and elegant and I wonder if Mark chose it to reflect the ivy that hugs the trees in the park outside our bedroom window. My heart swells as I turn it over and read the inscription inside.

To Saoirse, with all my love, Mark x

SEVENTEEN

APRIL

You make the best cakes but the worst coffee. Please stop poisoning me.

April brings brighter and sunnier mornings. I've stopped setting an alarm. It feels rather pointless when I'm usually awake for hours before it goes off anyway. My mind races in the early hours of the morning when the flat is eerily silent apart from the odd creak of pipes. I tell myself that I have a lot on my mind. Invoices, rosters, menus and such. But there is really only one thought keeping me awake. Saoirse! And Mark. Mark and *her*. For months and months, I'd felt Mark drifting away from me. His excuses were endless. Working late to do some bookkeeping even though his maths was terrible. Going for a run but he'd be gone long enough to complete a marathon. Missed his bus and returned smelling of perfume. Vanilla and something sweet. Whoever this Saoirse is, I have no doubt it was her perfume on Mark's collar.

I feel as if I have concrete in my socks as I shuffle into the kitchen. Avery and Becca are sitting at the table, laughing and munching their way through a raspberry and white chocolate cheesecake I brought home from work last night. They stop giggling and look up when they notice me.

'Don't worry, we kept you some,' Avery says, wiping away the sugary crumbs of the biscuit base that have gathered on her lips.

'No thanks. Not hungry.'

I don't miss the look Avery shoots Becca and I know they've been talking about me. Again. I hear their whispers late at night when they think I'm asleep.

'I'm worried about her,' Avery says.

Becca reminds her that I'm grieving and healing takes time. Then they discuss a trip to the cinema or a day in the park that they plan to drag me along on, as if I'm a small child whom they can coax out of a sulk with a nice reward.

'Was it late when you got in last night?' Becca asks. 'We kept dinner for you, if you want some? It's just shepherd's pie. But it should heat up okay.'

The thought of shepherd's pie for breakfast makes me want to heave. I don't reply as I walk past them, fill the kettle and flick it on.

'This is crazy,' Avery says. 'You haven't eaten properly in weeks.'

'I eat at the bistro.'

'No, you don't,' Avery says. 'I stopped by the bistro yesterday and you weren't there. Scott said he didn't know where you were or when you'd be back.'

'So now you're checking up on me.'

'I was hoping we could have lunch. I haven't seen you properly in ages.'

'Avery, we live together.'

'You're never here anymore. And when you are, you're stuck to your phone.'

'You're the one who said I need to get online,' I say, raising my voice to drown out the kettle as it begins to boil.

Avery stands up and scrapes her plate into the compost bin she bought for the kitchen, before putting it in the dishwasher. She fetches the tin of teabags from the windowsill, pops the lid and tilts it towards me. I take a bag and put it in my cup.

'If there's something wrong you can tell me,' Avery says. 'Is it Catherine? Do you need me to kick her arse?'

I lift the kettle and pour. 'It's not Catherine.'

'Is it—'

'It's not Scott. Or work. Or money or any of the other long list of things you have already asked me about.'

'She's just worried,' Becca says. 'You're not yourself the last couple of weeks.'

'How would you know? You hardly know me at all,' I snap, slamming the kettle down much too hard.

A splash of boiled water splashes up and scalds my hand. I yelp and bring my hand to my mouth, but the heat of my lips only makes it sting more. Becca hurries over and guides me to the sink, running my hand under cold water.

'It's not too bad,' she says, 'It might blister though.'

'I'll grab a plaster,' Avery says, hurrying towards her room.

When it's just Becca and me, I say, 'I'm sorry. I shouldn't have said that.'

'It's okay. You're right.' Becca nods. 'I was out of line.'

'Avery is lucky to have you to defend and support her,' I say, but I can't hide the slight concern in my tone.

Becca and Avery's relationship is moving at lightning speed. They finish each other's sentences, discuss their careers with one another and I overheard Avery talking about moving in together.

Becca sighs. 'I can only imagine how hard this is for you. You're going through something huge and here Avery and I are flaunting our happiness. I know the timing for a new relationship sucks. And I'm so sorry if seeing us together is making things harder for you.'

I snap my hand away from Becca and suck it again. 'Do you think I'm envious?'

'No. God, no.'

'Does Avery?'

'Does Avery what?' Avery asks, returning with a box of Disney princess plasters in her hand.

I look at Becca and she shakes her head.

'Does Avery fancy dinner together tonight?' I say, taking a plaster from the box. I cover the red patch on my hand with Snow White. It throbs, but inside my head throbs more. 'Last orders aren't until nine, but I could ask Scott to cook us up something delicious that I can bring home,' I add.

'Sounds good,' Avery says, smiling brightly. 'But nothing lumpy. Or green. Or anything avocado. Avocados freak me out, they're so shrivelled and bleurgh.'

'No lumpy green avocado. Got it,' I say. 'Is six okay for you, Becca?'

Becca looks uncomfortable as she returns to the table for her plate and scrapes the crumbs into the compost bin. 'Maybe I should leave you both to it. You've a lot to talk about.'

I suspect Becca is giving me an opportunity to tell Avery about our conversation before she does.

'Join us. Please,' I say, hoping this won't turn into a thing.

Becca secures a flyaway strand of curly black hair behind her ear and smiles, still looking unsure, but says, 'Six p.m.'

Desperate to cut the tension, I say, 'So, I got your email this morning, Avery.'

'Omigod. Is today April first?' Avery grabs her phone, checks the date and turns the screen towards me, shoving it too close to my face to focus. 'It is. It is. Look.'

'It's April,' I say.

'Bloody hell, time is flying.' Avery lowers her phone and

turns to gaze smittenly at Becca. 'Can you believe we've been together three months, baby?'

Becca smiles and nods.

Three months, I think. One quarter of a whole year. I can't quite believe Mark is gone so long. Sometimes it feels as if life is galloping and I can only just keep hold of the reins. Other times it's as though the days are laced with treacle, sticking me to the spot. And every day, fast or slow, my mind wanders to the bracelet that I buried back in the bottom of the desk drawer and the words inscribed on it. Simple words that have tarnished every memory I have of Mark and my relationship. *Who is she? Does she know Mark is gone? Who would tell her?* I hate that I think about this stranger often – too often. She occupies so much space inside my head that it's hard to function. I'm thinking about her right now; wondering if she's standing in her kitchen staring out the window just as I am. Is she thinking about him, just as I am? Does she check her phone constantly hoping for a text from him, or a call? Does she think his fiancée found out about them and he had to choose? Perhaps she's come into the bistro searching for him. She could have sat right in front of me sipping on a coffee and I would have no idea. But mostly I wonder, is her heart broken, just like mine?

There are countless Saoirses in Dublin, according to Facebook. Even if I had any idea what she looked like, without a surname she's invisible to me. I don't know Mark's email password or the PIN for his phone to search his contacts. I'm not ashamed to admit I've tried. Perhaps Saoirse will never know that the man who loved her enough to inscribe it in rose gold didn't choose me.

'Oh shit,' I say, suddenly realising the time. 'I'm going to miss the bloody bus.'

'But your tea,' Avery says, as I dash towards the kitchen door.

'It's grand. I'll grab some in work.'

'And coffee,' she calls after me as I race towards my room to grab my coat and bag. 'Don't forget about April's resolution. We have to start looking for better coffee.'

'Yeah. Yeah. Coffee,' I say, racing out of earshot.

April's resolution is the easiest yet. Food and drink wholesalers are constantly stopping by the bistro, leaving their cards and hoping to secure us as a client. I noticed a stack of them on Mark's desk. I'll pick one of those. I'll have better coffee for Avery by this afternoon.

'Dammit,' I say aloud when I can't find my phone.

I whip the covers off the bed and check the pockets of my dressing gown before I remember I left it on the windowsill in the kitchen. I stop outside the door as I hear Avery say my name.

'Tabs is really struggling, isn't she?'

Becca doesn't reply.

'She wasn't always like this,' Avery continues. 'She used to be so carefree and fun. I just want her to remember what it's like to be happy. I thought the resolutions would help. But I don't think she's enjoying them at all. She's just going through the motions like a zombie.'

'Is coffee fun?' Becca asks, confused.

'It used to be. Tabs and I made it through college on a diet of coffee and fig rolls. Sounds gross, I know, but they were the happiest days of my life. But then she met Mark and everything kind of went to shit.'

'People change all the time,' Becca says. 'It's not a bad thing.'

'I know,' Avery says. 'And sometimes people change back. I really, really want Tabby to change back.'

'Oh, love,' Becca says, sounding emotional. 'I'm not sure you can expect that from her. Neither of you are eighteen anymore.'

'I miss her.' Avery sighs. 'She's right here beside me but I miss her.'

I hear a cupboard close and the sound of the dishwasher coming to life. I tiptoe backward, knowing they're getting ready to leave. But before I make it out of earshot, Becca says, 'Give her time, eh?'

'Patience. Right. Yeah. Got it.'

I smile and turn to walk away, knowing that patient is one thing my sister certainly is not.

EIGHTEEN

No matter what time I arrive, Scott is always in work before me. Last week, I jokingly asked him if he slept here, and he laughed and said with rent prices in the city he could be tempted. He said after forking out for rent and commuting he's broke. Then he blushed and apologised because he felt his problems were nothing compared to mine.

A couple of days later I found Lyla, one of my favourite part-time waitresses, crying in the bathroom. She dried her eyes as soon as I walked in, excused herself and left. Later, I overhead some of the waiting staff whispering about how Lyla had failed an important college exam and now she had to repeat the whole year. Lyla couldn't confide in me the way I wished she would, because she knows I'm a broken thing now.

When I look in the mirror, I see regular old Tabitha Greenwood – slightly overweight, five foot tall on my tiptoes, hazel eyes and a button nose. But that's not what everyone else sees. Not anymore. They don't see a sister, or a boss or a friend. They see a new me, shaped by grief. Or at least that's what they think they should see.

The new shape makes people uncomfortable. This isn't

something I'm just discovering. When my parents died, I learned that when you lose someone you lose a whole circle of people along with them. Friends begin to watch what they say in case they accidentally make you cry. Neighbours drop lasagnes and apple tarts to your door, but avoid the usual small talk.

'A little something for your freezer,' they say, as if your new-found void can be filled with home cooking and a swift exit.

Even those who only vaguely know you feel obliged to build a wall.

'That's that girl I was telling you about,' they whisper. 'The one who lost her parents. Tragic. Poor thing. Anyway, more wine, Liz?'

Back then Avery and I shared our grief. We flicked through old photo albums together and laughed as we watched home videos that my father had filmed with a wobbly hand. It didn't matter if the circle around us bent out of shape because of their own overthinking. We had each other. Our own secure bubble.

Now Avery is on the other side of the circle and the walls are high. She tries so hard to scale them, but every whisper behind my back or squashed laugh as soon as I walk into a room piles another brick on top. Soon she won't be able to see me anymore.

This morning I had every intention of being first through the doors at work. It's early when the bus pulls up in the usual spot and Rashidi sees me in the window and waves. I wave back but, just as I'm about to stand, something stops me. I take a deep breath, close my eyes and wait for the bus to move again. I keep my eyes closed for a long time. I'm sure the other passengers think I'm sleeping, if they notice me at all or even care. I count stops silently in the back of my head, never once looking up to see where I am. When the bus reaches its final stop, I get off and switch to another. Then I close my eyes again and wait.

I must fall asleep because I'm startled by a hand on my shoulder, gently shaking me.

'Last stop, love,' the bus driver says as I gaze up at him groggily. 'You're in Wicklow now.'

'Ballynaffin,' I say.

'Ah good, you're not lost.'

'No.' I rub my eyes and slide out of my seat. 'I've been here before.'

'Right, well, I have to turn this thing round and get back to Dublin.' He taps his watch and rolls his eyes, but he continues to smile. 'So, if you wouldn't mind hopping off.'

I pull my bag over my shoulder and nod. By the time I step off, I can hardly breathe. I gulp in air until I feel as if my lungs might burst and when I let it back out, my head spins and I have to concentrate to keep my feet firmly on the ground.

The sleepy village at the foothills of the mountains is exactly as I remember. Emerald green fields cradle each side of narrow, winding roads and the sounds of sheep and cattle carry in the wind. It's postcard perfect and I could never understand why Mark was so anxious to leave the place he grew up. He couldn't wait to shake off the wellies and waxed coat of his family's farm life and reinvent himself in the city. He did an exceedingly good job. Ballynaffin is so at odds with Mark that it's hard to imagine him at rest here now.

I walk into the corner shop and heads turn as if I've arrived from another planet instead of just outside the county. I resist the urge to tell them I'm visiting someone as I search for flowers. There are several bouquets resting in a large bucket of water. I choose the largest one and it drips across the floor as I make my way to the counter.

'Fourteen ninety-nine,' the cashier says, her eyes on the puddle the flowers' stems are creating on the countertop.

'Could I get a tea too please?'

She pulls a box of tissues out from below the counter and

sets them next to the flowers before she turns round to make a takeaway tea. I take one and wrap it round the watery stems and I wipe the counter with another.

She turns back, places a paper cup of tea in front of me and smiles, seeing I've cleaned up.

'That'll be sixteen forty-nine.'

I tap my card and say, 'Could you tell me how to get to the graveyard, please?'

'Oh.' Her eyes flick to the flowers once more. 'First left after the pub. It's a mile or so up that road.'

'Thanks.'

I pick up the flowers, which immediately start leaking again.

'It's a bit mucky up there,' she tells me, as she leans over the counter to stare at my sky-blue Converse and skinny jeans. 'Here. These will help.' She passes me two plastic bags. 'Pop 'em over your shoes.'

I take the bags.

'Who ya visiting?' she asks, straightening up again. 'We don't get many people in here askin' for directions to the graveyard.'

I swallow. 'Mark Buchanan.'

'Oh Lord,' she says, her voice suddenly soft like summer rain. 'Catherine's boy. Gosh it was all so sudden. We're still in a bit of shock here.'

I grip the plastic bags in my hand tighter and plead with myself not to cry.

'Are you his sweetheart from Dublin?'

I think of the bracelet and Mark's loving inscription. I don't deserve this woman's condolences, Saoirse does.

'I was his fiancé,' I say.

'Oh, love.' She wipes her eyes and her voice cracks. 'I'm so very sorry for your loss.'

'Thank you.'

Outside, the midday sun has climbed over the mountains to

peek out between scattered clouds. But the wind is strong and I'm glad I have warm tea to sip as I make my way towards the pub. The muck is inches deep almost instantly when I turn left onto the narrow road that could actually best be described as a dirt track. I pop the plastic bags over my Converse and tie the handles into a bow. The sheep in the roadside field watch and judge me, bleating their disapproval as I pass.

The walk is shorter than I expect and it's not long before I come to a crossroads. The graveyard is not to be missed, on the far side of the main road with a bus stop just metres away from the huge, wrought-iron gates. I must have passed right by it on my way into town while I was asleep. I cross the busy main road and pull the mucky plastic bags off my shoes to toss them, and my empty teacup, into a bin. Mark would be laughing his arse off if he could see me right now.

'Google literally mapped out the whole planet for you, and you still get lost.'

The large gates are open on one side and it's not until I've passed through that I realise I've been holding my breath. The wind seems calmer on this side of the gate. Perhaps it's the shelter from scattered oak trees, bending in the middle as if to offer their respect.

I must spend an hour wandering between graves. Although newer graves are obviously towards the back, I can't find Mark's little patch of earth. Finally I stumble upon a caretaker and he kindly offers me directions, and his heartfelt condolences.

I'm surprised to discover Mark's grave marked out with a beautiful surround and headstone already. It's white granite, just like the countertop in our kitchen that Catherine chose shortly after we moved in. It reads:

Mark Buchanan
1989–2023
Loving son, cherished brother, caring friend.

Always loved. Always missed. Never forgotten.

I can scarcely see through my tears as I read the words over and over. My heart aches as I align the man I knew, and once loved, with the simple words that encompasses his importance to a special few.

But Mark was so much more to so many more. He was a business partner, a fiancé, and a lover. He was confident, charismatic, funny and sometimes a bully. He was human. He was real. He was here.

The grave is adorned with floral arrangements. Wreaths mostly in pastel colours. I wonder if anyone ever bought Mark flowers when he was alive. Some of the wreaths are dried and their petals droop and are tinged with brown. Others are fresh and beautiful. It's obvious someone visits often and I hate that I glance over my shoulder anxiously for any sign of Catherine. I crouch to lay my supermarket bouquet down. I don't know why but I stay down, as if it will make me feel closer. I place my hand on the top of the headstone. Sadness sits inside me like a physical thing – a knot, a ball, a rock. Something that I wish I could cut out and throw away. The pain is too great and a short, sharp yelp bursts past my lips as if I'm a wounded animal, trapped.

'I'm sorry,' I sob. 'I'm so, so sorry.'

I stroke the cold granite beneath my palm a poor compromise for the warm hug I wish for.

I cry for a while. Loud, angry sobs shake my whole body before I finally pull myself upright and together.

'Hi,' I say, starting over. 'Hey.'

It takes me a while to find more words but once I start they seem to tumble from my lips like dominos.

'I know about Saoirse,' I say, my voice cracking as I say her name. 'I think I've known for a long time. In a weird way it's sort of a relief, you know. A relief to know I wasn't going crazy. A relief to know our relationship wasn't working out. It was never going to work out.

'*I was cheating on you, Tabs. I didn't love you. I loved her.*'

I pause for a moment, realising what I just said and how huge it is.

'Were you happy? With her, I mean. I hope so. I hope she made you happy, the way we once made each other happy. We did, Mark, didn't we? There was a time when we were so much in love. Our little flat. Our beautiful bistro. Our shared dreams were so bright once upon a time. I'm not really sure when or why it all fell apart, really. Maybe it unravelled like a ball of wool, slowly and slowly until we were all tangled up. I loved you. I did. Right to the end. We weren't *in* love anymore. I think we both knew that. But I did still love you.'

I stop rambling and catch my breath. The clouds have finally parted and it's shaping into a particularly lovely spring day.

'I think I need to find Saoirse,' I say. 'I need to make sure she knows how much you loved her. I know how bloody crazy that sounds. Don't worry, I haven't lost my mind. But I've been thinking about it for weeks now. To be honest I've thought about nothing else. In the end it was Saoirse you loved and I hope she loved you too. I do. I mean it. I need closure, Mark. I need to know breaking up with you was the right thing to do. And I think only Saoirse can answer that. I guess that's what brought me here today. I wanted to tell you I know about her and it's okay. I'm okay. Or at least, I think I will be.'

A squeaking noise behind me startles me and I turn round to find that caretaker approaching with a wheelbarrow.

'Lovely day,' he says, letting go of the handles to drag a shaky arm across his brow. 'Didn't start out great, mind you. But it's a lot brighter now.'

'Yes,' I say, bending again to gather up the dying wreaths. 'It really is brighter now.'

He takes the wreaths from me and adds them to his wheel-barrow full of hedge trimmings and weeds and other, even browner wreaths.

'Haven't seen you here before, have I?' he asks, taking hold of the wheelbarrow handles again.

'No,' I say, and I can feel heat creep across my cheeks. 'It's my first visit.'

'Fair enough. Not always easy, the first time. The next time will be better.'

I swallow hard as I slowly realise there probably won't be a next time.

'Some of us find it hard to come. And others can't stay away. Like his mam.' The caretaker points towards Mark's grave as if I wasn't sure where to look. 'Poor woman is here every day. Rain, hail or shine.'

'Every day?' I ask.

'Well, would you look who it is,' the caretaker says, staring over my shoulder. 'Catherine, we were just talking about you.'

'Oh, I have no doubt,' Catherine says, as I turn round to face her. 'Hello, Tabitha. I see you finally made it.'

I don't have words so I simply nod.

'Right, best get on. There's rain forecast later,' the caretaker says, and his wheelbarrow wheel begins to squeak again.

'Wait. Wait,' Catherine says, edging past me and puffing out as she bends down to pick up my flowers. 'Take these too, will you?'

The caretaker shifts uncomfortably and says, 'I think the young lady—'

'They won't last,' Catherine says, as she tosses the bouquet in the wheelbarrow.

The caretaker and I share an understanding look before he nods and slowly walks away.

'Found us okay, did you?' Catherine asks when he's gone.

'Yes. I remembered which bus.'

'Good. Good. Because it's been so long since you were here.'

I want to tell her that I would have loved to visit Ballynaffin more often but any time I suggested it Mark shot me down. But of course I don't. Now is not the right time.

'It has been a long time, but the village is just as lovely as I remember,' I say.

'Have you eaten?' Catherine asks.

'Sorry?'

'Food,' she says slowly, as if I didn't understand the question.

I don't speak.

'Would you like to come up to the house for a bite of lunch? I made scones this morning.'

I can't think of anything I would dislike more.

'I'd love to,' I say, wincing. 'But I'm already late for work and if I don't—'

'Today isn't your day off?'

'No. But I had to come.'

Catherine's smile turns upside down as she says, 'Well, don't let me keep you. I'm sure I'll see you soon. At the bistro.'

'Yeah. Soon.'

NINETEEN

The morning plays over in my mind as I push through the front door of work. The smells of ragu and roux simmering on the hob make my mouth water. I don't bother to take my coat off as I head into the office. I flick through the business cards on Mark's desk, then pull open the top drawer and rummage through a stack of cards there too. There seems to be a card for everything except a coffee supplier. Eventually I find one, and punch the number into my phone. A generic voicemail informs me it's lunch break and if I'd like to leave my name and number...

I hang up and pin the card to the corkboard behind me – a reminder to call again later. I try to clear my head and think about today's menu and bookings. It's anyone's guess if I'll need more chocolate tortes than crèmes brûlées.

I'm about to pull on my uniform when I'm distracted by two bagels and a mini bottle of prosecco sitting next to the staff roster that I completely forgot to fill out for next week. There are yellow sticky notes on each bagel. There's another stuck to the desk that I guess was attached to the prosecco but has since peeled off.

My stomach rumbles as I pick up the nearest bagel and read the slightly-difficult-to-decipher handwriting.

The usual.

I place it back down and reach for the next one. I squint to make the words out.

Something different.

Lastly, I pick up the lost sticky note on the table.

In case something different is something disgusting, wash it down with this.

I'm laughing as, noticing there's writing on the other side also, I turn it over.

In case something different is something delicious, drink this to celebrate!

I glance at my watch. It's not quite 3 p.m. yet. Too early for prosecco, I decide. But not too soon to try something new. I open the wrapper on the *something different* bagel and immediately scrunch my nose. It smells like feet, and my instinct is to toss it in the bin. But I remind myself that many of our fine cheeses smell a little feety and they are bestsellers. I part the buns and peek inside, finding that it's green and mushy. Cheesy avocado, I decide, and I wonder who on earth would choose such a combination. Determined, I bring it to my lips and bite.

I'm on my feet instantly with my head over the bin. I'm spitting and spitting but I can't get the taste out of my mouth. I grab the bottle of prosecco, pop the cork with a loud bang and guzzle. I keep drinking until the dainty bottle is drained.

Scott appears at the door and he's laughing so hard he's bent in the middle and complaining that his sides hurt.

'Were you standing there the whole time?' I snort.

'Not the whole time. Just for the bin-spitting and prosecco-knocking-back part.'

His laughter is big and loud and it's hard not to laugh too, but I keep a straight face as I ask, 'What the hell was that? It tasted like vomit.'

'No idea. I asked Rashidi to make up his strangest bagel and that was the result.'

'Why? Why would you do that.' I shudder, still feeling the texture on my tongue.

'Because different is not necessarily better.' Scott shrugs. 'It's just different.'

'Oh God, couldn't you have proved your point some other way? That was gross.'

'I could, but it wouldn't have been as much fun. You should see your face.'

I shudder, but I can't hold my giggles in anymore.

We both laugh loud and long. I can't remember the last time I laughed like this. The sort of deep-belly, bend-you-in-the-middle laugh that even when you try and try, you just can't stop. It's a long time before we're all laughed out, and my face aches.

I reach for my uniform and am about to go into the bathroom and change when Scott produces another bottle of prosecco from behind his back. It's a full-size bottle this time.

'What's that for?' I ask.

'You.' Scott watches me for a reaction, but I'm like a rabbit caught in headlights. 'When was the last time you day-drank?' he asks.

'I never day-drink,' I say. 'And I absolutely never drink in work.'

'You've really never helped yourself to a quick wine from the bar after the lunch rush?'

'No. Never. Well, not until just now with the whole pros-ecco thing. It's really very nice. No wonder so many people order it.'

'I can't believe you never drink during the day. What about when you were a teenager? It's practically a rite of passage.'

'I had different teenage years to most people. I lost my mam when I was thirteen and my dad four years later.'

'Fuck. Sorry,' Scott says, lowering the bottle and his head.

'It's okay. It was a long time ago.'

'Still though, your parents. That's shit.'

'Oh yeah. Very shit. But I have my sister. It was just me and her for a long time. Then I met Mark and we opened this place. There was never time for boozy days.'

'Right!' Scott says, walking over to the desk and placing the bottle down. 'We're going to fix that right now.'

It takes me a moment to realise he's serious. 'God no. I can't. I've the rosters to do. We need to go over the new menu and I've some calls to suppliers to make. Not to mention all the bloody chocolate tortes I need to make for that after-bingo party coming in tonight.'

'I'll tell them we're all out.'

'Scott, seriously, c'mon.'

Scott's giddy body language changes and he looks at me almost sadly. 'Listen,' he begins, and it feels like the type of conversation where I might need to sit down is about to follow. 'I know we don't really know each other, so this almost defi-nitely isn't my place, but I've noticed how down you've been the last couple of weeks. Ever since Catherine had a go over the menus.'

I'm about to explain my mood has nothing to do with menus but Scott keeps talking.

'I don't know if I upset you. I didn't mean to go all weird knight in shining armour – if that's what you're thinking.'

'It's not.'

'Okay. But if there's something else I've done... if you hate the new ideas. If my beef bourguignon is fuck awful or if—'

'It's not you. I promise.'

Scott's tense arms relax.

'It's not even Catherine, believe it or not.' I take a deep breath before I say, 'It's pretty personal, actually.'

'Oh.'

'Yeah. So... if we could just have a normal work day, that would actually really help.'

Scott tilts his head to one side as if he's seeing me from a different angle. 'Okay,' he says.

I reach for my uniform again and it slips easily off the hanger. Then I eye up the bottle of prosecco by his side.

'Maybe we could have a drink after last orders? I could really use a drink today.'

'You're not a day drinker, I respect that,' Scott says, his eyes burning into mine. 'But I'm happy to make up for lost time after work.'

'Me too,' I say.

'After work,' he says.

Without another word we both head into to the kitchen and I begin to count down the hours.

TWENTY

It's unbearably busy all evening. By the time the last staff member leaves my feet are burning from standing for so long and I can't wait to get home and kick my Converse off. I think about a long bath and a good book. I catch Scott in the corner of my eye fetching two champagne flutes and some ice from the bar. I glance at my watch and realise it's after midnight. That bingo group were in no hurry to leave and other tables followed their example. Today is technically tomorrow and if I cancel now I won't actually be breaking our plans. But Scott is smiling as the flutes dangle from between his fingers and two extra-large pieces of chocolate torte sit on a plate in his other hand.

'Didn't we tell the bingo party we were all out of chocolate torte?' I say.

Scott shrugs. 'They were more crème brulée people anyway.'

I smile.

'C'mon,' he says, opening the office door with his elbow. 'I'm starving.'

We sit at opposite sides of the desk and Scott sets down the tortes and pops the prosecco. We both take a huge mouthful and sigh, exhausted.

'Busy out there tonight,' I say.

'Yeah. Yeah. Crazy,' he says.

'New menu seemed to go down well.'

'It did. It did.'

I take another sip of prosecco. He does the same. And then I try to think of something else to say. I could ask if he'd like me to roster in any time off for him soon, or if he's got to know all the staff yet. But everything feels jaded and small talk-like, so I continue to sip bubbles in silence and wait for him to strike up conversation.

'Another?' Scott asks, glancing at the glass I've already drained.

I nod.

He refills mine and tops up his and we continue sipping.

I'm not sure if it's the prosecco going to my head or my inability to take the silence anymore, but I suddenly blurt, 'I went to see Mark today.'

'Oh.'

'It was my first time at the grave,' I say, guzzling my prosecco as if it will wash the shame down.

'God. Right. Shit. That's big.'

'I know.'

'Why today?' he asks.

'What?'

'Sorry.' He cringes. 'That came out weird. I meant is today an important date. An anniversary or something?'

'No.'

'Oh.'

'It's complicated,' I say.

Scott clears his throat and I can sense his discomfort. 'Fair enough. It's not my business. I shouldn't have asked. Let's blame the prosecco, eh?'

I make eye contact with him for the first time since we sat down. He has a splash of Bolognese on his cheekbone that he's blissfully unaware of.

'You have a little something...' I point.

He taps his face.

'Up. Up. Right.'

He rubs but it doesn't budge.

'Hang on,' I say, opening the bottom drawer of Mark's desk, remembering that I saw a packet of tissues in there the other day.

The packet sits next to the velvet bracelet box and for a fleeting moment seeing it again takes my breath away. I grab the tissues and slam the drawer with unnecessary force.

'Here you are,' I say, pulling a tissue from the packet and passing it to him.

Scott wipes his face, his gaze on me the whole time, and he asks, 'Are you okay?'

'Yeah. Of course. This is really lovely.' I raise the glass of prosecco and tilt it towards him.

'It is,' he says, deflated as he watches me with concerned and curious eyes.

'A bit fizzy,' I say. 'But nice. I like fizzy.'

'Tabby,' he says, his chocolate eyes widening.

I puff out until I feel as if there is no air left in me and finally I say, 'Actually I'm not okay. Not really.'

'Do you want to talk about it?'

'I'm not sure.' I shrug. 'Where would I start.'

'The beginning is always a good place.'

'How Mark and I met?' I ask.

'Or before that,' Scott says, standing up. 'When did you know you wanted to be a chef?'

'Really? You want to go back that far?'

'I do.'

I smile and rewind my mind back over the years.

'Hold that thought,' Scott says, pointing a raised finger towards the door. 'I'm going to grab us another bottle.'

Memories explode like colourful fireworks inside my head as Scott returns with an open bottle of white wine and two long-stemmed glasses.

'Well?' he says, pouring a generous amount into one and passing it to me.

'Always,' I say, cupping my hand round the cool glass. 'Actually, that's a lie. I used to want to be Beyoncé, but since that job was already taken, I settled for the next best thing.'

'Me too,' he says, as he pours a glass for himself and sits back down. 'A chef, I mean. Not Beyoncé. I don't have the legs for all those short dresses.'

I smile and sip more wine.

'Life was so much simpler as a kid, wasn't it?' he says. 'You could make a decision based on nothing other than a sweet tooth, and presto – you had a life plan.'

'I have a life plan,' I say, my words starting to slur. 'It's all written down and everything. All I have to do is follow it and every zing will bef fine.'

'Really?'

'My sister wrofe it for me.'

Scott laughs.

I place my empty glass on the table and fold my arms. 'I'm serious.'

'Oh.'

Trying hard to be soberer and steadier, I explain, 'It's all about steps in the right direction. Right now, I'm s'posed to be finding a new coffee supplier.'

'New coffee is a life step?'

'Never mind. It's stupid. Just forget it.'

'What? No. Tell me, please,' Scott says. His eyes are glassy and most definitely drunk but they're also full of kindness. 'This is important to you and I want to understand.'

'It *was* important to me. Once-zupon a time. But, honestly, it's become a pain in the arse over the years. Do you know how hard it is to sthink of twelve ways of self-improvement every year?'

'Twelve is a lot. Couldn't you start with one and see how you go?'

'No. That's not how it works,' I say, trying not to become frustrated. 'It's a step a month for the year. It's a whole thing. See, I told zoo it was stupid.'

'It's not stupid,' he says, suddenly seeming sober. 'But it does sound hard.'

'It is. "Give up chocolate" has been on the list every year for over a decade and I've never once succeeeee... succeeded. I'm not sure I even want to give it up.'

'Why would you? You know chocolate releases endorphins that make people happy.'

I laugh.

'It's true. Look it up,' he says. 'Take a bite of that cake, and I bet in five minutes you'll be happier.'

'If only it were that easy,' I say, digging a fork into the torte.

'Isn't it?'

'My sister thinks so.'

'Maybe she's right.'

'Avery calls it The Remember Plan. Cos 'parently, I've forgotten how to have fun.'

'And have you?'

I take a deep breath. 'Yeah. Think so.'

Scott refills our empty glasses again and we talk and talk as we polish off the tortes.

'This was step one,' I say, pointing to my hair.

'Step one looks good on you. I didn't say it before, but I should have,' he says, with a slightly drunken smile.

'Sank you.'

I think I'm blushing. It's hard to tell. I'm so tipsy my whole face is tingling. 'Step two was a snew website and stwep three is better coffee,' I say.

'Good,' Scott says.

'Good?'

'The coffee here is shite.' He pauses and lowers his glass. 'Sorry, no offence.'

I shrug. 'None taken. I don't dwink the stuff. Not anymore. Mark said it made me cranky.'

'Wow.'

'I know. I know. No one wants a cranky girlfriend.'

'Not exactly what I meant, but okay.' Scott's lip twitches as he holds up his hand. 'Hang on, shouldn't April be step four? January. February. March. April.' He counts aloud on his fingertips as if he doubts his numeracy and must double-check.

'We skipped January,' I say, and I know for certain my cheeks are flushed now.

The office suddenly feels small and stuffy and I wish there was a window I could open.

Scott nods as if he understands January was difficult, as if he understands it's still difficult. His unwavering sympathy is hard to bear. If he asks me why, I'm not sure I have the sobriety or will to lie to him.

'Do you need some help?' he asks. 'If you don't drink coffee yourself, it's going to be hard to know what's good and what's not.'

'Yes,' I squeak, much too excited and loud for the small office. 'Help would bef great. Sanks. I found these guys.' I point to the business card on the cork board behind me. 'But I dunno if they're any good or not.'

Scott shakes his head. 'Why don't I call a friend of mine? She's a rep for a huge supplier. They do the coffee for most of the top restaurants in town.'

'Soundsss perfect. Thank you.'

'No problem.' Scott smiles. 'I'm surprised you don't already use them. I'm sure she must have called in touting for business. She works on commission so she scouts all the local places.'

I shrug. 'Mark usually took care of that side of things.'

'Sorry.' Scott shifts uncomfortably.

'Please stop saying that. Everyone keeps saying that. Every time I mention his name people tell me how sorry they are.'

'Okay.' Scott nods and I think he understands. 'I promise I won't say it again.'

'Thank you.'

Scott drinks the last of his wine and takes his phone out of his pocket. 'The Coffee Bean,' he whispers, concentrating as he flicks his finger on his screen. 'The Coffee Bean, The Coffee Bean, The Coffee... where the hell are you?' He flicks his finger the opposite way and squints. 'Ah ha, there you are. Saoirse@The Coffee Bean o86 674—'

'Saoirse?' I cut across him, not sure my drunken ears have heard him correctly.

'She's head of sales,' Scott says. 'We might as well go straight to the top. I'll call first thing in the morning. Saoirse will have us sorted in no time.'

He slides his phone back into his pocket and reaches for his glass again. The flash of disappointment when he notices it's empty would make me laugh if my thoughts weren't swirling in my head.

'Saoirse,' I say again, too drunk to whisper. 'It's her.'

TWENTY-ONE

Scott holds my hair dutifully as I lean over the bin and throw up. I can only imagine his eyes are closed – at least, I hope they are. I heave and hurl and the guttural sounds coming from me are primal and disturbing. Exhausted, I flop onto the floor as Scott lets go of my hair. He passes me a tissue from the desk just as I'm dragging a shaky hand past my mouth.

'Oh God.' I cringe as the feeling of torturous retching is replaced with equally torturous mortification. 'I really wish you hadn't seen that.'

'Me too.' He laughs.

I drop my face into my hands and rock on the spot.

'I can see why you don't day-drink now,' Scott says, pressing his back against the wall and sliding down until he's sitting next to me. 'You're a total lightweight.'

I scowl. 'I haven't eaten today.'

'Nothing at all?' he says.

'Didn't get a chance.'

Scott watches me expressionlessly and I wonder what he's thinking. It takes my drunken brain longer than it should to realise I should offer some sort of explanation or risk giving him the impression that I have some sort of disorder.

'Today started out shit and just when I thought it couldn't get any worse, it only bloody did,' I say.

'Crap-fests do kill the appetite all right,' he says, winking. 'You hungry now?'

'Um.'

I can taste sick in my mouth and when I close my eyes either the floor is spinning beneath me or I'm spinning on top of it, I can't tell.

'C'mon,' he says, standing up and reaching his hand out to me. 'I'm going to make you the best meal of your life.'

I take his hand and he pulls me to my feet. The sudden jerky movement disturbs my stomach and there's a loud, aggressive rumble.

Scott leads me into the kitchen by the hand as if I'm a small child. He turns a potato crate upside down and places it on the floor.

'Sit down,' he says, pointing at it. 'Maybe pop your head between your legs, it'll help with the dizziness.'

I sit on the very uncomfortable crate and lower my head. The ground beneath me seems to stabilise. I keep my head down and my eyes closed as I listen to the familiar sound of someone working in the kitchen.

Within a few minutes Scott says, 'Food's ready.'

I look up to find another crate in front of me acting as a makeshift table. On top is a plate of hot, buttered toast and a cup of tea with steam swirling out the top.

The irony makes me smile. I'm in a fancy kitchen, full of organic, seasonal produce, and yet I can't think of anything more perfect right now than tea and toast.

Scott places a second plate of toast and a cup of tea on the crate before sitting down cross-legged on the floor opposite me.

I bite into the toast and I don't just say it because Scott is an award-winning chef but the words, 'Omigod this is amazing,' burst out.

'So, do you want to tell me why your day was so shit?' he asks between bites of toast.

I slurp hot tea noisily as I peer over the rim of the cup, trying hard to focus my blurry vision.

'You'll be shocked,' I say.

Scott tilts his head and scrunches his nose. 'I've seen you throw your guts up. I'm not sure there's anything you can say at this point that will shock me more than that—'

'Mark was having an affair.'

Scott's eyes widen and he drops his half-eaten slice of toast onto the plate. 'Except maybe that.'

'See, I told you you'd be shocked.'

'Are you sure?'

I nod.

'How do you know? I mean, did you know before...'

'No. No. I just found out recently. The day Catherine blew up about the menus, actually.'

Scott nods with his eyes on mine and I can see him doing the maths in his head.

'That's why I went to the grave today,' I say. 'I needed to tell Mark I knew.'

'Right. Right. Yeah. Okay. I see.' Scott's head bobs as he speaks, and he's either too drunk or too uncomfortable to say more.

'I needed to tell Mark I forgive him,' I say.

'Is that because he's dead?' Scott says, and then he pulls a face, clearly horrified that his drunken brain let what he was thinking slip out.

'Do you know why Avery and I skipped January's resolution?' I say, my heart racing as I get ready to explain.

Scott shakes his head. 'You don't have to tell me that.'

'I want to.'

Scott's unsteady gaze focuses and he smiles, listening.

'Mark and I broke up just before the crash. My January resolution was to be single this year.'

'Wow. The puking thing really isn't so shocking anymore,' he says.

'I was so ready to grieve our relationship. But I was in no way ready to grieve him.'

Scott fidgets and clears his throat. 'I'm not really sure what to say.'

'Say you'll help me find her?'

Scott seems to choke on some crumbs. 'What?'

'Look, Mark's and my relationship was failing for a long time. Actually, I'm not sure it ever worked in the first place. But even still my heart is broken and I miss him. I don't know if this affair thing was a fling or if he really did love her, but I need to find out. There's something I need to give her. Something he wanted her to have.'

'You do know this all sounds a bit, erm...'

'Bonkers? Yeah. I know. But since Mark died, I have support from my family and friends – too much support, sometimes,' I say, with a sheepish giggle. 'But what if she has no one? What if she doesn't even know he's gone?'

'Okay, but how are you going to find her?' Scott asks. 'I don't imagine he left you a note – in case of my death please email mymistresses@WhoI'veBeenSeeing.com.'

Without a word I stand up and walk, still slightly wobbly, back into the office.

After a moment I hear Scott's footsteps follow me and when he reaches the office door he says, 'Tabby. I'm sorry. I'm drunk and that was—'

'Funny,' I say, shrugging it off.

'You're not upset?'

'Here,' I say, placing the velvety jewellery box on the desk.

Scott looks from the box to me, confused.

'It's okay. Open it.'

He picks it up, swaying slightly on the spot. The lid's creaks add a hint of melodrama as he opens it slowly.

'This isn't for you?' he says, as he stares at the pretty bracelet.

I shake my head.

'And this is what you want to give to her,' he says, as he separates the bracelet and box and then looks at them as if he's not sure how he will get them back together.

'There's an inscription,' I say.

Scott tilts the bracelet towards the light and squints. 'Nope. Too drunk, can't make out a word of that.'

'"To Saoirse, with all my love, Mark",' I say. 'And there's a kiss too.'

'Saoirse?' Scott says, dropping the bracelet. 'Shit, where did it go?' He's on his hunkers instantly, patting around the carpet with his hands. 'Got it. Got it.' In his hurry to stand up again he bangs his head against the lip of the desk. 'Ouch. Christ.'

Finally he's on his feet again, holding the bracelet in one hand and rubbing the back of his head with the other.

'Saoirse,' he says. 'As in coffee rep Saoirse? The one me and my big mouth suggested we approach as a new supplier.'

'I think so,' I say, taking the bracelet from his shaking hand to reunite it with its box. 'I mean, it can't be just a coincidence. You said she calls to all the local bistros and restaurants. Obviously Mark never mentioned her because, well, he was shagging her and it's not the type of thing you tell your fiancée.'

'Right. So. What now?' Scott says, wincing as his hand continues to stroke his head.

'That's going to leave a bump,' I say.

'Doesn't hurt too much.'

'It will tomorrow when you're sober.'

'Probably,' he says with a shrug. 'So, are you going to call her?'

'What? No. That would be weird. You're going to call her.'

'Me?' Scott taps his chest with his fingertip. 'And say what exactly?'

'That we're looking for a new coffee supplier,' I say, making a face. 'Because we are. And then when we meet her we can suss out if it's the right Saoirse or not. Even though we already know it is.'

'We?'

'Well, yeah.' I puff out air. 'I can't go on my own. And you already know her, so...'

'So you want to drag me into this.'

'Actually you offered to help, remember?'

'Yeah, but that's before you went all *Magnum P.I.* on it.'

'What's *Magnum P.I.*?' I ask.

'Seriously?'

I shrug.

'Tom Selleck, private investigator?'

I shake my head.

'It's a classic.'

'Nope. Sorry. No clue.'

'Right, we're going to rectify this right now.' Scott picks up the last of the wine and both glasses.

I follow him to reception, where he plonks onto the couch as if it's his living room. He sets the wine and glasses down on the tiled floor, stretches his legs out straight and takes his phone from his pocket.

'*Magnum P.I.* episode one,' he says as upbeat theme-tune music begins to play from his phone.

'Really? Here? Now?'

'Why not?'

I glance at my watch. 'It's two a.m.'

'You don't day-drink, fair enough,' Scott says, leaning forward to split the last of the bottle of wine between the two glasses. 'But don't tell me you've never stayed up past two a.m. bingeing Netflix.'

'Of course I have. But we have work in the morning.'

Scott stretches his arms out and looks all around. 'We're already here. We're just very, very early.'

'Which one's mine?' I ask, looking at the wine glasses.

Scott picks up the fuller glass and passes it to me, then pats the couch beside him. 'It's starting. C'mon.'

I sit beside him and tuck my legs under me. I sip wine and watch a man with a moustache and fancy sports car run around a lot. For the first time in weeks, I'm not thinking about resolutions or Mark and Saoirse. For the first time in a much longer time, I am a little drunk and fully happy.

TWENTY-TWO

The heat on my face is rather lovely as morning sunlight streams through the window. I yawn and open my eyes and for a moment I'm disoriented to discover I'm not in my bed. Scott's arms are round me and my head is on his chest as we lie stretched out on the couch. I gasp and untangle myself from him to sit up. The sudden movement makes my head pound as if someone is using my brain as a drum. The pounding grows louder and angrier as I stretch and rub my eyes and try to come to life. Groggy and with a blistering headache, I realise the noise is outside my head not inside. Slowly, I pull my gaze away from Scott's sleeping body and look outside to find Catherine, puce-faced, her fist pounding on the window.

Oh God. Oh God.

I shake Scott and he groans and turns over.

'Wake up,' I say as I stand up and the cold of the floor tiles nips at my bare feet.

I search for my shoes that I don't remember kicking off last night and I find them next to the knocked-over empty wine bottle and two empty glasses.

'Wake up,' I say again, louder this time, as I shake Scott's shoulder.

'What? What? What?' He snorts as his eyes spring open, wide and confused.

'Catherine's here,' I say, hopping on one foot as I try to pull on my socks and shoes. 'She's seen us. Oh shit! Shit, shit.'

Scott stretches and his spine cracks audibly.

'Calm down,' he says, yawning. 'We just fell asleep on the couch. There's nothing to be this worked up about.'

'You didn't see her face. She's fuming. Can you imagine what this looks like?'

'I can tell you what this looks like,' Catherine says, appearing behind me.

The realisation that she must have a back door key as well as the front one washes over me like a wave trying to drag me under. I turn round slowly, with one shoe on and one shoe in my hand.

'The shutter was up,' she says. 'You can see straight in from the road.'

My stomach knots.

'I can only imagine how many people passed by on buses this morning and got an eyeful of you two. And this... this scene.'

'We were just sleeping,' I say as I wrap my arms round myself, shivering.

'I left the back door open,' Catherine says, eyeing up my goosebumps. 'The stench of booze and morning breath in here is revolting.'

Scott gets to his feet and runs his hand through his bed hair.

'We had a couple of drinks after work last night and we must have fallen asleep,' he says.

Catherine exhales long and loud as if the sight of us exhausts her.

'Is that bistro wine?' she asks, pointing at the empty bottle next to Scott's feet.

The implication that we've taken something that belongs to her irritates me and I say, 'It's just one bottle. It won't be missed.'

Catherine jams her hands on her hips. 'If that's your atti-tude towards inventory, young lady, then we have an even bigger problem than this.' She drags her finger through the air to draw an invisible line between Scott and me.

'This is not what you think,' I say, pointing to Scott and then back to me. 'We drank some wine, watched some old telly and fell asleep. We were exhausted after a busy day.'

'Oh, you had a busy day all right,' she says, practically shaking with temper. 'Is that why you went to see my Mark after all this time?'

Scott's eyes are instantly on me and I know he's wondering why I didn't mention seeing Catherine at the grave yesterday.

'You've a guilty conscience because you've moved on,' Catherine says, and her anger suddenly seems diluted by how close she is to tears. 'Well, my God, it didn't take you long.'

Scott snorts and I hold my breath for a moment, terrified that he's going to jump to my defence and say something about Saoirse. Catherine eyes us both with such distaste I could swear the sight of us is making her stomach turn.

'Look,' Scott says after a moment of painful silence. 'We could all probably use a coffee. I know I certainly could. Tabby?'

'Tea please,' I say, trying to step aside out of Catherine's burning gaze, but her narrowed eyes follow me.

'Catherine?' Scott asks with a hint of anxiety stuck to his tone.

Catherine doesn't reply.

'Coffee, Catherine?' Scott repeats as he bends to pick up the wine bottle and glasses.

'Leave those,' she says.

Scott looks up, confused.

'I said leave them.' Catherine raises her voice.

Scott places the bottle and glasses back down and looks to me for direction. But I have no idea what to say.

'Get your stuff and get out,' Catherine says, taking a step back as if she's clearing a path between me and her.

Scott watches Catherine with a mix of sympathy and frustration.

'Did you hear me?' she says, angry saliva spraying past her lips. 'You're fired.'

'Catherine!' I say, stepping forward.

'Get the hell out!'

I open my mouth, ready to argue, but I feel Scott's hand on my shoulder and when I look at him he's shaking his head. I shake my head too because I don't understand. I don't understand why he doesn't want me to speak up for him. I don't understand why he's so calm.

'Okay,' he says, softly. 'Thank you for this opportunity.'

'Catherine, no,' I say. 'Scott, stop. Wait. Don't go.'

Scott pulls on his shoes, leans in to kiss my cheek and walks round behind reception to gather his stuff.

'Catherine, this isn't fair. Please. None of this is Scott's fault,' I say.

'Oh, I know whose fault this all is.'

Catherine's words hit me like rocks. Each word piles another stone on top. I want to beg her to reconsider. I want to tell her that Scott is the best thing to happen to La Bella Vita in a long time. But I can't. I'm slowly being buried under a pile of rubble. And even if I could dig my way out, I don't deserve to. Scott wouldn't be here if Mark was still alive. And Mark would still be alive if I had just kept my mouth shut. If only I had never said I wanted to break up then none of this would be happening.

'Are you crying?' Catherine says.

I pull my sleeve over my hand and drag a shaky arm across my eyes.

'Are you joking? I walk in to find the two of you like... like... like this...' Catherine jams her hands on her hips and angry red creeps across her nose and cheeks. 'I can't bear it. I just can't bear it. Mark wasn't cold in the ground when you were changing his menu. Now you're digging your claws into the staff. Good Lord, Tabitha, I never thought you'd stoop so low. Well, don't think this is going to be plain sailing. I tried, I really tried. I thought we could work together. I thought we could continue to be family.'

My tears fall faster than I can wipe them away.

'Families stick together, Tabitha. Where were you when they put my son in the ground? Where were you when I cried myself to sleep? You never once came to the house. Not once. Not even when I begged you to come yesterday. You've shown your true colours, that's for sure. I think it's clear to see we were never really family at all.'

'You're right,' I say. 'I'm sorry. I should have picked up the phone. But sometimes words aren't going to be good enough.'

'He was my son.' Catherine's anger melts into heartache as silent tears trickle down her cheeks. 'My son. My son.'

Scott slings his bag over his shoulder and walks slowly towards us. 'Thank you, Catherine,' he says, extending his hand, but she doesn't shake it. 'Goodbye, Tabby,' he adds.

The lump in my throat is too big to allow words past as I watch him turn and walk away.

'Clean this place up,' Catherine says, pointing to the wine bottle and glasses, as soon as Scott is out of view. 'And for God's sake clean yourself up too. You'll scare away our customers.'

TWENTY-THREE

'Scott, call me back when you get this, please? We need to talk,' I say, leaving a voicemail on his phone when I call for a third time and he doesn't answer.

I pace the office floor, trying to calm my racing thoughts. I stop sporadically to stare at my phone screen, willing it to ring and Scott's name to appear. But every time it vibrates in my hand it's another message from Avery.

Where are you?

You didn't come home last night!

Dinner was delicious, by the way

We waited ages.

Seriously, where the hell are you?

Do I need to call the police? Have you been kidnapped or something?

The usual noise of staff arriving trickles in from reception, distracting me.

'Morning.' I hear.

'Good morning.'

'God, I'm wrecked. How busy was that last night?'

'I know. Crazy. My feet have blisters.'

'Great tips though.'

'Yeah awesome.'

'Hope it's as busy again tonight.'

'Me too.'

Their chattering voices fade as they begin their shift and a lump swells in my throat and I don't think I can face a day in the kitchen. Not when it's all my fault Scott lost his job.

I leave Avery a quick voice message, apologising and promising to explain everything later. And then I rack my exhausted brain for a plausible excuse to hand the staff about why we are one head chef down when we are fully booked out for the evening.

There's a gentle knock on the door and Lyla's face appears as it creaks open. 'Tabby, erm, Mrs Buchanan wants you in the kitchen.'

'Okay,' I say like a naughty schoolchild being summoned to the principal's office.

Lyla's face looks worried. 'Are you okay?'

'Yeah, yeah, course.' I rub my stinging eyes. 'Just a bit tired.'

'Will I tell Mrs Buchanan that you're busy?'

I smile and swallow the bothersome lump that's been wedged in my throat since Catherine first arrived this morning.

'Thanks, but that's okay. I'll speak to her myself.'

Lyla watches me with trepidation and I can only imagine the staff have already picked up that something is not quite right this morning.

'Could you start getting ready for that fortieth birthday party we have coming in later?' I ask, knowing it's much too early. 'Push the tables nearest the window together and make sure there's somewhere for the guests to leave presents.'

I can tell Lyla is confused by my premature request. But she nods and smiles, obediently. She lets go of the door and turns to leave but, before she walks away, she twists her head back over her shoulder and looks at me with the concerned eyes of a friend.

'You know, I think you're amazing. We all do. Mark is only gone four months. It's okay to have bad days. It's normal, really.'

Lyla's kind words stab like a knife in my gut. The last thing I am is amazing. And absolutely nothing about my life is in any way normal right now.

'Thank you,' I say. 'That's a very nice thing to say.'

My phone vibrates and I glance down to find a message from Avery.

Glad you weren't kidnapped. Talk later x

When I look up again, Lyla is gone.

It's quite a while before I'm ready to face the kitchen. When I finally do, a hangover is setting in along with the pinch of not enough sleep. Catherine is standing with her back to me, staring out the tiny window that overlooks the alley between us and the pub next door. I pour a glass of water and the noise startles her.

'There you are,' she says, turning to face me.

I drink, instantly relieved.

'I thought you might have—'

'Left,' I say, reading her.

'Gone for a lie-down, actually,' she says, eying up the large glass of water I've drained.

'We're busy today. What did you tell the staff?'

Catherine glares at me as if I've just asked an absurd question.

'We have to explain where Scott is,' I say.

'*We* don't have to do anything. It didn't work out with that man, end of story.'

'We won't manage without Scott today,' I say, fighting the urge to guzzle more water. 'We're going to have to cancel some of our bookings.'

'We managed just fine before *Scott*.'

'But Mark was here then.'

Catherine clutches the edge of the countertop, suddenly unsteady on her feet, as if hearing Mark's name cracks her heart. But in a blink she's straightened herself. She can't bear to show her grief and I don't know why.

'I will put an ad in the paper this afternoon. We'll have a new chef by next week,' she says. 'Surely I can trust you to manage alone until then?'

'Catherine, please?' I say, noticing how despite her stiff upper lip and long neck, her fingers still wrap so tightly round the counter edge that her knuckles are white.

Part of me wants to reach out and hug her, although I know that would simply make us both uncomfortable.

'I know how hard this is,' I say, trying desperately to keep heartbreak out of my voice. 'And I'm so sorry if we've upset you, but you've misinterpreted what happened last night. We had a few drinks after our shift and fell asleep. I'm wrecked. I haven't been sleeping well.'

Catherine's gaze burns though me with such intensity it almost physically hurts.

'Scott is a fantastic chef,' I go on. 'Letting him go is a mistake. We've never been this busy before. Bookings are out the door, we're actually turning people away.'

'We will have a new chef by next week,' Catherine repeats.

There's so much pain behind her eyes that it strips my words from me. Finally, I pour another glass of water.

'I'm not feeling very well,' I say, truthfully, between mouthfuls. 'I think I need to go home.'

Catherine's wide eyes glare at me and I place the empty glass down on the countertop next to her hand.

'Don't be ridiculous,' she says. 'Who'll manage the kitchen?'

I shrug.

'Don't do this.' Catherine steps closer, pointing her finger. 'Don't you dare think you can bully me, young lady.'

I shake my head as the mix of emotion and last night's wine rumbles loudly in my stomach.

'I know what you're doing,' she says. 'You're trying to tie my hands.'

'Actually, I'm trying not to throw up in the kitchen. So, if you would please excuse me.'

'Tabitha, I am so disappointed in you.'

'I know,' I say, but for the first time Catherine's loaded words slide off me as if my skin is made of wax and I walk away without looking back.

TWENTY-FOUR

Back at the flat my first chore is to find a generic WE'RE CLOSED sign online. I copy and share the image on La Bella Vita's Instagram account. My fingers tremble as I add some sad-face emojis and the caption 'until further notice'. Shortly after, a stream of comments ensue.

L.Mac7 Oh God, how will I live without your chocolate cake? 😱
Fit.Fine.Life. Please tell me you're opening again soon!!
Pearson.Tom64 Not good enough. I have an anniversary dinner booked next month.
L.Mac7 @Pearson.Tom64 Next month? Book somewhere else. It's not rocket science 🙄
Pearson.Tom64 @L.Mac7 Mind your own business. Troll!

My initial and overwhelming instinct is to reassure Pearson-.Tom64 that we will most definitely be open next month. It's unbearable to think about the bookings we'll lose and the money we'll haemorrhage all because of Catherine's tantrum. My first thought is to call her and give her a piece of my mind. But I remind myself that she isn't thinking straight. That none of us are, and I take some deep breaths to calm down.

Lightheaded, I decide to call Scott instead. I want to tell him how sorry I am. I want to tell him that I'm going to fix this. Mostly, I want to tell him I don't regret last night even if it has played out the way it has. His phone rings out several times and finally, with a heavy heart, I give up.

The days that follow are a blur of calling staff to break the news that we are closed once again until further notice. I apologise and promise to pay their wages regardless. Although I have no idea how, and thinking about it breaks me out in a cold sweat. I try Scott again but there is still no answer.

Finally, I call Catherine. There's some small talk. Something about Mark's brother going on holiday to France and something else about the cows calving and some sheep getting caught in the hedge.

'It's hard work managing a farm,' she says, and her speech is slightly slurred and she's clearly had a couple of glasses of wine. 'I'm too old. I'm just too old. If only Mark and his father were still with us, they'd take care of me. And now a restaurant on top. I'm at breaking point.'

Catherine begins to cry and my heart hurts for her. Suddenly she sounds like a broken woman and not the strong matriarch of the Buchanan family I've known over the years. I hold the phone a little closer to my ear and sigh. 'Oh, Catherine. I know this is hard. I really, really do. That's why I think if you just rehire Scott, it will really help. At the very least we can get La Bella Vita open again and stop losing so much money.'

My palms begin to sweat as money worries take hold.

'Why didn't you drive on New Year's Eve, Tabitha?' Catherine says out of nowhere. 'You know how hard Mark worked – how tired he was. None of this would have happened if you were driving.'

My breath catches and my chest tightens and we both cry and cry.

TWENTY-FIVE

MAY

Time for a makeover. You are beautiful but your flat is not. Let your colours shine.

I stare at my emails and shake my head. Avery's resolution feels completely at odds with everything else in my life right now. The last thing I'm capable of is shining. Besides, every inch of my apartment is a reminder of Mark and Catherine and how I've remained a constant disappointment to the Buchanans over the years. The cream curtains in the sitting room are silk and handmade by one of Catherine's friends. I returned the shop-bought ones I chose without showing Mark. I knew he would rather the silk ones with the hem hanging slightly longer on one side than the other. The rug under the coffee table was an engagement present from Catherine's sister. The pile is thick and, no matter how often I vacuum, the dust trapped inside makes me sneeze. But Mark raved about the plush softness against his bare feet. Redecorating my apartment right now is the last thing I want to do. I can't cover up years of Catherine's disapproval with a lick of paint. And I can't gloss over the damage her tantrum is causing to La Bella Vita.

I didn't think my sleep pattern could get worse but I was wrong. Without a head chef La Bella Vita has been closed for three weeks and five days and with each passing day I grow more and more resentful. I blame Catherine. I blame Mark. But mostly I blame myself for letting Catherine push Scott away.

It comes as no surprise that Scott isn't speaking to me. But it is surprising that he seems to have fallen completely off the grid. I've left countless voicemails and WhatsApp messages and emails. And I've noticed his Instagram hasn't been updated in weeks. The last photo he posted is a rather unflattering selfie of the two of us, pretty drunk on La Bella Vita's couch. His radio silence worries me and despite feeling inappropriately stalk-erish I make the decision to call round to his flat. Unfortunately, this also means pulling up the shutter of La Bella Vita and going inside to find his address on the work computer. I convince myself that if I keep it together, I can be in and out before anyone realises I'm there.

I get dressed for the first time in days and put on a little make-up.

'Swit-swoo,' Avery teases when I walk into the kitchen. 'A tad overdressed to check out paint, but I like it.'

I glance at the table, where Avery and Becca are perusing colour charts. Thankfully Avery seems more zen than she has been recently. And I let myself think today might be the first day in a while that she doesn't hypothesise about causing Catherine physical harm on my behalf.

'Whatcha think?' Avery asks, pointing at a row of greens. 'Something like this for the kitchen?'

'Teals, aquamarines, turquoise. Greens are all the rage at the moment,' Becca says.

I smile. I like greens.

'The guy who did the show house for the estate I'm selling at the moment said he could call by later to take a look,' Becca goes on confidently, but she quickly adds, 'If that's okay?'

'An interior designer?' I say, opening the fridge and deciding on a bar of Cadbury's Whole Nut for breakfast. 'I can't afford someone like that.'

'It's cool. He owes me a favour,' Becca says.

'Oh.'

'Soooo will I tell him it's okay to call by today?' she nudges gently.

'Um.'

I glance around at the white walls, white cupboards and white drapes. I've never noticed before how clinical the kitchen seems. Mark liked everything to sparkle. He would wipe the countertops with antibacterial spray countless times a day. I often complained that it burned my throat but he argued it was a small price to pay for good hygiene. Once, I left the kitchen without noticing that my coffee cup had printed a semicircle stain on the table. Mark teased me that I was a slob. It was funny at first, but when he was still joking about it the next day it became another reminder that my standards weren't quite good enough. For weeks after Mark would eye up my morning coffee with disquietude.

'Did you wipe the bottom of that?' he would ask, pointing at my cup.

After a while I stopped drinking coffee in the mornings before I left the flat. But the snide comments followed me into work. Eventually, I stopped drinking coffee altogether.

'If you're not feeling green, how about yellow? Kitchens are always yellow, aren't they?' Becca says.

'Anything is better than this bloody white. I feel like I need to wear sunglasses in here, it's so bright,' Avery says, squinting.

She makes a good point. The morning sun is blasting in the

window and hitting the polished white floor with blinding intensity.

'I can't look at paint today,' I say, unwrapping my chocolate but not feeling particularly like biting it.

Avery sighs. 'Oh, come on, Tabs. Can't you just for once pretend to be excited about the resolutions.'

'I am excited.'

'Could have fooled me. We're almost halfway in and you've a face like a slapped arse most of the time.'

'Avery!' Becca says, feigning shock, but I can see her struggle to mute a giggle.

'Right. I'm off,' Avery says, standing up and leaning in to kiss Becca on the cheek. 'Talk to this one, will you?' She glances at me before turning back to wink at Becca. 'Maybe you can convince her to lighten up.'

Avery picks up her sketchpad and a box of pastels. 'I'll be just across the street in the park if you need me. Bird sketching today.'

'Sounds fun,' I say.

'Yeah, if I can get the little feckers to stay still for long enough.' She rolls her eyes. 'You eating that?' She snatches my chocolate before I have time to answer. 'Do birds like chocolate? One way to find out, I suppose.'

'I don't think animals are supposed to eat stuff like that,' Becca says.

'That's dogs,' Avery says.

'Pretty sure it's all animal types,' Becca says. 'Especially wildlife.'

'Okay.' Avery shrugs and bites off the top square. 'More for me. See you two later. Byeeee.'

Becca waits until we see Avery cross the street through the kitchen window before she offers to make us tea. We don't talk as she does. We sit at opposite sides of the kitchen table with a cup in front of each of us and strips of colour charts splayed like a fan in the centre between us.

'Are you okay?' Becca asks, at last.

'This colour is really nice.' I place my finger on a green that falls somewhere between sea green and turquoise.

'You know, if painting is too much you could start with little changes. Maybe some new cushions for the sitting room. Or new curtains.'

I sip tea as I try to find words.

'Avery really wants to help, but it's understandable that all your memories are tied up here.' Becca bend forward and scoops the colour charts into her arms. 'Changing the colour of the walls is a big deal and that's okay, you just need time and—'

'Could you sell the flat?'

Tea sloshes over the edge of Becca's cup. 'What?'

'I think I want to sell the flat. Could you do that for me, please?'

'I could, but...'

'Earlier, Avery said that we're almost halfway through the resolutions, right?'

Becca nods. 'Yeah. May. Five months into the year, can you believe how fast time is flying?'

'Exactly,' I say. 'Almost halfway through this year and nothing has really changed. But I want it to. I *need it* to.'

Becca shifts in her chair and I can tell springing this on her without Avery by her side has forced her out of her comfort zone.

'Look, I'm not saying I want to move today or tomorrow.'

Becca shakes her head. 'You know, usually we tell people not to put their homes on the market while they're grieving.'

'That's good advice.'

Becca looks on, confused.

'Do you know why Avery wants me to redecorate?'

Becca's smile returns and she's instantly lighter. 'Yes. She thinks you might enjoy brightening up the place.'

'She thinks I need to put my own stamp on the place.'

'I suppose.'

'Because it's never felt like it belonged to me,' I say, shocking myself as the realisation hits me. 'This was Mark's home. It never truly felt like I belonged. I think it's time to move on.'

TWENTY-SIX

There's a slight spring in my step as I get off the bus outside La Bella Vita. Summer is in the air as a gentle sun taps on my back.

'Good morning, Rashidi.' I startle him and he splatters a little mustard onto his apron.

'Well, look who it is,' he says, acting as if he hasn't seen me in years rather than days. 'The usual?'

'Not today, thanks.'

'Another day closed?' he asks as he glances over his shoulder at the shutter alienating La Bella Vita from the rest of the bustling street.

The rhetorical question saddens me.

'We'll be back in business soon.' I cross my fingers behind my back. My stomach rumbles loudly as I savour the smell of his delicious bagels.

'Good.' He winks. 'Because a lot of people be depending on you. Staff, customers, even that lady with the grey hair.'

'Catherine? Ha. No. She's technically my boss these days.'

'She might think she's the boss lady, but...' Rashidi shakes his head and points towards the closed shutter. 'Look what happens without you!'

I lean forward and kiss him on the cheek.

He smiles wide and nods, the way he always does, and then he pulls open the squeaky top drawer of his cart and passes me an already prepared bagel and a piece of folded white paper.

'How did you know I'd stop by today?' I say, taking the bagel in one hand and the paper in the other.

'I didn't.'

'Oh, Rashidi. Have you been making one of these all month? Oh my God!'

'I think that note is important,' he says, pointing to my closed fist.

I have to fight the urge to kiss his cheek again and hug him tight.

'I'll will have a bacon bagel ready again tomorrow,' he says with certainty.

When I try to pay him, he turns his back, curls his hands round the handle of his cart and moves along to his next spot on the road.

I replay the conversation as I unlock La Bella Vita's shutter. It creaks and groans, fighting against me for a moment before it finally rises. I open the door and step inside, glad to leave the noisy street behind me as I turn my attention to the piece of paper in my hand. I unfold it and read.

Dear Tabby,

Firstly, let me apologise for my handwriting.
Secondly, if you can make these words out, then know I am also so sorry I haven't been in touch. I left my phone in the office, and, since you haven't opened in a while, I've had no way to get it back.
Thirdly, I knew you could only do without one of Rashidi's bagels for so long.

Anyway, my new number is 082 8767572, it would be really, really nice to hear from you. And to get my phone back.

Scott

I hurry into the office and sure enough Scott's phone is sitting next to the unfinished roster on the desk. Unsurprisingly the battery is dead but I pick it up and stare at it nonetheless, as if I can will it back to life in my hands. Laughing at myself, and glad no one is here to see me, I take my own phone from my pocket. I lean my bum against the desk, stretch my legs out and cross them at the ankles. I stare at the piece of paper again and, with my heart racing, I dial the number Scott has shared.

'Hello,' a raspy, low voice answers.

I don't recognise the voice and I stand up immediately, almost tripping over my own legs.

'Hi. Hello. Is that, er... I think I have the wrong number. I'm looking for Scott.' I'm cringing so hard my face actually hurts.

'Scott's in the loo. Who's this?'

'Eh, I'm Tabby. Tabitha Greenwood.' It comes out all polite and reserved as if I'm trying to impress at an interview.

'Oh, right. Hey, I'm Richie. Scott's been hoping you'd call.'

'Oh good. Great.'

'You're that hot chick he works with. Or used to work with.'

'Oh. Eh...'

'Christ, you dick, Richie,' I hear Scott's voice in the background. 'Gimme the phone. Give it to me.'

'I've got to go now,' Richie says, 'it was nice talking to you, hot girl.'

'I'm going to kill you. I'm actually going to beat the shit out of you until you die,' Scott says, and then there is some laughing before his tone changes and I hear he's taken the phone as he says, 'Hi, Tabby, it's great to hear from you.'

'Hi.'

'Sorry about that. That was Richie. He *used* to be my friend.'

I can still hear Richie's laughter in the background.

I've no idea why, but I begin pacing the floor. If the heat of my face is anything to go by my face is no doubt fire-engine red. *Hot girl?* Did Scott really tell his friend I'm a hot girl? I don't think anyone has ever said that about me before.

'Richie seems nice,' I say.

'Yeah, he is. He's a great mate,' Scott says. 'And a pretty decent housemate if he'd just stop leaving his smelly socks in the hall.'

'Gross,' I say, and it's followed by an awkward giggle. 'Well, erm, I found your phone.'

'You've been into the bistro, then?'

'Yeah. Just now.'

'Why was it closed all this time?'

His question and the surprise in his tone take my breath away and I'm not sure what to say.

'Staffing problems, haven't you heard?' I joke, trying to lighten the atmosphere.

Scott laughs. I laugh too. But it's followed quickly by a heavy silence.

'I hear the coffee is shit there, too,' he jokes back finally.

'Yeah. It's total crap,' I say, pressing my free hand onto the top of my head as if it will help in some way.

The silence circles back and I find myself missing Richie's boisterous laughing in the background.

'Once I get my old phone back, I can text Saoirse,' Scott says. 'If you still want to go ahead with that. I'm sure she'd love to chat as soon as she's free.'

My brain is suddenly as on fire as my face.

'Maybe you could meet her. And just let me know how you get on?' I say.

'That might be a bit weird.' Scott inhales. 'Since I don't actually work at La Bella Vita anymore.'

'Right yeah. God, yeah, you're right! Sorry.'

My voice has risen an octave and I'm now actively wishing for Richie to come back.

'Look, it's just coffee,' Scott says. 'She's a rep and you need a new supplier. You don't have to mention anything else if you don't want to.'

'Will you still come? To meet her. With me, I mean.'

'Sure. If you want.'

'Okay. Cool. Great. Brilliant. It's a date. Well, not a date. Like a date in the calendar. Not a date, date. Something you mark with a circle in pen. Like an appointment. It's an appointment.'

'I'll text her,' he says.

'Do. Do. And let me know so I can mark it in my calendar.'

'With a pen.'

The heat from my face is travelling down my neck as I echo, 'With a pen.'

'I kind of need my phone to text her, though.'

'Oh God, yes. You do. It's here. Ready and waiting. Well, not exactly ready. The battery is dead. But it is waiting.'

'Will you be there tomorrow?' he asks.

I take a deep breath and glance at the unfinished roster on my desk. I think about my staff and how much I miss day-to-day life, chatting and working alongside him.

'What's the point?' I say. 'I can't open without a chef.'

'You're a chef.'

'I'm a pastry chef.'

'And a damn good one,' Scott says. 'But I bet you've managed on your own before.'

I *have* managed on my own before – when Mark would go away on a lads' holiday, or for training. In fact, I quite enjoyed those small windows of taking charge. The staff and I would laugh and giggle our way through prep and, when the final customer left, we would sometimes stay back for a well-earned drink and a chat.

'Yeah, for like a week,' I say. 'Nothing longer.'

'If you can manage a week, you can manage a month. And then a year. You can do this.'

I think about the mounting bills and disgruntled customers. I think about how hard Mark and I worked over the years building our reputation. Catherine would never forgive herself if she accidently put us out of business. Mark would never forgive her either. I have to get La Bella Vita running again and I have to do it on my own.

'I... uh... um... Rashidi has been making my usual bagel all month,' I blurt suddenly. 'He's been waiting for me to get back to work.'

Despite the lack of context Scott seems to understand.

'I guess you better not make him waste another bagel,' he says.

'I better not,' I say, smiling. 'I'll see you tomorrow.'

'Tomorrow.'

TWENTY-SEVEN

It's harder to get a meeting with Saoirse than Scott and I had anticipated. Apparently, she's been on sick leave on and off for a while, and she's not available until later in the summer. At first, we were both disappointed, but counting down the weeks gives Scott and me the perfect excuse to stay in touch. He keeps me up to date on his job search and I fill him in about my days at La Bella Vita. I have the odd wobble, but on the whole I've been managing, and Scott loves nothing more than to say, 'I told you so.'

Catherine still stops by sporadically. She updates me on her efforts to replace Scott and I update him.

Scott: More interviews today?

Tabby: Yup 😊 You?

Scott: Two. Wish me luck.

Tabby: Good luck ♣ I'd rather be on your side of the table.

Scott: Catherine still making life hard?

Tabby: Do you even have to ask?

Scott: 😶

Interviewing alongside Catherine is a unique form of torture. She is rude and condescending and it's embarrassingly obvious she knows very little about the real workings of a kitchen. Nonetheless, she manages to find fault in those who do. They're inexperienced or they're too experienced. They're lacking imagination or they're trying too hard. No one can fill Mark's shoes. At one point Catherine offers to step behind an apron herself, but luckily I manage to shoot the idea down with talk of insurance and safety regulations in the kitchen.

By late in the month there are no more applicants to meet and Catherine is stopping by less and less. Unfortunately, so too are customers. Catherine's reintroduction of Pizza Friday is less than a success. Suits are choosing to grab pizza slices from a corner deli rather than pay restaurant prices for similar. Things are gradually becoming so quiet that I'm worried I might have to let some of my part-time staff go.

On the other hand, earlier finish times give me more time at home. May's resolution is well under way and I have to hand it to Avery – redecorating the flat is a surprisingly enjoyable distraction from all the crap at work. Becca says fresh paint will add value when it comes to the sale of the flat and I couldn't argue with that. But her interior designer friend turned out to be insanely overpriced, favour or not, so we've taken on the task of revamping the flat ourselves. Unsurprisingly, Avery takes to the job like a duck to water. Becca, however, is most definitely a fish on dry land, and I fall somewhere in between. I had no idea so many memories were carved into the walls of my flat. The first power cut, when

Mark and I stayed up until morning playing Scrabble by candlelight. Our first big fight, when Mark told me I was fat. Our first time making up, when he said curvy was sexy and we made love all afternoon. Avery thought painting over all traces of Catherine's taste would fill me with satisfaction. And it does, I suppose. But mostly I'm filled with heartache, as I seem to be erasing part of Mark in the process. I shove the pain deep down in my gut. It wedges next to Saoirse, the bracelet and my last conversation with Mark.

'You okay?' Becca asks one evening as I stare at the half old white, half new soft lemon walls of my kitchen.

I nod.

'Happy?' Avery asks.

My breath catches. I know she's asking if I'm happy with the colour but the question seems so much deeper and more far-reaching.

I nod again and take my phone from my pocket. I snap a photo of the dual-coloured walls and send it to Scott, captioning it, 'May's Resolution'.

He replies with a smiley face and a thumbs-up.

I'm distracted from my phone by Avery's squeaky laughter as she points at Becca and says, 'Christ, you've more paint in your hair than on the walls. I could hold you by your legs and use your head as a brush.'

'I'd like to see you try,' Becca argues, head to toe in speckles and splodges. 'This painting business is not as easy as it looks.'

Avery shrugs. There's a tiny fleck of white ceiling paint on the bridge of her nose and a splash on the leg of her trousers that I'm almost certain was Becca's doing.

'I can't believe you'll be moving soon,' Avery says, dragging a large roller across the ceiling.

'If anyone wants to buy the place,' I say, trying to make rolling look as easy, but my arms are tired and I'm squinting so I don't get paint in my eye.

'They will. When they see this inviting flat, everyone is going to want to buy it.'

Avery is wildly excited about my decision to sell. 'Never liked this place much,' she says, craning her neck to admire her handiwork.

I could remind her that when she helped Mark and me move in she gushed endlessly about how it was the nicest flat she'd ever seen in her life. Instead, I listen as she complains about the inconsiderate birds in the park that fly away midway through a sketch.

'Feathery feckers can't sit still for five minutes. I bet birds in the countryside appreciate being painted. I bet they have a much better attitude than these stupid city birds.'

I nod, not really listening as I concentrate so as not to drip paint onto the countertop where the old bedsheets acting as dustsheets have parted.

'Oh my God, we should move to the country,' Avery announces.

I glance at Becca, who simply shakes her head.

'We should. Oh, wouldn't it be so fab? We could all live together in a big, old country house.' Avery begins to twirl, full of excitement, as if she's the heroine in a movie and she's just had that edge-of-your-seat epiphany moment that solves all the character's problems.

'I can see it now,' she says, coming to a stop as she gazes into the distance. 'A fixer-upper, that's what we need. We can spend our days by the lake and our evenings painting by candlelight.'

'There's a lake?' I ask.

'And no electricity by the sounds of it,' Becca adds.

'We're going to need dungarees,' Avery says. 'Old ladies in grand old houses always have dungarees, don't they?'

'Why are we old?' I ask.

Avery shrugs. 'People age.'

Becca returns to painting, much to Avery's disappointment.

In glaring contrast to Avery's excitement about my flat sale, Becca has been oddly subdued. She's been professional, of course. She's taken care of advertising and she has viewings lined up and ready to go the moment the paint is dry. But she has never once said whether she thinks moving is a good idea or not, and I don't know why.

'We *are* all going to live together, right?' Avery says, and I sense her disappointment that Becca and I aren't filled with excitement at the prospect of growing old in denim in the countryside.

'Have you thought about where you want to move to?' Becca asks.

I shrug. 'Not really. I thought I'd wait 'til I sell here before I start looking.'

Becca shakes her head and looks deeply concerned. 'Property in the city is being snapped up in a blink.' She clicks her fingers. 'You don't want to be in the situation where your flat is sold, you have to be out in six weeks, and you have nowhere lined up. I see it happen all the time. It's so stressful. Do you want me to start looking into some places for you?'

'Would you?' I say, a wave of excitement washing over me. 'That would be really great. Thanks.'

'No. No. No,' Avery says, dropping the roller into the tray. Paint sloshes over the side and onto the cloth.

I want to clean it up, worried it will sink through the cloth and stain the tiles below, but Avery looks upset. I think she might cry. Avery never cries.

'Tabs, why would you sell one flat only to buy another at the other side of the city or wherever? What's the point of that?'

'I have to live somewhere,' I say.

'Live with us. Please? I'm serious,' Avery says. 'It doesn't have to be an old country house. We can stay in Dublin, if you like.'

I glance at Becca, hoping for her to tell Avery that three

grown women growing old together in a country house – or a city home – is the stuff of fairy tales. But there is a twinkle in Becca's eye, as if there is already a plan afoot.

'Are you moving in together?' I ask, trying to read their excitement.

'More than that,' Avery says, her shoulders rising to her ears and a huge smile exploding across her face. 'We're getting married.'

TWENTY-EIGHT

I set my roller down in the paint tray and stare at Avery. I wait for her to start laughing and tease me about the look on my face. But she stares back, wide-eyed and brimming with elation. Suddenly the paint fumes sting my eyes and I rub them, but it doesn't help.

'You *are* joking, right?' I say.

Becca shakes her head and offers a half-smile.

'God. You're serious.' My eyes are beginning to burn. 'Oh my God, you're actually serious.'

Becca steps closer and speaks softly. 'We were going to take you to lunch this week and tell you then—'

'Lunch?' I cut across her, shaking my head, and I can't imagine this being much better coming over food.

'Tabs, what's wrong?' Avery says as the excitement drains from her face. 'I thought you'd be happy for us.'

'I'm just confused. It's so soon. I mean, you barely know each other.'

My voice wobbles and there's a stabbing pain above my eyes. Maybe it's the paint fumes, or the shock.

'We see each other every day,' Avery says, taking Becca's hand in hers and kissing the back of it.

I roll my eyes. 'Becca, surely you must see—'

'We love each other.' Avery cuts across me before Becca has time to reply, and her furrowed brows and sharp tone let me know she's pissed off.

'Look,' I say, pausing to take a deep breath to hide my emotion so this doesn't blow up into a whole thing. 'I am happy for you guys. I'm really glad you've found each other. But I don't see what the rush is for.'

'We're in love,' Avery says.

'You said that already,' I say, and my efforts not to sound snappy fail.

'Maybe I need to say it again, because you don't seem to get it. We. Are. In. Love,' Avery says, and then she looks away and whispers, 'You wouldn't understand.'

Avery's words hurt and I instinctively press my hands against my chest as if I can protect my heart. But it's too late. They've already cut deep. I make my way to the mound that is the table and chairs covered in a dustsheet. I uncover a chair and flop down.

'Avery, look, I know you live your life at a hundred miles per hour, but this is ridiculous,' I say. 'This is all just way too much, even for you.'

'Even for me,' Avery echoes, jamming her hands on her hips as her anger turns to disappointment.

I shift my gaze to Becca and wait for her to say something sensible. But she's avoiding eye contact. Her silence is even more irritating than the deep breathing and sighing Avery has taken to puffing towards me.

'This is too fast,' I say, and it comes out stiff and like a warning.

'Too fast,' Avery says, and I realise that maybe I should

become as silent as Becca, because it would seem Avery plans to repeat everything I say.

I nod.

'So what's your advice? Keep waiting?'

'Yes. Definitely. Just for a while. Until you're both really sure this is really what you want. Mark and I were together four years before he proposed.'

'Seriously? You did not just compare us to you and Mark.'

Avery's eyes are narrow and she's wearing an expression I've never seen on her before. I've seen other people make this face – that scrunched-up, nuanced appearance of hurt and angry combined – but never Avery. Not until now. And my heart aches even more than before.

'Maybe you're right,' Avery says. 'Maybe we should wait. How did you know you were ready? Was it all Mark's emotional blackmail? Or his constant criticism? Did you just wake up one day, no longer recognise yourself and think, *Yup. Now is the time.*'

'Avery,' Becca says, sounding disgusted.

'What?' Avery shrugs. 'I'm not going to pretend he was a great guy because he's dead. We couldn't stand each other.'

'Mark liked you,' I say, but it's a barely audible whisper.

'No, he didn't!'

She's right and we both know it. Sometimes, I'm not sure Mark even liked me.

'None of it matters now anyway. Becca is not Mark,' Avery says.

'Mark wasn't always like that. Everything was good at the start. It was great.'

'Becca is not Mark,' Avery repeats, shouting now. 'What the hell does she have to do for your stupid seal of approval?'

'Oh God, it's not like that,' I say, becoming upset. 'I'm just surprised things are moving so fast, you know?'

Becca nods and smiles with understanding eyes.

'I don't get it. I don't get you,' Avery continues, as tiredness creeps into her voice. 'Mark treated you like a sack of shit for years. Oh, don't cut your hair, Tabs, I hate short hair.' She puts on a deep, but in no way male-sounding voice. 'Don't drink coffee. You're too fat. I'm the boss at work. I'm the boss at life. And you're never going to stick up for yourself because you know I will laugh. I'm a big bloody narcissist, that's what I am.'

'Avery, it wasn't like that,' I say.

'And what about Catherine? The almost mother-in-law from hell. She's stomping her seriously ugly size seven loafers all over your bistro and you don't say a word.' Avery marches loudly on the spot. The sound of her boots pounding on the floor echoes in my head.

'She's the managing partner. She owns a larger share than I do.'

'That's a load of bollocks and you know it. You're running the place and you're still afraid to upset her. Or maybe you're just afraid *of* her.'

'That's not fair.'

Avery stops marching and makes an expression that's more herself. 'No! What's not fair is everyone else treats you like crap and you're grand with it. You wouldn't say boo to a bloody fly. But...' She shakes her head and throws her arms back. 'I tell you I'm the happiest I've ever been in my whole life and you want to shit all over that.'

'Is that really what you think?'

'Yes!'

I look at Becca again, hoping she will have finally found something to say, but her eyes are as teary as Avery's.

'I hope you're not envious, Tabs. You're not that kind of person,' Avery says. 'But something has crawled up your arse and if it's not envy, I don't know what it is.'

The combination of drying paint and the realisation that Avery is right brings on a headache.

'I'm going to bed,' I say, as I pinch the bridge of my nose. It offers slight relief. 'Leave this please. I'll clean up later.'

Finally, Becca finds her voice. 'It's okay. I've got this,' she says.

'Fine. Whatever. Night,' Avery says, staring at the ground, tracing shapes with her foot as she breathes heavily.

TWENTY-NINE

I don't turn on the light in my bedroom as I stand, staring out the window at a blinking street light, and hope for silence. A cat meows incessantly somewhere close by, a car horn honks, and there's rustling at the residents' bins. The familiar sounds that shape most nights outside my bedroom window; but tonight I wish they would go away. When I scrunch my face, I can feel the speckles of ceiling paint that dust my nose. The large splodges of yellow paint on the knees of my jeans have hardened and, when I flop onto my bed, they're stiff and uncomfortable against my skin, but I don't move. Not even to roll over.

I can't believe Avery is getting married. When Mark and I announced our engagement, she insisted that marriage was nothing more than an archaic ritual and a piece of paper. She said marriage wasn't measure of love. And part of me believed her. So, what the hell is this?

I close my eyes and wait for sleep to come, but instead there's a knock on my door. I groan inwardly. I don't answer, but I should know better than to hope Avery will go away.

'Tabs, c'mon. I know you're awake.'

I remain silent.

'It's almost twelve. I know you're going to stay up until midnight to read the next resolution.'

My breath catches. I haven't been keeping track of the date. I squint and try to make out the time and date on my watch in the semi-darkness. June first is minutes away. My fingertips tingle suddenly as I realise it's halfway through the year. Six whole months.

'Are you listening to me?' Avery says, knocking again, louder.

'Go away, Avery.'

'Ha. I knew you were awake!'

'Leave me alone,' I say, as I flop over onto my stomach and press my face into the pillow.

'I can't,' Avery says. 'Becca said I have to say I'm sorry.'

I exhale and sit up, wide awake. Avery doesn't owe me an apology. Everything she said is spot on. My whole life was built on a lie. Mark didn't love me. He loved Saoirse.

'I'm sorry I said all that mean stuff about Mark,' Avery says. 'And not just because he's dead.'

I hear her press her back against the door and I know she's sliding to the floor with her knees tucked into her chest and it reminds me of our childhood. We sat exactly like this often as kids. Me curled up on my bed, crying, and Avery with her back to the door rattling off an apology she didn't really mean and sometimes didn't understand.

When I was seven, or maybe eight, our parents bought me the coolest Tiny Tears doll for my birthday. She had pink dungarees and golden hair, and she was precious. Avery begged me to hold her, to touch her, but I couldn't bear to let her. Eventually, our mother couldn't listen to our arguing any more and she insisted that I share. Days later, Avery dropped Tiny Tears down the stairs and her head fell off. My father shouted, and I cried as our mother superglued the head back on. Avery sat outside my bedroom door for a long time that night. She said she was sorry over and over but I didn't believe her. I never played with Tiny Tears again. For a long time, I thought Avery dropped her on purpose. I was a teenager before I realised she didn't. Growing up, Avery never intentionally made a mess. But somehow she often managed to.

Avery's voice drags me back to the here and now. 'I love her, Tabs,' she says, and I wonder if she's bouncing on the spot like she usually does when she's excited. 'As soon as Becca asked me to marry her... as soon as I said yes... I wanted to tell you.'

I gaze at the door as if I can see Avery through it.

'I wanted to ask you to be my bridesmaid,' she says. 'Tabs, please? You will be my bridesmaid, won't you?'

I can hear the happiness in her voice even through the door. I want to tell her that of course I'll be her bridesmaid. It would be an honour, really. I want to tell her that I understand her excitement, because weddings are *so* exciting. But most of all I want to tell her not to do it. I want to tell her that some day everything you thought was wonderful will crumble around you and your life will be one big mess. We're not kids anymore. Superglue doesn't fix messes now. But instead I lie on my back, staring at the ceiling. The street light cast orangey shapes above me and I stare at them almost without blinking as I wonder how the hell I got here. Six months ago, I was planning my own wedding, and now look at me. Single. Lonely. And tired. I'm so incredibly tired.

'Okay,' Avery says, after a while of silence on both sides of the door. 'Okay. I'm going to go to bed now.' I hear her pull herself to her feet and, before she walks away, she says, 'I love Becca. She loves me. And we are getting married. No matter what, we are. I really hope some day you can let Mark and all his baggage go and learn to be happy again.'

The sense of rejection in Avery's tone saddens me.

'I'm happy that you're happy,' I whisper, too softly for her to hear.

I listen, sadder than ever, as her heavy footsteps carry her away.

THIRTY

JUNE

Keep shining. Remember how much you love to create. Time for art lessons.

I wait for a long time, until the sound of gentle snoring carries from Avery's room down to mine, before I get up and walk towards the kitchen. I'm glad to see Becca's coat still on the couch in the living area. The thought of her driving home this late worried me.

The kitchen is fully painted. There are the dustsheets, empty paint cans and used rollers scattered all around; but even still, the usually compact space seems bigger and more inviting. As I begin tidying up, I imagine new people moving in when the flat sells. I shake out the dustsheets and fold them as I think about a loving couple cooking their first meal in this kitchen. I imagine them chopping vegetables together, laughing and cuddling as they listen to music. A couple so very different to Mark and me. A couple so much more like Avery and Becca.

It takes me quite a quite a while to finish tidying, and I

enjoy the overwhelming sense of satisfaction when I step back and admire the bright and spotless, refreshed space. It's almost two in the morning when I fetch my laptop and make a cup of tea but I'm not tired. I have too much on my mind to sleep. I pull out a chair and sit at the table. Crossing my legs in my paint-encrusted jeans isn't particularly comfortable but I don't budge as I open my laptop and check my emails.

As expected, Avery's latest resolution has dropped into my inbox. The date stares back at me. Five months since Mark died. Five months since Avery and Becca meet. And five months since I was supposed to get my life together. Yet here I am, staring at my screen through teary eyes and with a heavy heart. Just as I did six months ago when I wrote my resolutions. I can change my hair and take up art classes, but deep down I'm still the same Tabby. I think about Avery's words earlier. Her cutting accusation that I put up with shit from everyone, always. I wonder how long Avery has considered me a pushover. She's never said it before. Not like that. And I wonder why, especially since she's not exactly built with a filter. Does Avery think I've spent the last five months making my life worse instead of better? If she does, she's probably right.

I try to see myself in an art class. I imagine a beret on my head and a paintbrush in my hand. And although I'm not expecting to be the next Picasso, or remotely as talented as Avery, art classes do sound fun. I look forward to the morning when I can tell Avery how excited I am about this resolution and show her that I do know how to enjoy myself. I close my emails, about to click into Google to search for local classes, but I'm distracted by my desktop background. I stare at the image of me and Mark arm in arm outside La Bella Vita on opening night. It's the same photo that hangs proudly in the hall. Mark and I are smiling brightly and the camera flash catches the sparkle of happiness in his eyes. They say a picture speaks a thousand words and I remember Mark's words just before the photo was taken. He said my dress was too tight and too short and I was embarrassing him.

'It's June, Mark,' I whisper as silent tears trickle down my cheeks. 'I'm going to art class. All Avery's idea, of course.' I tear my eyes away from the screen and drop my gaze to my jeans. 'You'd laugh if you could see me now – head to toe in yellow paint like a lemon drizzle cake. You'd probably tell me I'm wasting my time because I don't have an artistic bone in my body.'

I return my gaze to Mark's handsome face. I remember what it was like to feel his lips on mine, to run my hands through his hair or sense the warmth of his body next to mine as we lay in bed at night. I also remember what it felt like when his words sliced through me, cutting my confidence clean down the middle.

'I didn't give up this year,' I say, slowly realising that this photo isn't the epitome of success and achievement that I always thought it was. 'I didn't give up in March, like you said I would. Or in April, or May, or now.'

I tilt my laptop left, and then right, trying to catch the kitchen light to find a sparkle of happiness in my eyes, but it doesn't work. I can't find what wasn't there. I try to find a more recent picture of myself but I don't have any. Not even a selfie. I haven't taken a photo of myself in years. No one wants to see the fat girl with dull eyes.

I leave the kitchen and walk into the hall. I roll onto my tiptoes and try to take down the photo of Mark and me, but I can't reach. Deflated, I turn away. I yelp and nearly fall over when I see Becca standing behind me in Avery's old Nirvana t-shirt and a pair of slippers.

She begins to laugh.

I press my hand to my chest and my heart races. 'You scared the shit out of me.'

'Sorry. So sorry,' she says, between snorty giggles.

'Can't sleep?' I ask, worried that she's awake for the same reason as me.

'Snoring,' she says, rolling her eyes and still laughing.

'It's bad, isn't it?' I begin to giggle too as a loud, piggy snort erupts from Avery's room.

Becca nods but then immediately adds, 'Ah, I don't mind too much. Avery bought me earplugs for my birthday.'

I laugh more before I realise she's serious. 'Oh.'

'Fancy ones,' she explains. 'The same ones Jennifer Aniston uses.'

'Oh,' I repeat, unable to find a better word, as I hope Avery doesn't buy me the same for my birthday.

The laughter fades and we quickly become two people standing awkwardly in the hall in the middle of the night.

'How about you? What are you doing up at this time?' Becca turns her wrist to check her watch.

'I've a headache,' I say, quickly. 'Must be the paint fumes.'

'Um,' Becca says.

She doesn't believe me. It's written all over her face.

'Actually, I'm trying to take this down,' I say, pointing at the photo as my racing heart gradually returns to normal.

'Is something wrong with it?'

'There's no sparkle in my eye,' I explain.

Becca's sleepy expression emphasises her confusion. 'Need some help?' she asks.

I nod.

Becca reaches the photo easily on her tiptoes. She unhooks it and passes it to me. 'Are you okay?' she asks as she passes me the slightly dusty frame. 'Does this have something to do with earlier? Avery shouldn't have compared our relationship to yours and Mark's.'

'It's different,' I say, instinctively holding the photograph close to my chest. 'Mark and I were together a long time...'

'I know you think this is all wrong. Avery and me,' Becca says, stepping back to give me and my photo some space.

'It's just fast.'

'When you know, you know,' Becca says.

'Yeah. Sure.' My grip on the photo tightens until it becomes uncomfortable.

'You're so alike, you know. You and Avery,' Becca says.

I snort. 'What? No way. People always tell us how different we are.'

'People are wrong.'

I snort again, even louder this time, insulted. I'm insulted that Becca thinks I'm loud, and flighty, and wild. And then I sigh, disappointed in myself. Avery is my favourite person because of her traits, not in spite of them. Avery tells stories just like our mother. Sometimes with conviction so similar it's like watching a real live memory play out. They share a laugh too, something you never grow tired of hearing. Like your favourite song, that you just can't help sing along to.

'You both want the best for each other,' Becca says.

I can't argue with that. I've spent my whole life protecting Avery.

'She's my sister,' I say.

'I know. And I'm not going to pretend I get this intense, *we know what's best for each other* thing that you two have going on,' Becca says.

'I—'

Becca cuts me off. 'I don't get it. But I totally admire it. I wish I had someone in my corner who fights as fiercely for me as you do for each other.'

'She's my sister,' I repeat, gently.

'And you wish she was more like you.'

I shake my head.

'I don't want Avery to be like me,' I say, genuinely. 'I really, really don't.'

'She wishes you could be more like her.'

I sigh. 'I know.'

'Would that be such a bad thing?'

'Two Averys? I'm not sure the world could handle that.'

Becca smiles and I can tell she's wishing the world was full of Averys.

'Right,' she says, rubbing her sleepy eyes. 'I should get back to bed. I've a ton of flats to show in the morning.'

'I know you love her, Becca,' I say as I swallow the lump in my throat.

'I do. And I know you do too. Give it time. You'll see, this will all be okay.'

I nod, hopeful.

'Goodnight, Becca.'

'Night night.'

THIRTY-ONE

I've lost count of the number of nights I've lain in bed staring at the ceiling. It's certainly been often enough to notice fine hairline cracks in the plaster overhead. I'm not sure if they're new or I simply never paid much attention before. I've also noticed how there's a fleck of paint missing at the point where the lighting fixture attaches to the ceiling. Mostly I've noticed how the nights grow shorter and dawn arrives earlier and earlier.

Shortly after 5 a.m. my room is fully bright and I have to peel myself off the bed to close my curtains because superenthusiastic joggers will start whizzing by soon. I've noticed that too – brighter mornings mean earlier joggers. I wish I could be more like them: starting my day full of energy. Mark said I run like a penguin, with my arms by my side and my feet moving but my knees not so much. For once, his observation was on point. I am definitely not a natural runner. But despite my lack of sleep I feel surprisingly energised this morning as I sit, cross-legged, on my bed and power on my laptop.

I open my work emails and gaze at the inbox full of applications for the chef's position. I've read them all already, but I'm excited to revisit them with fresh eyes.

'Eeny, meeny, miney...' I whisper, as I swirl the mouse around and come to a random stop, '...moe.'

'Lizzie Parker,' I say aloud, recognising the name of a confi-dent chef who Catherine and I interviewed last month.

From: Lizzie Parker <liz.louise.Parker82@mymail.com>
To: La Bella Vita <info@labellavita.ie>
Date: May 11th
Subject: Head Chef Application

Dear Sir/Madam

I would like to apply for the role of head chef at La Bella Vita. I have almost eighteen years' experience and I was a huge fan of Mark Buchanan's work. I've long admired his creative menus and it would be an honour to follow in his masterful footsteps...

I roll my eyes and click out of the email. I was surprised when Catherine didn't want to hire Lizzie-the-lick-arse-Page. She said all the right things. And not just about food. She even complimented Catherine's hideous knitted cardigan. But still Catherine didn't want to offer Lizzie the job.

I scroll to the email below, but I have no memory of the next applicant, Zoe Zouch. I'm usually quite good with names and faces and I'm surprised that I've forgotten an applicant so quickly.

From: Zoe Zouch <Zoeinheels@yipmail.com>
To: La Bella Vita <info@labellavita.ie>
Date: May 12th
Subject: New chef at your bistro

To whom it may concern,

I kindly ask you to consider me for the position of chef in my favourite bistro. What I lack in experience I make up for in enthusiasm. I am ever learning, keen to try new recipes and menus and most of all I am a team player.

Regards and best wishes,
Zoe Zouch

P.S. My sister says I make the best raspberry and white chocolate brownie.

I skim through the chain that follows. Catherine confirms the date and time for the interview – my day off last week. I don't think Catherine purposely chose a day I wouldn't be in work. She simply didn't care enough to check that I would be there. Also attached are meandering, hand-typed directions instead of a link to our location on Google Maps. I scroll on to the final email...

From: La Bella Vita <info@labellavita.ie>
To: Zoe Zouch <Zoeinheels@yipmail.com>
Date: May 21st
Subject: Re: New chef at your bistro

Dear Zoe,

Many thanks for interviewing for the position of head chef. It is with regret that we inform you that we have gone in another direction. Unfortunately, we cannot engage in further correspondence; however, we wish you all the very best in your future endeavours.

Regards and best wishes,
Catherine Buchanan

Owner, La Bella Vita

I read through a handful more cover letters. And I remember many enthusiastic faces from the interviews. A variety of men and women hoping to join our team. Somehow Catherine found fault with them all. Someone was too old, someone else too young. Too tall, short, quiet, foreign. Catherine didn't hold back her criticism, insults or racism. I tried a couple of times to encourage her to rehire Scott.

'I'm sure he'd consider coming back if you apologised,' I said.

She looked at me as if she wanted to claw my skin from my bones and that's when I realised: it's not Scott's shoes she can't fill, it's Mark's. She hired Scott on a whim and he stepped into the role with ease. Too much ease. I think she's afraid that might happen again. Someone else might be as good as – or worse still, even better at the job than – Mark. I worry that Catherine would rather see La Bella Vita struggle and suffer than thrive without her son.

I circle back to Zoe Zouch's email and I begin typing.

From: La Bella Vita <info@labellavita.ie>
To: Zoe Zouch <Zoeinheels@yipmail.com>
Date: June 1st
Subject: Re: New chef at your bistro

Dear Zoe

I apologise for this email out of the blue. I believe you were told that your interview was unsuccessful, but that was a mistake. We would love to have you join our team at La Bella Vita. Could you come in today at noon for a chat?

All best wishes,
Tabitha Greenwood
Owner, La Bella Vita

P.S. My sister says *I* make the best raspberry and white chocolate brownie.

Before I shut my laptop, I send one more email.

From: Tabby Greenwood <tabitha.l.greenwood@
mymail.com>
To: Peter Lawlor <Peterpaints1988@arts4u.com>
Date: May 1st
Subject: Art lesson

Dear Mr Lawlor,

I would like to enquire about your beginners' art class. Do you
have any availability for the current term and, if so, how much
does it cost per lesson?

Many thanks,
Tabby Greenwood.

THIRTY-TWO

I stretch and yawn and try to wake fully. Bright sunlight is beaming in my bedroom window and a chorus of noisy birds encourage me to get up and start my day. I get up and open the curtains, squinting as it takes my eyes a moment to adjust to the beautiful summer's day outside. Traffic is heavy and barely moving. The footpaths are equally busy as people make the most of the sunshine, walking or cycling in their shorts or sundresses. I breathe in the joy that comes with good weather and I feel more alive. I know I will miss the hustle and bustle of life on this street when I move.

My phone beeps and I peel myself away from looking out the window reluctantly to check it. It's a message from Avery's hairdressers offering me 10 per cent off shampoo that I can't afford. I shake my head and turn my attention back to the glorious day outside, but then gasp as I catch the time on my phone screen out of the corner of my eye. It's almost eleven thirty. I can't believe I've slept the whole morning away. Suddenly, my lazy morning picks up pace as I throw on baggy jeans and a t-shirt and make a hurried attempt to brush my teeth and hair before I grab my bag and dash out the door.

Luckily, I round the street corner just as my bus pulls up. I'm breathless as I get on.

'Bleedin' roastin' out there, isn't it?' the driver says as I scan my ticket.

I nod.

'Too hot for all that running. You'd want to slow down before you give yourself a heart attack, love,' he adds.

'One of those days,' I say, as if that explains it all.

He nods and smiles. 'Some empty seats upstairs.'

'Thanks.'

I don't bother to go upstairs. Instead I make my way down the back of the bus and stand. I take my phone out of my bag and type, and wobble as the bus takes off.

Tabby: Hey. Is Catherine there?

Lyla: Hi Tabs. Yup. She's in the office. Why?

My heart races and I hate that I instantly regretted the email I sent to Zoe Zouch last night, because deep down I still know it was the right thing to do. I just have to hope I get to La Bella Vita before Zoe does.

Lyla: R U OK?

Tabby: Yeah. Just running late.

Lyla: OK. C U soon x

Tabby: Can you do me a favour? Someone might come in looking for me soon. Her name is Zoe. Can you ask her to wait in reception, please?

Lyla: No prob.

Tabby: Can you keep her away from Catherine?

...

Lyla is typing

...

Tabby: I'll explain when I get there. But it's very important Catherine doesn't see Zoe before me.

Lyla: I'll do my best. Promise.

Tabby: Xx

My palms are sweating and my phone feels hot to hold as I type another message.

Tabby: Hey. Are we okay? I really didn't mean to hurt you. I'm sorry.

I can see Avery reads the message and I wait for a reply. I wait and wobble and switch my phone from one clammy hand to the other, but still Avery doesn't type back. As I near my stop I type again.

Tabby: I love you x

I drop my phone into my bag and make my way to the front, weaving through the pillars of sticky and exhausted commuters all crammed on to this much-too-busy bus. As I get off the sun hits my already hot face. I squint and glance around. For a flashing moment I think I'm at the wrong stop – there's no sign of Rashidi. Every day for the last four and a half years the first thing I've seen when I arrive at work has been Rashidi's bright smile. Not a single day has gone by without that smile. I don't like the feeling that settles into the pit of my stomach without him.

My phone rings and I fish around in my bag for it. I'm flummoxed as I struggle to find it among lip balm and tissues and tampons. Finally I grab it and press it to my ear.

'Hello.'

'Hi, Tabby. Are you nearly here?' Lyla says, and I can tell from her tone she's almost as frazzled as I am. 'Zoe has just arrived and I'm not sure how much longer Catherine will be in the office. It's nearly lunchtime.'

'I'm right outside. Coming now.'

I can see Lyla shift into the window and she waves at me. I wave back as I hang up and hurry inside.

Breathless, I extend my hand towards the pretty young woman sitting next to the reception desk. 'Hi. You must be Zoe.'

She stands up and shakes it and says, 'I am.'

'Great, great,' I say, trying not to let my surprise at how young she is register on my face. I know she admitted in her cover letter that she didn't have much experience but she can't be long out of college. Still, her references checked out and I'm relieved to have her here. 'I'm Tabitha. Tabby. Thanks so much for coming in.'

'I was really surprised to get your email,' she says, and I can tell she's nervous. That makes two of us, and I wonder if she can pick it up from me too.

'We're delighted you're still available. Shall we go through to the kitchen and I can talk you through everything?'

Zoe nods as Lyla looks on, confused.

'Zoe is our new head chef,' I say.

'Oh, thank God you finally hired someone,' Lyla says. 'Zoe, you must be incredible, because we were beginning to think no one would ever be good enough—' Lyla's cheeks pinken as she quickly realises that, although she and the rest of the staff have understandably discussed the pressure of being understaffed, she probably shouldn't mention it in front of me. But I don't mind. It's actually rather funny watching her try to backpedal. And I could use some humour today for sure.

'You'll love it here, Zoe,' Lyla says now. 'Just don't be like me and keep putting your foot in your mouth.'

'Thank you,' Zoe says, as she turns round and picks up a Tupperware box from the seat behind her and holds it out.

'Brownies,' I say.

'The best raspberry and white chocolate brownies, as promised.'

The creak of a door opening behind us sets my nerves on edge and I hold my breath as I wait for Catherine to find us.

'Would you like to try one?' Zoe asks, taking the lid off the Tupperware box and nudging it towards me, thankfully oblivious to the building tension.

'Maybe later,' I say, looking over my shoulder for any sign of Catherine. 'Let's go through to the kitchen.'

Zoe is about to put the lid back on and follow me when Lyla says, 'Can I try one? They look amazing.'

Zoe smiles and tilts the box towards Lyla.

'Thanks, I'm starving. Missed breakfast,' Lyla says, taking a large brownie from the top. 'The bagel guy wasn't here today.'

'Rashidi wasn't here this morning either?' I say.

'Nope. It must be his first day off in for ever.' Layla speaks through a mouthful of brownie. 'Good for him. He deserves it.'

'Rashidi doesn't take days off,' I say, the gnawing pain in the base of my stomach flaring up again. It's the same feeling I got when I woke up in the hospital after the crash. The feeling I got when I found the bracelet for Saoirse. And when Becca and Avery announced their engagement.

'God, these are amazing,' Lyla says.

'What are amazing?' Catherine's voice comes from behind me and I physically jump.

'The new chef's brownies,' Layla explains. 'Could I take another?'

'Sure.' Zoe nods. 'I'm glad you like them.'

'Just wait until I tell everyone about these. They're going to be so excited you're working here.'

'Excuse me,' Catherine says, her voice edging closer and an octave higher.

'Zoe will be joining the team,' I say, reaching for a brownie as I try to feign cool and casual.

'Will she now?'

Catherine's eyes burn into the tasty treat in my hand.

'Zoe, you'll find your uniform in the kitchen, if you want to go on ahead,' I say.

Zoe looks at me, unsure.

'Lyla, will you show Zoe where to go, please?' I go on.

Lyla nods.

'I'll be through in a minute. I just need to speak to Catherine first,' I say to them both.

Catherine and I stand silently side by side until Zoe and Lyla have gone, then: 'You hired someone,' Catherine says, so much more calmly than I was expecting.

'We need help. We can't keep turning away bookings because we're short-staffed.'

'I'm glad to see you taking some initiative,' Catherine says.

My head spins, and I'm glad of the sugar as I bite into the brownie.

'I hope she's as good as you think she is,' Catherine adds, 'because if she's not—'

'If she's not, what? What will happen if she's not a great chef?'

Catherine takes a raspy breath and suddenly her age seems more apparent. 'Let's just hope she is great.'

I realise Catherine doesn't remember Zoe. I wonder if she remembers anyone she's interviewed or if the fog of grief is too thick to see through.

'She won't be as good as Mark,' I say, knowing she needs to hear it.

A tear trickles down her cheek and she smiles and turns to walk away.

'By the way,' I call after her and she stops and turns her head back. 'Did you see Rashidi this morning?'

'Who?'

'Rashidi. The bagel guy?'

Catherine squints and scrunches her nose.

'The elderly man with the bagel cart,' I say. 'He's usually next to the bus stop out front every morning.'

'Oh, that guy.' Catherine's confused expression turns to one of disgust as she remembers him.

'Did you see him today?'

'No. Thank God. Maybe he's finally gone.'

'What did you do?' I say.

Catherine rolls her eyes.

'Did you phone the council? He's just an old man trying to earn a living.'

'Right. I'm leaving,' Catherine announces as if there are more people here than just me. 'I have a hair appointment at two. Just so you know, I've taken bookings for two large parties tonight, one at seven and one at eight. It's in the book.'

'We're not taking party bookings right now,' I say, unable to peel my mind away from Rashidi and where he might be. 'We're understaffed.'

'Not anymore. We have brownie girl. Make this work, Tabitha.'

THIRTY-THREE

Thankfully everything with both of the large groups goes off without a hitch. It's our busiest night for weeks and to say we're run off our feet is no exaggeration. My ankles are swelling and my feet are pulsing, but it's so worth it for the chatter and laughter of a full bistro.

Zoe proves to be quite the perfectionist. And in some ways she runs her kitchen similarly to Mark. But unlike Mark she asks my opinion all the time. She'll ask if I think flavours are working or if there's anything I want to add to or exclude from the menus. And I feel the passion I once had for the kitchen reigniting in me. It does, however, take up more of my time than I can easily spare. But the enthusiasm and zest for life that Zoe brings to the kitchen is contagious. Waiting staff are smiling again, and returning to the kitchen often to announce that another table sends their compliments to the chef. Zoe hums while she cooks and we've played several rounds of Guess the Song. It's the first day in a long time that I've enjoyed being on the kitchen floor.

Even still, when the last table leave and all the staff are gone, I'm relieved. I pour myself a generous glass of Merlot. The really expensive stuff that very few customers order. It's not my favourite but I know that Catherine will go ballistic when she discovers a bottle is missing and there's something a little enjoyable in that.

I flop into the office chair with my wine in one hand and my phone in the other. My heart sinks when I see Avery still hasn't replied to my messages. She's read them and she's been on WhatsApp just minutes ago, but she clearly doesn't want to talk to me. I try another.

Tabby: Hey. Please talk to me?

...

Avery is typing

...

I stare at the screen and wait for her reply, but nothing comes through. Whatever she was going to say, she's changed her mind.

Tabby: If you're still up when I get home, maybe we could talk then?

Avery is offline

I sigh and stare into my glass for a long time before I touch a sip. Then I drink the whole thing, much too quickly, and pour myself another.

Tabby: Hey. How are you?

Scott: Hi. It's so late. Are you only finishing work now? 😴

Tabby: Shit sorry. Did I wake you?

Scott: Nah. Long day?

Tabby: Very. You free to talk?

Scott: Sure. What's up?

Tabby: Have you dropped by La Bella Vita recently?

Scott: Not in a while. Why?

Tabby: Rashidi wasn't here today and I was wondering if you'd seen him.

Scott: That's not like him. He never takes a day off. I think he works Christmas.

Tabby: Bet he actually does!! I'm a bit worried, think Catherine might be behind it.

Scott: Catherine doesn't scare Rashidi. He's as tough as yesterday's bagels.

Tabby: 🪨 Seriously? Stale bagels? That's the best you could come up with?

Scott: It's 1am. It's hard to be funny at 1am.

Tabby: I better let you get some sleep.

Scott: Rashidi will be ok. Try not to worry.

Tabby: Yeah. Hopefully he'll be back tomorrow.

Scott: Night Tabs.

Tabby: Night x

I swirl wine around my glass and watch as the deep burgundy leaves its mark around the circumference for a moment before it settles. I think about locking up and going home but a top-up of wine and a snooze in the office chair is more inviting.

Despite the booze it's hard to sleep and I scroll aimlessly through my phone. Facebook tells me that another one of the girls from my year in school is pregnant. She's posted photos of her gender reveal party. Lots of blue balloons, blue-topped cupcakes, and smiling faces. Other friends share engagement notices and over-the-top wedding photos. And of course, there are the usual holiday snaps: the French Riviera, Italian lakes, NYC – places Mark and I have also visited. Over the years my profile photo has regularly been of tourist hotspots. My subtle attempt to pretend I had the perfect life. Just like everyone else. I search the photo gallery on my phone and find a whiskey and chocolate chiffon with spun sugar topping. It took me five hours to make and it's still the creation I am most proud of. And most enjoyed eating too. Mark said it was dry. He always said my sponges were dry. And I believed him. But it doesn't look dry. It looks delicious, and I upload it to Instagram with pride. I add a filter and the browns and mustards instantly look better than they did in real life. Then I rattle off some hashtags: #Delicious #TryIt #BookNow #ChocolateHeaven #LifeSucks-EatCake #IUsedToLoveBaking #FianceSaidIWasntGoodE-nough, and post it. I drop my head back, close my eyes and sigh.

It's only seconds before I come to my senses and delete the post. My heart is pounding out of my chest. There weren't any likes, and at this hour of the morning I'm not sure there were any views. And yet, somehow, the brief moment of rebellion felt great.

I upload the photo again, adding just one hashtag this time: #NoFilter. I watch and wait but no likes trickle in. Suddenly the night feels darker and the only sounds are the low hum of the large refrigerator and the ticking of the second hand on the clock above the office door. Although I'm exhausted, sleep won't come. I check my emails.

From: Peter Lawlor <Peterpaints1988@arts4u.com>
To: Tabby Greenwood <tabitha.l.greenwood@mymail.com>
Date: May 2nd
Subject: Art lesson

Dear Tabitha,

Many thanks for your enquiry.
Unfortunately, we do not accept new students mid-term.
We are currently fully booked for the remainder of the year but I could add your name to a waiting list, if you would like?

All the best,
Peter

Disappointment brings sleep and I drift off with my phone in one hand and half a glass full of wine in the other.

THIRTY-FOUR

It's strange getting the bus from the bistro to my flat so early in the morning; usually I'm heading in the other direction. But never this early. I woke with a crick in my neck and my glass of red wine spilt on my jeans. I regret not going home last night and I'm so looking forward to a shower and change of clothes. My phone has been hopping all morning. The photo of the whiskey and chocolate crémeux that I shared last night has attracted unexpected attention.

@L.Mac7 OMG I need this in my life 😍

@Fit.Fine.Life Looks delicious. Do you do takeaway?

@YouLOL No filter my arse!

@PopK How do I book?

@JanShaw1976 Can you make a cake for my nephews birthday? He's 7.

@Pearson.Tom64 La Bella Vita was closed for our anniversary booking. Still waiting for an explanation and apology. NOT GOOD ENOUGH!!

@L.Mac7 @Pearson.Tom64 The owner died.

@Fit.Fine.Life. @L.Mac7 OMG so sad. RIP 😢

@Pearson.Tom64 @L.Mac7 OK. We still missed our booking.
@L.Mac7 @Pearon.Tom64 My God!! 😵😵

Messages come in faster than I can reply and I'm delighted of course, but there's an underlying sense of disappointment too. Disappointment that Mark isn't here to see how engaged customers are online. I want to share this moment with him. I want to hear him say, *'Well done, Tabs, your Instagram is great.'* I want to show him that sometimes I can make things work and work well.

By the time I reach my stop I'm overwhelmed. I turn my phone to silent, thank the driver and hop off. It's bright and birds are chirping, but for once I am all alone on the street. I'm up before even the most zealous joggers. I glance behind me at the park that I know will be heaving with runners and walkers soon. But right now it's sleeping and still and there's something eerie about its tall, old trees and empty paths. I find myself running towards my flat and turning the key in the lock with trembling fingers.

I kick my shoes off inside the door and head straight to the bathroom. It's busy inside my head. I hum a Britney Spears medley that Zoe got stuck in my mind yesterday and Catherine, Mark and @Pearson.Tom64 are all battling for space too. But I push them all aside and think about Avery. I shampoo my hair and think about the stack of her favourite American-style pancakes that I'll make as a peace offering.

Dressed but still sleepy, I wash blueberries at the kitchen sink and wait for the smell of freshly made pancakes to coax my sister from her room. I wait and wait, until I'm almost late for work. Then I hear a key turn in the front door. The sound is so familiar that for a moment I expect Mark to walk through the door. The realisation that he won't catches my breath. My heart aches with sadness but it beats quickly.

'Who is it?' I call.

'Becca. Sorry. Did I wake you?'

I walk into the hall with a spatula in my hand.

'Hey,' Becca says, standing in front of me in her work clothes and a full face of make-up.

'Hey,' I say, the fine hairs on the back of my neck standing on end as I grasp that she didn't sleep here last night; and I suddenly doubt that Avery did either.

'Something smells good,' she says.

'Pancakes.'

Becca nods.

'Want some?'

She nods again.

'Where's Avery?' I ask.

'The flat.'

'Yours?'

'Hers.'

'I didn't know she still had her flat,' I say, as batter drips from the spatula onto the hall floor. 'She's been here for six months. I thought she let the lease go.'

Becca looks at the sticky mess on the floor, avoiding eye contact as she says, 'She kept it. Just in case, I guess.'

'Just in case I told her her life was a joke, and made her so uncomfortable she had to scurry off in the middle of the night. This is so not what I wanted.'

'I know,' Becca says.

I sigh and lead us toward the kitchen, and Becca's face lights up when she sees the pancakes.

'Avery's favourites,' she says.

The tension eases slowly. Becca fetches the bottle of surface cleaner and a J-cloth from under the sink and heads back into the hall to clean up as I plate us up a couple of puffy pancakes each.

'Maple syrup?' I call after her.

'Yes please,' she shouts back.

'And blueberries?'

'No thanks, not a fan,' she says, returning to the kitchen and dropping the cloth into the sink.

I lead us towards the table and place a plate in front of each of us. Mine is piled high with blueberries, just as Avery's would be. We sit and eat and make small talk, but there's only so much weather we can discuss before the elephant in the room returns and I have to say something.

'This is bad, isn't it?' I say, pushing a blueberry around my plate with the back of my fork.

Becca winces mid-mouthful.

'Is she coming back?' I ask.

Becca's shoulders rise and fall as she puffs out. She shakes her head gently but she doesn't speak.

'What about her stuff?' I say, placing my cutlery down. My stomach churns and I regret every mouthful of pancake. 'All her stuff is here. Her paints and brushes. Even her easel. Doesn't she need them?'

'She does,' Becca says.

'Ah. That's why you're here.'

'It's not the only reason.'

'Is she still mad?' I ask.

Becca takes a deep breath as she glances at the final piece of pancake on her plate. 'No,' she says. 'She's not mad. She's just hurt.'

I puff out, my heart sinking. 'That's so much worse.'

'Give it time. It'll all be okay.'

'Will it?'

Becca places her fork back on the plate and the noise seems to startle us both.

'She knows I love her,' I say.

'Of course. Of course she knows that.'

'And I am happy for her. I'm happy for both of you.'

Becca nods and I hope she believes me.

'I just—' But I cut myself off. There's no point revisiting the same concerns. I'm sure Becca doesn't want to hear that's it's too soon. I don't even want to say it.

'I *am* happy for you,' I say instead.

'Thank you. But I'm not the one who needs to hear you say it,' Becca says. 'Why don't you stop by the flat later? You could bring her stuff.'

I shake my head. 'No, you better take it now. She needs it today.'

'Okay.' Becca nods. 'Will I see you later?'

'Yeah. Maybe.'

'Okay.'

Becca stands up and scrapes her half-pancake into the bin and pops her plate in the dishwasher. I do the same.

'I better hurry,' I say, as I ignore the rest of the clean-up. 'I'm already late.'

'The pancakes were lovely, thank you,' Becca says.

'No problem. Glad you liked them.' I pause for a deep breath before I add, 'Avery's stuff should all be in her room... eh, the spare room, I mean. Brushes and paints are in the top drawer and the easel should be standing in the wardrobe.'

'Okay. Cool.'

'I'm going to dash now. Would you mind locking up when you leave?'

'No problem.'

I take my bag from the back of my chair and sling it over my shoulder. I turn back as I reach the door.

'Oh, and Becca...'

'Yeah?'

'Thank you. It was good to talk.'

'It was.'

THIRTY-FIVE

JULY

You work too hard. Shake off your apron and grab your bikini. Spain awaits!

As expected, July starts with the next resolution dropping into my email inbox. I read Avery's words with a heavy heart. I can sense her excitement as she wrote them. I imagine us lying on the sun-kissed shores in Málaga or Costa Blanca.

'I don't need sun cream, I never burn,' Avery would announce proudly as she draped herself on a sun lounger with a pina colada in one hand and a book she had no intention of reading in the other. Then later, we'd spend all evening searching for a late-night pharmacy where we could buy burn cream. Our lack of Spanish and their limited English would mean Avery improvising with hand gestures and Google Translate. It happens every time we go away. And every time Avery is as surprised as the first that her porcelain-like Irish skin doesn't tan instantly.

Unfortunately, the timing for a holiday couldn't be worse.

Avery is still ignoring my calls and texts and she won't open the door of her flat to me. It's been more than three weeks. We've never gone this long without speaking before. I thought she might text this morning to see if I read July's resolution, but it's Becca who checks in.

I lie when she asks how I am, and I tell her I'm doing great. Then I leave the flat and try not to think about how badly I could use a holiday.

According to the weather app on my phone, it will be the hottest day of the year so far. It's already the hottest July on record for twenty years, or thereabouts. The smells of morning coffee and sweat hang in the air and it's a relief to get off the bus. There is still no sign of Rashidi. I've asked around in all the local businesses, hoping someone might know something, but staff are either as flummoxed by his disappearance as me or they hadn't noticed he was gone.

Work is particularly quiet at the moment, which unfortunately gives me more time to think about everything. The good weather means people are grabbing a coffee and a sandwich and sitting outside to enjoy an hour of sunshine on their lunch break. I watch them with longing as I stare out the window. As disappointing as an empty bistro is, I'm more disappointed that Rashidi is missing so much passing trade.

With nothing better to do, I check my Instagram. Avery has shared some new paintings. I recognise the trees and foliage in her work and it hurts to know that she's been so close, right across the street from me, in the park, but she is still avoiding my flat. And me. I check La Bella Vita's page. There are plenty of likes and shares over various dishes, but unfortunately no bookings.

I'm staring at my screen when a call from Scott flashes up.

'Hello,' I say, pressing my phone to my ear as I walk towards the office.

'Hey. You free to talk?'

'Yeah. What's up?'

'Where are you?'

'At work.'

'You busy?'

'No. Unfortunately not. Totally dead in here today. Bit shit, really.'

'Are you on your own?'

There's an urgency in Scott's tone that sets me on edge.

'I'm just walking into the office now. What's wrong?'

'It's Rashidi,' Scott says, clearing his throat before he adds, 'He's in hospital.'

'What?'

'I had a bad feeling so I started to ring around last week. I tried the police, hostels, pubs, you name it. I finally found him in St Martin's this morning.'

My breath catches when I hear the name of the hospital where Mark and I were taken after the car crash. My chest is tight and for a moment the memories that follow are overwhelming. It takes all my strength to pull myself back to the moment. Back to news of Rashidi.

'Oh God. Is he okay? What happened?' I whisper breathlessly.

'I don't know. They won't tell me anything.'

'That's crazy. Surely they could let you know if it's serious or not.'

'They can't, really. I'm not family. Just some random guy on the phone.'

My heart sinks. I know Scott is right.

'I thought maybe we could go to the hospital,' he suggests. 'They might tell us a little more in person, let us visit him.'

'Yeah. Okay. Good idea.' I nod as if he can see me.

'And if you're not busy...'

'Now? Do you want to go now?'

'Yeah, no point wasting time.'

'Okay,' I say, quickly. 'Will I meet you there?'

'I'm outside, actually.'

'Here? Now?'

'Mm-hm. I thought we could go together.'

I hurry back into the dining area and see Scott standing on the footpath outside. His concern and worry is scribbled into the lines of his forehead. He has no doubt grown close to Rashidi over time too. I wonder if they've shared important conversations and if Rashidi has imparted his advice. Maybe they even discussed Scott taking the job here. Maybe it was Rashidi who advised him to go for it. Rashidi might be the reason Scott is in my life now. I do hope so.

'I'm on my way. Give me two minutes,' I say. I watch as Scott lowers his phone and winks at me.

I duck my head into the kitchen and catch Zoe's attention. 'I gotta go,' I blurt.

'Eh, okay,' she says, looking up from her mixing bowl. 'Will you be back for the early-bird start?'

'Not sure. Can you manage?'

Zoe looks uncertain for a moment.

'It should be quiet. You've got this.'

'Yeah. Yes, of course,' she says, with a wobble. 'See you later.'

'Thanks.'

THIRTY-SIX

'You okay?' Scott asks as we walk through the main doors of St Martin's hospital. I walked out these exact doors six months ago with my life in tatters, and walking through again from the other side is a strange feeling.

'Yeah. I'm fine. Just worried about him.'

'Me too,' Scott says, squeezing my shoulder gently. 'But hopefully we'll know more soon.'

Scott breaks away from me to go speak to the lady on reception, and I stand to the side with my back against the wall. Everything is so painfully familiar. The smells of antiseptic cleaner mixed with tea and toast. The sounds of trolley legs being rolled along polished floors. White coats, blue scrubs and clipboards are all around. I shut my eyes and try to block it all out.

When I open them again, I see Dr Shapiro approaching in the distance. She's wearing a long, floral dress instead of her usual scrubs and she's walking alongside a man in plain clothes with a stethoscope round his neck. I smile as she gets closer but she's engrossed in her conversation and doesn't seem to notice me. It's not until she's right beside me that she smiles and does a double-take. I can tell she remembers my face but perhaps my name escapes her.

'Hello, Dr Shapiro,' I say, awkwardly.

She comes to a stop. 'Hello. How lovely to see you.'

'I'll catch you in there, Lauren,' the man says as he walks on.

Dr Shapiro smiles at him, and then at me as she searches my face for my name. I'm just about to prompt her when she says, 'Is everything all right, Tabby? Are you back with us today?'

Her kind concern makes my eyes sting with tears.

'I'm good. I've been well, thanks. It's actually my friend I'm here to see.'

'Ah.'

'Well, I hope I can see him. We're not sure what's happened.' I point to Scott, whose back is turned to us as he chats to the receptionist. 'We just know he's here. But we're not family so...'

'Would you like me to see if there's anything I can find out?'

'Could you? That would be great. Thanks so much.'

'No problem. What's his name?'

'Rashidi.'

'Rashidi...' she repeats in the way people do when they're waiting for you to add a second name.

I wince, and I can feel heat in my cheeks. 'I don't actually know his surname.' I giggle a little to hide my embarrassment.

'No problem at all. Look, I have a meeting now. Long, boring thing, I'm afraid. But I'll find out what I can after.' She takes a pen from her pocket and writes RASHIDI on the back of her hand. 'There's a coffee shop just round the corner, you probably remember.'

I nod. I do.

'I'll meet you there in an hour or so. If you're not there, I'll know you've found him yourself.'

'Thank you,' I say.

She takes my hand and squeezes gently. 'It's so lovely to see you, Tabby. I'm really, really glad you're well.'

Dr Shapiro isn't long gone when Scott returns, shaking his head.

'No luck?' I say.

'Nope.'

'What did she say?' I ask, linking his arm to lead us towards the coffee shop.

'Just that we should speak to his family for an update.'

'But he doesn't have family.'

'I know. What are we going to do?'

'Get a coffee and wait,' I say. 'One of the doctors here is looking into it for me.'

Scott stops walking and turns to look at me. 'How did you manage that?'

I shrug. 'I know people.'

Scott's intrigued expression makes me smile. I know he won't ask more, but, as we order a tea, a coffee and a couple of chocolate eclairs, I find myself wanting to tell him that I know Dr Shapiro because she was my doctor. I haven't talked about the crash, not to anyone. Not really. And, I want to. Something about being back in this place makes it all so fresh in my mind. If I have to be here with anyone, I'm glad it's Scott.

I'm surprised when I glance at my watch and notice a couple of hours have passed. Time seems to fly as we chat. I've had too much tea, and I should probably find the bathroom, but I don't want to leave in case Dr Shapiro arrives while I'm gone. So, Scott and I chat some more until his phone rings and he's distracted and silent as he stares at the screen, letting it ring for a while.

'Everything okay?' I ask.

'It's Saoirse,' he says.

'Oh.'

'I should take this,' he says, although he doesn't sound sure.

'Yeah. Course.'

Scott stands up and places the phone to his ear.

'Saoirse. Hi. How are you?' I overhear him say as he walks to the other end of the coffee shop to stand beside some empty tables where it's quieter.

I watch as he paces. It's not long before he lowers his phone and walks back towards me.

'What is it?' I ask, the look on his face worrying me instantly. My heart can't take any more bad news today.

'She's wondering if we could meet her tomorrow.'

'Tomorrow?'

'She knows it's short notice. She apologised. She's kind of squeezing me in as a favour. And I know the timing is so bad—'

'It's fine,' I say, catching my breath as if I've been running. 'Tomorrow is fine. It's good. I still want to meet her.'

'Are you sure?'

'I am.'

'Okay. I'll call her back. She said the morning, so how about eleven-ish?'

My heart is beating out of my chest. 'Yeah. Cool. Eleven is good.'

Scott steps away again and I sit, statue-like, watching him.

'Do you think I'm doing the right thing?' I ask when he returns. He sets his phone down face up on the table and I can't help but notice his lockscreen photo is him with his arm draped over a very pretty girl's shoulder.

'I think you're doing the brave thing,' he says.

'You know... something like this... it's just the kind of thing I'd tell Rashidi about. I'd go for my morning bagel, he'd say, *Any news, love?* Then there I'd be, half an hour later, still waffling on about my problems.'

Scott nods. 'I always take my bagel with a side of advice too.'

Conversation is harder to make after that and by the time Dr Shapiro arrives I have the caffeine shakes and I'm bursting to pee. I wave and smile, trying to catch her eye. She waves back and makes her way towards our table.

'I'm sorry. That took a little longer than expected,' she says.

'No problem. We don't mind waiting.'

Dr Shapiro's shoulders are rounded and she seems more tired than earlier as she glances from me to Scott.

'This is Scott,' I say. 'He's a friend of Rashidi's too.'

She nods as if she expected as much. Then she glances at our empty cups and melancholy seems to weigh her down as she takes a deep breath. I hold mine and search her eyes for the root of her sadness. I look away quickly when I find it. I know what she's going to say next. Déjà vu causes the fine hairs on the back of my neck to stand to attention.

A moment passes before I can bring myself to meet her gaze and then I say, 'You found him?'

'I did.'

'It's not good news, is it?'

'I'm afraid Rashidi Nasser died last night.'

'Omigod,' I hear Scott say, but I have no words of my own.

Coffee cups clatter in the background and there is the hum of conversations all around us but inside my head is still and silent, as if someone or something has hit me and all my thoughts and feelings have tumbled out.

'I'm so very sorry, Tabby,' Dr Shapiro says.

I notice Scott drop his face into his hands from the corner of my eye as I try hard to push words out. 'Thank you for letting us know. Is there anything we should do?'

Scott looks up and his voice cracks as he asks, 'Are there forms or anything? Should we call someone about the funeral or does the hospital do that?'

'His daughter was here with him, at the end,' Dr Shapiro says.

I look at Scott and I can tell he shares my surprise.

'We didn't know he had a daughter,' I say.

'I'm afraid I don't know much more,' Dr Shapiro says. 'But I'm sure she'll be in touch with funeral details. Or you might find them online later today.'

'Thank you,' I say, already getting my phone out to check. 'Thank you so much.'

'It was lovely to see you again, Tabby. I do wish it was under happier circumstances.'

'Yeah.' I swallow.

'Take care,' she says, nodding. 'And tell that lovely sister of yours I was asking for her, won't you?'

I smile but my heart is aching more than ever as Dr Shapiro gets up and walks away.

'A daughter,' Scott says, as the waitress comes to clear our table.

My fingers tremble as I search for funeral information on my phone.

'Excuse me, are you done?' the waitress asks. She reaches over my shoulder for my cup and plate. 'Only, it's after closing and I need to mop up.' She takes a step back and eyes us with care. 'Are you okay? Do you need a minute?'

'Thanks. We're okay,' Scott says, standing.

I get to my feet and look at my watch. It's almost 5 p.m. The early-bird sitting will start in the bistro soon. I should call Zoe to check how she's coping.

'I need to pee,' I say, as we leave the coffee shop behind and walk into the main lobby.

It's so much quieter than before. The silence is harder to bear than the busyness.

'Won't be long,' I say, pointing towards the toilets.

'Sure.' Scott takes his phone out of his pocket. 'I'll wait

here.'

'You don't have to. We're going in opposite directions, anyway.'

'I'll wait.'

I choke back tears. Glad.

THIRTY-SEVEN

The evening has brought a cool wind and my bare arms, in my summer dress, are lined with goosebumps. Scott leans close to me and drapes his arm over my shoulder.

'Bloody weather. Was roastin' earlier. Wish I had a jacket to give you,' he says as we walk towards the bus stop.

'S'okay. I'll be grand once I'm on the bus.'

"Will you?' Scott asks.

I come to a stop, knowing we're not talking about the weather anymore. Scott untangles his arm from round me and turns to face me.

'Did you know Rashidi had family?' I ask.

Scott shakes his head. 'You?'

'No. Never. He never once mentioned it.' I pause and sigh. 'I'm glad he'll have someone to miss him.'

'We'll miss him,' Scott says.

'I know. But I mean family.'

Scott takes a step back and a breeze whips between us, chilling me.

'You must miss Mark so much,' he says. 'You were family.'

My bus comes into view and I should hurry if I want to catch it.

'You don't talk about him much.'

I watch as the bus tucks itself next to the kerb and a couple of elderly ladies struggle with the step as they get slowly on board. If I ran now, I'd probably catch it.

'Don't I?' I ask, genuinely. Mark occupies so many of my thoughts. I'm surprised Scott doesn't know that.

'Is it too painful to talk about?'

'No, it's not that.'

'Only it seems...' Scott sighs and shifts his weight from one foot to the other. 'Nothing. Never mind.'

'What? Say it. Please?'

'It's just... it's just...'

I nod, encouraging him.

'It's almost as if you won't allow yourself to grieve, if you know what I mean.'

My chest tightens. I know exactly what he means.

'You make so many allowances for Catherine because she's lost her son but you won't seem to give yourself a break. You loved him and now he's gone. I can't imagine how hard that must be.'

The engine revs and the bus pulls away and tucks back into the flow of traffic.

'Mark and I broke up,' I whisper.

'I know, but—'

'No. No. You don't understand. It was just before the crash. Seconds before it, actually. I told Mark it was over and seconds later the truck hit. The last thing to go through Mark's mind was that I didn't love him.' I wait for the look of disgust to wash over Scott's face as he realises that the crash was all my fault. I don't deserve to grieve.

Scott steps closer again and it's instantly a fraction warmer.

There's so much sadness in his eyes and I can see how much Rashidi's death has hurt him.

'People break up all the time, for whatever reason. And then they go and live long happy lives away from each other. This was never what you wanted.'

'It's cold,' I say, shivering. 'Are you cold?'

Scott shakes his head, but I can see how he shivers too.

'You wanted Mark to live a good life,' he says, reading me as if I'm an open book. 'Maybe even with someone else. Maybe with Saoirse.'

I gasp at hearing her name, but I don't contradict him.

'Not at first, of course,' he says. 'But eventually.'

I sniffle and drag my sleeve under my nose. Fat, salty tears trickle down my cheeks as Scott gathers me into his arms and we sway gently on the spot. I drop my head onto his shoulder and I smile through my tears, because as resentful as I was, in the end, that is exactly what I wanted. I knew Mark and I couldn't be happy together. But I hoped that we could be happy apart. I even thought we could continue to run La Bella Vita together. I never, ever wanted him gone from my life completely. This is not the way it was supposed to be. Nothing is how it's supposed to be. My heart is broken into tiny pieces and I don't know how to put it back together.

It's not long before Scott's bus arrives and I peel myself away from him, wipe my eyes and say, 'You've got to go.'

'I'll get the next one. Or the one after that.'

'No. It's okay. I'm okay.'

Scott looks at me in a way that tells me he doesn't believe me.

'I have to go in to work,' I say. 'There's some stuff I need to take care of.'

I'm lying to myself as much as to Scott. I should go in to work. I should check on Zoe and glance over tomorrow's bookings – if there are any. But I won't. I plan to go straight home. In fact, I wish I was already there.

The approaching bus groans and puffs out as if it's an inconvenience stopping to pick Scott up. The door creaks open slowly and Scott takes a couple of steps forward before he turns to look at me.

'I'm fine,' I reiterate. 'Go. Go on. My bus will be along in a minute and I've some calls to make in the meantime.'

'Text me when you're on the bus,' he says, like a worried parent.

'Sure.'

'And I'll see you in the morning?'

'In the morning?'

'To meet Saoirse.'

'Oh God, yes. Saoirse.'

'Let's meet at La Bella Vita and go together from there?' he suggests.

'Sounds good.'

'And if you change your mind...'

'I won't.'

'But if you do—'

'If I do, I'll text you. Promise.'

'Mate, are you getting on or what?' the bus driver grunts, losing patience.

'Yeah. Sorry. Coming,' Scott says, moving again.

'See you tomorrow,' I say.

'Tomorrow.'

I watch as the bus pulls away and Scott wobbles down the aisle to find a seat. He sits next to the window and waves. I wave back, feeling colder and more alone than ever.

THIRTY-EIGHT

I stare at my reflection in the bathroom mirror. The bags under my eyes aren't as bad as I was expecting, considering I haven't slept a wink all night. I reached for my phone several times during the night to text Scott, ready to ask him to cancel our meeting with Saoirse today. But each time, I took a deep breath and put my phone back down. If I wasn't the woman Mark was going to spend the rest of his life with, maybe Saoirse was. If he was still alive, would they be together now? Was breaking up the right thing to do? Would he have broken up with me anyway? I'm so desperate for answers and Saoirse is the only person who can give them to me.

I layer on more make-up than usual and try on several outfits before I settle on skinny blue jeans, a grey t-shirt and a black blazer. I look for Rashidi through the bus window as I approach the stop at La Bella Vita and it takes me a moment to remember that he won't be here. The sadness that follows is all too familiar.

Zoe is already in the kitchen prepping veg when I arrive.

'Was everything okay last night?' I ask, glad to have company and a distraction.

'All good.'

'Sorry I didn't make it back,' I say, preparing an excuse that doesn't involve a long-winded recount of my shit day.

'No problem,' she says, slicing bok choy, unfazed.

'Were we busy?'

'Not really.'

I puff out, dispirited. I had hoped business would pick up in the evening.

'Oh by the way, someone left an envelope for you last night,' she tells me, placing down her knife and wiping her fingers on her apron. She crouches and pulls a slightly grease-spattered white envelope out from between stacked pots and pans on the shelves below her chopping board.

'Who?'

Zoe shrugs. 'No idea. One of the waitresses took it. She asked me to hold it for you.'

I take the blank white envelope and open it. I laugh as Zoe looks on baffled.

'Is that a fridge magnet?' she asks, glancing at the colourful martini-glass-shaped trinket in my hand that proudly boasts the slogan I LOVE IBIZA across the top.

'Yup.'

'Is that it? No note or anything,' she says.

I shake my head.

'That's weird. How are you supposed to know who it's from?' Zoe rolls her eyes.

'I know who it's from,' I say, my heart a little lighter than it's been in days.

'Oh...' Zoe smiles, intrigued.

'It's from my sister. She's reminding me that I have a trip coming up. A holiday to Spain.'

'Wouldn't a text or a call make more sense?' Zoe's confusion makes me laugh.

'Yeah. I suppose. But this is very Avery.'

My smile is so wide my jaw aches. I'm so relieved that even if Avery still isn't speaking to me, she is thinking about me. She's thinking about me and the resolutions and, as always, she is in the background supporting me. I feel guiltier than ever that I couldn't do the same when she told me she was getting engaged.

I take out my phone to text her, but before I have a chance to type anything, Zoe takes a deep breath and says, 'I drew up some menu ideas, maybe we could chat about them.'

I slide the magnet back into the envelope and try to concentrate on work stuff, but it's hard when I'm so excited about Avery extending this olive branch.

'I'm not sure pizza is working,' Zoe continues.

'Pizza is most definitely not working,' I say, wondering if Avery has booked something for us in Ibiza and hoping Becca will come. I'm already lying on golden sands in my head.

'Oh good. Great,' Zoe says. 'I was worried you'd be offended if I said something.'

'I'm not.'

I should tell her that Catherine will be, and Zoe will have a battle on her hands to change a pizza topping, never mind ditch them altogether. But I don't have time to get into any of that right now.

'Leave your ideas on my desk, will you? I have to pop out now.'

Zoe's eyes narrow and this time I can tell she'd like an explanation for my disappearing act.

'I'm meeting a new coffee supplier. But we can talk about the menus later, okay?'

'With Catherine?' Zoe asks, so full of misguided excitement.

'Yeah. Maybe.'

She nods and goes back to chopping and I head into the office to find the small red box that I've come for. I leave La Bella Vita with a takeaway tea and a coffee, and wait outside for

Scott. His bus drops him off within minutes and we walk towards each other, meeting in the spot where Rashidi would usually be.

'It's weird not seeing him here,' Scott says.

We both sigh and silence falls over us as we stare at the ground.

'Coffee?' I ask, after a while.

'Is that from La Bella Vita?' Scott makes a face.

'Yeah.'

'Okay. Thanks.' Scott takes the cup but he doesn't drink. 'Ready?'

There's so much to think about. Avery's magnet, Zoe's menu, terrible coffee and losing Rashidi. But my mind is focused on one thing. The rose gold bracelet. I tap my jeans pocket and feel the small jewellery box press against my thigh.

'Ready,' I lie.

THIRTY-NINE

'That's her,' Scott says, tilting his head towards the blond woman sitting at the window of a restaurant not dissimilar to La Bella Vita.

He continues walking, but I slow a fraction, taking time to notice how the woman overlaps her hands round a white cup and stares into space as if she has the weight of the world on her shoulders. She's younger than I expected – mid- to late twenties, perhaps. And she's pretty. Of course she's pretty; as if Mark would accept anything less.

Scott leads us inside and I follow with my head down. My hands are clammy when he squeezes one gently and asks if I'm okay. I look up, but before I can answer with a chirpy lie, Saoirse notices us. She waves and smiles and her rounded shoulders rise and push back. I know that pose. I've perfected it too, over the last couple of months. A straight body and bright grin that tell the world you're fine.

Saoirse doesn't stand as we reach her. Instead, Scott leans over the table and her empty coffee cup to kiss her cheek and to thank her for meeting us. There are three chairs at a table that would usually have four. Scott pulls one out for me and then he sits in the other.

Before we have an opportunity for any small talk a waiter arrives, hovering a silver tray just above Scott's shoulder.

'I've taken the liberty of ordering us some coffee,' Saoirse says, in a thick, country accent.

Her midlands twang surprises me more than it should. Maybe because Mark usually avoids everything and everyone that reminds him of growing up in a small village. I take satisfaction in the thought that despite her high cheekbones and arched eyebrows she's not his perfect woman, after all. And I instantly hate myself for it.

'They serve our latest blend here. That's why I chose this place, obviously.'

The waiter places a cup in front of each of us and asks if there is anything else we need.

'No thank you,' Saoirse answers for us all.

'Actually, could I get a cup of tea, please?' I ask.

'Tea. Sure.' He nods and walks away.

'Tea,' Saoirse echoes.

'Tabby doesn't drink coffee,' Scott says.

'Oh.'

I shrug. 'I used to. But I don't have the stomach for it anymore, unfortunately.'

'Then how do you know if your coffee is any good or not?'

'I don't.'

'Ah. That's where you come to the rescue,' Saoirse says, placing her hand over Scott's.

I suspect she's flirting, and when Scott blushes and pulls his hand away, I'm certain.

The waiter returns with my tea and I take a large mouthful. It's much too hot and my eyes water.

'Yummy,' I say, as Saoirse watches me. I won't give her the

satisfaction of revealing that my throat and the roof of my mouth are scalded to bits.

'So, I must say I was surprised when you called. I thought I'd be the last person you wanted to do business with,' she says, between sips of her coffee.

'Why's that?' I say.

Scott shifts uncomfortably, almost knocking over his coffee.

Saoirse places her cup back on the table. 'I am so sorry for your loss,' she says, so suddenly it shocks me. Her shoulders relax and her icy exterior starts to melt. 'We never meant to hurt you.'

I add a splash of milk to my tea, cooling it, and I try it again, calmly, as if my emotions aren't crippling me. *She knew about me. All this time she knew.*

'Mark said things weren't great between you for a while.'

I press my cup against my lips and peer at Saoirse over the rim. I blow occasionally, and the liquid inside ripples and I have to be careful not to blow too hard and send it sloshing over the edge of the cup. I've no idea what I'm doing. It's as if my body is here but my mind is somewhere else entirely. I wonder if this is how Avery sometimes feels when she fidgets with a button on her coat until it falls off, or becomes distracted by the shapes of clouds overhead on a midsummer's walk. I desperately want my mind and body to be one again, but right now they can't seem to align.

Saoirse continues, 'Mark said you had to stay together because of the bistro, but that it was a relationship of convenience.'

'And you believed him?' Scott asks.

'I had no reason not to.' Saoirse's voice begins to crack. 'I didn't know you were engaged until the funeral.'

'You were there?' I ask, lowering my cup.

'Yeah. But I stayed at the back. I didn't want to upset anyone. You wouldn't have seen me.'

'No,' I say, my thoughts and feelings colliding so suddenly again that I feel as if my head might explode. 'I wouldn't have seen you. I wasn't there.'

Saoirse's expression is blank.

'Tabby was injured in the crash. She was still in hospital when the funeral took place,' Scott explains.

Tears trickle down Saoirse's cheeks. 'Oh God. I'm sorry. I didn't know you were in the car too.'

'Do you miss him?' I ask, shocking myself as much as her.

Saoirse sniffles and stiffens. 'Do you?'

'Yes. Very much.'

'Did you love him?' I say.

Scott watches me as I watch her.

'I did,' she says, and her heartbreak is palpable. 'I know that's not what you want to hear. But I did. I loved him so incredibly much and I thought—'

'Then I'm sorry. I'm so, so sorry for your loss,' I say. 'It must be unbearable.'

'Really? You mean that?'

'Yes. I do. Mark was telling the you the truth. Our relationship had been over for much, much longer than maybe either of us realised.'

Saoirse crumbles and heartbroken sobs shake her whole body. Scott slides closer to her and drapes his arm over her shoulder as heads at other tables turn and stare at us. Saoirse sobs gently for a few minutes.

'I'm sorry,' she says, every so often trying hard to stop crying, but she just can't.

When she finally looks up her mascara is running and her cheeks are red and blotchy.

'He loved you,' I say.

'Did he say that?' she gasps, smiling through her tears, and I'm so glad I met her. I think she really needed someone to tell her that Mark loved her. I think she needs to believe it. The way I once did.

I reach into my pocket and pull out the small jewellery box that has been pressing uncomfortably against my thigh since I sat down. I place it on the table and push it towards her. She stares at it with confusion, as if she's never seen a jewellery box before.

'It's from Mark,' I say.

Saoirse's fingers tremble as she opens it, and she begins to cry again as she stares inside.

I point. 'It's inscribed.'

She lifts the bracelet and reads Mark's loving words and I can literally sense her heart swell.

It takes her a moment to gather herself, but she finally looks up with glistening eyes.

'Thank you. Thank you so much.'

'Here. Let me help you.' Scott takes the bracelet to drape it round her wrist. 'There,' he says, fastening it. 'It's beautiful.'

Saoirse stares at the bracelet, twisting her arm left to right in awe of how it shimmers when the light catches it. 'I knew this was never about coffee,' she says, her tear-stained face brightening once more.

'Actually, it was,' I say.

'Oh.'

'Our coffee is shite. Or so I'm told.'

I reach for my teacup again.

'Right. Okay.'

'So, if it wouldn't be too weird, maybe you could sort us out with some good stuff.'

'Erm... eh...'

'It really is the best coffee around,' Scott says.

'Okay. Sure.' She puffs out. 'I can pass you on to one of my colleagues.'

I nod, understanding.

'You sure we can't twist your arm to take care of it yourself?' Scott says, laughing a little to take the edge off his forceful nudge.

'I would love to. Honestly.' She spins the bracelet round her wrist, smiling. 'But tomorrow is my last day in the office.'

'Ah. Right. Forgot you said you're taking some time off,' Scott says.

Saoirse takes a deep breath and looks at me apologetically. 'It's just a little me time, before the baby arrives.'

Scott's wide eyes dart to me and I have to replay her words to make sure I heard them right. And, as if it has magically appeared right this second, I notice her baby bump, tucked under the table.

I catch my breath. 'Wow! Congratulations.'

FORTY

'Well, fuck,' Scott says, once we've said our goodbyes, and Saoirse and her round bump have walked away in one direction and we head off in the other.

We'll have to circle back soon, to our bus stop, but when I started walking the wrong way, Scott followed without question.

'I didn't see that coming,' he says, his mind very clearly blown. 'Holy shit. You okay?'

We pass by a street vendor and I inhale deeply. *Mustard, ketchup and onions.* I'm disappointed when the smell is hot dogs and not bagels.

'Tabby. Are you okay?' Scott stops walking and places his hand on my shoulder.

He doesn't ask me if I think the baby is Mark's, and I don't say that of course I do. I find myself wishing Avery was here. Rhetorical or not, she'd say it. She'd just blurt it out loud and not give a shit who was listening. I wish someone would say it out loud. I wish someone would say, *Mark is a father.* Or he would be. If he was here.

'Tabby, say something please,' Scott says.

I stop walking and fold my arms. 'Do you think Mark knew?'

'About the baby?'

I nod.

His nose scrunches. 'I dunno. Maybe.'

'Do you know how far along she is?'

'I have no idea. I didn't even know she was pregnant. I'd never have walked you into that if I knew. I swear.'

I tuck my arms tighter, folding myself like an accordion.

'I wish I had met her on her own now, like you asked me to,' Scott says. 'I'm so sorry you had to find out that way.'

'Do you want to come back to my flat?'

'What?'

'I could make us lunch. I don't want to be on my own.' I want to shovel the words back into my mouth as soon as they tumble out.

Scott looks at his watch. 'I've an interview at two. It's on the far side of town so—'

'No worries. No worries.' I wave my hand as if erasing the idea from the air. 'I should go in to work anyway. I'm pretty sure Zoe thinks I'm a complete scatterbrain, disappearing all the time.'

'Don't go in to work. Give yourself a break. Today at least.'

I nod. I had no real intention of going near La Bella Vita. Scott and I turn round and re-walk the way we came.

'Look,' he says, checking his watch again with nervous energy as we reach the bus stop. 'I'm going to hop on the 69b now, but I won't be long. I could come over this evening?'

'Okay. Later would be good.'

'How does five thirty sound?' Scott says, pointing as the 69b comes into view.

I nod.

'And you're sure you're okay?'

'Good luck,' I say.

'Thanks.' Scott smiles, stepping back from the kerb edge so the bus doesn't catch his feet. 'See you later.'

FORTY-ONE

I sit in my kitchen and stare at my freshly painted walls. Mark hated yellow. I wore a yellow maxi dress to his friend's wedding a few years back and, right before the speeches, Mark leaned in and whispered that I looked as if a sunflower threw up on me. I got very, very drunk after that. I still have the scar on my elbow from where I slipped in the emergency stairwell when I tried to go out for some air.

I think about texting Avery – there's so much I need to tell her. But instead, for over an hour, I flick mindlessly through my phone. Becca has posted my flat on homes4sale.ie. The photos look great. Each room appears deceptively larger than in real life. The view of the park is very clearly marketed as the icing on the cake. Becca has used a spring photo of cherry blossoms in full bloom, their vibrant pink branches hugging black wrought-iron railings as perfect as if someone had copy and pasted the opening scene from *Mary Poppins*. I will most definitely miss that view when I'm gone.

Tabby: Hey x

Avery *Last seen today at 16.19 p.m.*

Tabby: How are you?

Avery *Last seen today at 16.22 p.m.*

Tabby: I know you're there. Can't we talk? I've something important I need to tell you.

Avery *Last seen today at 16.24 p.m.*

Tabby: ~~Mark cheated on me. Mark knocked the coffee girl up.~~ ~~Breaking up WAS the right thing to do.~~ Rashidi died.

Avery: RIP

When the doorbell rings I glance at the kitchen clock. It's not quite 5 p.m. yet. Scott's early arrival has caught me off guard, as if I'm terribly busy and I've just been interrupted. My heart races as I walk towards the front door and the slow realisation that I've never had a guest in my flat before hits me.

Avery's been here regularly over the years, but she sort of invited herself. Not that an invite was ever necessary anyway. Where she went, I went, and vice versa. Recently, Becca's obviously been here. But as Avery's guest. She'd just stayed over one night and then we all went with the flow from there. Mark had guests over all the time. His friends stopped by all the time. And he threw the odd party. His mother was here too, of course. But I've never actually invited anyone in, or entertained anyone by myself before, and I'm suddenly nervous as I open the door and Scott stands, looking a little weary, on the other side.

'Oh no,' I say, stepping aside to let him brush past. I close the door after him. 'Interview didn't go well.'

'Interview was a load of balls. Some lad, half my age,

reading questions off a sheet that he clearly downloaded from the internet.'

I make a face. 'Ah crap.'

'Pay was shite too.'

'I'd offer to speak to Catherine again but we've hired someone new,' I say. 'Well, I did. I went a bit rogue, actually. Catherine is trying to be cool about it, but I know she's pissed.'

'Fuck her,' Scott says. 'And good for you. Show her who's boss.'

'I am sorry, you know. About how it all worked out. I really feel like this is all my fault.'

'It's not. I could never have worked around someone as toxic as Catherine for long.'

I nod.

'I'm sorry,' Scott says, stepping closer. 'I didn't mean—'

'Glad you got away, then?' I ask, wishing I could.

'Yes and no.'

'No?'

'I miss seeing you every day.'

'Ah, stop it,' I say, and laugh, knocking my shoulder against his. 'Right! Beans on toast okay for dinner?'

Scott's laughter drowns mine out before he cuts himself off, realising I'm serious.

'Don't you like beans?' I ask.

'I do. But I thought you wanted to cook up something fancy.'

'Show off, you mean.'

'Well yeah.'

'Do you want me to?'

'No, no. Beans on toast sounds perfect. I never cook dinner at home. Ready meals all the way. Or noodles. Throw on some boiled water and presto.'

'Mark hated lazy dinners like this,' I say, popping some

bread in the toaster. 'We usually ate at work, though, so it wasn't really an issue.'

'Frozen shepherd's pie isn't for everyone,' Scott says.

Conversation flows easily. Scott doesn't comment on the lovely decor or the view of the park the way everyone else does. In fact, I'm not sure he's noticed either of them. I'm almost disappointed when his phone rings, breaking our flow of chit-chat. He excuses himself and steps into the hall to answer. I'm plating up microwave-hot beans onto buttery toast when he returns.

'Everything okay?' I ask, unsure by his expression.

'Got the job.'

'Oh. The shitty interview with the shitty pay?'

'That's the one. Except, they've offered a bit of an increase.'

'That's great!'

'Nothing major. But I can afford rent again, so...'

I gasp and try not to let my concern show in my face. I hate that I didn't realise things were so tight for him.

'So, we should celebrate,' I say.

Suddenly the plates of beans on toast looks disappointing. I reach for a bottle of red wine from the rack above the fridge, blow the dust off and polish up the label with my sleeve. Scott fetches both plates of beans on toast as I pop the cork, and we meet at the table. A comfortable silence falls over us as we eat, although neither of us manages to finish.

'I'm really happy for you,' I say, pushing my plate to the side.

'Thank you,' Scott says, picking up both plates and setting them down beside the sink.

'Leave that. I'll clean up later.'

He nods. 'Weird day, wasn't it?'

'Yeah. It really was. New baby and a new job. They make Hallmark cards for this type of stuff,' I say.

'Are you really okay?' he asks.

I sip some wine before I say, 'I am. It's strange to think there will be a baby in the world with Mark's DNA. But that's Saoirse's life now, not mine. My life is La Bella Vita. And Avery and Becca.'

'And me, I hope,' Scott says.

I stand up, with our glasses of wine in each hand. I pass Scott his and lean with my back against the countertop, sipping mine.

'Do you think Saoirse will be all right?' I ask.

'I think so. She's tough.' Scott drinks the last of his wine and places the empty glass on the countertop next to the sink. 'Well, this was lovely, Tabby. Thank you. But I should probably get going.'

'Already?' My disappointment comes out squeaky and high-pitched.

'Won't your sister be home soon? I don't want to intrude.'

'No.'

'Oh.'

Scott tilts his head and I can tell that he guesses she's not simply out with friends or working late.

'We had a row. Stupid, really. And all my fault.' I sigh, exhausted. 'So yeah, she moved out. For good, I think. Not sure really. It's all a bit up in the air.'

'I thought you two were really close.'

I shrug and try to brush it off as if it's not the big deal that it is.

'What about your resolutions? Aren't you supposed to be doing them together?'

'Sort of. She made them up and I just have to give them a go. But it doesn't matter now anyway because I've already fallen behind. I missed last month. And this month is a definite fail too, so...'

'So, what did you miss?'

'You really want to hear this?'

'I do, actually.'

I pour more wine into Scott's glass and he smiles, reaching for it again.

'Avery wanted me to take an art class.'

Scott's eyes narrow as he listens intently. 'Go on...'

'I used to love all that stuff as a kid. Painting and pottery and all that. But life sort of got in the way. Avery is trying to remind me to make time for the fun stuff. But it doesn't matter anyway, because most beginners' classes are booked out for ever.'

'And what about this month?'

'Spain,' I say, before I slug a huge mouthful of wine. 'Avery thinks I need a holiday. I'm pretty sure she wanted us to go together. But not now, obviously.'

'And it wouldn't be much of a holiday sitting on the beach in silence,' he says.

I laugh. 'Avery wouldn't be able to do it. I think she'd literally explode if she tried to stay silent for a whole week.'

'It's a pity,' he says. 'Because I think she's right. I think you could use a holiday.'

'Do you want to go to Spain?' I joke as I stare into my wine glass.

I wait to hear Scott laugh too, but the kitchen is silent except for our breathing and the ticking of the clock above the door. I look up to find his eyes round and searching mine.

'Do you?' I ask again, not laughing anymore.

Scott's mouth opens but no words come out.

'It just... it would be nice to not be alone.'

Scott runs his hand over his bare head as he mulls it over. 'I'll have to talk to work. See what they want to do about a start date and all that.'

'Yeah. Yeah. Sure. There's no pressure. If it works, it works. And if not...'

I scrape the remains from our plates into the compost bin, feeling awkward and in desperate need of something to do.

Scott takes the plates from me and sticks them in the dishwasher. 'We'll make it work.'

Before I have time to think about it, I'm on my tiptoes, leaning forward to press my lips on his. They're warm and soft and in the moment it feels right. But only for a moment. Scott breaks away. We lock eyes and his gaze burns into me, but I don't look away.

'Are you sure you want to do this?' he whispers, breathlessly.

I lean in again and this time I feel him press his chest close against mine.

FORTY-TWO

The curtains in the spare room are thicker than in my room and they don't allow as much sunlight in. It's strange waking up in here. It's even more strange waking up with Scott's arm round me. Last night was wonderful and awkward and passionate and confusing. I lie wide awake with my eyes closed for a few minutes, thinking about it. I try to process how I feel but it's a sensory overload.

Mark was my first boyfriend. My only boyfriend. I never imagined I would ever be with anyone else, yet here I am, naked with Scott Wilson beside me. In Avery's bed. I couldn't sleep with Scott in the bed I shared with Mark. God, Avery would squeal like a schoolgirl if she knew. I open my eyes and take my phone from the bedside table to text her. But as I untangle myself from Scott and stand up, I change my mind and put it back down.

I grab a shower, get dressed and decide to head out to get some takeaway tea and coffee the way they do in all good romantic films after a hook-up. I write Scott a note in case he wakes up while I'm gone.

> *Morning,*
> *Getting us some sustenance.*
> *Be back ASAP.*

I hum and haw about adding a kiss. Then roll my eyes at how silly I'm being, considering where I added kisses last night. I scribble my name and two kisses and hurry out the door.

I get caught in the hustle and bustle of morning commuters and the queue at the coffee shop on the corner is long and slow-moving. When I finally arrive back at the flat with a tea for me and a cappuccino for Scott, he meets me in the hall. He's dressed and ready to go. I inhale deeply, slightly taken aback by the familiar scent of musky sandalwood.

'You smell nice,' I say, trying to figure out how the fragrance makes me feel.

'I used the stuff in the bathroom. I hope that's okay.'

'Sure.'

My inhales are deep and exaggerated as the scent transports me to a different time. A time when Mark was here smelling exactly like this.

'Oh, shit, that was probably Mark's aftershave. Of course it was.' Scott's face falls as he realises the obvious.

'It's okay. You couldn't have known.'

'I wasn't thinking. I shouldn't have used it. I'm sorry.'

'Coffee?' I say, desperate to change the subject before I start to cry. I tilt the takeaway tray towards Scott and he unplugs a cup.

'Might have gone a bit cold.'

'No, no. It's good,' he says without tasting it.

We stand in silence for a moment as aftershave and coffee mix in the air, bringing with them the familiar sense of many mundane mornings.

'Are you hungry?' I ask after a while. 'I could make us something.'

'I don't have time, sorry.'

I nod.

'Work want me to start today.'

My eyes are wide.

'I know,' Scott says, 'it's all a bit rushed. But to be honest, I'm glad. I need the cash and I can't spend another poxy day playing Xbox on Richie's couch.'

'Straight to the grindstone for you, so,' I say, trying to ignore how awkward everything about this morning is. 'Listen, about Spain?'

Scott swallows.

'It was a lovely idea, but you have a new job now and—'

'I'll talk to them.'

Tears glisten in my eyes. The smell of Mark's aftershave is becoming too much.

'I'll take care of it, I promise,' Scott says. 'I'll book us something, if you like. Two rooms, obviously. I get it.'

'Get what?'

'You have so much going on right now. I'm not expecting... I mean, I don't think...' Scott pauses, his face scrunched up as if gathering his thoughts physically hurts. 'We are friends, aren't we? I haven't completely fucked that up, have I?'

'No. God no. Of course not.'

'Good.' Scott sighs. 'It's just, I saw your face when you came home just now – when you saw I was still here – and, I thought, *Oh shit! What have I done?*'

'You haven't done anything. Nothing I didn't want. It's just that aftershave...'

Scott bows his head. 'I'm sorry.'

'Don't be,' I say, suddenly desperate to be alone so I can cry in peace. 'Now go. Have a great first day. I want to hear all about it, okay?'

'Okay.'

FORTY-THREE

A week passes and Scott and I have barely spoken. He says he's crazy busy with his new job, and we both pretend that's the only reason. But I know my reaction to Mark's aftershave in the flat scared him away. I wake every morning wanting to hear from him. And every night, when I go to bed, I'm secretly relieved that he didn't call. Because I don't know what to say. I like him. I think I *really* like him, and I don't know how that makes me feel. I don't know how that *should* feel. *Happy? Guilty? Confused?* All of it. I feel all of it. And the person I want to talk to about those feelings is Scott. Which is even more damn confusing.

Avery still isn't speaking to me either. I text her most days, and I try calling sometimes but she doesn't pick up. I talk to Becca almost every day. Usually, she's calling to set up a viewing of my flat with potential buyers, but the conversation always shifts to Avery. Becca says she sees all my messages but she isn't ready to write back yet, and part of me worries that she might never be.

When people come to view the flat, I go for a walk. Alone. Or I sit in the park. Alone. Or nurse a cup of tea in a local café for much too long. Alone. Always alone. I was supposed to be getting married this month. For so long I dreamed of a beautiful summer wedding. A white, backless dress. Mark in a smart, tailored suit. Avery wearing a teal bridesmaid's dress, no doubt, with hair to match. Instead, I'm lonely. So incredibly lonely.

I'm out back at La Bella Vita trying to sort out a mix-up with a seafood order when Lyla comes looking for me.

'There's a girl at reception asking to see you,' she says. 'Tall, kinda sad-looking.'

'Can you deal with it?' I ask, as the seafood delivery guy glares at me.

'She's not a customer, she says it's personal,' Lyla explains, as she turns her attention to the many, many crates of crab claws and mussels stacked beside me. 'Jaysus, we'll never use all that.'

'Catherine tripled our order by mistake.'

'Listen, love,' the delivery guy says, shoving an invoice and a pen towards me. 'I don't give a rat's arse who tripled what. I just want you to bleedin' sign here so I can get on with the rest of me day, right.'

I scribble my name and decide that we'll find room in the freezer to store the massive order, and I walk back inside and towards reception. I worry I'll find Saoirse waiting, and relief washes over me when it isn't her. But I do recognise the young woman waiting for me immediately. We've never met before, but her chocolate eyes and her flawless caramel skin are so familiar. And when she holds out her hand for me to shake and says, 'Hi. I'm Ida. I believe you knew my father, Rashidi,' I begin to cry.

Scott is the first person I text. I share the date, time and location of Rashidi's funeral and I say I hope he can make it – as if I'm inviting him to a summer barbecue or out for drinks after work.

I text Avery too. She sees the message but as usual she doesn't reply.

. . .

When the morning of the funeral arrives, it punches me in the gut as if it's snuck up on me and caught me by surprise. It hasn't, of course. The date has been firmly marked in the calendar on my phone. But my decision to go is less firm. The thought of walking into the church alone fills me with dread. I ring work, hoping for some catastrophe that means I'm needed immediately. It comes as no surprise when Zoe tells me it's all very quiet. I think about going in anyway. I could catch up on some admin work, or update Instagram with photos of recent cakes. Paperwork and Instagram aren't urgent though. In fact, they're stuff I could do from home; but at least if I'm in the office then I'm not alone. But so much worse than loneliness is knowing that I will never forgive myself for missing the chance to say goodbye to Mark. I can't make the same mistake again. I have to say goodbye to Rashidi.

The intimate church just off Parnell Street smells of incense and oils. But, it's seeing Avery that takes my breath away. Her sky-blue hair is refreshing brightness on such a dark day. Becca is sitting beside her and their back are towards me as they sit huddled in the centre pew. I take a moment to digest my surroundings before I join them. There are a handful of other mourners scattered around the church, enough to count on fingers. Scott is there. And Ida, of course. She sits in the front pew. Her head is low and her shoulders are rounded, but every now and then she looks up and towards the wicker coffin.

I can't help but think about Mark's funeral and a little acidy sick squirms up in the back of my throat. I stay close to the doors for now, just in case I throw up. Avery said the church was packed for his funeral. Mourners poured onto the road, it affected traffic and the guards had to come and direct people around the village. Every business owner from La Bella Vita's street was there, all anxious to say a final farewell to Mark. *Do they not want to say goodbye to Rashidi too?* I told every manager in every business along our street about Rashidi's passing. I gave them all the funeral details and asked them to pass the message to their staff. I'm disappointed they haven't come; but I doubt Rashidi would be. He would say something all profound and meaningful about the people here being the people who matter. But for once he'd be wrong. There was a time when Mark mattered most in the world to me. And even though I didn't sit in a pew, or read a prayer or watch his coffin go into the ground, it doesn't change that once upon a time I loved him very much.

Swallowing hard, and placing one wobbly foot in front of the other, I slide into the pew next to Scott, Avery and Becca.

'Hey,' Scott whispers, placing his hand on my knee.

'Hi,' I whisper.

Becca turns her head, smiles and mouths, 'Hello,' without sound.

I return her smile. Avery continues to look straight ahead, never once making eye contact.

Scott switches seats to slide in beside me.

'Hey,' he whispers, placing his hand on my knee.

'Hi,' I whisper back and I've never been so glad to sit beside someone in all my life.

The service is brief. There's no music or eulogy. And I only realise it's over when Ida stands up, shakes the priest's hand and walks down the centre aisle towards the door. I'm on my feet quickly to follow her.

'Ida,' I call after her, momentarily startled by the bright day outside. I place my hand above my eyes like a visor and call again, louder. 'Ida.'

She steps onto the footpath and turns towards the car park, picking up speed.

'Ida.'

She continues walking as noisy traffic whips past. Buses and trucks and cars. All filled with people getting on with their mundane day. People who perhaps drive this same road every day – pass this same church every day – oblivious that inside lies a man with no more days to pass.

'Ida, wait. Stop, please?'

Finally, Ida stops walking and turns round. 'Sorry,' she says. 'Didn't hear you.'

'You're leaving,' I say.

Ida's face pinches as if she's surprised that I'm stating the obvious.

'What about the burial?'

'The funeral director will take care of it. I don't need to be there,' she says. 'But you can go if you like.'

'Don't you want to be there?'

She shakes her head.

'Are you okay?' I ask.

'I am.'

I nod but I don't believe her.

'I'm so sorry for your loss,' I say.

Ida's stiff shoulders relax and she exhales slowly as we stand face to face. The street around us is bustling. A car horn honks in the distance, a man walks past talking loudly on his mobile phone, a toddler wails, squirming to free himself from his buggy. And, yet, it's the silence between us that seems loudest. Loss can do that; it has that power. The power to encapsulate you in a bubble, and for a moment nothing outside that shimmering, delicate exterior exists. Ida and I share a bubble now. And I'm happy to stand here for as long as she needs.

'I really must go,' she says at last, tilting her head towards the car park, popping our bubble with a bang. 'I'm already late. The babysitter can only stay until three, and in this traffic it'll take me over an hour to get home.'

'You have children,' I say, both shocked and saddened.

Shocked to discover Rashidi was a grandfather and saddened because I've never once heard him mention grandchildren.

'Two boys. Three and four,' Ida says. 'They didn't know him, Tabitha. The boys never met my father.'

'I'm sorry,' I say.

'Don't be. I'm not.'

Again, I nod. And again, I don't believe her.

'I think you'll miss him more than me,' Ida says. 'You certainly knew him better.'

I want to tell Ida that I don't believe a word out of her mouth. That I think she's full of bullshit, because I can see her heart breaking as clearly as if she was made of glass.

'I will miss him,' I say. 'And I know you will, too.'

'I'll miss the what-ifs,' she says, wiping away a single tear. 'What if we got back in touch? What if he got to know the boys? What if we grew close again?'

I want to tell her that what-ifs don't go away. They prick your skin late at night like tiny pins, waking you. What if we had more time? What if I never said what I said? *What if, what if, what if.* But I don't say anything. Ida will learn for herself soon, unfortunately. If not tonight then maybe next week, or the week after. But the what-ifs will come. I suspect they always do.

'To be honest, I don't think any of that was ever going to happen,' Ida continues. 'It would have been nice to be back in touch, but it just wasn't likely, you know. Too much water under the bridge, I suppose. I loved my dad, but really I lost him years ago. When we stopped speaking. The man in the church...' She pauses and shrugs as if shaking off her heartache. 'That man is a stranger to me. Has been for a long time. I'd be a damn hypocrite if I stood here crying about how much I'll miss him.'

'Why did you stop speaking?' I say, then clasp my hand over my mouth, but it's too late, the question is already out there.

Ida eyes me with apprehension, neither of us quite believing what I just said.

'Jesus. Sorry. It's none of my business. I don't know why I said that.'

My cheeks flush and I wish I had Avery's ability to be completely oblivious to asking an inappropriate question.

'It's okay,' she says, thankfully not taking offence. 'You're curious. I would be too.'

There's a moment of silence where she checks her watch. Then she looks up, sighs and says, 'Dad didn't want me to marry the guy I was seeing. We didn't have a huge fight or anything like that, that wasn't Dad's style. He never shouted. We just sort of stopped speaking. Eventually it became too hard to start again.'

'Did you marry the guy anyway?' I ask.

'As it happens, my dad was right. My husband was a bastard. Made my life bloody hell. But the worst part was, when it all fell apart, I couldn't tell my dad. My pride wouldn't let me.'

'I'm so sorry.'

She shrugs again. 'That's life though, isn't it? We never know if we're making the right decision – we just have to take each day as it comes.'

'You're so like him,' I say.

Silent tears spill down her cheeks as she smiles, nods and finally walks away.

FORTY-FOUR

'There you are,' Scott says, when I return to the church grounds.
'What happened? Did you catch Ida? Why's she leaving?'

'She only has her babysitter until three.'

I wonder if the look on Scott's face is the same as the look on
mine when I discovered Rashidi was a grandfather.

'God,' Scott says. 'I guess there was a lot about him that we
didn't know.'

'Where's Avery?'

Scott's expression changes. 'She had to go. Work stuff.'

'Really?'

'That's what she said.'

'And Becca is gone with her,' I say, more thinking out loud
than asking a question.

'She is. But she said she'd call you later. She has lots of viewings of the flat lined up for next week. She said interest is really
taking off. That's great news.'

'Yeah. Great.'

'Are you okay?' Scott asks, placing his hand on my shoulder.
It's the first time we've touched since we shared a bed. It feels

overwhelming and at the same time wholly comforting. 'Today must be hard for you. Bringing up all those feelings.'

'Do you think Avery and I will be like Rashidi and Ida?' I ask. 'Do you think we'll spend so long not talking that we'll eventually forgot how?'

'No,' Scott says, firmly. 'I don't believe that for a second.'

'Really? Cos right now it feels as if we might never talk again.'

'She was asking for you,' Scott tells me. 'Right before you came into the church. She seemed disappointed when I said I hadn't seen you all week. Like she can't bear to think of you on your own.'

'That's cos Avery hates to be alone,' I say, smiling as I realise that when she marries Becca she'll never really be alone again.

'She wanted to know if you're sticking to your resolutions.'

'Oh God. What did you tell her?'

'I showed her this.'

Scott takes his phone from his pocket and opens an email. My breath catches when I spot the Aer Lingus logo.

'Flights?' I say.

'Three nights in Ibiza,' Scott says, passing his phone to me so I can read the email. 'I wish it was longer but a long weekend was the best my boss could do. I'm still very much the new guy over there, so I didn't want to push my luck.'

I don't know what to say. Thankfully Scott keeps talking.

'Avery seemed really pleased. Not pleased that we're heading off, not exactly. More pleased that you're keeping up the resolutions. She really cares about you, Tabby. You know that, don't you?'

'Yeah.' I swallow hard, and then I start to giggle. 'God, she must be so jealous. She bloody loves Ibiza. All the sun, sea and sand. It's her dream place. Did you get a lecture about taking care of me?'

'Sort of,' he says.

'Sort of?'

'I got the sun, sea, sand – and the other "S" word lecture.'

'Sangria?' I say, quickly followed by, 'Oh, duh, sex. Oh God, she didn't warn you off, did she? I'm so sorry.'

'Actually, she warned me on...'

'Oh, right... Jesus. You didn't tell her we already...?'

'Fuck no.'

'Oh. Okay. Good.'

I can tell from Scott's tone that he considers sleeping with me a huge mistake, and I'm instantly having second thoughts about this holiday. I can't imagine it will be anything more than a big awkward mess.

'You don't have to do this, you know. Go to Ibiza with me, I mean. I know you said you would. But that was before...' I trail off. This is already awkward.

'And if I want to?'

'Do you want to? Actually properly want to. Not just because it's a resolution or whatever?'

'I want to. But I especially want to because it *is* a resolution. They're important to you and I want to help. I want to be a part of that.'

The sense of calm that comes with Scott's reassurance is chased quickly by excitement fizzing in my veins. I throw my hands in the air, lifting an invisible ceiling, and squeal, 'Ibiza. Hell yeah!'

Scott grimaces as he looks over my shoulder. I lower my hands and turn round to find the priest behind us.

'We're going to make our way to the graveyard now, if you would like to follow,' he says.

'Thank you, Father,' Scott says, composed and sombre.

When the priest has walked away and is out of earshot, Scott and I double over laughing. Both wishing we could share this story with Rashidi over bites of bagel.

FORTY-FIVE

AUGUST

I know you hate the camera. But please be in at least one holiday photo!

I take a selfie standing in my hall. I have one hand curled round the handle of my suitcase and I'm wearing a wicker hat with a large, floppy rim and a polka dot ribbon. My hair peeks out from underneath; it's growing out now and is already past my shoulders. I turn my phone round to check out the Instagrammable *I'm jetting off somewhere hot and fabulous* selfie. But all I see is my double chin and pale skin. I let go of my suitcase and flop my back against the wall. My knees bend and I slide onto the floor. I delete the photo and shove my phone into my bag next to my passport, which glares at me, judging me.

I told Catherine I needed some time off but I didn't tell her why. I didn't tell anyone why, because part of me feels Avery might have got this resolution all wrong. Should I be doing this? Eight months after Mark died, I'm jetting off on holiday. And worse still, I'm going with the man his mother hired to replace him. I'm no better than Mark. I'm a cheater too. Only I'm worse: I cheated death.

When a horn honks outside my window, I know the taxi is here. I'm on my feet as the horn honks again. And again. And again.

'All right. All right. I'm coming.'

I grab my case, hurry out the door and lock it behind me. Scott is standing next to the taxi, shifting from one foot to the other as if he needs to pee.

'I thought you were having second thoughts,' he says.

My breath catches.

'It's just when you weren't answering your phone?'

'You were calling me? I didn't hear it. My phone must be on silent. Were you out here long?'

Scott nods. 'A while. Joe here was convinced you'd stood me up.'

I glance at the taxi driver. His upper body is hanging out his open window and he has a huge grin plastered on his face, as if this is the best entertainment he's had in months.

'I would never do that, Joe,' I say, as if we're acquainted.

'Right ya are,' he says, tucking himself back behind the steering wheel. 'Have ye a plane to catch or what? Get in, will ya?'

Scott takes my case and puts it in the boot while I sit into the back seat.

'Ibiza, is it?' Joe says, as Scott joins me and we finally begin to drive.

'Yes. Ibiza,' Scott says.

'Lovely. Bloody lovely. Been there meself a few times.'

'It's a lovely island,' Scott says.

'You know what they say about Ibiza,' Joe asks, rhetorically.

'Hmm?'

'If ya can remember it, ya didn't do it right.'

Scott laughs. 'You should put that on a t-shirt, pal.'

'I should.' Joe chuckles too. 'Sure enough, that's how I'll make me millions.'

Maybe Joe has a point. Maybe that's how I should spend this weekend. Drunk off my tits doing God knows what and not having to feel a single ounce of guilt afterwards because I won't remember a thing. Actually, maybe that's how I should live the rest of my life. I laugh when I realise there's a term for this kind of problem-solving – alcoholism!

FORTY-SIX

I've never been in a five-star hotel before. Mark always said he wasn't paying a fortune for an extra star and a lousy chocolate on your pillow. I think about him as I lower myself to sit on the edge of the bed, suddenly too exhausted to stand. I wonder what he'd say if he could see me now.

'Bikinis are for abs not flabs, Tabs.'

There may well be a floral bikini packed in my case but I wonder if I kept the receipt. I'll return it when we get home. I sit for a while not thinking about anything and thinking about everything all at the same time. It's a while before I notice there isn't a chocolate on each pillow. Instead, there's a small box of chocolates on the dressing table, next to two bottles of water. One sparkling and one still. And there is a handwritten note on a white card with the hotel name embossed at the top.

Dear Tabitha,
Happy Anniversary.
We hope you enjoy your stay at White Sands Resort and Spa.
Kind regards,
Keesha.

There's a knock on my door and I answer with the card still in my hand.

'Hey. You settling in okay?' Scott asks.

He's changed into neon orange swim shorts and a floral, short-sleeved shirt. I try not to laugh as I remember the night he introduced me to *Magnum PI* and how much he looks like he could star in the show now.

'Your room is bigger than mine,' he says, craning his neck to peer past me.

'Is it? We can swap if you like.'

Scott grins.

'It's really nice here,' I say. 'Thank you.'

'Did you get the choccies?'

'My anniversary chocolates? Yeah, I got them.' It's hard to keep a straight face.

'Anniversary?'

I pass Scott the fancy card.

'Ah, bollocks. I said Happy Resolution on the phone. Must be the language barrier.'

'Happy resolution,' I echo. It all makes much more sense now.

'Well, anniversary or resolution, they taste the same so...' Scott shrugs.

'It's a fail. A nice try but a definite fail,' I joke, trying to hide how much I appreciate the sentiment and how emotional it's making me.

'Do you know what's not a fail? Happy hour!'

I stare at Scott, trying to guess if he's serious or not. I think he is, so I check my watch.

'It's not even midday yet,' I say.

'And?'

'And we've been up since stupid o'clock.'

'And?'

'And... erm... I don't have another and.'

'Sounds like you need a drink to me. Anyway, you heard what Joe the taxi driver said. When in Rome and all that.'

'But we're in Ibiza.'

'Ha. Ha.'

'Okay. Give me a few minutes. I need to change.' I say, comparing my tracksuit to Scott's tropical look.

Scott sighs. 'Yeah,' he says, shaking his head. 'This room is definitely bigger.'

'We really can swap. It's the least I can do since you won't let me pay half.'

'Well.' He shrugs. 'If you're sure.'

I'm taken aback that he's serious, but I smile and say, 'It's no problem, really.'

'Okay cool. I'll leave you to get your stuff and I'll meet you at my room.'

Scott dashes away, without another word, almost falling over his flip-flops.

There isn't much to gather up. I hadn't begun to unpack yet. I fetch my case and the box of fancy chocolates and the water that I've no intention of leaving behind and make my way to Scott's room at the other end of the long hotel corridor. I raise my hand and knock three times.

'Just a sec. Give me two secs,' Scott shouts from inside.

I wait. An elderly couple pass behind me. Their bodies are shaped like question marks but they're linked arm in arm like a couple of love-struck teenagers. I've seen Avery and Becca walk like this. Their spines, admittedly, straighter, but their infatuation the same. I wonder how many years this little old man and little old lady have been linking arms, and I find myself hoping that Avery and Becca are linked for just as long.

I raise my hand to knock again, but the door opens and Scott stands grinning and giddy in the gap.

'Come in. Come in,' he says, stepping aside so I can pass.

My hands cup my face. 'Oh my God. This is huge.' I spin slowly on the spot, taking in the size and luxury of what is clearly a suite, and then I stop moving and stare at Scott. His smile is so huge it takes over his whole face. 'But you said my room was bigger. You said you wanted to swap.'

Without a word Scott takes me by the hand and I leave my case by the door as he leads me into a connected room.

'Wow. Holy shit, wow.' The huge back wall is made entirely of glass to appreciate the stunning sea view. 'This is amazing. But... but... something like this must cost a fortune.'

'Oh yeah, absolutely. But I'm not paying.'

'You're not?'

Scott leans his shoulder against the door frame and crosses his feet at his ankles.

'I know the manager,' he says.

'You must know him pretty well to get all this for free.'

'Her.'

'Oh.'

'An ex-girlfriend. She never really got over me so, for a few sexual favours, the room is all mine.'

I glance over my shoulder at the bed and cringe.

'I'm joking.' Scott belly-laughs. 'But you should see your face. My sister runs the hotel and you have the room for one night only. Sort of a Cinderella deal. It's back to basics tomorrow, I'm afraid.'

'Ah, I remember you mentioned a sister.'

'I've two actually. One older, one younger. But we're not close the way you and Avery are.'

Me and Avery.

'We see each other at Christmas and for the odd family occasion, that sort of thing.'

Scott's confession saddens me, I can't bear the thought of only seeing Avery a couple of times a year.

Scott drags himself away from the door frame slowly and walks over to slide back the enormous glass door. Salty sea air rushes in and I take deep, satisfied breaths.

'C'mon,' he says, beckoning for me to follow as he steps into the sunshine on the balcony.

'Jesus, it's boiling out here,' I say, as the heat outside wraps around me like a hug from a long-lost friend. 'I've no sun cream on.'

'There's shade round this side,' Scott says as he turns the corner where the balcony wraps around.

And, again, I follow. I find him standing next to a large easel, paper and paint. It's pointed towards the sleepy sea that stretches to infinity, yawing every so often and stirring up a frothy wave.

'Is this for me?' I say, tapping my chest with my fingertips.

'I thought you could paint the view or something. I know you couldn't book an art class for your June resolution. But maybe just picking up a brush is enough to remind you that you like to paint. Isn't that the point?

I want to tell him that this is the nicest thing anyone has done for me in years. I want to say that I'm so grateful. And I want to paint. I really, really want to paint. But my feet are stuck on the spot and all that passes my lips is a groggy and indecipherable 'eh'.

'It's corny. I knew it was corny,' Scott says, running his hand over his head the way I've noticed he always does when he's second-guessing himself.

'It is very corny,' I say, finding my voice. 'But it's perfect.'

Scott's cheeks are a little pink, and I'm not sure if he's blushing or sunburnt already.

'Right,' he continues. 'I know you're not a day-drinking kind of girl—'

'I can day-drink, you know,' I say, feeling an overwhelming

need to remove the metaphorical stick Scott seems to think I have up my arse.

He raises his hands above his head, surrendering. 'Hear me out... See that beach hut down there?' He points to a bandstand-shaped café at the edge of the sand.

I nod, thinking how it seems like the perfect place to fritter away an afternoon.

'I'm going to go down there now. Have a few beers and maybe catch up with my sister.'

'Oh, okay,' I say, suddenly feeling as if I would be intruding if I joined him.

'You take all the time you need, okay?'

I stare at the blank paper. 'I haven't picked up a paintbrush in years. I wouldn't even know where to begin. You know, Avery is trying to make a point with her resolutions. She wants me to remember who I was a long, long time ago. Actually, I think she wants me to *be* who I was a long, long time ago. And not only is that person gone, I'm not really sure I'd want her back even if I could.'

Scott's eyes narrow and his confidence seems to wobble for a moment. 'If this is too much' – he points to the easel – 'if I've got this all wrong, I can pack it away and we can go back to the other room.'

'Could you take my photo? Me and the easel,' I say.

Scott's face scrunches, confused.

'August's resolution is to be in a holiday photo,' I explain. 'I'm sure Avery meant something on the beach or in front of some landmark building. But this is so much better.'

'But it's blank. It doesn't count.'

I snap my arm back down by my side and pull myself straighter and taller.

'If you don't actually paint something you're skipping a resolution.'

'Oh, c'mon. You don't seriously think I can paint a view like that.'

'Did Avery specify what you had to paint?'

'No.'

'Well then. What you paint is up to you. Paint something that makes you happy. Isn't that the whole point? Remembering how to be happy.'

I clasp my hands as if in prayer and tap my index finger against my lip, thinking, then I squeeze some yellow paint onto the tray, pick up the brush and draw a circle. I add two round blobs inside for eyes and finish with a big, curved line for a smiling mouth.

'Done,' I say, satisfied, as I place the brush down and fetch my phone from my bag.

Scott laughs. 'I see what you mean. You are most definitely not a painter.'

'Just take the feckin' photo, will you?'

I pass Scott my phone and he takes a couple of steps back, still laughing. I stand next to the easel with my thumbs up.

'Say sangria,' Scott says, raising my phone, ready to snap.

I smile as brightly as my painting. 'Sangria.'

'That's one for a frame,' Scott says, as he gives me back my phone.

Surprisingly, I love the photo. Scott has captured a boat on the horizon, tiny in the distance. The water sparkling under the sun, golden and inviting. The beach hut, the balcony and the easel. But most of all he's captured my happiness. That sparkle in your eyes that the camera searches for and that you can't fake. My sparkle was missing for a long time but now my eyes glisten as brightly as the shimmering sea.

'This is perfect. Thank you,' I say, and I wonder if he knows I'm talking about much more than the photo.

'Glad you like it.'

'Right,' I say, turning my back on the easel and the sea. 'Get out.'

Scott's face falls. 'What?'

'I have to change. I can't meet your sister for drinks wearing this.'

FORTY-SEVEN

Ibizan time seems to tick by differently. Mornings are long and lazy. Afternoons are sun-soaked and full of conversation and laughter. And the evenings over dinner, or moonlit strolls with sand between my toes, make me wish I could bottle how I'm feeling and bring it home with me.

On the last day of our brief holiday, I sit on a sun lounger overlooking the Mediterranean. I have a cocktail in one hand. A fancy one in a tall glass with a pink sugar-coated rim and matching paper umbrella. My phone is in my other hand and I'm staring at the screen. I find myself coming back to the photo of me, the easel and the smiling face often. My artwork is laughable, my face is flushed and sweaty and I must have spilled something on my top because there's a stain next to the collar, but Scott is right, I think I just might frame this one. I caption the photo, 'Living my best life', and with shaking fingers I finally send it to Avery. I take a deep breath when her reply is instant.

Avery: Nice self-portrait

Tabby: 😂

...

Avery is typing

...

Avery is offline

...

Avery is typing

...

Avery is offline

I stare at the screen until my vision blurs and I wait and wait for Avery to find her words. When she doesn't, or can't, I take the lead. I send her another photo. I catch the bottom half of my legs, slightly pink as they soak up the last day of sunshine before I return home, the sugary top of my cocktail glass and the sea that stretches for miles.

Tabby: This place 🌊 Best resolution ever!

Avery: 👍

Tabby: Thank you.

Avery: I think it's Scott you need to thank.

Tabby: A holiday was your idea. Thank you for helping me to be happy.

There's a long pause with no reply and my heart sinks until a shriek of laughter pulls my attention away from my phone. A couple giggle and play beach tennis together. They're particularly terrible and the ball flies everywhere except at their rackets. But they seem to enjoy themselves anyway, howling with laughter as they chase after a runaway ball. Mark and I rarely attempted sports together, especially ball games. Mark was athletic with natural ability and I was decidedly not. My butterfingers drove him crazy and he would insist that I try harder or concentrate more. I'm trying to remember the last time I picked up a ball when my phone beeps and I check the screen again.

Avery: Are you happy?

When I look up again, the couple have moved. They've chased their ball further down the beach, stopping to kiss and cuddle when they've caught it. They move again, taking their ball and their laughter with them, and I shift my gaze out to sea. There's a cruise ship passing in the distance. It's miles away, but even from here it looks big. As big as Avery's simple question. *Am I happy?*

Avery: You still there?

Tabby: I'm here.

Avery: So are you happy?

My face aches and it takes me a moment to realise it's because I'm smiling so hugely.

Tabby: I am.

Avery: Good. You deserve to be.

Tabby: So do you. I hope you will be sooooo happy with Becca.

Avery: Do you really mean that?

Tabby: You're going to be the best wife. I wish I said that sooner.

Avery: 😊😊

Avery: I'm not the only one who's going to be sooooo happy with Becca. You're going to bloody love her when you get home!

Tabby: ??

Avery: I'm not supposed to say anything yet...

Tabby: But???

...

Avery is typing

...

...

...

Avery: Nope can't. Never mind. Forget I said anything.

Tabby: FFS you've never kept a secret in your life. Don't start now. Tell me!

Avery: OK. But it wasn't me who told you.

Tabby: Fine. Now what is it?

Avery: Becca really wanted to be the one to tell you herself.

Tabby: Avery I swear to God if you don't spit it out...

Avery: There's an offer on your flat. A big one. Like A LOT over the asking price.

Tabby: OMG!!

Surprise ripples over me like the waves hugging the shore. I can't quite believe someone wants to buy my flat. I can't quite believe that some day Mark's and my ground-floor space, on the corner of a pretty street, will no longer be the place I call home. I can't put my finger on how it makes me feel. I'm excited, I think. But I'm also nervous and unsure. My life is changing so quickly. For years I wrote New Year's resolutions hoping to change my life. And ironically, now, New Year's resolutions seem to be the only the only fragment of my old life remaining. They may not solve any problems, but they are me and I am them and I am more determined than ever to cling to them.

Avery: You should celebrate.

I send her another picture of my near-empty cocktail glass.

Tabby: On it 🍸 🍸

Avery: Have you told Scott? What did he say?

Tabby: He's at the bar. I'll tell him when he gets back.

I crane my neck and pick out Scott's floral Magnum PI shirt among the group of equally awful shirts queuing for drinks at the beach hut bar.

Avery: What's the story with you two? Have you shagged him silly ways yet?

...

Tabby is typing

...

Avery: Oh my God you have. I bloody knew it. Everyone has sex in Ibiza!!!

Tabby: Not me.

Avery: What are you waiting for? Your flight isn't for another few hours. There's still time to hop on him.

Tabby: 😳😂

Avery: Sex is the best way in the universe to celebrate. Technically you have to do it otherwise the universe will know and your flat won't sell. Don't piss off the universe.

Tabby: See you soon xx

Avery: Not if you're too busy shagging and miss your flight.

Go. Hop! Hop! Hop! 🐰🐰

Scott returns from the beach hut with a beer and another cocktail for me just as I drain my glass. He takes my empty glass and twists it into the sand at the end of my sun lounger.

'That's impressive, Ms Greenwood,' he says, standing back to observe.

I crane my neck to peer over my toes and over the end of my sun lounger at the row of empty glasses lined up.

'You certainly know how to make a point,' he says, flopping onto the lounger next to me. 'I will never doubt your ability to day-drink ever again.'

I raise my glass to my lips and sip on the lime-green liquid. I decide green is nicer than blue and pink but not as nice as red.

'My sister said she'd drop us to the airport. Save us taxi fare,' Scott says. 'Her shift finishes at four so we can leave then.'

I glance at my watch. It's almost one.

'You okay?' he asks.

'Yeah. I think so.'

'You look like you've seen a ghost.'

'Someone wants to buy my flat.'

'What? Holy shit, that's fantastic. I'm so happy for you,' Scott says. 'Does Avery know?'

'She's the one who told me.'

'You two are talking again?'

'I think we are.'

Scott takes a mouthful of beer and smiles as if it's the best-tasting beer he's ever had. 'That's great. Balance has been restored to the universe at last.'

'What did you just say?'

Scott shrugs and shifts around in his sun lounger trying to find that sweet spot to relax. 'Balance has been restored. The stars have aligned, yada, yada, yada.' He lowers his beer and shakes his head. 'What? You're looking at me like I'm crazy. I saw it on a documentary. Scientists say it's a real thing. Keep the universe balanced and life just sort of stays on track.'

'You know, you really need to spend more time with my sister. I think you'd totally get along.'

Scott nods and sips beer. 'We could all go out when we get home. Celebrate your good news.'

Avery's words play on repeat in my head. *Everyone has sex in Ibiza.* I close my eyes and try to block them out. The sun lounger spins. My head spins. My stomach spins. There is way too much spinning. But I keep my eyes closed and go with it because I know it's just the booze. When the rum and vodka and whatever that green syrup stuff is wears off, I'll be steady again. I don't know about the universe being in balance, but for now my life finally seems to be changing. And as tempting as it may be, I don't need the *sex in Ibiza* club throwing me off course.

FORTY-EIGHT

SEPTEMBER

The little black dress is so last year! How about a red one?

I nearly break my neck trying to get out of work on time, but nevertheless I'm running late and I practise my apologies on the bus on the way. When I arrive, for a moment I think I've missed my stop. I do a double-take and realise that Flaherty's Pub is under new ownership. The gaudy, light-up TIME FOR GUIN-NESS sign is gone and the whole building has been repainted in cool cream and warm teal. I never noticed what a commanding building it is before, but its facelift has changed the entire façade of the street. It's funny how a makeover, however subtle, can change a person or place. I think about my hair that's calling out for a root touch-up now and my revamped flat that will soon belong to someone else. I decide I like change, or I'm okay with it, at least. And I look forward to seeing what old Flaherty's looks like inside.

Inside, I'm deflated to find that new Flaherty's looks exactly like old Flaherty's. Mismatched chairs dotted haphazardly around tables. Two lonely chairs at some of the tables, five chairs fighting for space around others. The ruby-red carpet is worn to a pale pink and threadbare in patches and a horseshoe-shaped bar takes pride at the centre, overseeing it all. It smells of stout and mashed potatoes. The familiar smells of Saturday afternoons frittered away here over the years, watching rugby with Mark.

Tonight the place is packed as people enjoy a carvery dinner and a GAA game on the big screen. I glance at the telly as players chase a sliotar with their hurl. Kilkenny versus Dublin, I see, from the colour of the jerseys. The spectators in the bar are decked out in matching attire. There are at least three sky-blue Dublin jerseys for every single black-and-yellow Kilkenny one. A crowd of twenty-somethings yelling 'up the Dubs' every so often drown out all other cheering and, occasionally, the commentary on the TV too.

I lap the bar a couple of times trying to find Avery and Becca or Scott. I finally spot Avery and Becca in a booth at the back, thankfully away from the telly and, hopefully, the noise. They're kissing and cuddling and it almost feels as if joining them would be intruding. But Becca spots me and waves. Avery waves too as soon as she notices me.

'So loud in here,' I say, covering my ears.

'The all-Ireland semi-final is on,' Becca says.

'Kilkenny are kicking our arses,' Avery adds, rolling her eyes. 'Bastards.'

I laugh. I don't think I've ever seen Avery watch a game before but she and Becca are kitted out in matching blue jerseys, fitting right in. Meanwhile my skinny jeans, oversized floral blouse and wedges stand out like a sore thumb.

Scott arrives moments later. I'm glad to see he's wearing regular clothes too, complete with a bourguignon stain on his pale pink t-shirt.

'What did I miss?' he asks.

'We're losing,' Avery tells him.

Scott looks confused for a moment before he glances over his shoulder to seek out the TV screen.

'Well, I'm not,' he says. 'I'm from Kildare and we never feckin' win anything so...'

'Speaking of winning, what did you think of this month's resolution?' Avery asks, poking my shoulder.

Before I have time to answer the game ends. Kilkenny have won by an embarrassing number of points and there's lots of booing, some cheering and plenty of cursing. And quickly, as if it's a choreographed routine, people get up from their tables, slip on their hoodies or jackets and begin to leave.

I like the quieter atmosphere better as we drink and laugh and chat. As I suspected, Avery and Scott get along famously and watching them enjoy each other's company is wonderful and refreshing.

'Right, the suspense is killing me,' Scott says, turning towards me, once he and Avery have caught their breath after laughing for much too long at one of his terrible dad jokes. 'It's September fifth and you haven't said a word about this month's resolution yet.'

'Have I not?'

'No. You haven't,' Avery says.

'Are you excited?' Becca asks, and I can tell she is.

'Sure.' I shrug. 'I don't wear dresses much. But I'm getting good at this whole trying-something-new thing.'

'You haven't a clue what the dress is for, do you?' Avery says.

She crosses her legs and bounces her top leg, shaking the bench we share. I glance at Becca, hoping for a clue. But she shakes her head, graciously remaining button-lipped so Avery can lead the conversation.

'A red dress,' Avery says, making a strange face with her eyes wide and her head jutting forward. 'Red.'

I nod. 'Red. Yes. Okay. I like red.'

Avery rolls her eyes. 'It doesn't matter if you like it or not, jeez. The colour is a clue. Red is a clue. C'mon, Tabby, can't you at least try to guess?'

'Guess what?'

'Oh, for God's sake.' Avery throws her hands over her head. 'You're bloody useless at this. Scott, tell her.'

'Don't look at me,' Scott says. 'I haven't a clue where you're going with this.'

'Think the Oscars. Except for food...' Becca says, drawing an invisible circle in the air as if she's encouraging the cogs in my brain to turn.

I stare back, blankly.

'Ah here,' Avery says, folding her arms and puffing out as if she's a teacher disappointed that her naughty pupils have failed another test. 'It's for the Little Red Book awards.'

'No way,' Scott says, almost knocking over his pint with excitement. 'How on earth did you get tickets? They're like gold dust.'

'Not if you're up for an award, they're not,' Avery says, smiling towards me. 'La Bella Vita has been shortlisted in the best pastries category.'

'Are you serious?' I'm barely able to catch my breath. 'Oh my God. Oh my God.'

'Yup. And you're totally going to win too,' Avery says. 'The food Oscar is in the bag.'

'Ah, food Oscar. I get it,' I say turning towards Becca, who seems pleased that I've finally caught on.

'Avery explained what a big deal the Little Red book awards are,' Becca says. 'I'm so excited for you, Tabby. No one deserves it more. You work so hard.'

'It is. It is. Only the top eateries in the country get their names in the book. Well, get their names on the website. It's all online now. But back in the day it was an actual book. But it's still as big a deal as ever to be included. Bigger maybe,' I explain, so quickly and excitedly I make myself breathless.

'Hang on...' Scott says, counting dates on his fingers. 'Nominations for the Red Book Awards open in March with the shortlist published in August, right?'

'Right,' Avery says.

'But you wrote this red dress resolution all the way back in January. How did you know La Bella Vita would make the shortlist back then?'

'I just knew.' Avery winks and knocks her shoulder gently against mine. 'But to be fair, I also thought Tabby would put two and two together when she saw the resolutions, so I'm not always right.'

'Avery, this is huge,' I say. 'I don't know what to say.'

'Ah, it's no big deal. I set a reminder in my phone to apply in March, as soon as the competition opened. And they said they'd send an anonymous judge to eat in La Bella Vita some time in May or June. I didn't tell you because if you were expecting them, you'd probably have shat yourself, you know what you're like.'

There's so much more to it than that, and I wonder if Avery knows I'm familiar with the complicated application process. Mark applied several times over the years and La Bella Vita never made it past the preliminary rounds.

'To be honest, I'd forgotten about it,' Avery says. 'Until the committee wrote to me early last month to let me know you'd made the final cut. Normally it would kill me trying to hold in news like that in, but we weren't talking so it was grand.'

I laugh. 'I'm glad us not talking made it easier for you.'

'Ah yeah, it definitely did,' Avery says, missing my sarcasm.

'So we're going shopping then?' Becca asks.

'Hell yeah,' I say. 'I have a little red dress to buy.'

I wrap my arms round Avery and kiss her cheek.

'Thank you. Thank you so much.' I say. 'I love you.'

'Love me enough to try karaoke?'

'Definitely not that much.'

'Oh, c'mon,' Scott says, getting to his feet and reaching for my hand. 'Karaoke is a laugh.'

'No,' I bark, folding my arms. 'Karaoke is everyone laughing at you.'

'They're not laughing at you. They're laughing with you. The worse you are, the funnier it is.'

I'm not convinced. 'You do it then,' I say.

Scott shrugs. 'You really won't join me?'

'Not in a million years.'

Scott makes his way towards the front of the pub and the big screen switches from after-game commentary to chunky, bold font on a bright blue background. Someone passes Scott a microphone and when he taps it there's a loud *thud, thud* sound, calling everyone's attention.

'Evening, folks,' Scott says. 'I'd like to dedicate this song to my friend Tabby. The best baker in Dublin. And soon she'll have an award to prove it.'

Scott points and heads turn to look at me. And, although my face feels hot and my cheeks are no doubt red, I'm not embarrassed.

'Wait. Wait,' I say, hopping to my feet and racing past tables to join him.

His smile is bright and encouraging as he places the microphone between us and the music begins. We start singing 'Living on a Prayer' on the wrong beat. Our voices are like nails on chalkboard as we sway on the spot. Scott holds the microphone in one hand and waves his other arm over and back above his head as enthusiastically as if he's at the best rock concert of his life. Within minutes most of the pub has joined in, and we all murder a Bon Jovi classic, and laugh and laugh.

FORTY-NINE

On a slightly chilly autumn morning Avery, Becca and I sit on a low wall across the road from Buttons and Bows, a corner boutique, and sip hot chocolate. Fashion isn't really my thing and Avery's taste is much too eccentric for me, so this ornate-appearing boutique was Becca's suggestion.

The shop doesn't open for another ten minutes and I can't feel the tips of my toes anymore. I would have happily ordered a dress online, as I usually do. But, last week over lunch, Becca said, 'I'm so excited to be part of a resolution at last.'

Avery took her hand and kissed it, saying. 'Me too. I'm crazy excited too. Are you excited, Tabs?'

And I said, 'Yes. Yes. I really am.'

It's true. I am. I'm grateful and happy. Grateful that Avery nominated La Bella Vita for such a prestigious award and happy that the tension between her and me finally feels gone. I knew the moment I told Avery about Mark and Saoirse's baby and she joked about how Mark's nose would look on a newborn that we were fine. We were better than fine. We were us again. No one except my wonderful, colourful, bright sister could make me belly-laugh about my dead fiancé fathering a baby with a woman I didn't know existed a year ago. But, oh how we laughed. Avery even snorted. I did too.

Becca seems relieved that Avery and I are back on track too. And I think this shopping trip is less about the perfect dress and more about the perfect day. All three of us spending time together. As a family. Gentle encouragement from Becca that I'm not losing a sister, I'm gaining another.

'I hope you find a dress you love,' Becca says, between mouthfuls of hot chocolate. 'They really have some fab stuff in here.'

'They do,' Avery adds. 'I heard Beyoncé got her dress for the Grammys here.'

'Really?' I say, sarcastically. 'Beyoncé shops on St Francis Street now, does she?'

'She does.' Avery nods with stubborn conviction. 'Honest to God. It's true. She probably shops in a disguise or something. S'pose you'd have to if you were that famous. Imagine if we bumped into her today. Wouldn't that be mad?'

'How would we know it's her?' Becca asks.

'Everyone knows her,' Avery says, her eyes wide and sparkling as if a day with Beyoncé waits for us on the other side of Buttons and Bows' front door.

'But if she's in a disguise...' I say.

A marshmallow sticks to Avery's front teeth and I watch as she tries to free it with her tongue. It's hard not to laugh, but Becca steers the conversation away from A-list celebrities and on to updates about my flat sale.

The buyers are a retired couple. They used to live in Dublin, years ago, but they moved down the country when their kids were small. Their kids are all grown up now so they're downsizing and moving back to the city. They want something cosy and central and my flat is the perfect fit.

Avery frees the marshmallow, swallows it and joins the conversation.

'That's just the circle of life,' she says. 'You move away to find yourself, chase your dreams, make your money, that sort of thing. But people almost always end up coming back to where they started.'

'I don't ever want to go back to where I started,' I say as I shake my head and think about the resolutions. I'm reminded that they are the reason I'm here right now with a warm paper cup in my hand, a bright smile on my face and butterflies in my stomach. Deeper in my mind are the emotions that come with completing each one. Each resolution feels like my personal Everest and I've never been higher. I don't want to climb back down. Ever.

The light comes on inside Buttons and Bows and we hop off the wall, throw our empty cups in the bin and make our way across the busy road. Inside smells of peaches and vanilla and everything is cream or white. The plush carpet, the walls, the cash desk. Mark would love this place, I think, almost afraid to touch anything in case I leave a stain. And when the glamorous sales assistant glides my way with swishing hips and says, 'Good morning, Ms Greenwood,' I suspect I won't be able to afford a thing in here.

'Morning,' I say, regretting my hot chocolate as it starts to repeat on me.

'I'm Siobhán and I will be your assistant. We have you for an hour this morning, is that right?'

I look from Avery to Becca, unsure.

'It's fittings by appointment only here,' Becca explains.

'We're usually booked up for months in advance,' Siobhán says with a casual shrug. 'But how could I say no to Becca?'

'Siobhán was a client of mine last year,' Becca says.

'Becca helped me find this place,' Siobhán says, turning on the spot and looking all around as if she's seeing her little boutique for the first time.

I nod.

'So what are we thinking?' Siobhán asks. 'Cap sleeve, puffy sleeve, no sleeve? Halter or sweetheart neckline? Fitted or flowy?'

'Eh... em... red,' I say.

'Of course,' Siobhán says with an enthusiastic clap of her hands. 'Let's try a few different styles and shades and I guarantee we'll find your perfect dress in no time.'

I try to catch Avery's attention to tell her that there's no way I can afford this place and maybe we should try Penneys instead, but Avery has already made herself comfortable on the kidney-shaped white couch and is sipping the complimentary prosecco, at 9 a.m.

In the changing room, I love every single dress I try on. Siobhán didn't ask my size but all the dresses she chooses fit like a glove. Some with sleeves, some without. Long, short, lacy, plain. Each more beautiful than the next – and all without a price tag.

'Oh my God. That's the one,' Avery says when I pull back the curtain of the changing room for an umpteenth time. 'Isn't that it?'

I spin on the spot, wearing a long-sleeved ruby dress with a corset bodice and full, swishing skirt.

'You look like a princess,' Avery tells me, and I feel like one too. 'You have to buy it.'

'It really is stunning on,' Becca says.

'How much is it?' I whisper.

'No charge,' Siobhán says. I didn't realise she was in earshot. My cheeks turn the colour of my gown. 'But perhaps you could give Buttons and Bows a shout-out on La Bella Vita's social media? And if you could mention us in your speech too, that would be fantastic.'

'My speech,' I say, suddenly feeling pressure.

'If you win. And if not, some photos on social media would be fine. Don't forget to tag us, of course.'

Becca nods, clearly well versed in the mutual back-patting that is Instagram shares and tags, and I wonder if I'll ever be as savvy a businesswoman as she and Siobhán are. I hope so.

'Great, Siobhán, thanks. But let's call it a loan? I'll borrow the dress for the event and return it after,' I say, confidently dipping my toes in the savvy businesswomen water.

'Oh no. Not at all. It's yours to keep,' Siobhán tells me with a dismissive wave of her hand. 'I can't resell a used dress anyway.'

I cringe and, as beautiful as the dress is, I can't wait to take it off and leave. In the changing room I struggle with the zipper and call Avery for some help.

'Damn thing is stuck,' she says, tugging.

She tugs harder and harder and my shoulders jerk back.

'Careful. Oh God, please be careful, if this thing rips—'

'Shh. Shh. Shh,' Avery says, cutting across me. 'You hear that? Someone's here.'

'What?'

'We're supposed to have the place to ourselves for another ten minutes,' Avery huffs.

Her inconvenienced expression is hilarious and I wonder if she knows I can see her in the mirror.

'It's grand. They're just a little early. We're finished now anyway,' I say, wriggling and trying desperately to set myself free.

'What? No. There's another glass of prosecco out there with my name on it.'

The zipper finally releases and I stand in my bra and knickers as the dress falls to the ground around my ankles.

'It's not even ten o'clock and you're on your third glass and —' I stop and listen, hardly believing my ears as I recognise the voice of the woman talking to Siobhán.

'I know what time it is,' Avery says, reaching for the curtain. 'It's free prosecco o'clock.'

'Wait,' I say, grabbing her hand and pulling her against me so roughly we both almost topple over.

'Jesus Christ. Fine. You can have the prosecco. No need to pull my bloody arm off,' Avery says, rubbing her shoulder as if I've actually hurt her.

'Shh,' I say, placing me finger over my lips and tilting my head towards the curtain. 'Do you hear that?'

'Told you someone was here.'

'It's Catherine,' I say. 'I'd recognise that voice anywhere.'

'No way.' Avery pulls the curtain back, revealing Catherine standing next to the couch and exposing me in my underwear. Thankfully, I snap the curtain shut again before anyone notices.

I scold Avery, and dress quickly, all while straining to listen as Catherine and Siobhán speak in hushed tones.

'So, yes, your dress finally came in yesterday,' Siobhán says. She's gushing, and I can't tell if it's over Catherine or the dress. 'And it looks even better in the flesh. I'm just finishing up with a customer now. Then we'll get you into a changing room. Can I get you some prosecco while you wait?'

'My bloody prosecco,' Avery says, pulling the curtain back again and marching forward.

'Oh hello,' Catherine says, as I race after Avery without time to tie the laces of my runners.

'Hi.' I grimace.

'This is a pleasant surprise,' Catherine says, glaring at Siobhán, determined to let her know she's inconvenienced by our presence.

I don't know what to say as I glance back at the beautiful gown that, in my hurry, I've left strewn on the changing room floor.

'If you'd like to take a seat, Mrs Buchanan, I'll be right with you,' Siobhán says.

Catherine checks her watch. I do the same. It's a couple of minutes past ten now. Our shopping window is technically over and we're clearly encroaching on Catherine's time. Without another word Catherine sits, crosses her legs and reaches for the glass of prosecco. Avery's face is a picture and I'm uncomfortable leaving her next to Catherine as Becca tilts her head towards the checkout desk and encourages us to approach together.

At the desk, Becca chats to me excitedly while we wait for Siobhán, but I'm not fully listening. My eyes are on Avery and Catherine, who seem to be deep in conversation. Avery's knees are bouncing slightly, but her upper body is straight and poised and I can tell that whatever Avery is saying, she's not simply making small talk. Catherine seems to be listening; she nods and occasionally smiles. But no matter how hard I strain I can't make out what they're saying.

'This is fantastic, thank you,' I hear Becca say, and my attention shifts back to the checkout desk.

Siobhán has arrived behind the desk. A white suit bag is draped over the countertop, zipped down slightly to reveal the neckline of the ruby dress I left on the floor now hanging inside. Becca takes out her phone and snaps some photos.

'Can you twist it to the right,' Becca says, taking a step back and holding her phone a fraction higher. 'I just want to get the Buttons and Bows logo in the shot.'

Siobhán rearranges the bag so the boutique's name, printed on the front of the bag, is visible.

'Perfect,' Becca says, stepping forward again to share her phone screen with Siobhán.

'Ah, brilliant. Looks great,' Siobhán says, zipping the bag up. Then she walks round from behind the desk to pass it to me. 'Can't wait to see you in this next week, Tabitha. I'm sure you'll be the belle of the ball.'

'Thank you.'

I take the bag, a little swamped by its size and awkward-to-carry shape.

'Oh, fuck off!'

Avery's outburst is loud and abrupt. When Siobhán, Becca and I turn to face the commotion, Avery is on her feet and Catherine is sitting crouched and vulnerable as if she's afraid of Avery. But I know Catherine isn't afraid of anyone.

'Go on, say it again,' Avery says, looking at Catherine but pointing at me. 'Say it to Tabby's face.'

The searing heat in my cheeks is instant, and I want to run out the door.

'Avery,' I say, my eyes pleading with her not to embarrass us any further.

'Catherine is here to collect a dress. A red bloody dress,' Avery says.

'For the Red Book Awards,' Catherine says, uncurling herself to look me in the eye.

I haven't seen Catherine since I found out about the nomination. I haven't had an opportunity to share the good news. I glance at Avery, wondering if she told her. Avery shrugs. And the heat in my face is beginning to sting.

'You heard,' I say.

'No thanks to you.' Catherine rolls her eyes. 'Thank God that Zoe girl you hired can't keep her mouth shut. She was bragging about the shortlist to some of the waiting staff. I quizzed her about it, of course, and she spilled the beans. I don't suppose you were ever planning to tell me?'

'Honestly, Catherine, it's not like that. I didn't even know Avery had nominated me and then—'

'Nominated La Bella Vita,' Catherine corrects with a strained smile.

I nod. 'Yes. La Bella Vita. But it's not really a work thing for me. It's all part of this personal journey, you see. It's something Avery is helping me with. I know that all sounds a bit—'

Catherine raises her hand into the air like a Garda signalling for traffic to stop.

'I've contacted the committee to fix the mix-up,' she says, exhaling sharply.

'Mix-up?'

'With the tickets. They didn't send me one.'

The sense of longing on Catherine's face breaks my heart. Mark's memory is entwined in La Bella Vita; understandably, Catherine would like to be included.

Avery shrugs. 'As I already explained, Mrs Buchanan, there's no mix-up. They asked me how many tickets I needed and I said four.' Avery holds up four fingers and as she tips each one, she assigns a name. 'Becca. Me. Tabby. Scott.'

'Scott Wilson?' Catherine's eyes widen. I can tell she didn't know we are still in touch.

'We've become friends,' I say, feeling an explanation is due.

'Right.' Catherine's shoulders push back and her neck juts forward. 'Well, as I already told your sister, I will attend the awards in Mark's place.'

Avery shakes her head, but I don't think Catherine is being unreasonable.

'Maybe you could get in touch with them, Avery,' I say. 'Let them know we need another ticket.'

'Tabb-byyy,' Avery says my name in that sing-song voice that used to drive me crazy when we were kids.

'Please.'

'Fine. But when Mrs Buchanan runs up on stage and steals all your thunder, don't say I didn't warn ya.'

I laugh and say, 'I really don't think...' but the serious expression on Catherine's face pierces my giggles like a pin popping a balloon.

Catherine gets to her feet and places her hand on my shoulder, consoling me as if Avery has just painted an accurate picture of the future.

'I would like to dedicate the award to Mark,' she says.

'And...' Avery says, and I realise that whatever Catherine is about to say Avery has already heard. I'm certain it's the reason for Avery's outburst. I brace myself for the impact.

'And...' I echo.

'And I think it's important that I go onstage to collect it.'

I'm pleasantly surprised by the reasonable request.

'Absolutely.' I bob my head several times. 'If we win, it would be lovely if we both—'

Catherine sighs. 'Actually, I think it would be more appropriate if I was alone.'

'See,' Avery says. 'This is why I asked for four tickets not five. Four! Thunder-stealer.'

Catherine ignores Avery and says, 'Tabby, sweetheart, I know you hate the spotlight. Remember that one time you sang karaoke?'

'Mark told you?'

'I'm trying to remember his exact words,' Catherine says, squinting as if trying to see the memory in the distance. 'Second-hand embarrassment... yes, that was it. He was so embarrassed by the whole fiasco he wasn't sure he could ever go back to that pub again, poor thing.'

Avery lunges forward and I yell, 'Stop,' before she can gouge Catherine's eyes out.

Catherine takes a step back and glares at Avery as if she's a wild animal that she's slightly afraid of. In the moment, I'm slightly afraid of what Avery might do too.

'I don't want to see you embarrass yourself. Not again,' Catherine says. 'I care about you too much for that, darling.'

'Care about La Bella Vita, you mean,' Avery snorts, stepping forward and forcing Catherine to take another step back. 'If you gave two shits about her, you'd leave her alone. Mark treated Tabby like crap while he was alive. I used to think you turned a blind eye cos he was your son. But you didn't have to. You never even saw it, cos you're just like him.'

Catherine looks as if she's been winded and needs someone to catch her, but I don't move.

'Oh, Tabitha, tell me this isn't how you feel. My Mark adored you. Worshipped the ground you walked on.'

'He did in his shite,' Avery says, and it's impressive that a voice so big and commanding can boom from such a small body.

'Avery, stop it. Please,' I say, as Becca and Siobhán look on, open-mouthed

'If La Bella Vita wins, Tabby is collecting the award. End of. It's her bloody bistro. You're not even a chef, for fuck's sake.'

'I own more than half,' Catherine says, like an indignant schoolchild.

'Tabby could buy you out. She has money now.'

I gasp as the idea explodes in my mind like a firework.

'Ha!' Catherine snorts.

'I'm serious,' Avery says, jamming her hands onto her hips. 'Tabby sold her flat so she has lots of money. More money than you.'

My face falls into my hands and there's a sharp pain my stomach as I wait for Catherine to explode. Instead, there is silence. When I finally look up Catherine is glaring at me. I recognise her expression. Mark looked at me with the same hurt and shock in the sea-blue eyes they share when I told him I wanted to break up.

'Is this true?' Catherine asks. 'Have you really sold Mark's flat?'

I nod.

'What about his stuff? His clothes and things?'

'I thought maybe I could give some stuff to charity. And of course, if there is anything you want, you're more than welcome...'

'All of it. I want all of it.' Catherine's voice cracks. 'Oh, Tabitha, what have you done?'

She wraps her arms round herself, folding herself inwards as she turns and walks towards the door.

'Mrs Buchanan,' Siobhán calls after her, 'What about your dress? Mrs Buchanan, wait. Please?'

Catherine doesn't listen. She charges out the door. I follow her, but as I reach the street she's getting into a taxi and they drive away.

FIFTY

'So, do you think she'll sell?' Avery asks, joining me as I stand on the quiet footpath.

I stare down the street and watch with a heavy heart as Catherine's taxi disappears round a corner.

'Why did you tell her about the flat?' I ask.

'Why *didn't* you?'

I take a deep breath.

'Are you afraid of her?'

'What? No. Of course not.'

'You know even if you'd told her sooner, nothing would be any different. She'd never have given you her blessing. Or worse, she'd have convinced you not to sell.'

'I know.'

'She's not a nice person, Tabs. She never has been.'

'I know that too. But I should have told her about the flat. She has a lot of memories of Mark there—'

'Mark isn't there anymore. And she still has her memories.'

'Yeah. Me too,' I say.

'Oh, Tabs.' Avery slides her arm round my waist and pulls

me close. I let my head fall onto her shoulder. 'Are you really going to give her all his stuff?'

'Yeah. Of course.'

'Even that watch you bought him for his thirtieth?'

'Even his watch,' I say, remembering how blown away Mark was when he opened the box.

'Jesus Tabs,' he'd said, staring inside with wide eyes, almost afraid to touch it. 'It's great. I mean, I'd have probably gone for a blue face not a black one, but this is still great. Thank you.'

'But it was so expensive,' Avery says.

'It was. I saved for ages because I wanted to get him something special. Something he could keep and cherish for ever. It's not mine to take back.'

'She doesn't have to know.'

I roll my eyes, but I'm smiling.

'I'm starving. Are you hungry?' Avery asks, and before I have time to answer she adds, 'Let's go for brunch. Somewhere with pancakes. I really want pancakes. And maple syrup. And blueberries. I want lots of blueberries.'

I'm still smiling as Avery skips back inside, no doubt to inform Becca of the pancake plan. Then my phone rings. Scott's name appears on the screen.

'Hello.'

'Hey.' He sounds groggy, almost sleepy.

I check my watch. It's 10.30. I'm surprised he's not in work.

'How are you?' he asks.

'Good. Just dress shopping.'

'Find anything nice?'

'Think so. It's a bit puffy but Avery and Becca like it so...' I trail off. I can tell he's not listening. 'Is everything okay? Is it work?'

'No, no, work is good.' The nuance in Scott's voice rattles me.

'But there is something wrong...'

'Erm... Saoirse had her baby this morning. A boy.'

'A boy.'

'She's calling him Marc,' Scott says, almost whispering. 'But spelled with a C instead of a K, apparently.'

'A boy.'

'I thought you'd want to know.'

'I do. Thank you. I'm happy for her.' My voice sounds strange, like it belongs to someone else.

I can hear Scott's deep inhale on the other end.

'I *am* happy for her. It's a new life.' Tears trickle down my cheeks. 'A little piece of Mark back in the world.'

I hear giggling behind me and I turn round to find Avery and Becca approaching, linked arm in arm.

'I have to go,' I say into the phone. 'Avery wants to go for pancakes.'

'You sure you're okay?'

'I'm sure. Call you later, yeah?'

'Yeah. Later.'

'Bye.'

'Bye.'

'Who was that?' Avery asks.

'Scott. He was calling to let me know Saoirse had her baby today. A boy called Marc. Marc with a C.'

'Can you spell Mark with a C?' Avery asks.

'I suppose you can spell it any way you want, can't you?'

'Well, no. If you spelled it B-E-N, then that would be very confusing.'

'Are you okay?' Becca asks.

'I think so. It's kind of nice to think there is a little Mark now. Maybe with his eyes or his chin.'

'Hopefully not his nose,' Avery says, squeezing hers. 'He had a bit of a honker, didn't he?'

'Does Catherine know?' Becca asks.

My breath catches. 'Catherine doesn't know about Saoirse.'

'So, she has absolutely no idea that she became a grand-mother today?' Becca says.

'No, I don't think so.'

My head is spinning. Moments ago, Catherine raced away consumed with fear. Losing the bricks and mortar of my flat meant losing another part of her son. Little did she know that at the same time a living, breathing part of Mark had joined the world. Babies bring such joy with their arrival, but I imagine Marc-with-a-C brings more than most.

FIFTY-ONE

OCTOBER

*Happy birthday, little sister. No baking your own cake this year.
You deserve a rest!*

I read October's resolution sitting on my couch surrounded by
countless cardboard boxes and I wish two things.

1. that I had time to rest.

   And

2. that Avery doesn't bake me a cake by herself.

   I knew packing up to move would be exhausting. Or at least
according to TV shows and movies it is. Usually, the protagonist
scurries around her flat in a flannel checked shirt, tracksuit
bottoms and a messy bun that seems to sit exactly centred on
the top of her head. My hair is still too short to twist into a bun
and I don't own a flannel shirt. As I pack up Mark's clothes, I'm
reminded that neither did he. Mark's blue-and-white pinstripe
shirts still smell of him and I hold each one to my face and

inhale before I fold it and place it in a box. Some, like his sky-blue shirt with a white collar, conjure an instant memory. The time we picnicked in the Phoenix Park and a baby deer got separated from her mother. I wanted to wait for the mother to come back, but Mark said she wouldn't return if we stayed. I lay awake most of that night thinking about the poor little thing and wondering if her mother came back for her. Mark said of course she did, because that's what parents do. They always come back for their kids. I have never wished that to be truer than I do now, as I so desperately wish Mark could come back for little Marc.

I lose track of time as I pack until, finally, somewhere between pants, jumpers and baseball caps, I fall asleep. I wake to knocking on my front door. Bright morning light streams in through the curtains I forgot to close last night and I rub my eyes and peel myself off the floor. My back is crumbled like an accordion and when I stretch it pops audibly.

'I'm too old for this shit,' I tell the spot where I slept as if it's a living thing that has somehow offended me.

Knocking turns to banging, loud and almost angry, and I huff as I open it, expecting to find Avery or maybe Scott. My breath catches when I find a man I don't know on the other side.

'Mornin',' he says chirpily as if he hasn't just tried to bang my door off its hinges with his bare hands.

I blink. It's offensively bright outside.

'I'm Kevin Sharp,' he says, pausing for me to recognise him. 'From Carpet King. We spoke on the phone yesterday.'

'Oh yes, of course. Come in. Please.'

I run my hand over my frizzy hair, embarrassed. The new owners want to have carpet fitted throughout. They asked Becca if they could send someone to measure up and Becca asked me. Kevin, the carpet king, called yesterday to arrange a time but it had gone completely out of my head. But he's here now with a takeaway coffee in his hand and a pencil tucked above his ear.

'Where do you want me to start?' he asks, pulling a measuring tape form his pocket.

'Wherever. Sorry the place is a bit of a mess,' I say, pointing to small selection of boxes packed and sealed in the hall.

'Ah don't worry about it. I'll work around it. When are you moving?'

'Not for another few weeks but it feels like there's so much to do, I want to get a head start.'

Kevin glances into an open, half-packed box. Inside are some of Mark's things. Thrillers he never read, a couple of bottles of aftershave and a folded leather jacket.

'I bet himself is no help.'

'Sorry?'

'We're just not good at that sort of thing.'

I stare blankly for a moment and then join Kevin's dots to realise he's talking about men. As a whole. As a different species.

'The missus boots me out the door when she's packing. And that's just suitcases for a holiday. Says she'll have it done in half the time without me. She's right too. I'd only get in her way.'

'Sounds convenient,' I say.

'Ah, look. I won't lie. Suits me just fine.'

I smile. At least he's honest. Chauvinistic but honest.

'I have my uses, mind.' He shakes his measuring tape. 'I bet himself will be the same when you're in the new place.' He stares into the box as if he'll find Mark hiding at the bottom. 'And if you're in need of carpet...'

'I haven't found somewhere to move to yet.'

'Cutting it a bit fine, aren't ya?'

'I might stay with my sister for a while, so...'

Kevin glances around at the boxes once more and then stops talking. I'm guessing he has now assumed a break-up, and I don't correct him. Especially since it's partially true.

'Right, best get on. Okay to work my way from room to room?' he asks.

'Yeah, that's fine. Leave the bedroom until last, please. I need to get dressed.'

'Sure. Grand. Sure. No bother,' he says, his eyes darting to the floor as if I'd just implied that I am naked instead of standing in front of him in an old tracksuit.

I offer Kevin some tea and I'm relieved when he declines and gets straight to work. I make myself a cup and take it into my bedroom. I'm tempted to flop into bed and grab a nap before I return to more bloody packing. But, even if there wasn't carpet royalty in my flat, I don't have time. My phone dances on the bedside table, vibrating as missed calls, emails and messages pile up. I've no doubt they're mostly updates from Zoe about work stuff. Nothing major, she's just a tad overzealous and likes to keep me informed. She hasn't quite got the hang of sieving the big stuff from the little stuff yet. I wonder if I will be able to take time off ever again. Really off. With my phone switched off and my racing mind switched off too. I hover my finger over the power button but I can't bring myself to press it. Instead, I check WhatsApp.

Zoe: Catherine's looking for you.

Catherine and I haven't spoken since the boutique, over a week ago. And she hasn't come in to work, either. I've compiled many text messages. But I deleted them all without sending.

Tabby: It's my week off.

I'm happy to remind Zoe as much as Catherine.

Zoe: She says it's urgent. Something about tickets? I don't think she's going to leave until she speaks to you.

Tabby: She has my number. And she knows where I live.

Zoe doesn't reply and that suits me fine. Catherine is fully aware that I take the first week in October off every year for my birthday. Mark's and my birthdays were days apart. The second and fourth respectively. Mark was exactly two years and two days older than me. We shared the celebration in the early years.

'It's so special,' Mark said when we first started dating. 'Something we share that other couples don't.'

It felt special. When either date fell close to the weekend we would book a couple of nights in a fancy hotel, just the two of us, and we'd savour each other's company and look forward to another year of growing older together. Over the years the cele-bration gradually felt less special and certainly less shared. Mark would insist that it was a joint party but his name was the only one on the cake. And the balloons would advertise his new age. Twenty-six. Twenty-seven. Twenty-eight. As the years rolled on my birthday gradually fell into the shadows. Avery remembered, of course. Always. And two days after Mark's party, as I cleaned up the flat while he nursed a hangover, Avery would stop by and we would bake a cake together and eat the whole thing while watching *The Notebook* for a one-millionth time. I doubt we'll do the same this year. Avery has Becca now. But I leave the old DVD on my bedside table, careful not to accidently pack it up, hopeful.

I finish packing the last of Mark's stuff and find Kevin in the bathroom to let him know the bedroom is free to measure up whenever he's ready. He nods and continues to run his measuring tape round the bath. I can't imagine why anyone would want carpet in their bathroom but I say nothing as I remind myself that soon this flat will no longer be mine and the new owners will put their own stamp on it.

I'm about to make a start on sitting-room packing when

there's a knock on the door. A gentle knock, nothing like Kevin's fist-pounding, and I know before I open it who's outside.

'Hey,' I say, swinging the door back, and as expected I find Scott on the other side.

'Hey,' he says, and he seems unusually shy, standing with his hands in his pockets and his shoulders rounded.

A sudden breeze whips by to inform us that winter is fast approaching. I step back to let him in but he doesn't budge and after a moment I realise he won't until I actually ask.

'Come in. Come in.'

Scott smiles and steps inside and I close the door. We meet Kevin in the hall as he leaves my bedroom. The look on Scott's face is priceless. Kevin smiles and his stiff upper lip softens as if he can finally relax now that another man is here.

'Right,' he says, as he shoves the measuring tape back in his pocket and tucks the pencil above his ear.

Scott's expression softens too as he catches on.

'All done,' Kevin adds. 'Thanks again for letting me in.'

'No problem,' I say, turning to open the front door again.

When I twist back Kevin shoves a business card at me, but he's looking at Scott as he says, 'Like I was saying earlier if you need any work done when you find a new place, we offer twenty per cent off to new customers so...'

'I'll keep it in mind,' I say.

'And good luck in the sister's place. I'd rather you than me, mate.' Kevin chuckles and pats Scott on the back as he leaves.

I close the door and Scott says, 'Who was that guy?'

I scrunch my nose. 'Ah, just someone Mark would have really got along with.'

'Right,' Scott says, seeing the picture I've painted of Mark's friends, and we both know there's no need to say more.

I lead us towards the kitchen.

'Day off?' I ask.

'Nah, just the morning off unfortunately.'

I sigh. Disappointed.

'Tea? Or coffee? Think I have some bikkies here too. Somewhere. If I can find them with all these damn boxes.'

'No. Thanks. I don't have long.'

'Okay. No bikkies.' I sit, getting the sense that bad news is coming. I hope he's not going to say he can't get time off to come to the Red Book Awards.

I don't want to go without him.

'I have something to show you,' he says, pulling out a chair next to me at the table.

He takes his phone from his pocket, places it face up on the table and slides it across to me. I stare at the picture of a cute baby. Red-faced and wrapped in a blue blanket.

'Marc,' I say.

'Saoirse sent it to me yesterday. He's just a couple of hours old in the photo.'

'He's beautiful.'

I stare at his cute button nose, nothing like Mark's. But he has Mark's eyebrows and chin.

'I didn't want to forward it to you. Felt a bit weird. But I thought you'd like to see him.'

I nod and choke back tears. I run my fingertip over the screen as if I can feel the silky softness of his newborn wrinkled skin.

'Does Saoirse know you're sharing this with me?'

'Yeah. And she's cool with it. She said she can send some more photos, if you like. As he gets bigger and stuff.'

I swallow hard, unsure. I'm so glad Scott is here showing me a photo of Mark's son. My heart is light and soars. But I'm not sure it could bear following the journey of little Marc's childhood.

Scott checks his watch and says, 'Crap. I gotta go.'

He reaches for his phone, pausing to look at me, and I nod, letting him know it's okay to take it.

'Could you do me a favour?' I ask as he stands.

'Sure.'

'Do you know where Saoirse lives?'

'Eh...'

'Don't worry. I don't want to go all weirdo stalker or anything.'

Scott doesn't seem so sure and I contemplate taking offence. Instead, I shake my head, sigh and re-ask my question. 'Do you know where she lives?'

He nods.

'Okay. Great. Can you give her something for me, please?'

'Eh...'

I don't wait for a reply. I hurry into my bedroom and pick up an old shoebox that I've left segregated from the other boxes next to the bed. When I return Scott is standing and waiting by the kitchen door, and I can tell the idea of being late for work is making him anxious. I really wish he liked his new job more and feel a pang of guilt.

Scott reaches his arms out and I pass him the light box with a Nike tick and a half-torn-away price tag on the side.

His eyes are full of questions but he just nods and says, 'I'll give this to her.'

Then, I walk him to the front door and he leaves. He could easily open it and peek inside but I doubt he will. Even if he did the stuff in there wouldn't mean much to him; but I'm certain it'll mean a lot to Saoirse.

Inside the old shoebox is the bottle of aftershave Scott accidently wore and the watch I gave Mark for his thirtieth birthday. Some day, maybe on Marc's own thirtieth birthday, Saoirse might like to pass the watch from father to son. Folded on top is a grey shirt with black buttons. Mark bought it last summer for a hiking trip in Kerry with the boys. A shirt seemed like an unusual choice for hiking but I didn't question it at the time. I was even more confused when I bumped into a couple of

Mark's friends in town that weekend. They tried to cover for him, of course. One of them even thought it was funny. Mark and I had a huge fight when he returned. I accused him of lying to me and he accused me of spying on him. We didn't speak for days after. Looking back, I knew. I didn't know her name, or even if there was a 'her'. But I did know it was the beginning of the end for us. And somewhere, deep down, I believe Mark knew it too. A break would be messy, but it was the only healthy option. Mark would never do it. He hated mess. And for a long time, I thought, neither would I. But as soon as I made a break-up my January resolution, as soon as I committed those words to paper, there was no going back. I wonder if the shirt is one of Saoirse's favourites. A memento of their getaway. I should hate this shirt. I should want to cut it up or set fire to it, or something equally dramatic. But all I want to do is give it to Saoirse. I've packed away countless shirts but none are as important as this one. This shirt is Mark. This shirt is a man who spent a weekend away with another woman. A man who made a baby with her. A man who told me I was fat and sometimes stupid. A man who was not right for me. I knew I had to let Mark go. But I wish so hard it wasn't this way. I wish I could rewind the years and replay them differently. I wish I was stronger sooner.

Finally, tucked in the sleeve of the shirt, I have enclosed a small yellow Post-it with a phone number written neatly across the front. Above it I have written, *Mark's mum's number x*

FIFTY-TWO

On Saturday, 4 October, the morning of my thirty-fourth birthday, I awake to the sound of my doorbell. I rub my eyes and check my phone, cursing under my breath when I discover it's not quite 7 a.m. yet. I swing my legs over the edge of the bed and my body takes a long time to follow. Finally, in slippers and a silk dressing gown that isn't warm enough for the changing weather, I drag myself towards the door.

I can hear the out-of-tune chorus of 'Happy Birthday' and I hurry, hoping to drag Avery inside before she wakes my neighbours. I'm startled to find Becca and Scott next to my teal-haired sister.

'Happy Birthday,' Avery shrieks, throwing her arms open and lunging towards me to envelop me in a bear hug.

'What's going on?' I say, peering over Avery's shoulder at the pink-and-purple polka dot cake box that Becca holds against her chest and the cluster of several helium balloons that Scott grips tightly. They're rainbow-coloured and some proudly advertise *Happy Birthday* in swirly silver font and others simply display two digits. 3 and 4.

'Becca's in work at nine, and Scott has to be gone around the same time, so we have less than two hours to have the best party ever,' Avery says, punching the air as she adds, 'Whoop! Whoop!'

'Sorry. She made me do this,' Becca says, smiling.

I laugh. 'And what's your excuse?' I ask, my eyes meeting Scott's.

'Avery said there'd be cake.' He shrugs. 'She also said she'd kick my arse if I didn't come and I believed her.'

Becca and I both nod. Because she would.

Inside, I make tea and coffee and we sit round the kitchen table tucking into a delicious lemon drizzle cake that thankfully Avery has shop-bought instead of baking. We chat and chat. Mostly about mundane things like work, shitty commutes, flat prices and selfish birds that won't sit still long enough to be painted. And all the while I smile because it's the loveliest birthday party I've ever had.

All too soon Becca and Scott have to leave for work.

Becca kisses my cheek and says, 'Good luck with the rest of the packing. Don't let Avery get Sellotape stuck to her lip the way she usually does.'

I nod, wishing I could promise, but it's highly likely that Avery will do just that at some point when my back is turned.

Scott copies her and kisses my cheek too, lingering for a moment. I hold my breath and don't want to pull away. But he straightens and says, 'Happy birthday, Tabitha.'

'Thank you.'

Later, after Avery and I watch *The Notebook* and cry as always, we sit cuddled together on the couch. We order pizza and wash it down with Diet Coke and polish the remaining cake off too. I stay in my pyjamas because Avery says birthdays should be jammies days and I agree.

'Have you heard from Catherine recently?' Avery asks, catching me off guard as I scoop the last of the zesty lemon icing into my mouth.

'Eh, yeah. I texted her two days ago—'

'For Mark's birthday,' Avery finishes for me.

I swallow hard. 'I thought she should know I was thinking of him... thinking of her.'

'Did she reply?'

'She did.'

Avery doesn't hide her surprise; if anything she exaggerates it, pulling a face as she asks, 'What did she say?'

'She said she got a ticket for the Red Book Awards.'

'That's it? That's all she said?'

'That's all she said.'

'Has she texted you today?'

'For my birthday?'

Avery nods.

I sigh and shake my head. 'No. And I'm not expecting her to. She never has before.'

'Maybe she always thought Mark would pass on her best wishes.'

'Maybe.'

Avery and I both know that's not true. But, perhaps because it's my birthday, or perhaps because we're both exhausted from a long, lovely day, we don't say another word as we pretend that it is.

FIFTY-THREE

It's so much harder than I thought it would be to pack the last of Mark's things. Every boxed-up saucepan or wooden spoon, every soap tray or shower gel feels like reaching a final chapter in a book and all the pages are stuck together so I can never read it. It wasn't the best book ever. There were some dark and difficult chapters. But there were some wonderful and enjoyable ones too. And, without doubt, it is heartbreaking to realise I've finally reached *The End*.

The last item to pack up is a t-shirt. A simple, round-neck grey t-shirt. Nothing fancy to look at. The smell of Mark is gone, washed away and replaced with the faint hint of clean-linen-scented fabric softener. But nonetheless I can't seem to let it go. Mark wore this t-shirt that last time we made love. It was months before New Year's Eve, some time in the summer, I think. He'd just come in from the gym all sweaty and red-faced. He dashed straight into the shower and retuned with his hair still wet and wearing old, navy tracksuit bottoms and this t-shirt. We cooked together that night. Fajitas, I remember. I chopped peppers and onions while he fried chicken and I sang along to an Ed Sheeran classic playing on the radio. I was out of tune and forgot most of the words but Mark didn't criticise. We ate, drank wine and made love twice on the couch. I was happy that night. So happy. I cradle the t-shirt like a baby as silent tears trickle down my cheeks. It's quite a while before I'm ready to face the box again, and when I do I set the t-shirt aside as I seal it up with lots and lots of sticky tape. Later, I tuck the t-shirt under my pillow and sleep well.

A blink later it's morning. Becca is at my flat just after 8 a.m. We pack the boxes neatly into the back of her car and she asks me over and over if I'm okay. And I lie and tell her that I am.

An hour and a half later we're driving through the Wicklow countryside and every so often Becca says, 'Are you sure we're going the right way? This doesn't seem like the right way.'

'It's the right way. Trust me, Ballynaffin isn't somewhere you ever forget.'

'Okay,' Becca says, her accent a little thicker than usual, emphasising her uncertainty.

'Next left,' I say, contradicting the satnav as the mountains come into view.

Becca doesn't argue as she turns left onto an even narrower road. High above a valley, we wind around bend after bend until finally the familiar sight of Ballynaffin village comes into view. Becca's eyes widen as she takes in the view of multi-coloured cottages with baskets of heather and winter pansies dotted outside each one.

'Left again,' I say, my ribcage pressing against the seatbelt as my deep breathing fills my chest up. 'The house is just up this road.' I point and Becca stares ahead as if she'll find Catherine's house, the house Mark grew up in, on the horizon.

Becca seems reluctant to leave the sleepy village behind as the sounds of sheep and farm machinery beckon in the distance, but cautiously she drives on. Her knuckles whiten as she grips the steering wheel.

'This is it,' I say when a small farm gate appears, tucked between bramble bushes.

Becca turns in and the colour slowly returns to her knuckles. The sound of wheels rolling over loose driveway stones announces our arrival and Catherine hurries outside before we are out of the car. Her floral apron, sprawling silver hair and flour-dusted cheeks surprise me.

'Oh, good Lord,' she says, wiping her face frantically as Becca's and my feet crunch against the stones. 'I forgot you were coming.'

I believe her and I apologise for startling her.

'Come in. Come in,' she says, leading the way as she reaches her hands round her back to untie her apron strings.

The smell of freshly baked bread and melting butter greet us at the door and make my mouth water.

'Omigod, yum,' Becca whispers.

Overhearing her, Catherine says, 'You'll stay for lunch, won't you? Or do you have to rush away as usual?'

'We'd love to stay,' I say.

'Oh.' Catherine makes a face. 'Well, this is a surprise.'

We reach the kitchen and, in silence, Catherine sweeps her hand through the air and towards the table and I think it means she wants us to sit. I sit first and Becca copies. There's no talking as Catherine fills two bowls of soup from the large pot on the stove and places them, and a platter of brown bread, on the table in front of Becca and me. Without a bowl for herself, she pulls out a chair and sits down. I stare at the blank space in front of her.

'I'll eat later with family,' she says, reminding me very clearly that I am very much not, and never have been, considered a part of the Buchanan tribe.

The root vegetable soup is delicious, as is the brown bread, but I find it difficult to eat as I choke on stilted conversation. I wish Avery was here to break the glacier-like ice. Becca tries to help, but she's not acquainted with Catherine and it's all painfully awkward.

Finally, when I can't take it anymore, I say, 'We should get the boxes.'

Catherine nods, then stands and takes our dishes to the sink.

'There's quite a few,' I say. 'Where should we put them?'

'Mark's room, of course,' she says as if I've asked a painfully stupid question.

Becca and I unpack the car boot and begin moving the boxes inside. Some are light and easy to manoeuvre. Other are heavy and hurt our backs as we share the load between us. The final box is the largest and heaviest. I take the front, shuffling backward as Becca holds the other end and follows my lead. Catherine stands in the doorway of the bedroom at the end of a long corridor. She barks instructions like a frustrated foreman on a construction site.

'Put this one here. Put that one there,' she says, pointing to the corners.

It's only when the last box is stacked that I finally pause to look around. Mark's bedroom hasn't changed in two decades and the time-hop startles me. The ghost of a teenage life gone by is forever encapsulated. The wall above the single bed proudly sports a Wicklow GAA poster. The colours have aged, faded by the sun, and the sticky tape on all four corners is peeling. The carpet is deep blue, as are the curtains. The walls are just a couple of shades lighter. I wonder if blue was Mark's favourite colour as a teenager. I don't know his favourite colour as a man or if he even had one. My eyes are drawn to the line of trophies on the small desk under the window. They vary in size but they are all gold. *Best Player. Rising Star. 1st. 1st. 1st.* I pick one up and blow away the dust gathering at the base. Catherine takes it from me, polishes it off with the sleeve of her blouse and sets it back down. She picks up another and begins dusting and polishing it and I wonder how often she comes in here, to complete the mundane chore.

'Did you know Mark was seeing someone else?' she blurts as she runs her hand over the largest of the trophies, as if the swirly gold top can reassure her that her son was a champion and not a cheater.

The dust catches in my throat and I begin to cough. Catherine watches me with enquiring eyes and waits for me to reset my breathing.

When I stop coughing, I expect Catherine to ask the question again but instead she says, 'She called me. That girl. The one he'd been seeing. All of a sudden and out of the blue she called. She said her name is Saoirse.'

'Yes. That's her.'

'Did you know her?'

Catherine's voice wobbles slightly. Perhaps it's the realisation that her perfect son wasn't quite so perfect after all; that I wasn't always the villain, no matter how he liked to tell the story.

'I only found out about Saoirse after Mark died,' I say.

'After he died.' Catherine lets go of the trophy and clutches her chest as if she is hearing for the first time that Mark is gone. 'But it must have been going on for a while. Long enough to make a baby.'

'Yeah. I guess so.'

Catherine looks at me with weary eyes, and at first I think it's her usual disdain or disgust with me that she never bothers to hide. But slowly I realise this expression is different – it's pity. And it's so much worse.

It's the same look Avery and Becca gave me when I told them about Marc's arrival. It's the way Scott looked at me when I told him about the bracelet. I see it in the eyes of the staff at work too. People feel sorry for me because I have a broken heart. But these past few weeks I've realised that their glances and looks and whispers are all misplaced. My heart is heavy but it is not broken. It's battered and bruised but it is not broken. Mark's death didn't break my heart. And I have to live with that guilt every single day.

'It's Mark's baby,' I say at last, confirming what Catherine so obviously and so desperately wants to be true.

Catherine swallows hard and I see the lump make it way down.

'A baby. A tiny little baby,' she says.

'Your grandson.'

'Yes. Yes. My grandbaby. Mark's baby.'

Catherine's euphoria is palpable and I smile, happy for her. If we were two different people, I would reach out to her and hug her. But I can't hug Catherine. Not even today.

'Have you seen him?' she asks.

'I've seen a photo.'

'A photo,' she says, as if she's in awe of the idea.

'He has Mark's eyes.'

Catherine beams. 'Can I see?'

I shake my head. 'I don't have it. I saw it on Sc— on a mutual friend's phone.'

Catherine sighs, disappointed. 'Not to worry. I'm meeting them next week.'

'Oh,' I say. I'm surprised but I don't know why. It makes perfect sense for a grandmother to meet her grandson.

'I'll take lots of photos then,' Catherine continues. 'I'll bring them into La Bella Vita to show you.'

As my once-upon-a-time-almost-nearly mother-in-law smiles at me, I feel the twinge of desperation to escape this life completely. To untie myself from the Buchanan family strings. To separate my future from this complicated past. 'I'd rather not see any more photos of the baby,' I say.

Catherine's eyes widen. But I don't backtrack. I am firm on my decision that I do not want Mark's son in my life, nor do I want to be in his, and that includes swooning over cute newborn photos.

'Right. Well, I suppose when you're not a mother yourself you don't understand how precious these early weeks are,' Catherine says, folding her arms.

Her loaded remark doesn't have the same effect as usual and when I roll my eyes I'm sure she notices.

'Have you thought any more about selling your share of La Bella Vita?' I ask, and Becca's mouth gapes, surprised I've chosen this moment, wedged between Mark's trophies and twenty-year-old curtains, to go there.

'My God.' Catherine tucks her folded arms tighter against her chest and inhales sharply. 'You and that sister of yours just can't wait to push me out the door.'

I try not to let the exasperation in her tone throw me as I say, 'With the baby now, you'll probably want more free time.'

'I'll decide for myself what I want, thank you very much. But, you did the right thing putting that girl in touch' –

'Saoirse,' I say.

Catherine ignores me – 'but passing on a phone number doesn't entitle you to half a business. More than half.'

I wonder what else Saoirse told her. Did she tell Catherine about the box I gave her, and all the things I placed inside? Or did she mention that Scott and I met her for coffee before the baby was born? I hope not.

'I don't feel entitled to Mark's share of our bistro,' I say. 'As I said before, If you want to sell I would be more than happy to pay market value—'

'If! *If*... I want to sell,' Catherine interrupts me. 'I don't. And I don't want to discuss this again.'

'We better get going,' Becca says, and I nod. The tension has reached boiling point.

I sigh and say, 'Thank you for lunch.'

'Yes. Yes.' Catherine waves her arms, shooing us like a pair of unwelcome flies.

Outside, Becca sits into the car first. As I open my door Catherine takes my hand, squeezes gently and says, 'I'll send you some photos of the baby.'

I slowly slide my hand away, sit into the car and close the door with a bang. Becca places her hand on my shoulder and shakes her head.

'That woman,' she says, twitching her lips to one side. 'Wow.'

The engine purrs to life and loose driveway stones crackle like Rice Krispies in fresh milk as we roll forward. An angry grey cloud bursts overhead just as we drive through Ballynaffin village and the pitter-patter of heavy raindrops falling on the car roof soothes my racing mind. I glance in the side mirror as we leave the flower boxes, terraced cottages and rolling hills behind us. There's something oddly liberating about leaving this place. Something about leaving the boxes of Mark's things back in his family home where they seem to fit and belong so effortlessly. Something about leaving Catherine standing on her porch waving, her face full of excitement at the thought of meeting her grandson. Something about knowing I might never be back as we leave behind bendy, tricky-to-navigate roads and rejoin the busy motorway leading us home.

FIFTY-FOUR

Every day for a week I wake up to a message from Catherine on my phone. No words, just a picture of baby Marc in various cute babygros and poses. In his mother's arms. In his grand-mother's arms. Asleep in his bassinet. Occasionally, I type up a message telling Catherine how cute the baby is or how I see Mark in his eyes, but I never send it. Instead, each morning before I get out of bed, I delete the newest photo from my phone. But not until after I run my finger over my screen and marvel at how beautiful his tiny little face is and how much I wish Mark was here to meet his son.

I have stopped expecting to see Catherine in work. She doesn't text about orders or bookings or staff anymore. I've come to think of her as a silent partner and I like it that way.

I've taken today and tomorrow off work. Today so I can pamper and prepare for the party, and tomorrow so I can recover. Avery, Becca and Scott have all done likewise and the 'This Is In The Bag!' group chat that Avery created on What-sApp is full of messages, emojis of crossed fingers and four-leaf clovers and gifs of celebrities kissing Oscars. Zoe and Lyla and

all the staff at La Bella Vita have sent countless message of
support and wishes of luck too and their excitement is palpable.

Unfortunately, a day of pampering is much less relaxing
than I imagined. I cut my shin shaving my legs in the shower
and my hair seems determined to knot and frizz despite using
half a bottle of conditioner. I grow increasingly hot, flustered
and nervous and I curse Avery more than once for this damn
resolution.

With just minutes until Scott is due to arrive at the door, I
give myself the once-over in the mirror. My reflection stares
back. My hair has dried out sleek and shiny. It's finally reached
shoulder length again and I've returned to my more natural
mousy-brown colour. Black patent high heels offer some much-
desired height and the beautiful red dress from Buttons and
Bows hugs my waist and accentuates my curves in all the right
places. The mirror sees a woman ready to party. It doesn't
reflect the woman inside whose heart races and stomach somersaults. I run my hand over my hair as I remember that last time I
stood in this very spot all dressed up with a full face of make-up
and forced smile. The memory of New Year's Eve punches me
hard. So hard I bend forward in the middle and for a while I'm
not sure if I can straighten up again. But slowly, with some deep
breaths, I peel myself upright and look at the woman staring
back at me. She looks believably like she has her shit together. *I
can be her,* I think. I can keep it together. I have to.

I fetch my phone and snap a shot of my reflection. I take
several more photos, tilting and twisting the camera until I am
happy that I have a picture in which my dress appears full-
length. Then I scroll through the photo gallery on my phone to
find the photo of me in my work uniform that Zoe took a couple
of days ago. My hair is tucked completely into a net and my face
is make-up-free and a little pink from the heat in the kitchen.
This time last year I wouldn't have dreamed of posting a photo
of myself online. And certainly not one in my unflattering

uniform. I wouldn't have seen past my weight or the splashes of raspberry coulis to see the proud professional like I do today. I post both photos, side by side, on Instagram.

#TheRedBookAwards!
All scrubbed up! Wish La Bella Vita Luck 🍀

@Tom.Pearson64 Nice buns 😏
@L.Mac7 @Tom.Pearson64 Don't be gross. Don't mind him Tabitha Greenwood. You look great!
@Tom. Pearson64 @L.Mac7 I was talking about the buns on the shelf behind her in the kitchen FFS.
@L.Mac7 @Tom.Pearson64 Oops 😳😂
@Tom.Pearson64 @L.Mac7 her boobs look great too tho.
@L.Mac7 @Tom.Pearson64 😳

The comments make me smile and thankfully lift my mood. I stare in the mirror again and decide that my both my buns and my boobs do look good. I'm laughing to myself as the doorbell rings.

When I open it Scott is standing outside with a gigantic bouquet of red roses and a bright smile.

'Thank you,' I say, taking care not to let water from the damp stems drip onto my dress.

Scott follows me into the kitchen, where I search for the vase but eventually decide I must have packed it. I improvise by filling a large saucepan with water and placing the flowers in it. Scott smirks but he doesn't pass comment. I place the saucepan of flowers on the windowsill and stand back to admire them.

'I thought they'd be a good match for your dress,' he says.

'They are. They're almost the exact same red.'

'You look amazing, by the way,' he says.

I glance at the red roses, my red dress and my red nails and

I've no doubt my cheeks are growing red too as I say, 'Thank you.'

Outside, as we walk towards the bus stop, heads turn, their curiosity written on their faces.

A little girl points at us and asks her mother, 'Where are they going?'

'Somewhere fancy,' her mother tells her.

'Is she a princess?' the little girl asks.

'Yes. Tonight she is a princess.'

The mother and daughter pass by hand in hand. The little girl skips happily and says, 'I want to be a princess when I grow up too.'

It's cold at the bus stop. My teeth chatter as I look around at everyone else in puffy coats and woolly hats. Scott takes off his jacket and drapes it round my shoulders.

'Wow. You smell incredible,' he says.

'What?'

'You smell great.'

I shake my head.

'Did I say something wrong?' he says, shoving his hands into his pockets as he looks a little lost.

'I don't think I can do this,' I say.

'Do what?'

I run my hands over the silky fabric of my dress as my heart tries to pound right out of my chest.

'It was one of the last things Mark and I talked about,' I say. 'The smell of my perfume.'

I hear Scott's sharp inhale.

'He didn't like my perfume. I hated it too. I only wore it because his mother bought it for me for Christmas and I thought it would make him happy.'

Scott looks at me, confused. I don't blame him. I'm confused right now. Thirty seconds ago I felt like a beautiful princess, and now, because of stupid perfume, I want to run back to my flat, rip off this dress and tuck myself up in bed.

'It was the last nice thing he ever said to me. *You smell lovely.*'

A single, fat tear trickles down my cheek and Scott steps closer to catch it.

'You don't have to do this,' he says. 'If dressing up and going to a big fancy party is too much, you don't have to. We can stay home.'

I sweep my eyes over him from head to toe, taking in his ill-fitting shirt and unpolished shoes.

'We can stay home, order pizza and watch the whole thing online. There's a link for people who didn't get tickets. The entire event is being live-streamed,' he goes on.

I swallow hard. I didn't know that.

'And at least this way, we can skip the speeches.'

'What about Avery?' I say.

'She'll understand.'

I shake my head. 'She's gone to so much trouble.'

'You don't have to go,' Scott says. 'Not if you don't want to.'

I sniffle. I want to go. I do. And not because of a beautiful dress, or a resolution. I want to go because I've worked so hard for this.

'It's impossible to be happy, Tabs, if you don't give yourself permission to be. You're a princess tonight. I believe it. Avery believes it. That little girl believes it. Please allow yourself to believe it too.'

I roll onto my tiptoes and kiss Scott's cheek. He presses his fingertips against his cheek and smiling, he says, 'What was that for?'

I shrug. 'Just something princesses do.'

FIFTY-FIVE

'Holy shit, there's a red carpet. Did you know there'd be a red carpet?' I say, as we reach the large, granite steps of the convention centre.

Scott doesn't reply but the startled look on his face tells me he. Did. Not. Know.

'And press. Do you see all the photographers everywhere?' he says.

I link his arm tightly, as if I might topple to the ground without him. We make our way up the steps, pausing at the top to show our tickets and ID to a very stern-looking man in a suit and earpiece and with sunglasses despite the fact that it's getting dark.

'Good luck,' he says, as he smiles and waves us on.

'Where are you from?' someone shouts over my shoulder.

I turn to find a camera pointing and flashing.

'La Bella Vita,' I say, blinded.

'Have you a quote for *Food and Life* magazine?'

'Erm... erm... we're delighted to be here and we wish all our fellow nominees the very best of luck.'

'Nice, thanks.' The man lowers his camera and takes a small

notepad from his pocket and scribbles down my words. 'And you, sir,' he says, turning towards Scott. 'Anything you'd like to add or has your partner said it all?'

Scott doesn't correct the man's misconception about our relationship, working or otherwise. Instead, he pulls me closer and says, 'I think Tabby speaks for us both. It's a very exciting evening.'

'Lovely. Lovely,' the man says. 'Well, best of luck, folks. Enjoy yourselves.'

'Thanks. We will,' I say, as we turn away and finally enter the lobby.

Stylish red dresses and chic tuxedos dot the grand open space haphazardly like a giant game of chequers. Intimate groups of people chat and laugh, tossing their heads back, so full of joy and anticipation. Champagne flows and everyone holds a glass in their hand, whether they're sipping from it or not.

Within seconds, Avery has spotted us, and she races towards us with Becca in tow.

'Oh my bloody God, this place is unreal, isn't it?' she says, shoving a glass of bubbles into my hand.

Becca gives a glass to Scott too.

'It's something all right,' Scott says, still linking my arm.

'Are you here long?' I ask.

'No. Not really,' Avery says. 'We got here about ten minutes ahead of you. Just enough time to use the loo and grab some drinks.'

I nod as nerves fizz inside me.

'Speaking of the loo,' she continues. 'I overheard two women talking about La Bella Vita. They couldn't say enough good stuff. They actually thought I was you and they went on and on and on about bisque this and pomme-something-or-other that. Nothing in English, I'll tell you that. I thought I'd never get away from them.'

'I think they were judges,' Becca says.

'Really?' The nervous fizz in my stomach suddenly feels explosive.

A bell dings and slowly chatter and laughter turns to a low hum, followed by lots of shushing, and finally silence falls over the entire lobby.

Somewhere a commanding voice says, 'Ladies and gentlemen, thank you all for joining us at the fortieth annual Red Book Awards...'

Loud applause and some cheering erupts, filling every inch of space with noise and energy until it feels as if the roof might lift right off. It's a while before there is more shushing and the slow, inevitable fall back into silence.

The voice continues, 'If you would like to make your way through the doors behind me, dinner awaits. Good evening.'

I can't see the owner of the articulate voice, lost somewhere in the sea of red and black chequers, but I can see the large double doors as they draw back and we are swept up in the wave of people ushering forward.

'That's us. That's us,' Avery shouts, sloshing some champagne over the edge of her glass as she points towards a large, round table near the stage and next to the dance floor.

Each table is clearly assigned. *The French Café. The Pan and Pot. Chateau One. Our House.* The best in Irish cuisine, almost all with a nod to the Mediterranean, are dotted around me. It's both humbling and mind-blowing to see La Bella Vita among them.

I feel a hand on my back and Scott whispers, 'Are you okay?'

'Can you believe we're here?' I ask.

'Can I believe *you're* here?' he says. 'Yes. I absolutely can.'

Scott's hand stays on my back as we walk towards the table. Catherine is already seated and seeing her takes my breath away – but not as much as finding Mark's older brother, Alan, sitting next to her. The bridge of Catherine's nose wrinkles as she surveys Scott up and down. Then she and Alan share a look that tells me they've already discussed Scott's presence and neither of them approve.

'Alan. Wow. Hi,' I say, consciously pulling his attention away from Scott.

'Tabs. Hey,' he says, in his deep voice so much like Mark's my knees buckle at the sound.

'It's good to see you. It's been so long...' I trail off, wishing I hadn't said that, as I remember the last time I saw Alan was in the hospital just after Mark died.

Alan nods but he doesn't say anything more.

Scott pulls a seat out for me and I sit. Then he pulls one out for Becca. Avery glares at him and he steps back as she pulls her own seat out and sits down.

Catherine gives me the once-over and points towards my hair. 'Oh yes, this is much better.'

Instinctively I run my hand over my head.

'The blond didn't suit you at all,' she adds.

I don't tell Catherine that I agree. Although I do. In February a blond bob couldn't possibly have suited me better. It was a drastic change from the same mundane style I'd had for twenty years. Now, months later, I'm brunette again. And while the colour might be the same as before, the person I've become underneath definitely is not.

'The Best Pastries Award is eighth on the list,' Catherine says with a sigh.

She stares at the itinerary for the evening printed a thick, cream card with embossed gold font sitting at an angle on top of each plate.

'Eighth,' she repeats, tutting. 'We'll be here all night.'

'Doesn't dessert usually come at the end?' Avery says, glaring at her.

'Who's working tonight?' Catherine asks, ignoring Avery and turning towards me.

'Do you mean in La Bella Vita?' I ask.

Perhaps it's the champagne on an empty stomach but I very much enjoy how the corners of her lips curl and her nostrils flare at her disapproval of my rhetorical question.

'Yes. Of course,' she says, folding her arms on the edge of the table. 'If you're not there and I'm not there—'

'You're never there,' I say, and I can feel a glare burning as Alan sets his narrowed eyes on me. I shake my head as if I can shake him off. 'Zoe is working tonight.'

'And she knows what she's doing?' Catherine says.

'She's hasn't a clue,' Avery cuts in before I have time to reply. 'It's a total shitshow over there. But hey, if Zoe burns the place down at least you have insurance, right?'

'Avery,' I scold.

'I can see you haven't changed a bit, Aves,' Alan says, and for the first time, not only do I hear Mark in his tone, I hear Catherine in his words.

'What you see is what you get.' Avery shrugs.

Thankfully a waiter appears at our table and we order drinks. Followed swiftly by food. And soon we're eating and drinking and almost enjoying ourselves. Every now and then I look across the table at Catherine and Alan and I'm reminded not to relax too much.

Ironically for an event celebrating the best cuisine, the meal is pretty mediocre. Avery decides to make up for bad food with good drink and orders round after round of tequila shots. It doesn't take much convincing to get Alan to join and by the third round his arm is wrapped round me and he's telling me how much he misses me and how I was the best thing to ever happen to his brother.

I notice Scott isn't drinking and when I ask is everything is okay, he says, 'Yeah. Yeah. All good.'

We drink and eat until I feel as if I might explode. Staff

clear our table and top up our glasses of water, and then the lights dim.

'Woo,' Avery says, waving her arms as if she's swimming in the foggy glow of stage lights.

The winner in each category is announced and acceptance speeches and thank-yous follow. Avery orders more drinks as winner after winner takes to the stage.

Finally, Scott nudges my arm gently as the Best Pastries nominations are projected on the giant white board behind the maître d'.

'This is it,' he says.

I take a deep breath and hold it, and as I look around the table I'm certain everyone else is holding theirs too.

'And the award for the Best Pastries goes to...' The maître d' pauses for effect.

I honestly think I might pass out before he finally says, '... Chateau One.'

I breathe out to the sound of whooping and cheering from the table closest to us.

'Congratulations,' I shout as they stand.

I don't think they can hear me over the cheering. Their cheering. And everyone around us. I clap and clap until my hands are sore. Avery claps. Becca too. And Scott. Catherine doesn't clap. Neither does Alan. They sit with serious, long faces. Catherine swirls some Chardonnay around her glass and glares at the stage as the management and some of the staff of Chateau One climb the steps and stand, very shakily, around the podium.

My eyes are on the stage, focusing on the variety of beautiful red dresses, as a firm squeeze of my shoulder summons my attention. I pull my gaze back to our table and find Catherine standing behind me.

'You want me to sell my share of the bistro,' she says, and it's very clearly a statement not a question.

I shrug. Not just because brain fog and tiredness has set in but because I don't want to have another conversation with Catherine about Mark. Or La Bella Vita.

Grateful speeches and excitement fade into the background as Catherine squeezes my shoulder a fraction harder and says, 'You said you wanted to buy me out.'

'I did.'

She stares. 'So, can you actually afford it?'

I glance around the room at the mixture of expressions. The mood has changed over the course of the evening. Anticipation and excitement has been replaced with either satisfaction or disappointment. Tables are divided into winners and losers. Winning tables proudly display their shiny, glass award in the centre. They clink glasses off one another and wrap arms round each other and they smile and chat as if they haven't a care in the world. The tone at the losers' tables is entirely different. People sit slouched in their seats, their hands curled round a glass of wine or a tumbler of whiskey. They chat too, of course, but mostly to console each other and wallow in their disenchantment. It's so sad to think that a shiny, glass trophy, or lack of, can suck the happiness out of them like a vacuum. Award or not, La Bella Vita has been sucking happiness out of me for years. I think it's time it stopped. I think it's time I stopped letting it.

'We should talk numbers,' Catherine says. 'I won't be swayed because La Bella Vita didn't win tonight. I think we all know it's not the type of place to win awards. Maybe a few months ago, but not now.'

'I thought we stood a good chance,' I say.

'Oh, sweetheart, I'm sure *you* did.' Catherine rolls her eyes and turns towards Alan. 'Do you see what Mark was talking about now?'

Alan nods sympathetically as he looks at me with round eyes. The same round eyes he shares with his mother. And

Mark. Buchanan eyes. Eyes that suggest they are winners and everyone else is a loser. Eyes that could once make me believe that I really was a loser. But I don't have to look into these eyes anymore. I can walk away if I want to. And I finally realise that is what I want. I want to walk away. I tried on New Year's Eve but it all went wrong. I need to try again. I need to walk away from Mark and everything and everyone attached to him. Including La Bella Vita.

I cast my gaze towards my sister and her fiancée dancing the macarena. I laugh and Catherine edges closer.

'So, shall we meet in the office first thing on Monday morning to discuss the sale of my shares?' she repeats.

Avery almost falls over as her knees and elbow jerk in a crazy dance move. Becca catches her. I can only imagine what it's like to have someone ready to catch you. Dancing or not.

'Tabitha,' Catherine says.

'I don't want to buy your shares,' I say. 'Not anymore.'

Alan suddenly looks as if he needs more to drink and Catherine exhales sharply, her Chardonnay breath hitting me hard.

'What exactly is it that you *do* want, Tabitha? Because for the life of me, I have no idea.'

'I want to be happy. I want to stop worrying about what other people think or how other people see me. I want to be Tabitha Greenwood. Not Thunder-thighs Tabby. Or can't-sing-karaoke Tabby. Or the fiancée-who-gets-cheated-on Tabby. I want to be the girl I was before. But most of all, right now I want to leave.'

Without another word, I pick a glass of untouched white wine up from the table and stagger slowly away.

FIFTY-SIX

I receive more compliments in the ladies' bathroom than I know what to do with.

'No man is worth your tears, love,' a very drunk stranger tells me as she looks in the mirror and tries to apply mascara with a wobbly hand. 'You're gorgeous and he's not worth it.'

'Oh, hun, don't cry. He's a dick, I bet,' someone else says.

'Your dress is fab.'

'Your hair looks great.'

'I like your shoes.'

I stare in the mirror behind the row of sinks and let the kind words fill me up. I'm lost somewhere tranquil and washing my hands endlessly when I hear a familiar voice.

'Why do you want to move?'

I glance up to find Becca's reflection standing behind me.

'Why are you selling your flat?'

'What?'

'It's done now, I know,' Becca says. 'But I never asked you why, and I think I should have.'

'I'm drunk.'

'I know,' she says, and I'm embarrassed to realise that she's not even tipsy.

'But you're also crying on what should be a very special night.'

'Am I?' I ask, running my fingertips under my eyes.

'You're turning your life upside down this year,' Becca says, pushing one of the stall doors open to gather some tissue that she passes to me. 'Following all these resolutions, selling your flat... it was all supposed to make you happy but—'

'But you don't think any of it worked.'

'I'm sorry La Bella Vita didn't win tonight. You deserved to.'

'Oh God. I swear that's not what this is.' I cringe. 'The judges thought Chateau One deserved it more. And that's okay. I'm okay. I never needed to win. It's an honour just being here.'

'Then why the tears?'

'Honestly,' I shrug, tossing the damp tissue into the nearby bin, 'they're happy tears.'

'Happy tears?'

I nod. 'I'm happy because this is me. This is my life. I don't always win. And that's okay. I don't need to. Pretty soon I will officially be homeless because I don't have a plan. And that's okay too. I don't always need a plan. This is me. I lose, I don't plan and I cry sometimes. And for the first time, possibly ever, I'm okay with that.'

A smile tugs at the corners of Becca's lips and she looks at me as if she's meeting me for the first time. Meeting the real me. And I think she likes me.

Suddenly, Avery thunders in. Her long floral dress is pulled above her knees as she exclaims, 'Christ, I'm bursting.'

Becca laughs as Avery hurries into a stall, slamming the door behind her.

'Could you do me another favour?' I ask.

Becca nods.

'Please God find me somewhere to live. My fancy speech

may have sounded great, but I really, really don't want to be homeless.'

Becca nods and laughs as a toilet flushes and Avery emerges. She washes her hands and without a word links her arms into Becca's and mine and leads us to the dance floor to funky-chicken the night away.

FIFTY-SEVEN

On Saturday lunchtime, just as Zoe and I prepare for what we hope will be a busy service, Lyla hurries into the kitchen with her hands on her hips. She shakes her head and tuts as she calls for my attention.

'There's a lady here looking for you, I think she was here before. She says her name is Ida Nasser.'

My breath catches.

'She has two little boys with her. And, they don't have a booking.'

I place down my spatula next to the carrot cake I was icing. 'That's a nice surprise,' I say, smiling. 'And she brought her children with her.'

'She doesn't have a booking,' Lyla reiterates. 'And we're packed, Tabby.'

'Lyla, please. I know you can make something work.'

Lyla tuts again and shakes her head as she walks out of the kitchen muttering something about magicking up a table out of thin air. I shake my hair loose from the hairnet, and dust some flour off my cheeks.

'Will you be okay on your own for a while?' I ask Zoe,

knowing I'm putting her in the awkward position of having to say yes whether it's true or not.

'All good, boss,' she says, nodding, but she doesn't take her attention away from the filo pastry she is hand-rolling.

I'm delighted Ida is here, booking or not. And I'm especially glad she brought her children. Rashidi's grandchildren. I didn't think I'd see her again after the funeral and it hadn't seemed appropriate then to ask for her number. But I have thought about her since, usually when I get off the bus in the mornings and look at where Rashidi and his cart are so poignantly missing from his usual spot.

Thankfully, Lyla does seem to conjure a table from thin air. It's not in the best spot, wedged between two much larger, noisier tables. But Ida is smiling as she peruses our lunch menu. Her sons sit either side of her, colouring contentedly with our new La Bella Vita colouring packs.

'Ida, hello,' I say, reaching their table.

'Tabitha. I'm so glad you're working today. I wasn't sure. And we've come all this way—'

'Mummy, Mummy, can I have fizzy orange,' the older of the two boys says, tugging on her sleeve.

'Me too. Me too,' the younger boy chirps. 'I want fizzy orange too.'

'Maybe. If you're good,' Ida says, tapping her long nails on the half-coloured paper in front of them, redirecting their attention back to their task.

'Sorry,' she says. 'They're just excited to be here. I told them their grandfather used to work nearby.'

'Yes he did,' I say, knowing the boys are still listening. 'He made the best bagels in the whole world.'

'I want a bagel,' the eldest boy says.

'Oh, me too. Me too,' the younger boy says.

Ida's eyes sweep the menu once more and she shakes her head. 'You know, I don't think they make bagels here.'

I play the menu over in my mind. Soft cheeses, game, Mediterranean vegetables. All with fancy names and even fancier prices. Certainly not appealing or appetising to two little boys.

'We have the most amazing chef here. Zoe is her name and—'

'There's a Zoe in my class,' the youngest boy tells me. 'She's nice.'

'Well, Zoe, our chef, is nice too and I bet if I ask her she could whip up two of the yummiest bagels ever.'

'And fizzy orange,' the young boys says. 'I realllyyy want fizzy orange too.'

'And fizzy orange,' I say.

'Thank you,' Ida says. 'Do you think you could join us or are you too busy?'

I look around the packed-to-capacity bistro. 'Um...'

'Please,' Ida says with longing in her eyes.

She doesn't say that she's come out of her way to be here and it isn't for bagels and a soft drink.

'I can spare a few minutes,' I lie.

I catch Lyla's eye and she nods, picking up that I will be joining the Nassers' table. She returns moments later with a stool from my office, the only chair she could find.

I sit gratefully and say, 'The boys would like some fizzy orange, please. And bagels.'

'Bagels?' she says, dropping her eyes to the menus stretched out in front of Ida and her sons. Menus that Lyla knows by heart. Menus she knows don't include, and never have included, bagels.

'I'll have a bagel too please. Three BLTs,' Ida says.

'Just a tea for me, thanks, Lyla,' I say.

Lyla exhales and walks away shaking her head.

'How are you?' I ask as the boys continue their colouring. 'How have you been since...' I trail off, unable to find the right words.

'Since my father died,' Ida finishes for me.

I nod.

'You're the only person who's asked me that. No one at home, none of my friends and colleagues know he died ,so...' She shrugs as if it's no big deal but her sad eyes tell a different story.

'You didn't tell anyone?'

Lyla returns and places a couple of glasses of bubbling orange with bright red straws on the table, one in front of each child. The boys drop their crayons and reach for them.

'Ah-ah, where are your manners?' Ida scolds.

'Thank you,' the boys say in unison as they look up at Lyla.

'You're welcome,' she says, smiling. 'I'll be back with your bagels soon.'

Ida waits until Lyla is out of earshot before she says, 'You're probably wondering why I'm here.'

I am. Of course I am, but it doesn't feel right to admit it out loud.

'My father didn't have a will. Surprise, surprise,' Ida says. 'But they found me nonetheless. They told me all his stuff is mine now.'

I wonder who *they* are. People in government, is my best guess. People who step in to tidy up the affairs of the lonely after they're gone. My heart is filled with sadness that Rashidi needed *those* people.

'He didn't have much,' Ida says. 'A small flat in a not-so-great part of town. Clothes, a watch and his bagel cart.'

The boys slurp orange through their straws. They stop to catch their breaths and slurp again. It's loud and irritating and the sound fills the gap where my words should be, but I have no idea what to say. I'm not sure why Ida is telling me all this.

'I'm going to sell the flat,' she continues. 'I'm not sure what

I'll get for it. But whatever it is I'm going to put it into a savings account for the boys for college.'

I smile. I think Rashidi would be really pleased to know he's contributing towards his grandchildren's education.

'I'm throwing the clothes out. They're too worn out to give to charity. The watch is nice though, so I'll keep that.'

I glance at Ida's wrist, where a chunky, silver watch wraps round. It's not particularly fancy or stylish and I doubt it has any monetary value. I decide Ida must be keeping it for senti-mental reasons and my smile grows.

Lyla once again returns to our table. She places plates of doorstop-thick sourdough bread cut into perfect circles and stuffed with bright green lettuce, juicy red tomato and crispy bacon. Zoe has pan-fried the bread until it's crisp and she's garnished it with herbs, dressing and edible flowers.

'Ew, gross,' the youngest boy says, pushing his plate away.

The older boy takes longer to appraise the plate of food in front of him but then he reaches the same verdict and shakes his head.

'I'm sorry,' Ida says. 'They're used to simpler dishes.'

'Can we get McDonald's instead?' the younger boy asks.

Ida places her finger to her lips and suggests he returns to his colouring. I am confident that means there is a McDonalds in their future.

Ida on the other hand tucks into her bagel. Between bites she says, 'I want you to have the cart.'

'Oh, I couldn't possibly.'

'I don't have any use for it and I thought you might.'

Once again, I glance around my bistro. Although La Bella Vita has never claimed to be a fine dining establishment, it certainly tries to boast a near experience. I have absolutely no idea what I would do with a bagel cart.

As if Ida can read my mind, she says, 'I just wanted to ask before I threw it away.'

'No, no. Don't throw it away,' I find myself rushing to say. 'I'll find somewhere for it. Some use. Just please don't get rid of it.'

Ida swallows hard, shoving down a mouthful of bacon, lettuce, tomato and bread that she certainly seems to be enjoying. 'Consider it yours, then.'

FIFTY-EIGHT

NOVEMBER

Go On A Date!

Tabby: Soooo Avery and Becca are only feckin' trying to set me up.

Scott: Anyone decent?

Tabby: No. No. And no. Mr I like tattoos. Captain I'm divorced 3 times. Creepy guy who wants to know if I'd like to share nudes.

Scott: That bad?

Tabby: Actually no, not really. I'm sure there are lots of nice guys out there. But I'm just not feeling it.

Scott: Tinder not your thing, then?

Tabby: Not really. Avery thinks I'm a dinosaur.

Scott: And what's the story with the flat?

Tabby: I'm out next week and I still have nowhere to go.

Scott: Sh!t, really? Can I help?

Tabby: I'm looking a place later today. Maybe you could come? I'd love a second opinion.

Scott: I'm in work until 4. After that any good?

Tabby: Perfect. Appointment is at 6 but it's a bit outside town. Maybe come here first and we can get the bus together?

Scott: Sounds good. See you later x

Tabby: xx

I slide my phone into my pocket and sigh. I've made it all the way to November and it pains me to fail now, but I don't think I can see this resolution through.

'Is it because of Mark?' Avery asked when I told her.

'Is it too soon?' Becca added, concerned.

'It's not because of Mark. I swear.'

It's the truth. It's not because of Mark. It's because of Scott. I don't want to date because the guy I want is right in front of me, but I don't think he sees me that way. And I can't handle the rejection of finding out. I think one heartbreak a year is about all I can deal with, resolutions or not.

At 5 p.m. when there is still no sign of Scott, I text him. When there is no reply I send a couple more. At 5.15 I ring and ring but he doesn't pick up. Then I call Becca.

'Hello.'

'Hey. It's Tabby.'

'Oh, hey. Everything okay?'

'I'm going to be a few minutes late. I'm still at work.'

I hear Becca's inhale. She knows as well as I do that I am definitely going to be more than a few minutes late. The property I plan to view is in the suburbs. In rush-hour traffic there is no chance I will get there in forty-five minutes.

'I'm so sorry,' I say. 'I asked Scott to come along and he's late and now he's not answering his phone and I don't know what the story is. I'll leave now, so I should get there—'

'Wait for him,' Becca says. 'He probably just got held up in work or something.'

'Aren't you supposed to be going to the karaoke bar with Avery tonight? She'll kill me if I hold you up.'

Becca laughs. 'She'd kill both of us. That's why I'm not going to be late.'

I sigh. 'Okay, no problem. We can reschedule. I'm really sorry.'

'Don't be silly,' Becca says, softly. 'I'll leave the key under the mat for you and you can let yourself in whenever. Stay as long as you like. Get a real feel for the place.'

'But the owners...'

'They live in Spain. They're not planning on coming back. It's why they're selling.'

'Thanks so much.'

'Call me later and let me know what you think. I'll keep my volume turned up so I can hear my phone over Avery's beautiful singing.'

We both laugh and I thank Becca again before I hang up and try Scott again.

'Hello,' he says, and I can hear tiredness in his voice.

'Hey. You okay?'

'Oh God, Tabby, I'm so sorry. There was a mix-up with an

order and then the boss went apeshit. Had to stay late and grovel.'

'Oh no, sounds like you've had a horrible day.'

'The bloody worst,' he says. 'I hate this job more by the day. I've messed up your whole evening. I'm sorry.'

'It's okay. Maybe another time.'

'Is it too late to go now?'

'No. Becca says we can head over any time.'

'Oh. Good. That's great. I'm walking out the door here now...'

'But you're so tired—'

'Tabby, please. I've had a really shit day and the only thing that kept me going was the thought of spending the evening with you.'

'An evening in the suburbs viewing a house.'

'It sounds like a perfect evening to me.'

I smile.

'I'm getting on the bus,' he says, and I can hear his breath quaking and I imagine him racing to catch it. 'I'll be there in no time.'

'Okay,' I say. 'I'll see you soon.'

FIFTY-NINE

The house is two bus rides away from work. Scott and I change at the main bus depot in the city. The weather is particularly awful. Strong wind blows the heavy rain sideways, hitting our faces despite our trying to shelter under a golf umbrella. The weather app on my phone says to expect thunder and lightning and the angry sky overhead agrees.

I wait in line for the bus that isn't here yet while Scott fetches us something to eat from the nearby street vendor. It's a while before he returns.

'Sorry, no bagels,' he says, as he passes me a hot dog and a can of Diet Coke.

I nod and I know we're both thinking of Rashidi.

We're too tired and hungry to make conversation while we eat. We both inhale our food and chug down our cans. Finally the bus arrives and cold, exhausted and wet commuters file onboard.

The fifty-minute bus ride out of the city and into the suburbs passes surprisingly quickly. Scott seems recharged after his hot dog and conversation flows. He tells me about his horrible boss, the long hours and impossible menu. He never once says he's unhappy, but he doesn't have to. I tell him about Ida's visit and Rashidi's cart.

'This is our stop... I think,' I say, staring out the window at sparsely spaced-out street lights that bathe the narrow path below in their orangey glow.

Scott shuffles out of his seat first. I miss the warmth of his body next to mine immediately as I shiver in my damp clothes. I stand up and follow him to the front of the bus.

'What time is the last bus?' Scott asks the driver.

'Eleven thirty usually, but I'm not sure it'll be going.' The driver points out the windscreen to where angry wind shakes the long, knobbly branches of leafless trees.

A stream of rainwater gathers at the corner of the road, running steadily downhill, dragging with it leaves and stones and sludge. Oversized raindrops pound the roads and paths, bouncing and rippling.

'There are already reports of trees and electricity poles down on other routes. And we haven't seen the worst of the wind yet,' the driver continues. 'The country is in for a battering tonight, I tell you. I'd stay in, if I were you. Not worth heading out in this for any reason.'

Lightening suddenly flashes through the sky like Poseidon's trident forking the ground.

'Sweet Jesus,' the bus driver says, as the bright purply-blue light is followed by a mighty rumble of thunder.

'Wow,' Scott says, his mouth gaping as if he's in awe of a beautiful painting. 'Did you see that?'

'Maybe we should go home,' I say.

'Are you afraid of lightning?' he asks.

'No. But I am afraid of buses not running. We should come back another day.'

'We're here now.' Scott shrugs and tilts his head towards the bus door.

The driver opens it and I take a deep breath and prepare to step into the inclement night.

'Stay safe,' the driver calls after us.

'Goodnight. Thank you,' I call back, and I follow Scott onto the path.

I try opening my umbrella but the wind shakes it inside out. Rain is everywhere. In our eyes, running down our faces, soaking through our clothes. More lightning and thunder follow.

'Isn't it beautiful,' Scott says. 'Like nature's light show.'

I wince as icy rainwater soaks into my Converse and nips my toes. 'We should hurry before the weather gets any worse. I think we need to take a right, a left and then two more rights,' I say checking the directions that Becca sent me.

Scott reaches for my hand and says, 'Right, let's run.'

'Run?'

'The faster we run the warmer we'll be.'

I'm about to tell him that I don't run, but he takes off with my hand in his and I have no choice but to keep up. Our feet pound the ground, splashing water up the backs of our legs. It's surprisingly satisfying and I begin to smile and laugh. The messier it gets the more I laugh. Scott laughs too. By the time we round the final corner I have a painful stitch in my side and I can barely draw breath, but I am still smiling.

'This is it,' I say. Two-storey, red brick terraced houses line each side of the road. 'Number twenty-seven. The blue door.'

The rows of identical houses are defined only by their colourful front doors that open directly onto the footpath. Red, green, yellow, purple. It's obvious the postcard-pretty buildings were once a long row of homes; but, over time, most have been upcycled into business premises. A dentist behind the red door. A nail bar and lash salon behind the yellow door. From what I can see someone still lives behind the purple door, and there seems to be building work going on at the green door. Overall, the street feels sleepy and relaxed and the change from residential to commercial seems slow and maybe reluctant, but I imagine this is what other parts of Dublin were like forty or fifty years ago. The street where La Bella Vita is located was once a row of townhouses too and today it's a bustling hive of activity. I try to imagine a similar future here.

'Are we going in?' Scott says, as rain trickles down his face and falls off the tip of his nose.

I bend down and lift the front mat that seems to belong more to the street than to the house. I jump back when a wood-louse crawls out and Scott bends to pick up the small, bronze key. He turns it in the lock and the blue door creaks open.

Inside, I listen to rain batter the windows and pound the roof. The storm seems fiercer from the sanctuary of an empty house. Wind howls through every crack and, there seem to be many, many cracks. A smell of damp hits me hard and I turn my face into the collar of my coat, trying to escape it.

'How old is this place?' Scott asks.

'A hundred years. Maybe more.'

'It's cold. How is it possible to be colder inside than outside?'

'No one has lived here for a while,' I explain.

'Do the lights work?' Scott asks, flicking the switch on the wall. A hall light rattles and flickers to life. 'They do.'

In brightness the house seems even more run-down. Most of the small terracotta hall tiles are cracked or missing. Paint flakes off all the walls and doors and mould gathers in every corner. And yet I feel overwhelmingly excited to look past it all, at what may be. Scott shares my enthusiasm as we wander from room to room.

'This place has so much potential,' he says.

'It's a whopper of a fixer-upper.'

He takes my hand and squeezes. 'But just think how great it will be.'

His fingers feel warm curled round my palm. I like it. I close my eyes and let my imagination run wild.

All too soon he lets go and wanders into the kitchen.

'This is a great size. And if you knock out the wall between the two front rooms, that will give you a huge dining space. There's even room for a small reception and bar area. It won't be as big as La Bella Vita but it will be cosy and maybe even better.'

My breath catches. I never told anyone I planned to convert the downstairs of my new home into a bistro. Not even Avery and Becca.

'How did you guess?' I say.

'Because it's exactly what I would do.'

'Catherine and I accepted an offer for La Bella Vita last week,' I say.

Convincing Catherine to let La Bella Vita pass into the hands of strangers was easier than I thought it would be. She has taken her obsession with Mark's bistro and replaced it with adoration of her grandson. She continues to send the occasional photo of Marc. And unlike before, I don't delete them. Instead, I search for all the parts of Mark in his little face and savour them. Sometimes I text Catherine back and tell her how cute the baby is. I text because she needs to hear it and it no longer hurts me to say it. For a long time I tried to fit into the Buchanan world and it hurt. I tried to squeeze and bend and pour myself into a mould. And it always pinched. Always. When Mark died, the mould broke. There is no one to bend myself out of shape for anymore. Slowly, I am unfolding.

'I'm so excited for you, Tabby,' Scott says. 'No one deserves to be happy more than you.'

'Well,' I sigh, managing his expectations and mine. 'It won't be easy. By the time Catherine takes her share and we pay fees and suppliers and God knows what else, it's not as much as I was hoping.'

'Oh, Tabs.'

'It's okay. I have the money from the flat too. And if I pool them together, it's just about enough for this place. I was thinking I could live upstairs, and down here – well, you said it.'

'Down here will be great.'

'It would mean putting every penny I have into this project and if it doesn't work out...' I clutch my chest. If it doesn't work out doesn't bear thinking about. 'I'm scared,' I say, and it feels good to admit it out loud.

Scott drapes his arm over my shoulder and pulls me close to him.

'You're freezing,' he says.

I shiver. He feels like ice too.

'We should get going,' I say, pulling away from him. 'We need to catch the bus before they stop running them.'

'Nobody lives here,' Scott says, looking around as if he's double checking that the owners aren't hiding behind a curtain or an ajar door.

'Not anymore. The owners live in Spain. And with this weather, who can blame them?'

'So, we could stay here,' he says, with a cheeky smirk.

My teeth chatter.

'It's bloody freezing outside and we could wait for an hour or more for a bus that may or may not turn up.' Scott shrugs. 'Or, we could just stay here tonight.'

I shake my head.

'I noticed a bucket of logs in the kitchen. I could get a fire going. We could get out of these wet clothes and—'

'We can't. It's not our house.'

'But it will be your house, won't it? I mean, I can see the excitement in your eyes.'

I don't have words.

'I'm cold and hungry,' Scott says. 'And I know you are too. I spotted a Chinese takeaway on the way here.'

My mouth waters at the thought of fried rice.

'We can set an alarm for first thing. We'll be gone before anyone even knows we were here.'

I'm so cold that I can't feel the tips of my fingers or toes anymore. My stomach rumbles every so often, reminding me that all I've eaten all day is a hot dog and an apple.

'What do you say, Tabs? Are we staying?'

This is madness, I think; but somehow I find myself nodding.

A bright smile lights up Scott's whole face. 'Welcome to your first night in your new home.'

SIXTY

While Scott sets out for food, I lay my coat on the threadbare carpet in the sitting room and try to ignore the smell of years of smoke and neglect worn into the pile. I strip down to my underwear and gasp as the amber glow of a crackling fire wraps me in its warmth. I stand still for a long time. Finally, defrosted, I gather up my wet clothes. Without anywhere to hang them, I shake them out and place them flat on the ground as near to the fire as I can get without risking burning them. Then, I sit cross-legged on my coat and text Becca.

Tabby: I love the house.

Becca: Have you found your new home?

Tabby: I have. And so much more. Thank you!

Becca: Xx

Some day someone else will sit here eating their dinner. They won't be sitting on the ground. They'll sit in a comfortable chair at a neatly dressed table. They'll wear their favourite outfit and sip their favourite wine and order their favourite food. And they'll come back to do it all over again. And again. And everything will be all right. It has to be.

I hear a key turning in the lock and stand up quickly, pulling my coat around myself as I hold my breath.

'Scott. Oh my God, it's only you.'

Scott peeps his head round the sitting room door as rain trickles off his face and coat and onto the wonky tiles in the hall.

'Who did you think it'd be?'

I shake my head and breathe in the smell of Chinese food wafting from the paper bag tucked under his arm.

'The owners are in Spain, remember?'

'They are. They are,' I remind myself and my thumping heart calms.

'How's our fire doing?' Scott pushes the door back to step inside fully.

I step aside to allow him space in front of the glow. He places the soggy and ripping paper bag of food on the ground and lines himself up in front of the fire. He holds his hands towards the flames, turning them front-to-back and back again as he looks at my clothes spread out on the ground.

'I was so cold.'

He nods. 'It's a good idea. You'd get sick if you kept those on.'

'You're soaking too,' I remind him.

Scott peels off his coat and I can see the rain has seeped through it. I look at his wet clothes as he looks at my near-naked body wrapped in my coat. I feel heat in my cheeks, but I think it's the warmth of the fire more than embarrassment.

'It's warmer with them off,' I say, pointing at his dark navy jeans that started the evening light blue.

Scott strips to his boxers and doesn't bother to wrap his coat around him; instead he turns it inside out and places it on the ground.

'C'mon,' he says, sitting cross-legged on it. 'Let's eat.'

He pulls some containers and two plastic forks from the bag and sets them down beside him.

'Aren't you going to sit down?'

I glance at the grubby carpet, take a deep breath and unwrap my coat from around me. I place it inside out on the ground facing Scott and sit down.

All I can think about is facing him in a mismatched bra and knickers. I think about the last time we spent the night together. I'm desperate to know if he's thinking about it too. He must be, but his eyes don't give me any clues.

'Tabs, aren't you hungry? Is everything okay?' Scott places his hand on my bare knee and when he leaves it there, finally, I know what he's thinking.

I lift the lid on the fried rice and say, 'Everything is great.'

SIXTY-ONE

We don't need to bother with an alarm. The morning sunlight shining through the windows with no curtains slaps us awake. Thankfully too. Because in the time it takes Scott and me to rouse fully, the street outside has become busy with people walking by. Luckily, many are staring at their phones or are deep in conversation with someone, but the odd person glances through the window to see two people stretched out naked on the floor.

We hurry to pull on our clothes, which have mostly dried overnight. We gather up our rubbish that we both regret not tidying up last night and hurry out the front door. The storm has blown over and left behind a clear blue sky. It's still Baltic, but fresh, and I imagine waking up on winter's mornings here for many years to come.

'Shit, that was embarrassing,' Scott says as we walk towards the bus stop. 'Did you see the face on the old lady with the big scarf. She stared right at us. I thought she was going to rap on the bloody window at one point.'

I laugh. 'I didn't see her. I think I was too busy trying to shove my legs into my jeans.'

'I've never gotten dressed so fast in my life. I still have a wedgie,' Scott says.

We reach the bus stop faster than I was expecting. It seems closer in daylight and without rain. I find myself disappointed when the bus almost immediately comes into view.

'Perfect timing,' Scott says.

'Are you in a hurry?' I ask.

Scott tosses me a quizzical look.

'I just mean, are you rushing off for work or do you have some time? Maybe we could get breakfast somewhere?'

'I could use a coffee,' he says.

'Cool. Let's catch the next one, then,' I say as the bus pulls up and the people in front of us get on.

'There's a café next to the Chinese takeaway.'

I look at him.

'What?' he says, 'I saw it last night. Looks nice. Actually, this whole area seems nice. I think you're going to love it here.'

I link Scott's arm and let him lead the way towards the café. We saunter along and I take in the sights as we walk. Both sides of the main street are lined with pastel-coloured shop fronts like a tray of appetising macarons. I'm disappointed to discover there are already a couple of elegant bistros on each side. Scott must see them too because he squeezes my arm and quickens his pace.

The café is small, but inviting. Scott says the coffee is good and I like the tea. We order a couple of pains au chocolat and they're delicious too.

After some awkward small talk as we actively avoid the topic of what happened last night – again – Scott says, 'Did you see the restaurants on the main street?'

'They look good.'

'They do. But there's always room for great.'

'Actually, I've been thinking,' I say, sliding my empty teacup aside so I can fold my elbows on the table.

'Um?'

'What about if I didn't do anything fancy?'

There's a flash of something in Scott's eyes. Intrigue. My stomach somersaults, excitedly.

'I told you about Ida's visit,' I begin.

'More coffee?' a waitress says, interrupting us as she appears at Scott's shoulder.

'Oh God, yes. I've a feeling this morning calls for lots of coffee.' He winks at me and adds, 'Tea too, yeah?'

'Yes. Please. More tea please,' I say, as the girl turns towards me.

'Tea and coffee. And you're okay for everything else?'

Scott looks at me and I nod.

'We're okay. Thank you,' he says. He waits until she's returned behind the counter before he says, 'Go on...'

'I wanna use the cart,' I say.

'Rashidi's cart?'

'Yes. I can't bear to see it go to the dump or go into storage or something. But I can't be a street vendor. For one thing, you saw my hair last night, it hates the bloody rain.' I run my hand over my head and down my usually straight but definitely-frizzy-today hair.

'Yeah. It takes a certain kind of someone to handle all weathers,' Scott says.

'So, I was thinking... what if I didn't turn the downstairs of the new place into a *fancy* restaurant?'

Scott seems unimpressed as the waitress returns with our tea and coffee.

'Thank you,' he says.

The atmosphere is tense and I can sense her discomfort at disturbing us. She walks away without another word.

'Is this about last night? Do you not want to turn it into a restaurant now because we... we...'

'No! God no. It's not that.' My face is hot. I take a moment and tear open a sachet of sugar and empty it into my cup.

'Because if I'm rushing you...' Scott runs his hand over his head, like always. 'Look, I know I fucked up with the aftershave. And I tried to give you some space. But last night, seeing you in the firelight—'

'Last night was great. Honest.'

Relief washes over his face.

'I'm not fancy,' I say.

Scott's lips move but before he has time to reassure me that I'm perfectly fancy I keep talking.

'Last night was great. There wasn't furniture or even knives and forks and yet it was one of the nicest evenings I've had in longer than I can remember. It was simple and perfect. My life hasn't been simple in a very long time and I want it to be.'

Scott raises his cup of black coffee and sips casually.

'People like fancy things. Food, cars, flats. People like the Buchanans,' I say.

Scott nods.

'But more people, a lot more people, like simple things. An open fire, running in the rain, comfort food. People like me. And Avery.'

Scott nods again and says, 'Food like bagels.'

'Well, yeah,' I say, thinking of the disappointed faces on Ida's two little boys when a gourmet, slightly improvised bagel presented itself on their plate. 'I think if I can find that balance between great taste and simple food, I might be on to something.'

'You're really doing this?' Scott says, lowering his cup, which I see is already half-empty.

I pull my shoulders towards my ears and hold them there. 'Yes. I hope so. You know when I tried the first few of Avery's resolutions, I couldn't see the point. I couldn't see how such small, simple things would help with such big, complicated problems. What good would a haircut, or painting, or a new dress do?'

'Did they do good?' Scott says. 'Are you happy?'

'Yes. I remember now who I was before life became complicated. And I know who I want to be now that it is. You are right. You cannot be happy unless you allow yourself to be. It has taken a long time but I am finally giving myself permission.'

'Then good for you, Tabs. Bloody good for you.'

'Thanks,' I say, finally lifting my teacup and hoping the tea is cool enough to drink. 'I was sort of hoping you'd join me.'

'I am happy,' he says.

'Erm.' I blush. 'I sort of mean join me at the new restaurant.'

'Work for you?'

I lower the cup again, deciding it's still too hot. 'Well, yeah. Or with me really. I know we got off to a rocky start the last time we tried to work together—'

'That's putting it mildly.'

'I know you hate your job,' I continue.

'I do.'

'So...'

'So,' he echoes, but there's a flatness to his tone that saddens me.

'Please,' I say. 'Just say you'll think about it.'

Scott shakes his head.

'You won't even think about it?'

'No,' he says, barely above a whisper.

I push my tea aside. Suddenly I can't stomach it.

'We should get the next bus,' I say.

I take a deep breath, ready to stand up, but Scott places his hand over mine and looks at me with round eyes. I let my breath out slowly and slouch. I look at his hand on top of mine and he pulls it away, unsure.

He folds his arms on the table and leans a fraction closer as he says, 'I can't work for you. Not after last night.'

I puff out, hurt, and place some money under my saucer.

'We should get going,' I say

Scott pushes his chair back and half stands, just enough to catch my arm before I turn away.

'This month's resolution is to start dating,' he tells me as if he's sharing something I didn't know. 'Then, how about a date with me?'

My eyes narrow.

'I can't work for you, Tabs. I can't work for you because I'm crazy about you. I can't make impartial decisions or be at my best in the kitchen because every day I would be thinking about pressing you against something hot and steamy and kissing the shit out of you.'

'Oh.'

'Mostly...' Scott continues, locking his eyes on mine, knowing he has my full attention. '...I don't want history to repeat itself.'

'Me and Mark?'

Scott doesn't say anything. He doesn't have to.

'And what if I say I don't want to date you?' I say, trying to sound serious, but my heart is racing and a smile is tugging at the corners of my lips.

'Then my answer is still no.'

My eyebrows pinch.

'Because nothing will have changed for me. I will still want to touch you every time I see you.'

My head is spinning. I pull my teacup back and curl my hands round the warm china.

'You know I'm going to have to text Avery about this?' I say.

Scott pulls a face. 'To ask for her advice?'

'To tell her to take my profile off bloody Tinder.'

'So, we're going on a date?' he says.

I lift my tea cup to my lips and stare at him over the rim. 'Aren't we already on one?'

SIXTY-TWO

DECEMBER

You made it. Congratulations!

I am currently homeless. Or at least that's what Avery calls my stay at the Waldmort Hotel on St Stephen's Green. I turned the key in the door of Mark's and my flat for the last time three days ago. Avery and Becca were by my side. I pressed two fingers against my lips, kissed them, and held them to the door. Then I turned to Becca and placed the key into her hand.

'You'll be okay,' she told me.

'I know,' I said, and I believed us both.

I have two weeks to wait until I receive the keys to my new flat. Everything moved quicker than we could possibly have hoped. The sellers have been wonderfully accommodating and Becca says it's the smoothest sale she's ever handled. My solicitor said the same.

'Six weeks from an offer to moving in,' he said, sitting in his tall-backed leather chair, chewing on the back of his pen. 'Must be a record. I guess some moves are just meant to be.'

'Some moves are just meant to be,' I echoed.

But nothing feels as if it's meant to be this morning. Avery is sprawled on my hotel bed with her face mushed into my pillow and one leg hanging over the edge. A champagne breakfast sits, untouched, on the bedside table next to her. I glance at my watch. The wedding photographer will be here in an hour to start snapping us getting ready and Avery's loud snores rattle the room.

I yank the covers off her and wait for the cold to finally rouse her.

'What the hell?' she says, sitting up and rubbing her eyes.

'Good. You're awake.'

Avery glances at the breakfast that arrived almost two hours ago.

'Um. Yum,' she says, shoving a piece of toast into her mouth. She spits it back out quickly. 'Uh. Gross. Cold.'

'Sleep okay?' I ask, pouring her a cup of coffee from the silver pot on the tray. It's barely lukewarm but she takes it gratefully and drinks.

'Like a baby,' she says, finally getting to her feet. 'You?'

Avery's snoring kept me up half the night but I say, 'Yeah. Great. How are you feeling?'

'Bursting,' she says, dropping a bitten piece of toast onto the tray and dashing towards the bathroom.

Alone, I begin to tidy up the room. I fold the towels Avery has left draped over the chair and I pack her scattered clothes back into her suitcase, ready to move everything to the room she will share with Becca tonight. I'm about to pour two glasses of champagne when there's a knock on my door. I'm beyond relieved when I find the hotel concierge waiting on the far side and not an eager photographer.

'Post for you,' he says, shoving a gold envelope towards me.

I glance at the handwritten address on the front.

Ms Tabitha Greenwood,
Room number unknown,
The Waldmort Hotel,
St Stephens Green,
Dublin 2

'I'm between houses at the moment,' I explain. 'I sold my flat a few weeks ago and my new house isn't ready to move into yet so I'm staying here. It's just short-term...' I trail off, realising that my long-winded waffle is as painful for him as it is for me.

I reach for the envelope and say, 'Thank you.'

He nods, smiles and walks away.

I open the envelope and slide out a Christmas card. There is a photo of Catherine on the front. She's sitting in a leather armchair next to a huge, heavily decorated Christmas tree. She wears a colourful Christmas jumper and her perfect-as-ever silver hair peeks out from underneath a Santa hat. A little boy sits on her knee. Marc. He's bigger now, with chubby cheeks and pudgy fingers. His powder-blue dungarees bring out his beautiful blue eyes and he wears a bib that proudly states, *I love my grandma.* Above their heads in jolly red font that fits the season perfectly reads, *Happy Christmas from the Buchanan family.*

I open the card, take a deep breath and begin reading.

Dear Tabitha,

Happy Christmas, Sweetheart. I hope you are not too lonely this festive season. Christmas without our Mark will be a challenge for us all. But I thank God every day for baby Marc. He's three months old now and growing quickly. I am very much enjoying retirement and spending precious time with my grandson. I am sure you will find something to fill your time soon.

All best wishes,

Catherine.

I close the card and pull it close to my chest. And I imagine words between the lines in Catherine's note. *My heart is breaking this Christmas without my son. I miss Mark. Nothing will be the same again.*

For a moment a wave of almost unbearable emotion washes over me. I glance up at Avery's wedding dress hanging on the outside of the chunky oak wardrobe and I think about how truly nothing will ever be the same again. Mark is gone. Our flat is gone. I imagine the new owners setting up their Christmas tree in their choice of spot – next to the window in the sitting room or perhaps closer to their new couch. Soon, I will close La Bella Vita's door for the last time. We are booked out on New Year's Eve. Our final sitting. And in a little over three hours my sister will be a married woman. Something I never, ever thought she would be. Something I hope she loves and enjoys every moment of. Nothing will ever be the same again; it just might be better.

The loo flushes and Avery reappears. A crisp white towel sits like a turban on her head, pulling her hair off her face. An oversized fluffy dressing gown emphases her petite height and her skin is bright and glowing. She's positively beautiful.

'You, okay?' I ask.

'Nervous,' she says.

Avery's confession surprises me. I haven't known my sister to be scared of anything. Not since I fell out of a tree and broke my leg when we were young.

'What if I mess up – forget my vows or say something inappropriate?'

'Then Becca will probably laugh,' I say.

'What if I fall over? Just do a complete face-plant right there in front of everyone.'

'Then we will probably all laugh.'

I was hoping Avery might laugh now, but her face is pale and her hair that she's dyed her natural colour – dark brown – falls around her face in jagged layers, emphasising her wide, worried eyes.

I fetch one of her wedding shoes, custom Dr Martens with a lace trim and hot-pink laces, and wave it above my head.

'These things are like concrete blocks,' I say. 'I really don't think you're going to topple over.'

'But what if—'

'Avery,' I say, cutting her off as I toss the shoe onto the bed and then walk over to pull her into my arms. 'Today is going to be great. The best day of your life.'

'As long as it's the best day of Becca's life that's all that matters.'

I kiss her cheek and let her go.

'My God, Becca is a lucky woman,' I say. 'I know people say stuff like that all the time at weddings but I really mean it. Anyone who gets to spend their life with you is lucky, Avery. I certainly was.'

'You know I'm not actually going anywhere?' Avery says. 'Our new flat is something like a thirty-minute drive from your new house.'

'I know. I know,' I say. 'But everything will be different once you're married.'

'Why?' Avery asks, pulling away from me, and I can tell she's deeply concerned that I've picked something up wrong.

'Because that's just the way marriage works.'

'No, it's bloody not,' she says. 'If marriage was going to change anything in my life, I wouldn't do it.'

'But, Avery—'

'I'm not marrying Becca because I want to show her how much I love her. I'm marrying her because I want to show the world. I want to introduce her to a stranger as my wife and see that look in their eye when they think about how incredibly lucky I am to share my life with such an amazing woman. That's what I think marriage is. It's a big, fat announcement to the world that you've finally found your favourite person. I've known from the day I met Becca that I love her; marriage...' Avery pauses to catch her breath. 'Well, it's just icing on an already delicious cake.'

I smile. I'm so deliriously happy for my sister that I can't find words.

'Is Scott your icing, Tabs?'

I take a deep breath and glance at Avery's beautiful dress again. 'Actually, I think he might be the whole cake.'

SIXTY-THREE

NEW YEAR'S EVE

Mark loved snow. He said the family holidays he had skiing in the French Alps were some of the happiest times of his life. We talked about going skiing all the time, but as busy restaurateurs we never found the right time. I wonder what he would say if he could see the snow gathered in the corners of La Bella Vita's sash window now, like icing sugar sprinkled heavy-handedly on a Belgian waffle.

It started snowing early this morning, before dawn, I'm guessing, because when I woke up and pulled back the curtains in my hotel bedroom, there was already a thick white blanket covering the street and the footpath outside. I marvelled at its beauty before footsteps and car tracks disturbed it.

I skipped the bus and walked to work instead, poking my tongue out every so often to catch a falling snowflake as if I hadn't a care in the world. I stand outside La Bella Vita now for quite a while. Long enough for snow to pile on top of my knitted hat like vanilla ice cream on a cone. I sweep my gaze over its postcard-perfect face and, despite the weather, I am tingling and warm.

Finally, I push open the door and walk inside. Chunks of

snow fall off me and onto the ground and litter around my feet like balls of cotton wool. I glance around the dining room, with tables set for the busy day ahead. La Bella Vita's last day. I take a deep breath and drink it all in. Mismatched chairs around oval tables. A single silver candlestick in the centre of every table. Polished cutlery and shining Delft on every table. A sight that for so long filled me with pride and joy and worry and stress. I spent the happiest of times here. Opening night. My thirtieth birthday. Anniversaries. But I also experienced some of the hardest times in my life here. Long hours in an understaffed kitchen while Mark attended a friend's wedding, or birthday, or baby's christening, that we couldn't both go to because someone had to stay and work. Days of few to no customers and bills mounting. Days of wishing my life was different. La Bella Vita was certainly a roller-coaster ride and my heart is aching knowing today is the day I get off the ride and walk away.

I make myself a large pot of tea, certain that I will drink it all, and settle into my office for a long day of phone calls. I call the staff first: Zoe, Lyla and the others.

'Hey,' I say when a groggy Zoe answers the phone.

'Hey,' she says.

'Just a quick call to let you know we're not opening today.'

'What? But it's our last day.' Zoe's disappointment is palpable and it take all my self-control not to cry.

'I know,' I say, 'but it's not safe. The roads are glass and they're saying on the news not to travel unless necessary.'

I hear Zoe shift about and I assume she's climbing out of bed.

'Holy shit, that's heavy snow,' she says, obviously staring outside for the first time today.

'I'm sorry,' I say. 'I know how much we all wanted tonight to be great.'

'We did.' Zoe sighs.

'We'll just have to make sure our first day in the new place is even better,' I say.

'I can't wait. Tabby's Table is going to be the best. I'm so excited,' she says.

'Me too.'

'Happy New Year, Tabs,' Zoe says.

I take a deep breath, choke back tears and say, 'Happy New Year.'

The rest of my calls to my staff play out similarly. Everyone reassures me of their excitement for the opening of Tabby's Table and they wish me a happy new year.

Next, I call customers. Most people agree that closing tonight is sensible. They tell me of their plans to fetch a local takeaway and have a night in front of the TV. There's the occasional disgruntled customer. Some shout, some curse, and they all seem to blame me for the weather.

Finally, I make the call I've been dreading all day. I dial Catherine's number and pray she doesn't answer.

'Hello,' she says.

'Hi, Catherine. It's Tabby.'

'Tabitha,' she says, sounding surprised, as if she didn't see my name or number appear on her screen.

'How are you?' I ask.

'I'm okay, sweetheart. I'm okay.' She inhales, sharply. 'Thank you for the Christmas gift. Unfortunately, it was too big, but I was able to exchange it.'

I don't ask how the scarf I sent could possibly be a wrong size. I move on. 'I was just calling to say—'

'Yes, yes, I'm coming,' Catherine says, speaking to someone in the distance and not me. 'I'm sorry, Tabitha. I really must go. We're having a family get-together. You know, for Mark's anniversary.'

I hear a baby cry in the background and I swallow hard as I realise Saoirse and baby Marc are there. Of course they are, they are family.

Before I have time to find words Catherine says, 'Bye-bye, Tabitha. Take care.' And the line goes dead.

'I was just calling to say that I'm thinking of him and of you and I hope you will be okay,' I say out loud as if she can still hear me. But I know even if she was still on the line Catherine wouldn't hear me. She never did and she'll never change. I take a deep breath and delete her number from my phone. 'Good-bye, Catherine,' I say as I slide my phone into my pocket with a bright smile on my face.

Then I leave my office, wrap myself in my coat and hat and scarf, taking care not to slip where the snow has melted and left a wet patch on the floor, and I step outside. My boots sink ankle-deep in fluffy snow as cold air pinches my cheeks. The sounds of the usually busy street are missing. No cars, or buses or horns honking. No music trickling onto the street from busy bars and cafés. But there is something beautifully poignant about the silence. As if the whole road has stopped to hold its breath as I close the doors of La Bella Vita one last time. I turn the key in the lock, clasp it tightly between both my hands as my heart tries to beat out of my chest.

A man and a women approach, arms linked. Three children, with heights like steps of stairs, in matching coats and hats and wellington boots, trail after them, tossing snowballs at each other.

'Happy New Year,' the couple chirp together as they pass.

I smile as a snowball narrowly misses me. 'Happy New Year,' I say.

When silence returns as the family take their laughter and chat with them, I stare up at the sky. Snow has finally stopped falling and there's a sense of calm and freshness. I pull my hands close to my chest and my heart, feel the key between my icy fingers, take a deep breath and push it through the letter box.

'Happy New Year, Mark,' I say, 'I'm going to be okay.'

EPILOGUE

It's 11.45 p.m. The bus journey from town to my new house that usually takes fifty minutes today takes an hour and a half. Despite snowploughs clearing the roads and spreading salt, traffic is a mess as nervous drivers struggle.

Avery, Becca, Scott and I agreed to meet at my house at eleven and I've no doubt that I'm the last to arrive. I'm also the one with the keys. Technically it's not officially my house just yet, but the new owners have been beyond kind, allowing me to move my stuff in piecemeal over recent weeks so I'm not paying for storage while I stay at the hotel. Firstly we moved everything to Avery and Becca's flat and slowly, bit by bit, we move it out here. Several evenings after work Scott and I made the round trip by bus to drop off a couple of boxes. Light stuff like clothes, or bedsheets, things that we could manage to carry. Avery and Becca packed bigger, heavier boxes into Becca's car and also made several trips. Tonight, we're all making our final trip of the year, but the only things I'm carrying are a bottle of expensive red wine and a vanilla chiffon cake.

'I'm sorry. I'm so sorry,' I say, trying to race up the street.

Avery, Becca and Scott stand at the door huddled together

like frozen statues. Thankfully they all begin to laugh at my comical attempts to hurry in deep snow.

'You guys must be so cold,' I say, feeling awful that I've kept them waiting.

'I can't feel my feelings,' Avery says, shivering.

'Don't mind her,' Becca says, slapping her arm playfully. 'We're not here long, and Scott arrived after us.'

Scott nods and I sigh, relieved.

'I brought us some goodies,' I say, raising both my hands.

Everyone smiles.

I tilt my hip towards Avery and says, 'Key's in my pocket, can you grab it?'

Avery looks at Becca nervously before she reaches in and pulls out the key. Scott watches wide-eyed as she turns the key in the lock.

'What's going on?' I say. 'You all look as if you've seen a ghost.'

'Nothing. Nothing,' Avery says, bouncing on the spot, and I know it's not just because she's cold.

'Oh God, what have you guys been up to?'

Avery barges past me and closes the sitting room door before I can see inside.

'You have to close your eyes,' she says.

'What?'

'Close your eyes, Tabs,' Scott says.

I shake my head but I do as they say. I feel hands on my waist. Scott's, I think. And I hear the sitting room door open again.

'Okay,' Avery says, 'You can look now.'

I open my eyes slowly and I can barely breathe when I see Rashidi's cart sitting in the middle of my sitting room. It's been polished until it gleams in the light, catching the reflection of the window on its side. I smell bacon bagels and I can't believe I didn't notice before now. Tablecloths are draped across several boxes, and a single tea light candle sits in the middle of each one, transforming them into makeshift tables.

'I know it's not quite the La Bella Vita New Year's Eve you were hoping for,' Avery says.

'No, it's not.' I shake my head in disbelief. 'It's even better.'

I wander over to the old cart that looks so new and strangely as if it belongs right here in this spot. I press my hand against the cool, shiny metal.

'How? How on earth did you get this in here?'

'With great difficulty. We had to take it apart and put it all back together. It's taken us all day.' Avery says.

'It's taken Scott all day,' Becca corrects.

'You did all this for me?' I say, looking at Scott.

'And for Rashidi,' he says. 'He'd be so proud of you.'

Fat, silent tears trickle down my cheeks.

'You were right, Tabs,' Scott says. 'This is a great idea. Bringing the street vendor experience inside. People are going to love this place.'

'God, I hope so,' I say.

'Right,' Avery says, walking round behind the cart and fetching some bagels. 'Are we going to eat or what?'

We take our place at the cardboard-box tables, cross-legged on the floor. Avery passes us a bagel each and I unscrew the cap on the wine. We pass the bottle around and take a large slug each. Avery looks at her watch and says, 'Oh my God it's five minutes until midnight.' She reaches into her handbag and pulls out a pen and paper. 'Quick. Quick, Tabs. You have just enough time to jot something down.'

I stare at her.

'New Year's resolutions for next year.'

I take the pen and the paper and set them down on the table next to my bagel.

'I only have one resolution this year,' I say. 'New Year: remember to be myself.'

Avery nods. And Becca and Scott too. And we eat and drink until suddenly Avery stands up with her phone in her hand and starts to count loudly. 'Ten... nine... eight...'

Becca stands and joins her, counting at the top of her lungs. 'Seven... six....'

Scott stands. 'Five... four...'

He pulls me to my feet and we all chant. 'Three... two... one.'

I feel his lips on mine. Warm and safe and wonderful, and when he pulls away my heart soars as I hear the best first words of the year, 'Happy New Year, Tabitha Greenwood. Let's make it one to remember!'

A LETTER FROM THE AUTHOR

Huge thanks for reading *Memories of You*, and I hope you were hooked on Tabby's journey. If you want to join other readers in hearing all about my new releases and bonus content, you can sign up for my newsletter!

www.stormpublishing.co/brooke-harris

If you enjoyed this book and could spare a few moments to leave a review that would be hugely appreciated. Even a short review can make all the difference in encouraging a reader to discover my books for the first time. Thank you so much!

Like Tabby, I read an article about New Year's resolutions and why, although we start the new year with great intentions, almost all of us give up when it becomes too hard/life becomes too busy/the results aren't happening fast enough. I began to wonder what would happen if someone, a regular someone, with problems and dreams, stuck it out. Would their life really be so different this time next year? It was so fun writing Tabby and her wonderful sister and friends and finding out. I hope you enjoyed sharing her year as much as I did.

Thanks again for being part of this amazing journey with me and I hope you'll stay in touch – I have so many more stories and ideas to entertain you with!

Brooke

ACKNOWLEDGMENTS

Every book begins with a writer sitting all by themselves at their desk and ends with a whole team of people coming together to bring that book to the shelves. I was fortunate to work with a truly talented team on this book.

My wonderful agents at the Madeleine Milburn Agency – Hayley Steed and Hannah Todd. Hayley thank you for developing this idea with me, and Hannah, thank you for your clever suggestions to it make shine.

To the lovely Oliver Rhodes and Kathryn Taussig at Storm Publishing – thank you so very much for wanting to work with me. And to the trailblazing Emily Gowers, how incredibly lucky am I to work with you? Your emails always put the brightest smile on my face. Working together on this book has been a pleasure every step of the way and I even learned a lot about curly hair, lol.

To my fantastic family and friends. I adore you all. I am sorry for missed coffee mornings or skipped Pilates class because I suck at time management and it's always a rush in the end to meet a deadline.

Finally, to my amazing readers. I've been blessed in this business and I have quite a few books under my belt now. And absolutely none of it could happen if people like you didn't spend your precious free time reading my words. Thank you! Two small words, but I say them with HUGE gratitude. Thank you, thank you.

Made in United States
Orlando, FL
26 October 2023

38274419R00224